Katy Regan joined *Marie Claire* as features writer in 2002. 'Highlights' in that position included spending ten days in the buff on a nudist resort and becoming a footballer's wife for a week – all in the name of investigative journalism.

In 2004, at the height of her career as the office roving reporter singleton, she fell accidentally pregnant by her best mate (who just remained a friend). Seeing the creative possibilities in this unconventional situation, her editor commissioned her to write a column – *And then there were three . . . sort of* which proved so successful it ran for two years. She has now taken her loyal following to her blog: *The State She's In* on the *Marie Claire* website www.marieclaire.co.uk. *One Thing Led to Another* is Katy's first novel, a laugh-out-loud and very poignant debut based on her column. She lives in south London and shares care of her son Fergus with his dad who lives across the road.

Find out more about Katy and her novel by logging onto www.marieclaire.co.uk/KatyRegan

KATY REGAN

One Thing Led
to Another

HARPER

Harper
An imprint of HarperCollins*Publishers*
77–85 Fulham Palace Road,
Hammersmith, London W6 8JB

www.harpercollins.co.uk

This paperback edition 2009
1

A catalogue record for this book is
available from the British Library

ISBN-13: 978 0 00 727 7377

Set in Sabon by Palimpsest Book Production Limited,
Grangemouth, Stirlingshire

Printed and bound in Great Britain by
Clays Ltd, St Ives plc

Acknowledgements

Well, One Thing Led to Another, and I only went and wrote a novel! It would definitely never have happened without so many wonderful and talented people. Special thanks go to my agent Lizzy Kremer for her unerring belief in this book, her boundless ideas (all the brilliant ones are hers! I must come clean . . .) and for generally being a total delight. To my editor, Claire Bond – the most modest genius I know. How you manage to make it look so easy and remain so calm, I'll never know. I am very lucky to have you.

I want to thank everyone at HarperCollins and David Higham Associates. I've been blown away by the support and enthusiasm everybody has shown for this book.

To Marie O'Riordan and Charlotte Moore – the column would never have happened without you, and therefore definitely not the book – I am forever indebted. To all the team past and present at Marie Claire and at www.marieclaire.co.uk, for your encouragement and enthusiasm.

To my mum and dad; sisters, family and all my wonderful friends. See! I wasn't lying, I really was writing a book, even if it took me seventy-five years. Thank you for your support and love, So much of this book was inspired by times we've shared.

Big thanks to Louis: My friend, father-to-my-child, first reader, and so much more. You bigged your part up as 'first editor' and so you should! For giving me the time to write; the confidence to do it and the good sense to tell me when the writing was 'dull, dull, dull!' I don't deserve you.

Last but not least, my biggest thanks go to Fergus, the best surprise of my life.

This book is for you.

For Louis and Fergus

Prologue

Two minutes it says to wait, two minutes and bam! Your life changed forever. Imagine that. No God, on second thoughts, let's not. Let's just calm down, breathe deeply and concentrate. I take off my watch. It's one of those underwater sports ones. Great for boiling eggs and ideal for timing how long my mother can monologue on the phone whilst I m doing something else.

I never dreamt I'd be using it for this.

I set it: 2.00. The numbers glow neon in the darkness, a countdown to my fate. Could I be? If I really thought I was, surely I'd have chosen somewhere better than a self-cleaning toilet in the middle of SE1 to have such a life-changing experience.

1.45

It was only once. Once! Out of only a handful of times that we'd even bloody done it in the first place – that we thought we'd . . . how can I put this . . . leave it to Jim's impeccable timing and wing it.

1.40

But there's winging it and winging it, isn't there? And the more images of that night come at me like film stills on double

1

speed replay, the more I'm thinking the odds are stacked against us.

1.35

There's the position for a start. Oh Shit. Me on my back, legs wrapped around his neck in possibly the most sperm receptive position of all time, on day 16 (I know, I've counted, about a million times) of my cycle.

1.00

And then there were the knickers: black satin tie-at-the-side jobs, and on a school night. I mean, what kind of whore am I? And the fact I can't drive. If only I could drive, this could all have been avoided. If my mother had just bought me driving lessons at seventeen like every other reasonable mother in the whole world, if she had just trusted me, not assumed I was an accident waiting to happen (quite literally), I would have driven home, safely home, very probably in a thoroughly un-alluring pair of Bhs briefs, and been tucked up in bed by 11 p.m. instead of flat on my back with my legs around Jim Ashcroft's neck.

0.40

Please God, I'm begging you. I cannot be pregnant. I don't even have a boyfriend. Jim and I are just good friends. So good, admittedly, we tend to fall into each other's beds after one too many on a Friday night when the proposition of a cuddle seems like a good idea, but still, we are 'just good friends'.

0.27

I know this because after each encounter (and for the record there's been more than could constitute 'a one off' but less than could constitute 'seeing each other') we don't spend all weekend together. We don't visit garden centres or use cutesy voices on the phone. And I certainly *never* buy his mother's birthday present on his behalf.

0.20

Having stayed the night at each other's houses we get up then go our separate ways. Me back to my girly shared house in Islington and Jim to his south London bachelor pad. Two single people, two ends of London, two different lives. So you can see if this test is positive, it's hardly going to be Swiss Family Robinson.

0.15

But once is all it takes isn't it? And what if the man I decided to take a chance with had a Superhero sperm? A bloody non-conformist little sperm that when the masses herded in one direction, turned on its tail and butterfly stroked in the other shouting, Vive La Revolution! That would be typical of Jim. He's the most non-conformist free spirit I've ever met. And it only takes one. One sperm, one chance, one moment, for all the other moments in the rest of your life to be changed forever.

But anyway . . .

0.07

We're about to find out . . .

0.05

I pick up the test.

0.04

I hold it under the light of my phone.

0.03

I'm looking at it now, reading it feverishly like I remember looking for my degree results on a board of thousands.

0.02

All I can concentrate on is the sound of my pulse throbbing but I'm glaring at it, gripping it tight in my hands and I'm trying to see straight and . . .

0.00

Beep beep beep

. . . I AM! Shit I am! There's two lines! There's two . . .!

3

Oh. No.

But there's not.

I'm not. Because there's two lines, but there's no cross. Which means it's negative. No baby. Thank you Lord.

CHAPTER ONE

'Seven weeks before I was due, the silly bugger got down on one knee whilst I was washing up. We tied the knot at Lancaster Registry Office, with a lollipop lady as the witness and Eddie with a daffodil in his buttonhole. My waters broke, just as we were about to consummate our wedding in a B&B in Lytham St Anne's. Eddie has never forgiven Joel for the timing, and he's thirty-three now.'

Linda, 56, Preston

I'd always believed that sleeping with your male best friend would have one of two outcomes. Either it would be a unanimous disaster, from which your friendship would never recover. Or it would be an epiphany. You'd wonder why on earth you'd never done this before.

I'd experienced the first: Gavin Stroud, Manchester University, 1998. Gavin was my best mate on my French course, until a moment of inebriated madness – round about the four-pint point, the point at which I obviously believed I was irresistible to all members of the opposite sex. That's also the point at which I should have gone to bed, my dignity still intact. But no, it was at this point I decided Gavin Stroud needed to know this: that my French oral in class wasn't half as good as that in the bedroom and that I looked erotic dancing to *Purple Rain*. We went back to my room in halls, shut the orange and brown curtains and poured each other glass after glass of cheap white wine. With each glass, the edges of his face grew more blurred as did any good judgement I'd ever possessed. After an hour of *Purple Rain* on repeat play and even longer trying to get a comatosed Gavin to maintain an erection long enough to get a condom on, we passed out. When I woke up, head feeling like someone had mown over it, the blackheads on his nose rather too close for comfort, I knew it had been a big, huge, no . . . *colossal* mistake. The five-minute walk across campus to our first tutorial that day was one of the most excruciating experiences of my life. How can you act normally when you've just spent the night wrestling with your (I think I could now safely say) *ex* friend's uncooperative penis? Trust me. There's no coming back from there.

But Jim is different. Sex with him is never a disaster, it's just it has never been a light-bulb moment either. It's just, you know, nice. Like getting into a warm bath after a freezing day, or finding a twenty pound note in your jeans pocket.

We met in November 1997, second floor of the John Rylands Library, Manchester University, both of us wading through our very first English essay in Critical Theory (critically dreary more like). At eighteen years old I was a dangerous mixture of ecstatic and terrified to be officially 'independent'. Two years my senior, Jim seemed like he'd been knocking around on his own all his life. He was sitting opposite me with his head buried in *The Death of the Author* by Roland Barthes as was I (and probably every other first year English Lit student in there). But it was the intense frown that really made me laugh, it told of utter and total bafflement. My feelings exactly!

6

'Is that making about as much sense to you as it is to me?' I said, hoping this guy with legs so long his feet were nearly touching mine under the table was in need of distraction too.

Jim looked up.

'I.e. none whatsoever?'

'That's the one!'

He smiled, broadly.

'Put it this way,' he said. 'If this death of the author lark means it's all down to the reader's interpretation then I'm screwed because I haven't got the first clue what this French nutter's on about.'

'Me neither,' I whispered back. 'I thought I'd be studying books, literature – you know, novels innit . . .' Jim laughed. 'But it's all structuralism this and post-structuralism that, seminology . . .'

'Semiology,' he corrected.

'Yeah, that's what I meant,' I said, feeling suddenly embarrassed.

That was it, we were off. Couldn't shut us up for two whole hours. We sacked off work and went for a pint in the end because neither of us could fathom what 'Barthes Simpson' as we christened him that day was on about and we were having too much of a good time chatting. When I stepped out of the student union into the crisp November air, I felt like we'd cracked the secret to something that afternoon, Jim and I. Life, probably, or maybe that was just the beer. But for all the personality fireworks I didn't fancy Jim that day, still don't, maybe that's why sex with him has never been a big deal. It's not that Jim's un-fanciable, far from it, he's just not my type. He's cigarette-thin with Scottish skin and dark hair that flicks out at the sides and on top due to cow licks and various double crowns. He's got nice full lips – if a little gormless on occasions; a sturdy, prominent nose – attractive on a man I've always thought; and green, sparkly eyes that

7

crinkle up so much when he laughs they almost disappear. But I've never felt the urge to tear his clothes off.

And so if you had told me on that day we met (or any other day during the next eight years and six months which is how long it took us to kiss, never mind have sex: hardly a whirlwind romance) that one day James Ashcroft and I would be occasional shag partners, I'd never have believed it. But we are and it's strange, most of all because I don't really get why it *did* take us so long. Until one warm weekend last May to be exact.

It was supposed to be two days' hard graft cleaning up my parents' caravan, which along with fifty or so other caravans on the tiny site in Whitby hung precariously off a cliff like a stranded sheep. I'd agreed to give it a makeover in return for a hundred quid from my dad and Jim was the only person I knew who had a power drill, but from the first moment we got there, it felt more like a holiday than hard work.

I've never known lager taste so good as that first, exhausted pint drunk with Jim at the end of day one. We sat on a bench outside a pub in the town – the Flask and Dolphin – a prime spot with harbour views, and seagulls fat as milk jugs squawking round our feet. I remember the vinegary smart of fish and chips in the air, the lull of bobbing boats, the warmth of the sun on my chest and the feeling that I'd not been so happy for a long time. I told him all about my childhood holidays spent here in Whitby. He told me about endless summers holed up in Stoke-on-Trent, playing Connect Four in his front porch, bored out of his mind.

One pint turned into two, into three, into four, until suddenly it was almost dark and we were surrounded by towers of empty glasses and a sense of anticipation as sharp as salt air.

Jim sighed. 'This rocks.' he said, lifting his face to the sinking sun. 'I've had the best day I've had in ages.' Then he turned, his head resting on the wall and he added, 'With you'.

And it didn't feel awkward. I didn't get that feeling I was going to regret this in the morning. I just put my glass down, threw my legs sideways over his knee and snogged him like we'd been going out for twenty odd years and this was one of those rare romantic nights made for rekindling the flame.

We'd kissed now, what the hell – sex back at the caravan seemed like the most obvious next step. Afterwards, we sat and talked on the beach until a red dawn flooded the water. 'I've never met anyone like you,' said Jim. 'I'm probably closer to you than I am to anyone.' And the thing was, right at that moment, I felt exactly the same.

When I opened my eyes late the next morning to find the sun in slices on the floral duvet and the North Sea wind whistling in through the windows, I felt strangely and yet wonderfully at home and at ease.

'So, Jarvis, that was going to happen all along, was it not?' I remember Jim muttering as he stood in his palm tree underpants pouring coffee into two chipped mugs. And I agreed. 'Predictable as death,' were the words I mumbled from underneath the duvet.

After all, if you rate one another highly enough to be close friends in the first place, then chances are, if you're opposite sexes, it's only a matter of time. That's not to say there aren't consequences. A quick scan of the carnage when I finally emerged that morning revealed my bra was hung on the back of a chair, my knickers gusset-side-up on the caravan hob. There were CDs scattered all over the floor, ransacked in a frenzy of drunken delight, not one in its case. We'd danced to Take That, to George Michael, to Billy Joel for crying out loud! I'd made five thousand times the fool of myself as I had with Gavin Stroud and yet I wasn't one bit embarrassed.

I don't know what I expected after that night. I suppose I would have been happy to give a relationship a try, but then I was also petrified of ruining what we had. In the end,

Jim made that decision for me, and I would be lying if I said I wasn't a little deflated.

I called him on the Monday, the night after we got back. 'I had a brilliant time this weekend,' I said. Good opening I thought, perhaps this is where he says he couldn't agree more and asks me out?

Or not.

'Me too,' he giggled. 'It was right laugh. I have particularly fond memories of you doing a routine to 'Relight My Fire' wearing only your pants.'

Brilliant, I thought. Absolutely typical. Could it be, perhaps, that I failed to give off the right signals?

But maybe that was no bad thing. Maybe there's a reason we felt no embarrassment whatsoever after our antics. So unembarrassed were we, in fact, that, a year later, we seem to have fallen into a habit of just 'doing it' whenever the need for a little no-strings nookie grabs us.

'Think of it as a way of extending the fun we're having,' Jim always says, usually naked which doesn't exactly help, 'like going to an after-hours bar.'

And this suits me too, because I don't think I know what I want. I can't fathom the workings of his brain either if truth be told. All I know is that Jim Ashcroft and I have crossed the line. We are no longer purely platonic, nor lovers either. We're just two misguided fools frolicking about in a vast sprawling, savannah-sized space commonly known as 'The Grey Area'.

It's a week since the pregnancy scare and frankly it's a good job it was just a scare since all I seem to have done since then is accompany people to the pub. Such is the curse of the unattached I've always thought. What with no fall-back

10

plan – no flat/wedding/dog to save up for – we, The Unhooked, are expected to attend everything.

Take tonight for example. 'I may kill someone if I don't get drunk this very evening,' was Vicky's raspy threat down the receiver that I, in a mid-afternoon slump, had cradled between my head and the desk. Dylan had decorated the walls with macaroni cheese, she said, Richard had come home from a hard day's work as zoo keeper at London Zoo chatting to kids about the mating habits of camels to find his own kid, the two foot rhino, bulldozing around the house in a toddler rage and his dear, lovely wife, coiled like a cobra, ready to pounce at any time.

I love Vicky, which is weird because it was far from love at first sight. In fact, thinking back to that first day we met in Owens Park Halls when she introduced herself in her Yorkshire, 'this-is-me-like-it-or-lump-it' way, I'm ashamed to say a little part of me withered with disappointment.

How could I, Tess Jarvis, owner of:
- Old Skool Trainers (various)
- New (but artfully battered) leather jacket
- Entire works of Bob Dylan
- *Ministry of Sound: The Annual,* volumes two and three (because at eighteen years old I am both artily intellectual and just mainstream enough, you understand)
- Poster of Che Guevara (because I care about other countries and Politics)
- Obsession with Ewan MacGregor
- Occasional marujana habit that I fully intend to upgrade to 'moderate'
possibly be sharing a room with Victoria Peddlar, owner of:
- Fluffy penguin slippers
- Fake designer sweatshirts worn over stone washed jeans (various)

11

- Entire works of Take That
- *That's What I Call Power Ballads 1, 2* and *3*
- Poster of Patrick Swayze (because nobody puts Vicky Peddlar in the corner)
- Obsession with *Dirty Dancing*
- Moderate horoscope-reading habit (soon to be upgraded to borderline obsessional).

But it was true and I was utterly gutted. Especially since I'd just met a girl called Gina who had already designated her room as Smoking HQ. A room I wished I was sharing more than anything else in the world. Gina was the coolest girl in our halls and a guaranteed route to mischief, every night of the week. She had big curly hair that she wore in low bunches, boasted a dragon tattoo that snaked across her stomach, said 'wicked' a lot and owned a bong. And as if that wasn't enough to make your average eighteen-year-old fresher practically pay to be her friend, she had about a million of her own friends from boarding school who were all as cool as she was.

It's easy to see how this Peddlar girl didn't even get a look in during those first few days at university.

'Rich says I can go out . . . I just need someone to go with and guess-what? You're the lucky lady!' Vicky shouted over Dylan. I don't mind really, Vicks often inspires in me selfless acts of love. When she was holed up in hospital, thirty-seven weeks pregnant, ankles as fat as an elephant's, blood pressure soaring, I travelled half way across London to bring her the only thing that would satiate her queer, hormonal taste buds. Deep fried aubergines served up on a silver platter (well, a polystyrene tray, anyway).

I'd soon found out there was far more to this girl from Huddersfield than first met the eye. She could really put it away, for one. A childhood spent pulling pints in her parents' pub saw to that. She had real talent too, which whoever you are, I've always thought, can only add to your credibility.

I will never forget the last night of Freshers' Week, the night of the Owens Park talent competition. Vicky stood up, dressed in her Benetton sweatshirt, swinging her mousy ponytail. She took the mike in one hand and holding a pint of cider in the other, she began to sing. It was 'Cry Me a River', and it was utterly brilliant. Nobody moved or spoke, everyone just stared at this girl, this Big Bird of a girl who was suddenly possessed by the ghost of Ella Fitzgerald. She finished the song, put the mike down on the table, gulped down the rest of her cider and sat down. There were five seconds of dumbfounded silence, save for Gina whispering 'fucking hell' next to me. Then we began to clap, first slowly and then uproarious applause. It was brilliant, mind-blowing, made the hairs on the back of my neck stand on end and even then, as stupid and self-absorbed and inexperienced at life as I was, I knew that you didn't sing a song with soul like that if you hadn't experienced things which, I knew instinctively, I hadn't. Things like your mum walking out on your dad for a man half her age and then dying of ovarian cancer two months later; things like watching your dad go from jovial pub landlord to suicidal recluse; things like bringing up two little brothers pretty much single-handed as well as singing in your dad's pub in the evenings for the tips. So yes, there was a lot more to Victoria Peddlar. Gina got the Vicky thing too, eventually, and we had things to teach each other back then. Gina and I taught Vicky how to skin up, accentuate that splendid bosom with something other than sweatshirts and basically be an irresponsible teenager – something she'd kind of missed. And Vicky was our surrogate mother when we needed one most, I suppose. Always the one with the plan of action, the best hangover cures. And the fact she'd seen a lot in her short life meant you waking up in some inappropriate bloke's bed with no recollection of the night before was no big deal. 'Look, nobody died, did they?' Vicky would say, sitting on my bed as I growled under the duvet with shame. 'And look on the bright side, at least you didn't get so drunk you shat yourself.' (Ever since a girl called Julianne Breeze had, actually, got so drunk she shat herself, this had been the scale against which we measured all mortifying events. After all, nothing could ever, ever be that bad.)

A fortnight into term one, Gina, Vicky and I were pretty much inseparable. By late November I'd brought Jim into the fold and we'd became a proper gang. Or as my dad put it, 'A foursome to be reckoned with.'

And I loved my friends, I idolized them, still do. Tonight one of them is simply asking me to accompany her to a public house, her first baby-free night for weeks, for a couple of quiet beers on a Thursday night. I can usually think of nothing I'd rather do, it's just tonight, I could do with a little help. I need Jim.

From: tess_jarvis@giant.co.uk
To: james_ashcroft@westminster.edu.uk
Peddlar needs beer. I need bed. Help?

It only takes a few seconds for the reply to pop into my inbox which means Jim must be in the staff room.

From: james_ashcroft@westminster.edu.uk
To: tess_jarvis@giant.co.uk
No can do, have hot date. I can come for the first hour to ease the pain but then I have to shoot. Going to see *Swan Lake*??! (help)

The thought of Jim watching the Dying Swan, whilst wondering when he's going to fit in a pint and a snog brings a smile to my face. Still, an hour of his support is better than nothing so I call Vicks back and say, 'You're on.'

CHAPTER TWO

'The day we brought Jen and Ming home from China was the happiest day of our lives. I was forty-four. We'd been trying to become parents for almost two decades, and had travelled half way across the world to adopt a baby. Three months later, I had a routine scan about my polycystic ovaries. "Mrs Freed," said the doctor his face waxy white. "Were you aware you were pregnant? With twins"?'

Jenny, 46, Southampton

So here I am again, fifth night out on the trot, in the Coach and Horses, Soho, a warm smoky pub that smells of damp coats and stale beer, with Vicky and Jim, my very best mates.

'Wine for the lady, Stella for Sir in the corner,' I say, passing Jim his pint.

'Aw thanks, you're a beauty.' He downs half of it in one go. 'Chaucer and fourteen-year-olds, I tell you, it does me in every time.'

'So Jimbo,' says Vicky, pouring herself a bowlful of wine. 'How come your "loverrrr", or is she your girlfriend?' Jim groans at this. 'How come she's managed to drag you to *Swan Lake*? When we went to see *Les Miserables* you said

– and I quote – "It was just a load of old women with massive jugs, bounding about the stage for what felt like days."'

Jim looks up at me from his pint, a moustache of froth on his top lip. I raise an eyebrow.

'Did I?' he says, genuinely incredulous. 'Sorry Vicks, what an absolute knob.'

'Apology accepted – even though it was my birthday, if I remember rightly – but anyway, you still haven't answered the question.'

'What question?'

'How come you're going to the ballet when you don't even like musicals?'

'I don't *not* like musicals,' says Jim, nervously pulling on his jacket collar. 'I just don't like all of them that's all.'

'So exactly what musicals do you like?' says Vicky. I can tell she is enjoying this line of questioning.

'*Chicago*,' Jim shrugs.

'*Chicago*?' Vicky splutters.

'Yeah, *Chicago*. You know, the one that was made into a gangster film.'

'The one with loads of chicks in suspenders and stockings, you mean?' I cut in.

'That's the one,' winks Jim.

Vicky nods her head sagely.

'Ah yes,' she says. 'I should imagine you like that one.'

Jim looks at us, gives a short laugh, then looks away, shaking his head.

This is his 'teacher' face. It says, 'will you all just grow up'. And the thing is, annoyingly, it kind of becomes him. Whereas everyone else went through – and came out the other side of – the 'I want to become a teacher' stage (spurred on by fantasies of standing on tables making inspiring speeches like Robin Williams in *Dead Poets Society*), Jim actually did it. And he was a natural too. So much so that in less than

16

three years of teaching English to the little tyrants at Westminster City School he had been made Head of Department. Jim can talk about Shakespeare like he's talking about *Neighbours*: he knows his stuff, is genuinely mad about the subject and yet manages to never sound like a pretentious wanker. Well, hardly ever . . .

'Look,' Jim says, wearily. 'This girl's quite nice, she happens to like ballet, she quite likes me and she wants me to go. Since when is it a crime for a man to indulge in some culture anyway, and what is this? The Spanish Inquisition?'

'No, it's just, it's quite girlfriendy, going to the ballet just because "she likes it".' I poke his arm playfully. 'Selflessness, I'd say, is the first sign of true love.'

Vicky folds her arms industriously.

'Annalisa won't be best pleased,' she chips in.

Annalisa is that rare thing: a holiday fling that goes on being a holiday fling. Jim met her in Rimini on a lads' holiday a few years ago and they've had an 'understanding' (basically to be each other's bit of no-strings fun when he visits Italy or she visits London) ever since.

'Give it a rest will you.' Jim sinks back in his chair. 'Annalisa wouldn't care and anyway, Claire's a lovely girl but she doesn't want anything serious anymore than I do. You two are just jealous. I've got a date, I'm going somewhere interesting. Meanwhile, you're in this rubbish pub talking about makeup and periods. Probably.'

This is what we do, us lot, wind each other up. Sometimes I forget I've had sex with Jim. I forget he has seen me naked in all sorts of compromising positions. I don't remember how he's caressed my boobs, taken baths with me and commented on my rather relaxed upkeep of hair removal. It's like we are experts at compartmentalization. When we're having sex, we're tender and intimate. When we're not, we're mates. That's all, nothing more, nothing less. Just mates.

17

I look at Jim.

'So, what are you wearing for your "hot date"?'

'What do you mean?'

'I mean when are you getting changed, you know, into your going-out clothes?'

Jim examines his attire. Then looks at Vicky. He actually looks a bit hurt. A little part of me wants to give him a hug.

'This is it,' he says. 'This is what I'm wearing.'

'You are kidding,' I say. Vicky erupts, spraying scampi fries everywhere. 'This is the ballet, Jim. You'll get chucked out looking like that.'

'Like what? What's the matter with me?'

'Like an Austin Powers/raver cross breed?'

'Aw, give over Tess. He looks alright, don't you Jimbo?' Vicky puts an arm around him, trying not to laugh.

Jim looks at me.

'What?' he says, a smile curling at the sides of his mouth. 'It's a bloody good jacket this, I'll have you know. It's Ellesse, not your Top Man bollocks. Top notch.'

Vicky and I are pissing ourselves now. Jim's had that jacket since about 1991. Which was about the time Ellesse was last cool.

'Where's your whistle and your acid tabs?' I joke. 'And I bet it's still got that fag burn in the back.'

Jim sticks his bottom lip out in a mock show of hurt.

'Come 'ere, I'm only kidding,' I say, getting his head and putting it into an affectionate head-lock. 'You look cool. Honestly. You really do. Kind of . . . what would I say? Sports casual with a seventies twist.'

We all laugh but the fact is, he does look cool, in a Jim-eclectic kind of a way. It's a mish-mash of decades, what with the Ellesse jacket, the seventies tank top and cords, but there's something attractive about a man who doesn't try too hard and Jim's certainly not guilty of that. In fact Jim doesn't so much 'do' fashion as happen upon it when by the laws of probability means he does, occasionally, pull something OK out of his wardrobe.

Jim stands up, zips up his jacket and announces he's going. 'Well, thank you, Fashion Police,' he says. 'But I'm now going to get myself some refined company. A woman who knows how to conduct herself, a woman who appreciates cutting-edge style when she sees it.'

Kylie's 'Spinning Around' comes onto the jukebox. Jim stands up and shimmies to the bar, his small bottom wiggling.

'Nice moves, Ashcroft!' I shout after him. 'The girl won't be able to resist!'

With this, he downs the rest of his pint, puts his glass on the bar, flashes us a V-sign and dashes out of the door. I watch him as he goes, bouncing along the pavement on his Reebok Classics, hands in pockets, head down.

When I turn back, Vicky's staring at me.

'What?'

'You're smiling,' she says.

'Am I?'

'Yeah, you're really smiling.'

Here we go again.

A night out with Vicky is a bit like that film *Groundhog Day*. From the moment I walk in to the moment she disappears into the night only just catching the last train to Beckenham by the skin of her teeth, I know exactly what's coming: as many bottles of house red as we can fit in and the obligatory 'but-you-are-really-secretly-in-love-with-Jim, aren't you?' conversation.

Vicky has a huge soft spot for Jim. 'So, are you two like fuck buddies? I mean, is that how you'd define yourselves?' she asks, looking at me over her wine glass.

She no doubt got this awful term from some sordid programme about weird peoples' sex lives hosted by Jenny

19

Éclair, but she has a point: 'Friends who have sex', that's exactly what we are. But we're not, either, not in my eyes anyway, because 'fuck buddy' suggests it's all about the sex and not much about the friendship and Jim and I are the complete opposite to that. 'Fuck buddies (if ever there were such a grim thing) are all about sex on tap without the emotional complications that come with actually caring about someone,' I say to her. 'And I do care about him, I love him to bits.'

'*I know you do,*' she says, over-enunciating the words as though I am deaf. 'And he loves you – hello! – a lot.'

'But not like that,' I say, staring into my glass. I always feel uncomfortable when she starts on this one. 'As disappointing as that is – and believe me, I'm disappointed too, it's not like that. Jim and I are just mates. Mates who occasionally shag and probably shouldn't, I know, I know; but we're still just mates.'

Vicky shakes her head, defeated.

'Pretty weird ones if you ask me.'

And on we went. Until I found myself stumbling out of the pub, at almost midnight, into the crisp ring of night air and no hope of getting home before one a.m.

I decide to pass on the cab and walk through Soho, to catch a bus on Oxford Street.

There's nowhere quite like Soho at night. It's like the set of a West End show itself, alive with movement, light and noise. As I walk down Old Compton Street, the gay guys sit outside French patisseries with one leg snaked around the other, scarves wrapped tight around their necks, sipping their espressos. Steam from the last washing up of the evening rises from the basements and bar workers settle in for their end of shift beer.

I cut across Dean Street towards Wardour Street, snaking through the crowds of people queuing for late-night bars, members' clubs and restaurants.

20

This part of London, it's the playground of the free. A zone for those who don't have to make any decisions yet, the circumstances of their lives still unravelling, for those still playing.

And just for now, I'm playing too. But I've got a funny feeling that for me, the game's almost over, the final whistle is nearly up and I have to make some decisions and sort out what I actually want from life.

It's ludicrous to think I could have been pregnant with Jim's baby last week. Besides anything else, as I held that test in my hand, the potential father of the potential baby was on a date, just as he is tonight, and that can't be right, can it?

I had been tempted to send a text. HELLO, DADDY-TO-BE would have served him right, out gallivanting while I was in a self-cleaning toilet having a near nervous breakdown.

But I couldn't do it in the end. 'It's negative,' I texted. 'You're off the hook.'

I didn't even get his reply until I was standing at the bar in the Camden Head an hour later: 'Thank fuck for that. And you had me believing that paunch was all baby.'

Cheeky git! So much for sharing the weight of responsibility.

I turn into Wardour Street where a herd of twenty-somethings, the boys all moulded hair and skinny jeans, the girls with sultry, smoky eyes, are careering across the street, singing and laughing. One of the girls is sat on what must be her boyfriend's shoulders, lanky arms in the air, swigging a bottle of beer. Still high on the buzz of London, I think: we were like that; that would, once, have been me, Jim, Gina and Vicky, strutting our way from one late bar to the next, back to someone's place, more beer, maybe some drugs, not caring about the next day, masters at navigating a day's work on no sleep.

We still give it our best shot (even Vicky, who I sometimes think would sell an organ for a good night out). It's just, sometimes I get the feeling that I've accelerated through most of my twenties in a beer-fuelled haze, only to arrive at almost thirty *still* accelerating in a beer-fuelled haze, when really I should be putting the brakes on, or at least starting to look where I'm going.

*

'Next question,' says Gina, adjusting her bikini top. Her boobs jostle about in the water, like dumplings in a boiling pan. 'Marcus?'

Marcus licks the spliff he's holding and sticks it down, then gestures to Gina for the lighter.

'OK,' he says, 'I've got a good one. What's the worst thing you've ever said in an interview?'

Jasper cracks open a beer with a fizz.

'I once asked an interviewer when the baby was due,' he mumbles from beneath his trilby.

'What's wrong with that?' I ask.

'She wasn't pregnant.'

I almost wet myself laughing at this one. I don't know why, it's just the thought of Jasper attending an interview – like, ever – is suddenly hilarious. Jasper is an artist. He does 'installations'. This is absolutely no disrespect to people who are actually artists, who do, actually do installations. But in Jasper's case, it roughly translates as 'on the dole'.

Ooops, so much for the contemplative mood brought on by my life-affirming walk through Soho. It's now two a.m. and I am in the Jacuzzi with Gina (now my flatmate) her current shag Jasper and a man I have never met before in my life. This is all too often the case these days; I don't plan to have a large one, it just sort of happens. It's one of the perils of having a Jacuzzi in the basement of your house.

Gina and I didn't plan to live together this long; that just 'sort of happened' too. In our second and third university years, all four of us shacked up in a house in Rusholme. Then when we graduated, we all moved down to London together. Jim did his PGCE and then because he was now officially one of London's 'key workers', got a 'part-ownership' deal and put down a deposit on a flat with money he'd saved from his weekend job selling padded cards in boxes with messages like 'To the One I Love'. Gina, Vicky and I moved into 21 Linton Street in upmarket Islington, and that was it.

At that point I, having spent an awful lot of time watching tragic documentaries about people with ten-stone tumours, was doing a diploma in magazine journalism, with a view to interviewing people about stuff like that all the time. I thought I'd made it living in N1, a career in the media at my fingertips. Trouble was, with its crumbly black steps and security grating, our house looked like the Hammer House of Horrors on an otherwise elegant row of white Georgian townhouses. But we loved it. And we loved our landlady almost as much. Mrs Broke-Snell had her hair blow-dried every other day and only ever shopped in Harrods Food Hall. It's a shame she didn't pay as much attention to the upkeep of her properties as she did to herself but at least she had the genius idea (and a sufficient level of insanity) to install DA-DA-DAR!! THE JACUZZI.

Doubtless the most ingenious popularity device ever known to man, the Jacuzzi comes complete with wooden surround, massage jets, and a film of mould growing around the outside. 21 Linton Street has always been THE back-to-mine post-party house, scores of people padding their soap-sudded feet from the hall to the basement and vice versa, to shrivel up in our Jacuzzi and have drunken conversations about where we'll all be in five years time. The trouble is, those five years are up now. You'd think that the novelty of having deep and meaningfuls in our swimwear would have somewhat worn off but we're still at it.

Though Jim took my room when I went travelling in 2002 – he rented his flat out for some much needed cash – it was always very much a single girls' pad. Then Vicky committed the ultimate crime (in Gina's eyes anyway) which was to not only marry Richard, but have his babies. It was, of course, totally predictable but still, Gina and I didn't expect to be here nearly a decade later. In fact Gina was so convinced that whatever bloke she was shagging at the time was about to ask her to move in with him, she didn't buy a bed for two years.

And I thought I'd be long gone by now, married, living in a garden flat, but we're both still here, maxing up the rent so we don't have to get in a third person. Gina continues to go out with tossers (the sort who talk about moving in together by week three, and who have dumped her by week five). And I just coast along quite happily, cheered by the odd shag with Jim, wondering how I wound up, twenty-eight and a half, living like an ageing student.

When I eventually recover from my laughing fit I realize Gina's glaring at me. Gina doesn't like people laughing at her boyfriends, even when they offer up the jokes themselves.

'Tess can do better than that, can't you Tess?' she says, playfully. 'What's the worst thing *you've* ever said in an interview?'

Here we go, Gina loves to wheel this one out at every social occasion. 'Do I have to?' I groan.

'Yes, you have to. It's genius. Go on.'

'I once told the Head of a PR company that I was fluent in Italian,' I sigh. 'Which would have been fine, if I hadn't failed GCSE.' Everyone waits for the punch-line. 'And she hadn't been Italian.'

Gina claps her hand with glee. 'Love it! Cracks me up every time! I wouldn't mind,' she continues, hardly able to talk she's laughing so much, 'but her name was fucking Luisa Vincenzi!!'

And I have to admit. It is quite funny.

It is only when Marcus starts to get fresh, playing footsie in the water, I come to my senses, realize I am shrivelled like a prune, and am utterly and totally shit-faced. When I eventually make it to the sanctuary of my bedroom it's gone three a.m. I climb into bed, sink back into the coolness of my pillow and exhale, slowly, deeply. Outside I can still hear cars whizzing past, the faint sound of engines revving, London still alive and throbbing. I don't know how I'm going to get up tomorrow, or make it through the day on four hours' sleep.

The other thing I don't know, is that somewhere deep inside of me, cells are multiplying, life is just beginning.

CHAPTER THREE

'Funnily enough, Chris was watching football when I came home. "Right," I said, "do you want the good news or the bad?" "Good news," he said. "I'm pregnant," I said. "And the bad?" "It's due in June." I called him immediately after Grace was born, but he didn't pick up. When I heard Pearce and Bates had both missed penalties, I punched the air. Needless to say, divorce proceedings were already underway.'

Laura, 25, Leicester

The next morning, I'm sitting on a stool drinking tea in the kitchen when Gina wanders in with Jasper, still complete with trilby.

'God, rough as a bear's arse,' she yawns, reaching above my head to get mugs out of the cupboard so I have to duck, spilling tea all over my nightie.

I wince slightly as the heat hits my skin. 'Don't feel too clever myself. How about you Jasper? You feeling rough? You've got the right idea with that hat, that's for sure.'

Gina raises an eyebrow, she knows I'm being sarcastic but he doesn't hear me anyway. He's got his hands down his pants and his head in last Saturday's copy of the *Guardian* Weekend.

Gina wanders over to the kettle, coughing, or rather hacking, and switches it on then pulls her curvaceous little frame up onto the worktop. There's a flash of red knickers from underneath her dressing gown.

'Jesus, I need to give up the fags,' she says, when she's eventually recovered from her coughing fit. She's been saying that for ten years. I got her four sessions with a hypnotist once, in return for being in a health feature in *Believe It!* magazine. It did nothing to help her kick the habit, but she did gain a new one: the hypnotist. Blaise Tapp he was called, and that was his real name. She ended up shagging him for three months.

'Tea or coffee Jasper?'

'Er, coffee. But only if it's proper coffee. One sugar please.'

He leans back on the kitchen chair, stretching his arms above his head. He's wearing a string vest, so I can see his thick, dark underarm hair sprouting forth like those fake moustaches you get in joke shops.

I get up to put my bowl into the dishwasher and realize I'm wearing no bra and my nipples are probably on show.

Gina opens her side of the cupboard. We did try sharing everything once, but due to our clashing eating habits, i.e. I eat like a horse and she eats hardly anything, it didn't work out that well.

'Fuck, no coffee,' she mutters under her breath.

'Have you got any real coffee I can borrow Jarvis?'

I get it out of the cupboard and hand it her; she doesn't say thank you.

Gina can be a bit like this: brusque, bordering on rude. It gets people's backs up sometimes. Jim goes into teacher mode and tells her off and Vicky just steers clear. And me? Well, I'm well practiced I suppose. Gina may act like a tough little cookie, but she's soft as treacle inside, sensitive as anything. I definitely blame the parents: palmed off to nannies as a

27

baby, sent off to boarding school aged eight. I suppose earning £70,000 plus in the City it's not as if Gina needs someone to give her financial security, but it doesn't take a genius to work out that even though she resists it like an exhausted toddler resists sleep, she just needs to be loved. Which is why I worry about her choice of men.

Jasper excuses himself and goes for a shower, his jeans hanging off his arse to reveal the start of a most unsightly hairy crack. I worry I'm turning into my mother.

'He's such an interesting guy, isn't he?' says Gina, walking over to the kitchen window and putting her nose to the glass. Outside, the morning light is cobalt blue, like a church window. 'So creative.'

So obviously a prat, I want to say, but I don't. I couldn't. I mean it's not that he is an evil person or anything, he just isn't boyfriend material. And Gina, more than anyone else I know, could really do with a boyfriend.

I am getting out of the shower when I hear my mobile. Oh for God's sake, piss off! Who can possibly have something so important to say, that it needs saying at eight a.m.?

I get to the phone on the fifth ring.

'Hello?'

'Tess?!'

Even though she has known me and my voice for nearly thirty years, my mother still behaves as if I am Terry Waite, and this is the first time she has spoken to me after twenty-five years in captivity. I wouldn't mind, but this level of drama can be quite exhausting, especially when she sometimes rings twice a day.

'Oh it's you. Hi mum,' I say, sitting down on my bed. I am only wearing my towel and am dripping wet through.

'Oh, thank God. Thank *God* you're OK,' she says breathlessly.

28

'Why wouldn't I be?'

Had there been a national disaster whilst I was in the shower? A bombing, a military coup? A tsunami perhaps?

'I just worry about you down there, that's all. There's always that part of you when you're a mum – you'll see when you become one! – that worries something might have happened in the night.' Remembering the near miss I had last week, I wince at this, hold the receiver away from my head.

Welcome to the world of Pat Jarvis. Fifty-four, happily married to Tony Jarvis, two wonderful children, Tess and Edward, the loveliest woman on earth, and pathologically pessimistic, especially when it comes to the safety of her own children.

If there had been a train crash in, say, Cardiff, my mother would not rule out the chance that I had been interviewing someone in Wales that day and am therefore lying dead and mutilated on the rail-track. If I am not able to get back to her within half an hour of her ringing, she'll imagine me bound and gagged in the boot of a crack-dealer's car, as my phone rings futilely in my coat pocket. When I was a little girl, she would refuse to let me help her bake in case I got my hand mangled in the whisks of her electric blender or my jugular slashed through with a bread knife. To cut a long story short, my mother is constantly amazed that at twenty-eight years old, I am still alive. Such is her faith in my ability merely to survive.

'I was just calling you to remind you about your brother's birthday. But before we talk about that, I'm afraid I have a bit of bad news.'

Now there's a surprise.

'David Jewson died yesterday. Sixty-two, dropped dead in his garden, just like that.'

She awaits my reaction as I trawl through my brain, trying for the life of me to remember who David Jewson is.

'That's terrible. But . . . um . . . who's David Jewson?'

Mum sighs. This is not quite the reaction she was hoping for.

'Oh come on, you do know David Jewson, Tessa. You went to school with his daughter, Beverley. Lovely girl, very pretty, works at Natwest in town.'

Beverley Jewson had middle-aged hair and once won Young Citizen of the Year (need I say more?). That doesn't make it any less terrible for her to lose her dad, of course, but why does my mum insist on banging on about the merits of other people's children all the time? Wasn't I pretty? Wasn't I intelligent? (Wasn't I deplorably childish and should pull myself together?)

'Oh yes, I remember Beverley now,' I say, biting my lip. 'That's awful. Absolutely terrible.'

'Well it was Tess, it really was,' she says, perking up. 'The thing was, he was perfectly fine last week. I saw him in the Spar as I was buying your dad a chicken Kiev for his tea. There I was, digging around in the freezer section when I felt this hand on my back and heard this voice say, "Hi Pat, is that you?" I felt awful because I had my bi-focals on at the time and I didn't recognize him and . . . '

Bla bla bla . . .

I am only roused from the catatonic state brought on by one of my mum's monologues when I hear her say . . .

'And your dad's fifty-seven this year and he's not getting any younger. And, he's in one of his "funny moods" again.'

Dad gets in what mum calls his 'funny moods' every few months. He goes a bit quiet, watches telly a lot and potters around his greenhouse more than usual, but that's about it. I don't know why she gets all stressed about it. You just have to know how to handle him, i.e. leave him alone and stop nagging him, poor man.

'For God's sake, mum, dad's not going to drop down dead.

30

He's got more energy than you and me put together.'

This is true. My dad owns a construction company so he's up and down ladders, lifting sacks of cement daily. On top of that, he's on the golf course every weekend and last year he ran the Morecambe 10K race dressed as a shrimp for Cancer Research. What my mum lacks in get up and go, my dad makes up for ten fold. If anything it's my mum whose health is dodgy, the amount of time she spends sitting on her backside scoffing stilton and watching *Emmerdale*.

'You're right lovey, you're absolutely right,' she sighs. 'But the mind does boggle. I mean, alive one minute, dead as a doorpost the next. He was just mowing his lawn at the time, can you believe it? Who'd have thought mowing your lawn could kill you.'

I chuckle to myself at the characteristic lunacy of this comment. If mum had her way, we would all be bubble-wrapped and crash-helmeted in order to protect us from the potentially life-threatening nature of grass cuttings.

It's ten more minutes at least before she shows any sign of hanging up and allowing me to get ready for work.

'Now, don't forget Ed's birthday will you? It's next Monday so make sure you post a card on Saturday because there's no post on a Sunday and . . .'

'Yes mum. Contrary to popular belief, I am not a complete imbecile.' I hold the receiver under my chin as I attempt to put on knickers. 'I'll speak to you soon. Bye! Bye . . .!'

I press 'end call' and feel instantly guilt-ridden. Poor mum. Living in London, I never seem to have the time for leisurely phone calls with her anymore and I sometimes worry she feels jealous that I manage it with my dad. It's just, me and dad have an understanding. Whereas my mum and my brother were born with a tendency to gossip and dramatize, to expect the very worst and then delight in going on about it when that prophecy is fulfilled, me and my dad have always come

31

at life rather more sunny-side-up: in the belief that everything and everyone is good, until proved otherwise.

I finally leave the house at 8.40 a.m. thinking I'll just have time, if I'm quick, to pop into Star's before catching the bus. Star's is the dry cleaners on New North Road. Its run by a family of Turkish Cypriots, headed up by Emete, whose numerous spare tyres and racoon-ringed eyes belie an energy level so phenomenal, you wonder if this woman could pop out another five babies to add to her brood this week, and still get the whole street's ironing done.

The bell sounds as I push open the door. Emete bustles to the front of the shop, a tape measure around her neck.

'Tessa, my love. What a wonderful start to the day!' She opens her arms – each the size of one of my thighs – and places an enthusiastic kiss on both cheeks.

'Hi Emete. Morning Omer!' I shout, peering through the rows of plastic bags to the back of the shop where Emete's husband sits, coffee in hand, reading the newspaper. He raises a hand without looking up.

'Now angel, what can I do for you?' Emete pins a pink ticket to somebody's jacket and hangs it up on a rail to her right.

I hear the doorbell go again and am half-aware of a presence beside me.

'It's this shirt,' I say, taking the linen shirt out of the bag and laying it out in front of us. 'It was in my last lot of dry cleaning but it's not mine, there must have been a mix up.'

Emete puts the safety pin she was holding between her teeth and holds it up to the light. 'How strange,' she says.

'Very strange,' says a voice. I recognize it instantly. 'I've got the same problem.'

Another item of clothing appears on the counter.

I stare at the white linen dress in front of me, and then at the hands placed on top of it· tanned, big, with slender fingers and round, shell-pink nails. I'd know those hands anywhere. I trace the arms, lean, boyish, a perfect covering of fine, black hair and then the face, I'm looking at the face. My hand goes to my mouth, my heart starts to race.

'Laurence?!'

Brown eyes, behind which lie albums and albums of memories of us, are staring at me now, flickering with disbelief. He covers them with his hands. Those oh so familiar hands. 'Tess?' He uncovers his eyes again. 'Shit, it *is* you.' He looks at the shirt. 'And that's my shirt!'

Emete, prone to fits of the giggles at the best of times, is doubled up now, great wheezy laughs making her bosom heave.

'You know her?!' Her bulbous eyes are round as gobstoppers. 'You know him?!' She summons Omer from the back of the shop. 'In fifteen years, Omer! I've never known . . . oh! How wonderful!' Omer shuffles forward, puts his arm around his wife and gives a silent, toothless grin in appreciation of the moment.

We exchange clothes – Laurence gives me my white dress, I try to give him his shirt, but my hands are shaking so much that I drop it, at his feet.

'Sorry, whoops.' (What sort of a word is whoops?!)

'It's alright, I've got it.' He picks it up. When he stands up, his face is so close to mine I can see the subtle bumpiness of this morning's shave. Laurence has hardly aged at all. Hairline slightly retreating perhaps, but only to reveal two sun-kissed Vs and some fine laughter lines around those lazy, pretty eyes. I hold his gaze for as long as I can bear, then look away, embarrassed.

'Hello,' he says.

'Hi,' I say. Then we look at each other, but we're flabbergasted, half laughing, not having the slightest clue what to

33

say. I haven't seen him for five years. Not since that freezing November morning at Heathrow airport.

'It really is you' he says eventually.

'I know, I know!' I say, giggling like an idiot and wishing I'd at least had time to put some mascara on this morning.

'I cannot believe . . .' He steps back, as if to get a better look at me.

'Nor can I!' I look at Emete, who's still shaking with laughter like a mountain in an earthquake. 'It's totally freaky!'

We stand there, all four of us laughing, not really sure what we're laughing at except that this is turning out to be the most extraordinary, wonderful, glorious morning.

Omer finally speaks and when he does, it's worth every syllable.

'So how do you two know each other?' he says, flashing his gummy smile.

Laurence takes hold of one of my hands. He looks at me from under those heavy lids.

'She was my girlfriend,' he says finally, proudly even. 'We went out together, for two years. Till I went and ballsed it up.'

Laurence and I met in April 2000 – the unseasonably warm spring of our final year – and all I was doing in Manchester was lazing about campus with Gina, sipping beer out of plastic glasses.

'Do you fancy coming to this party?' Gina asked one day.

'Er, yeah!' I said. (Was the Pope a Catholic?) 'What kind of party? Count me in.'

'A garden party,' she said. 'At my mate Laurence's parents' house in Sussex. They have one every year.'

She said Laurence was studying media studies at Leeds University and was a mate from boarding school. I can't say that 'garden party' really got my pulse racing but as with most things involving Gina, there were a few surprises in store. For starters, any preconceptions I had about 'parents' and 'garden party' were swiftly eradicated the moment we accelerated up to the main gates in Gina's Fiat Bravo (the purchase of which I hold entirely responsible for me delaying learning to drive). There was some kind of French rap music, the sort you expect to throb from Parisian banlieue, reverberating from their huge, sprawling farmhouse as we walked up the long gravel path. Huge red and gold lanterns adorned the front of the house. A barefoot, wild-haired woman wearing a sequinned waistcoat and holding an enormous glass of red wine almost ran towards us, arms out-stretched. 'Bienvenue and welcome!' she cried, kissing Gina then me on both cheeks. (I immediately had a personality crush.) She was Laurence's mum – or Joelle as she insisted we call her – something which seemed biologically impossible since she looked about thirty. She'd been in England for twenty years, even though her French accent was still treacle-thick. Joelle and Laurence's dad, Paul, had met when he was a student in Aix-en-Provence and Joelle was working as a life model (so French! I loved her even more). Now he was a lecturer in French at the University of Sussex and skulked about the house wearing Woody Allen-style glasses and smoking Camel Reds. Joelle poured us equally huge glasses of wine. 'Make yourselves at home,' she said. 'All my boys are outside.'

At that point, a bare-chested young man sauntered into the kitchen, wrapped his arms around Joelle, who was stirring something sweet and spicy on the Aga, and kissed her on the cheek. 'And this,' she said, reaching on her tip toes and kissing him back, 'is my most beautiful and most idle one.'

I should have let that be my warning, but I fell in love – well, it was all-consuming, primeval lust at that point – on the spot.

Laurence was six foot two with closely cropped black curls which looked like they would spring to life like his mother's if he let them, sultry dark eyes with languorous lids and an exquisite dimple in his left cheek. He was wearing Levis twisted jeans and white flip-flops that showed off the most perfect tanned toes. I remember curling mine, complete with chipped purple nail varnish and the odd unsuccessfully frozen verucca, inside my trainers.

We're standing outside the dry cleaners now, Emete and Omer still watching from the window.

'So what are you doing now?' Laurence says it as if we have options.

(A coffee maybe? Stiff G&T? I suppose a quick session back at mine would be out of the question?)

'Oh, work, unfortunately,' I say, hoisting myself back down to earth. 'And you?'

'Yeah, work,' says Laurence.

'What kind of . . .?'

'Bar manager. I manage a bar in Clerkenwell,' he says, hands in pockets. 'My dad's gutted I'm not a lawyer or a doctor or a fucking philosopher come to think of that but you know me.'

'I know you.'

'Never one to do as I'm told.'

We shuffle from foot to foot grinning inanely and not knowing quite what to do with ourselves.

'So God, I mean, how come I've never seen you around here before?' I say, wanting to keep him here, not wanting this to end. 'Where are you living?'

'Not here. I mean, here for now, but not usually. I'm staying at a mate's. And you? You live with Gina of course, for which you clearly deserve a medal.'

'She's alright, is Marshall,' I laugh. 'You've just got to be strict. We live on Linton Street. You come out of that dry

36

cleaners and turn first right. Bit of a party house as you can imagine . . .'

'So I'm told,' says Laurence. 'So how is work in the big bad world of publishing? Still tragedy correspondent?'

'Tragedy correspondent?'

'Yeah, Gina said you earn a living hearing other people's sob stories.'

'Cheeky cow!'

He backtracks with a smile.

'In a good way.'

'It's "triumph over tragedy", get it right. Even if they've been taken in by a polyamorous cult, had all their limbs amputated and all their family have been massacred by a crazed gunman, there's always a positive angle. And if there isn't, we just make one up.'

'Like?'

'Like he didn't like his family anyway. Or his legs come to think of it.'

Laurence laughs. I find my face reddening with pleasure.

'I forgot how funny you are.' He studies me. 'And quite how foxy.'

It's a good job we both see a bus trundling towards us at that point, otherwise I might have had to react to that statement and it would definitely, have been idiotic.

'Well, this is me,' Laurence says, taking his wallet out of his pocket. 'But here, here's my card.'

'And here's mine,' I say, hastily rummaging in my bag and handing over my fuscia pink business card with *Believe It!*'s slogan emblazoned all over it: *From the touching to the twisted, every single week!* Classy.

'Thanks, um . . .' As Laurence reads the card I see his eyebrows flicker and inwardly cringe. He says, 'Just ring the bar, I'm usually there. Well, I come and go.'

Like a cat. An elusive cat.

He gives me a kiss on the cheek

'Bye,' he says.

'Yeah, bye,' I say dumbly.

Then he runs across the road, and I keep watching him. He's almost jogging now, his rucksack over one shoulder, his jacket riding up. Cute arse. Gorgeous arse. Round and perfectly formed and slightly uplifted and filling out those jeans like an arse should. He still makes the blood rush to my nether regions. He still makes my head surge with indecent thoughts.

It's 8.30 a.m., barely an hour since I got up, and I am walking to work in broad daylight, wondering how the hell we buggered that one up.

CHAPTER FOUR

'When I said my vows, "In sickness and in health", little did I know how far that would be tested. But when I saw Howard in hospital bandaged and bloodied, his face unrecognisable from the burns, there was no doubt in my mind that he was still my Howard. Freddie was born three weeks after the bomb and it's been so hard. But even now, I look at both my boys and all I see is that they are the spitting image of each other.'

Dee, 32, London

I stride into the atrium of Giant Publishing with, miraculously, fourteen minutes to spare. 9.16 and already the place looks like Piccadilly Circus only shinier.

I get into a lift with two people: one is Justine Lamb, the Editorial Director, head to toe in cream cashmere. The other is Brian Worsnop, owner of the lowest hairline in trichological history, currently devouring a Ginster's Scotch Egg, very noisily.

He beams at me, revealing bits of sausage meat between his dentures.

'Super night last Friday wasn't it? You looked a little merry, to say the least, I particularly liked your . . .'

'Yes, OK, Brian.' I smile, tight-lipped. Justine Lamb does not need to know about my drunken impressions of Blanche Jewell, our MD, complete with a pair of enormous false teeth.

I landed my job as writer on *Believe It!* magazine in 2003, as soon as I got back from what turned out to be a pretty traumatic year travelling. It was the least glamorous title in Giant Publishing's portfolio and was edited by Judith Hogg, a pigeon-chested tumour of a woman who couldn't feel empathy if her life depended on it. However, it was a proper job in journalism and with stories like *'I lost my nose but still sniffed out love'* it was hard not to see the funny side. The relentless interviewing of people with such shit lives meant you couldn't help but think your own was maybe not that bad. It was the perfect distraction from a broken heart, too. A heart broken by Laurence Cane.

Bing! The lift door opens and I stride out, into a pool of morning sun which drenches the office in an orange-pink glow.

'Morning Tess.'

'Morning Jocelyn.'

Jocelyn, our receptionist, is from Perth in Australia. She has a shocking-red bob that swings around her face when she walks or even moves (mainly due to a sort of wave effect brought on by her sheer size) and a bottom as wide as her homeland.

I feel I can say this and not sound fattist because Jocelyn is far from embarrassed about her body. In fact she accentuates her 'womanly curves' with sleeveless, bingo-wing-revealing tops in lurid prints and tight, white, cellulite-enhancing trousers.

'May I say Tessa, you look fintistic today,' she trills, biting into a ham and cheese croissant. 'Off on a date tonight by any chance, met someone nice on the Internet again?'

Ever since I made the grave mistake of telling Jocelyn I

had a date with a guy from Match.com, she has asked me this question on average twice a week.

'No, not tonight, Jocelyn,' I say, hanging up my coat. 'I've gone off men from the Internet anyway, all they ever seem to be into is skydiving and bungee jumping if their photos are anything to go by.'

'Quite right too,' says Jocelyn. 'I've never been one for adrenaline sports myself.'

Back at my desk, I hear Anne-Marie busily relaying the latest in the saga of Vegan Boyfriend to someone on the phone. 'He won't even kiss me if I've eaten a bacon sandwich, you know,' she's saying proudly, pop-sock-clad feet up on the desk. '*That's* how committed he is.'

I give her a little wave, she gives me one back. I turn on my computer and see the little red light is flashing on my phone.

'You have two new messages,' says the automated voice.

Beep.

'Hiya . . . is that Tess? This is Keeley. You came to our house last week to interview me and Dean. Fing is, yeah, we woz a bit pissed when we did the interview. Dean had just bought me that bottle of Asti to help with the nerves and now we're worried everyone's gonna find out . . .'

Oh dear. Another second thoughts casualty. You'd think what with the tape running and the photographer turning up, people might realize the larger ramifications before they start blabbing about their boyfriend's penis enlargement to the national press.

Next!

I try to concentrate but thoughts of Laurence are like a swarm of butterflies in my brain.

Next is a message from a woman from Dudley. Her husband is forty-three stone and bed-ridden, can we do a campaign to save his life?

'Before I ballsed it up,' he said. I can't stop those words from circulating in my mind. Admittedly, there had been a brief moment when I felt like punching the air – it is only right he should have suffered a bit after what he did to me. But that was years ago now and anyway, let's face it, I ballsed it up too. If I hadn't been so flighty, if I hadn't done a Tess special and buggered off around the world, assuming everything would be hunky dory when I got back, maybe we would be together now, in love, married, maybe even a baby on the way.

I've got seventeen things to do on my desktop To Do list but I all I can do is day-dream. The fact is, when I look back to my two and a half years with Laurence the entire era reverberates with a huge WHAT IF. What if I had engaged my head as well as my heart, what if I had not been so naïve, what if I had been thinner, more demure, more exotic. What if, for example, I had not got caught having sex with Laurence Cane the very first time I met him, by Mrs Cane herself? At *her* garden party. Maybe it was jinxed from the start.

I blame the sun. That and his liberal parents who plied us with an endless flow of Beaujolais. (My parents would have provided two boxes of Asda's best, announcing, 'and when that's finished, it's finished, Tessa.') By three a.m. everyone who was going home had gone and Gina had passed out on the sofa-bed in the spare room. So, it was just the two of us, talking and drinking at the kitchen table.

'Your mum's so cool,' I slurred, nursing about my eightieth glass of wine, my teeth black as a peasant's. 'So exotic and bohemian.'

Laurence laughed. 'Everyone says that,' he said. 'And yeah, I suppose she is.' Then he paused, hesitated, then said, 'But she's not as cool as you.'

That's when he turned to me, took my face in his hands

and started kissing me, passionately and urgently. 'You're funny,' he said.

'Funny?'

'Yeah, and kinda sexy, you make me laugh.'

I wasn't quite sure what to make of that. But what did it matter anyway? I was snogging a Thierry Henry look-alike.

He reached inside my top and placed his hand on my breast. 'Come here,' he whispered, fixing me with eyes that told me how much he wanted me. Then his hand was suddenly in my bra and he drew me close and we were kissing, harder this time, our tongues exploring each other's mouths hungrily, hot, quick breath moist on my skin. He gestured for me to hold my arms up, he removed my top. He removed my bra. And not with a teenage fumble, but in one, smooth, masterful stroke, as if he undressed women for a living.

Then, pulling me upwards, never taking his lips from mine, he put his hands around my waist and picked me up, sitting me on the table in front of him. His hands were big and warm and as they explored me: my shoulders, my neck, my stomach, the nerves in my groin suddenly sparked into action.

'Should we be doing this?' I looked at him, eyes shining under the table lamp.

'Don't you want to?'

'Yes, yes, of course I bloody want to!' I said, which came out far more eager than I had anticipated.

'Well that's good then,' he said, looking at me from under canopy-sized eyelashes.

He swept my hair back from my face, then gently pushed me back onto the table, never diverting from my gaze.

'Stop it!' I giggled. 'Your parents might come down, your brothers might hear!'

'So what,' he said, 'I don't give a shit.'

He undid my jeans and I undid his, my hands trembling, and we were kissing all over each other's faces and necks and he ran his hands through my hair, pushing it back from my face and kissing me again. Then he was flicking his tongue all over my nipples and I was moaning and half laughing at the same time and pulling him into me and we were going at it hammer and tongs over this huge oak table and I'd already decided it was true what they said about French men. And the lamp above us was creaking slightly with the motion of us, and I felt like Vanessa Paradis in one of those late-night saucy films. Then:

'Putain de merde Maman! Qu'est ce que tu fou?!'

Doing a course in French, I knew this loosely translated as 'What the fuck are you doing?'

Then Laurence leapt off me, his erection waving about like a rather awkward third person and pulled up his jeans.

'Oooh la la.' I noted the distinct lack of humour in his mother's voice. Then in her face. She was standing right in front of us. 'It's three a.m. And you have a bedroom to go to, Jesus Laurence, have some respect.'

And then I said the weirdest thing, to this day I don't know what possessed me.

'Merci beaucoup!' I shouted after her. Just like that. No joke. I nearly died.

'*What* did you say?' Laurence said incredulously. Eyeing me up like he'd just spent the last half an hour getting off with a mutant.

But I couldn't say anything. I covered my face with my hands.

My stomach churns at the memory. I turn back to my inbox and there it is.

From: LCane@blackberry.co.uk
To: tess_jarvis@giant.co.uk
I was wondering, now we have our glad rags back, you free tomorrow night?

I am now!

I am on my way back from lunch, after reciting the email word for word and relaying the whole dry cleaners scenario to Anne-Marie and Jocelyn and basically the entire office, when I feel the growling vibration of a text message in my pocket. It's Jim.

Warren. House party tomorrow. Keep it free.

Presumptuous or what! Now I get my own back. I text:

Sorry, no can do, have hot date with sexy ex. Ha! Kiss that! One all. I do have a social life of my own, you know.

My phone rings immediately. 'Jim' flashes up.
'Oh, now that is lame,' he says.
'Come again?'
'Resurrecting an old boyfriend. I don't think that counts.'
'Sorry, I didn't realize this was a competition!' I laugh.
'You started it. You're the one who said "one all".'
Jim is always like this when he is on school holidays. Too much time on his hands, gets very childish.
'It's a date isn't it?' I say. 'He's a bloke isn't he? He fancies me, I fancy him, what's not to like?'
'Fine, it's just, you know, take your good friend Jim for example. Not one to resort to dredging up old flames when in need of a bit of excitement, I travelled far and wide for romance and found an Italian corker who can offer me first class stays at exquisite hotels with no strings attached.'
'Annalisa found you, remember? White as a sheet, having just barfed in a bin in Rimini town centre you were so hungover, I seem to remember.'
'She didn't know I'd just barfed in a bin.'
'Bet she did, bet she could smell it on you.' (I always sink to Jim's level eventually.)

'No, I was gentlemanly and paid for her coffee actually and anyway she fell for my northern charm and quick wit.'

'Whatever.'

'Yeah, whatever. The point is, I thought you hated Laurence?'

'What makes you think it's Laurence?! I know it's hard to believe but I have had other boyfriends, you know.'

'Not ones you'd call your "sexy" ex, you haven't.'

I protest but Jim's right. I would not call any of my other exes my sexy ex. Not because they weren't sexy at all (I like to think I have upheld some standards in my life) but because Laurence was THE sexy ex. The One. Or as near as damned as I've ever been to it.

'Anyway,' I continue, feeling ever so slightly triumphant, that Jim has even thought about my past relationships enough to even make this observation, 'I never said I hated him.' Did I? He broke my heart; I was gutted for a while. OK, maybe I hated his guts for a while but I never actually hated him. 'We were young, I expected too much. That was like, seven thousand years ago now anyway. Give the guy a break.'

'I've got nothing against Laurence,' protests Jim. 'It was you that he upset, or have you forgotten the night you got back from travelling and demanded I come round, having drunk a bottle of wine in about half an hour feeling practically suicidal? What makes you think he's changed is all I'm saying.'

'Jesus Jim, it's just a date, he didn't ask me to marry him.'

'OK. Well that's OK then,' says Jim, cheerily now. 'Have a good time and make sure you give old Cane a damn good seeing to.'

I hang up, walk back to work smiling to myself. Jim really is weird sometimes.

I text Gina 'how's the evil hangover?' And look at my watch: 1.53 p.m. There's seven minutes till lunch officially

46

ends. Still, a lot can happen in seven whole minutes. I go to the Ladies and then, I don't know why, perhaps it's women's instinct that draws my attention just then, to something in my bag. Shimmering among the bus tickets and leaflets about cultural events I know I will never get round to attending, the blue wrapper containing the other pregnancy test from the pack of two I bought glints at me from the bottom of my bag. I'm not pregnant, I can't be, I had a negative test. (Shelley Newcombe told me back in Year 9 that you can never have a positive after a negative.) But it cost me fifteen pounds and I really don't like waste. And so I go into a cubicle and I get it out. It's less of a conscious decision, more of a cleaning-up exercise, just as you might eat the one left-over stick of Kit-Kat that was making your desk look untidy. I wee on the little stick and balance it on top of the toilet roll holder, not thinking, just doing. Then I set the timer on my watch for two minutes.

1.50

This is ridiculous, I've even got PMT: sore boobs, knack-ered, short fuse, the Works

1.30

No period though and that's a fact, I'm a week late; I'm never a week late

1.00

I am stressed though, that's also a fact and I bet two seconds after doing this negative test, I'll come on (ruining my best knickers it's always the way)

0.45

I glance at the test, yep, just as I thought

0.30

Two lines emerging, God, I hate wasting money, especially due to paranoia

0.25

Misplaced, neurotic, paranoia

47

0.14

I pick up the test and tear off some toilet roll – I'm wrapping it up now, to throw in the bin

0.10

But then the light catches it – the breath catches in my throat

0.08

It can't be, can it? *can it?* oh my God! tell me it can't!

0.06

I feel like I might throw up, I swallow, take a deep breath, exhale slowly, then look at it again

0.04

But it's still there

it's *still* there . . .

a *cross,* a *bright blue fuck-off cross!* I'M PREGNANT! I'M FUCKING PREGNANT!! and I can hardly breathe, I can't get my breath – help me! – my lungs won't expand, and all I'm aware of, apart from this sensation, is a great surging, flooding of blood to my head . . .

If it wasn't suddenly rush hour in the toilets, I might be making much more noise by now. But I can hear someone in the cubicle next to me, blowing their nose, and I know – she even does that in her own special way – that it's Anne-Marie, so I don't, I don't make a sound. I just stay where I am, hand clasped over my mouth, my world having just shifted on its axis, and me hanging off the side by one finger-nail.

My first concern (which points towards promising maternal impulses at least) is that I must have pickled whatever is there, if it really is there, by the alcohol consumed last night, the sambucas at Greg's birthday drinks, the drugs. Shit, the drugs! I had a spliff with Gina last night and I am overcome with a murderous guilt, a guilt I am wholly and completely unprepared for. And then comes the shock, it hits

48

me like a wall. Shock, guilt, shock, what the hell do I feel? The emotions seem to thrash over me, like merciless ice cold waves, pinning me to the back of the toilet door and stealing my breath.

There's the sound of flushing next door, the taps running, the pad-pad of Anne-Marie's hemp boots and the creak of the door as it shuts behind her. I'm feeling a whole kaleidoscope of emotions now but what are they? Am I happy? Is this elation I'm feeling? Or is it horror? I don't know. I can't think.

I hold the test in my hand, my breathing shaky, my palms moist, and suddenly I'm very angry. Angry that the other test lied to me, even angrier for doing this – getting pregnant in the first place, and now I'm angry at myself for handling this so badly.

Then it occurs to me. This cannot be right. No, it must be the alcohol from the weekend, turning the test positive. Like litmus paper. But I'm clutching at straws of course; I don't really believe that. Plus, something instinctiv tells me I am pregnant. I feel different. In that moment, the whole toilet cubicle in which I am standing seems to spin and to distort, as if everything I have ever known, ever experienced as my life, the feeling of just being me, is annihilated and I feel utterly disoriented.

I have to speak to Jim. Now. But I can't face seeing someone I know, so I don't take the lift down I take the stairs, two at a time.

Outside, everything looks different, as if I'm looking at it for the first time. It's raining, pelting it down, and so I run, clutching my phone, to the doorway of a recruitment company at the end of the road. My hands are shaking as I find Jim's number. I'm pregnant, I'm fucking pregnant!

It rings and rings and then he finally picks up.

'Hello.'

His voice sounds muffled, sleepy almost.

'Jim it's me again.'

'I know. Listen, can I ring you back?' he whispers. I hear a woman cough.

Oh brilliant, Annalisa's there. I am phoning him to tell him I'm carrying his child, and his Italian F.B. is in his bed on one of her impromptu visits to London, almost definitely naked. I met her once, his gnocchi nookie, on one of her 'romantic' breaks to East Dulwich.

'You should get togezzer with Tess, she is adorable!' she apparently said to Jim afterwards. 'You're an English lost boy,' she always says to him. (She means loser, but she never quite gets it right, and 'lost boy' sums him up so much better I always think.) I have nothing against her. I really couldn't care less if she was in his bed four times a year, but now? 'Christ Jim!!' I want to say, but I can't, because it's not his fault. I mean I know it takes two to tango and all that, and that if I am pregnant (I am still hanging onto the fact this might all be a very large mistake), it's his doing as much as mine, but I can't start going all jealous wannabe girlfriend on him now. It's just ... stood here, his DNA fusing with mine, it's in slightly bad taste, that's all.

And so I say, 'It's really pretty important. I do need to speak to you. Now.'

'OK, hang on,' he says, and there's a few seconds where he obviously puts his hand over the receiver and explains he has to take the call.

I can picture him now. He is getting out of bed, hair sticking up, skinny legs making for the door, holding his privates. He is slipping on his dressing gown, going into the kitchen and picking up the other phone.

'So what's wrong, hey?'

The concern in his voice makes me well up, my voice starts to wobble.

'I am pregnant after all.'

Silence. He swallows.

'What do you mean? You did a test, it was negative.'

'I did another, it was positive.'

'How do you know?'

'There's a cross.'

'What sort of cross?'

'A blue one.'

A pause. Just the sound of his breathing.

'Are you sure you've read the instructions properly?'

'Yes. I'm sure, I'm not that stupid.'

There's another silence and then when he speaks again, there's a tone in his voice I've never heard before.

'Is it mine?' he says softly. And as the tears finally fall, and I say, 'Yes, yes, of course it's bloody yours,' I realize that the tone in his voice, was hope.

We arrange to meet outside the Tate Modern after work; I'll bring the test so he can see it for himself. I put the phone down and walk back to the office, under a cloud, through a city sheathed in rain. I imagine that everyone I pass: a group of smokers huddled outside their office, a queue outside the post office, can see inside my womb, red and illuminated. And I have never felt so extraordinary in my entire life.

When I get in the lift for the third time today, who should step in behind me but Julia, my ridiculously glamorous friend from Journalism College, who is eight months pregnant herself. She's features editor of *Luxe* now, having actually worked her way up rather than got to the first place that would have her and never moved again, so we often bump into each other like this and have some awkward conversation about how I should send her some features ideas, which of course I never get round to.

'Hi,' she says, but I'm not really listening, I'm too fixated on the words that bubble threateningly in my throat. 'I'm pregnant too!' I want to say. 'Help! What do I do!?' But I don't obviously, that would be ludicrous. So instead I say, 'Had a good week?'

'Yeah, chilled out,' she says, stroking her bump. 'It's all I can do to haul myself off the sofa these days. Fraser's started calling me The Rock, because I'm so hard and big and immovable,' she laughs. Then she says, 'Oh God, don't. My pelvic floor isn't quite what it was.' Then she laughs again and I do too on some very obvious delayed reaction.

I imagine she can sense it, smell the fact I'm pregnant. They say pregnant women have heightened senses. I know any minute now she's going to say it and it's making me nauseous with anticipation. I run through what I'm going to say in my head, how I'm going to explain.

'Tess?' she says eventually.

'Yes?' I gasp. Oh shit, here it comes.

'I said have you?'

'Have I what?'

'Have you got anything planned for the weekend?'

'Oh right! I say, letting out an almighty sigh of relief. She's frowning at me now.

'Yeah, quiet.'

I can sense her looking at me, but I stare at the floor. She giggles.

'You've met someone haven't you?' she whispers in my ear. 'Go on, I can tell by that face.'

I don't stop staring at the floor.

'Oh no! I know! You've finally got it together with Jim – that's it isn't?'

'No!' I snap, making her start back ever so slightly.

'Oh right. It's just, you were looking kind of shifty that's all.'

Thankfully it's then that we get to the eighth floor and

52

Julia waddles out as I mumble something about having a hangover.

I rush to my desk, the email's there. I didn't send it. Thank fuck I didn't send it!

To: LCane@blackberry.co.uk
Yes I'm free, if I haven't been taken in by a polyamorous cult by then.

(Or if I haven't been impregnated.)
I press delete.

By some miracle, I make it through the rest of the day, the sun sinking behind St Paul's by the time I meet Jim outside the Tate.

He's sitting on one of the black rubber benches when I get there. His gangly legs are stretched out in front of him and he's carrying a bunch of freesias with foil wrapped around the stems.

He looks up when I say hello and squints into the light.

'These are for you,' he says holding out the flowers. They smell amazing. 'I'm sorry about before.'

'About what?'

'Er, for being in bed with Annalisa when you rang to tell me you're pregnant? I feel awful.'

'Don't worry, honestly I've forgotten already.' A picture of her, nude, black hair flowing all over the pillow pops into my head. 'Was she naked?' I ask.

'I thought you'd forgotten,' says Jim. 'Sorry,' I mumble. 'I have, I have.'

I sit down beside him. The evening sun flickers like embers on the river in front of us. 'Anyway,' I say. 'Look at this.'

I undo the front pocket of my bag, take out the test and hand it to him. He unwraps it, looks at me, squeezes my thigh, then holds up the test to the light.

'Mmm. There's definitely a cross there isn't there?'

'Really? Oh God, I was hoping . . . Do you think?'

The reality hits me, there's no getting away from this now. I burst into tears, tears of pure shock.

'Sorry,' I say, 'I just don't know what to do. I cannot believe this is happening, what are we going to do?'

Jim rubs his face with his hands then puts an arm around me and we don't say anything for a while, just stare blankly at the water. Then Jim says, 'I don't know. But whatever happens it will be alright, OK? I promise. Whatever happens, I'm here for you.'

In reality there never really was any question of whether I was going to keep the baby.

'It's your decision,' Jim said, as we walked across Millennium Bridge. 'I'll stand by you whatever you decide.'

It felt like I was alone at that moment. As if the glittering towers at either side, the Gherkin glowing orange like a burning rocket and the river below us were holding their breath, awaiting my decision.

But the truth was, I had already made my decision. The decision was made the moment the blue cross emerged. If I was eighteen, I wouldn't think twice, I'd have an abortion. But I am twenty-eight, a grown woman and besides, the way things are going lately – Laurence showing up out of the blue and now this, the second earth-shattering event of the year and it's only April – half of me wonders whether life is trying to tell me something and I should sit up and listen.

'I want to keep it,' I say. And even though I mean it, I still want to gobble all the words back again as soon as they've left my mouth.

'You do?' Jim stops, turns and looks at me. He looks . . . what is that look? . . . *delighted*?! And for a fleeting second,

I think what a brilliant dad he'll make and maybe, just maybe this isn't so terrible after all.

'Yes,' I say looking at him. 'It's scary as hell but I do. I mean, it's not sunk in yet, and this isn't conventional. Actually it's utterly mental! But . . .'

But what? I think.

'But to have an abortion would feel like the coward's way out,' I say, and for that moment I really believe what I'm saying. 'It would feel like not choosing life. Not just literally in terms of the baby, but for me, for us.'

Jim gets hold of my hand. We're right on top of the bridge now and the wind is blowing our hair sideways, making our eyes sting.

'I agree, Tess, it's alright, I agree . . .' He says beaming at me now.

'And the main reason,' I add.

'What's the main reason?' Jim asks.

'In the future, the years to come, I couldn't deal with what could have happened, you know?'

'I know, I know.'

'I couldn't deal with what might have been.'

CHAPTER FIVE

'I knew as soon as I set eyes on Mac that I was in big trouble. At fifty to my twenty-six, he was way too old. But he was so bloody sexy – a big hairy bear on wheels, how could I resist that? People stare when he's pushing Layla down the street in his leathers and old enough to be her grandad but I don't care. He's not what I expected, but he's a kitten. The most loving dad Layla could ever wish for.'

Georgie, 27, Brighton

I could tell Jim was secretly delighted by his own virility – by the fact that he shot and he scored. But I also knew, despite his usual optimism, that he was freaked out beyond belief.

The days that followed were totally surreal. We were both – we still are – in a state of shock and took to calling each other sometimes three times a day with phone calls that went a bit this.

Me: Hello

Jim: Hello

Long pause

Jim: How are you feeling?

Me: Weird. How are you feeling?

Jim: Yeah, weird

Long pause

Jim: I'm going to be a dad, I can't believe it

Me: *You* can't believe it!? Try being the one who's got to carry the thing for nine months

Jim: I thought I wouldn't be able to have kids though, that I'd have killed all my strong swimmers with all the booze I've quaffed

(See, I was so right about the virility thing)

Me: Well you can and it's true

Jim: I know, I just can't believe it though, it's like it's happening to someone else

That particular line was not that encouraging. And I told him so.

We're on the fourth floor of Borders on Oxford Street in the Parenting section.

I need to say that again.

We're on the fourth floor of Borders on Oxford Street in the Parenting section.

Nope. Still sounds ridiculous.

I lean against the bookshelf leafing through a book called *Bundle of Joy: 101 Real Stories of Motherhood* as if I do this every day, as if I do, actually, belong to this weird species, most of them mutant-shaped, milling around the shop floor, hand in hand: 'The Expectants'.

But I am not expectant. At no point did I ever *expect* this! When that positive test emerged it was categorically the most unexpected thing I have ever experienced in my life. Things like this don't happen to me, they happen to the people I interview – everything happens to the people I interview, but not to me.

My life has been one big cushy ride so far, which is why I've always blagged it when it comes to taking precautions against life's eventualities. After all, the less stuff happens to you, the less you think it will, don't you? I never did lie awake at night, dissecting my last session of oral sex and panicking that I hadn't listened in Biology and it was perfectly feasible to get pregnant from a blow job after all. I rolled my eyes at Mrs Tucker our 'personal health' teacher – you can imagine what she got called – who said you could get pregnant by withdrawal – something that evoked all the risk of a banking transaction to me.

Some would say I'm reckless (my mum would, but then my mother thinks caffeine after five p.m. is reckless). I would say I've always been relaxed, optimistic. OK, I admit it, veering towards winging it and hoping for the best. And yet, here I am, and the thing that's caught me most off guard, aside from the stampede of hormones currently taking over my body like an occupying army, is that I've been caught out. My winging it wings are out of fuel, my Bank of Blag is cleared of funds, my cat's nine lives are all used up. Game's over Tess Jarvis. You've officially fucked up.

It's late afternoon, ten past five, and the sun is pouring in through the floor-length window, illuminating a column of dust particles which swirl to the ground, a reminder of the passing of time, of the seconds, minutes and days since my news. In the bookshop café to my right, there's the clatter of tea cups and saucers, normal people getting on with their normal lives.

Two aisles in front, I can just see Jim's head of dark, over-grown hair buried in a book and I am immediately transported back to the day we met. He was stood like that then too, the first time I saw him, on the second floor of the John Rylands Library, head buried in the *The Death of the Author*, bathed in autumn sun.

I remember thinking, just as I do now, he looked a bit vacant with those full lips hanging slightly open. But I liked his slim, defined face too, this guy with the hair that had its own mind.

I squint to read the title of the book Jim's reading: *You're Pregnant Too Mate! The Essential Guide for Expectant Fathers.* And have a sudden inexplicable urge to blow out the brains of the author. He's been reading it since we got here. Don't ask me how we got here either, it wasn't a conscious decision. One minute we were buying his mum a present for her birthday. (Already made the seamless transition from friend to mother-of-child, side-stepping girlfriend and wife as I go . . .) The next, we'd wandered in here, on auto-pilot really, me looking as shell shocked as if I'd just emerged from a national disaster, a look I've been sporting for more than a week now.

I go back to my book – a cheery story of a woman whose morning sickness was so bad she would dry heave at Tesco's cheese counter – but the words start to blur, I can't concentrate. Everything in here is too loud, too bright.

Ever since we decided we were definitely going ahead with this, the whole world has felt like this: like I've woken up in a different one.

I go home, I watch TV with Gina, I go to Star's and sip sweet Turkish tea and chat to Emete whilst she mends my trousers. I do everything I've always done, and yet it doesn't feel like me doing it. It's like someone has hijacked my body. Someone pregnant.

'Hey, listen to this,' says Jim, leaning over the bookshelf. 'It says here that at six weeks pregnant, your baby is the size of a shrimp – how cool is that?'

'Right, yes, very cool,' I say, trying to sound enthusiastic. 'Although I don't much fancy the idea of a sea creature setting up home in my body.'

'Right,' nods Jim and goes back to his book.

'A shrimp,' he mumbles when I don't say anything else. 'Maybe that's what we can call it, "shrimpy".'

'Jim, shut up,' I mumble. I feel bad for being so moody. I can't help it though. In less than a fortnight, we seem to have gone from best of mates – two people who actually have fun – to me weeping at not being able to work the tin opener.

Jim sidles off to the other side of the bookshelf, taking his book and dragging his feet in mock rejection. I bite my lip. I feel awful.

The fact Jim seems to be taking this so well isn't helping. Despite the shock, ever since we found out, it's weird, he's had this look on his face; a look of boy-like wonder that says, 'I just got the best surprise of my life.'

But me? I don't feel like that. I don't even know how I feel.

After the official showing of the pregnancy test, I mainly lay on my bed, listening to the strangely comforting soundtrack of inner city London, or did cool, long lengths at the outdoor swimming pool, anything to stop the noise in my head.

Both Vicks and Gina must know something's up though. I've refused wine for three nights at home. I told Gina I've got cystitis, but I don't think she's buying it. 'Cystitis?' she said. 'Likely story. You must be pregnant.' She was joking, but I nearly fell off my chair. Plus when Vicky called me at work the other day, my voice was doing strange things. 'What's up with you?' she said. 'What's happened? You can tell me.'

'I'm pregnant!' I wanted to shout. 'I'm up the bloody spout, what the hell do I do ?!' But I promised Jim I'd wait until the twelve-week scan before I went blabbing to everyone. In that typical male way, he likes to do things that don't concern him by the book but I'm not sure I can wait that long.

'How pregnant are you now?' enquires Jim, looking up from his book.

'Oh, I don't know, about six weeks I think, why?'

'Nothing.'

'Why?'

Here we go again.

'Because it says here that by seven weeks, the baby's internal organs are in place, its brain is fully developed, and the body measures around two point five centimetres long.'

I almost gag.

'That's around an inch,' I squeak, in disbelief. 'How can it be?'

How can it be? I've barely got my head around any of this and yet its brain is a week off being fully formed? Its entire personality practically in place! There's still a part of me too, who doesn't really believe it. Even though Dr Cork threw her head back and laughed when I told her I'd done three tests, I can't accept it.

'For heaven's sake my girl!' she spluttered, in that soup-thick Irish accent. 'I think we can safely say you're expecting, can we not?' But I didn't believe it. Not really. Even when she scrolled down on her calendar, looked at me over her half-moon glasses and gave me a date: December fourteenth. 'Ah! A little Christmas baby.' I didn't believe it was true.

I pick up another book, *A Bloke's 100 Tips for Surviving Pregnancy*.

'Your partner's pregnancy may mean that you both rethink your domestic situation,' it says. 'It is still common for partners co-habiting and expecting a child to decide the time is right to get hitched.'

Right. But was it common for those 'partners' to be friends and not lovers? Was it common for them not to be co-habiting, or ever likely to be? Should we, after all, be rethinking our domestic situation and just get hitched anyway? Where were the rules for us? The top tips for us? I didn't need *My Best Friend's Guide to Pregnancy*, I needed, *Help! I'm Pregnant, and it's my Best Friend's!*

I look around me; the place is swarming with couples, the

61

men protective of their girlfriends and wives who house the offspring that soon will make their nuclear, normal families. I look at Jim, still nose in his book. What were we? A pair of frauds.

I decide to take the *Bundle of Joy*. I figure some real-life tales may help with the denial. I go to the till and stand in the queue of couples, two-by-two, Noah's bloody Ark.

I'm aware that my heart is beating but it's only when I feel Jim's hand on my shoulder, then his arm around my back that I realize I'm crying – again – that tears are rolling down my face and the woman at the till is staring at me.

'Come on,' says Jim, softly, stepping in front of a sea of staring faces and paying for the book. 'I've got an idea. Let's go to Frankie's.'

Frankie's is an old jazz club on Charing Cross Road. Jim and I stumbled upon it a couple of years ago, a night that ended up with us dancing ourselves sober to a Bossanova swing band. It became our place after that. 'Would madam care to dance ce soir?' Jim would call and ask me, then we'd get all dolled up and we'd hit Frankie's, dance the night away.

But I don't want to go now. Frankie's won't make this any better.

'I dunno,' I say, as we glide down the escalator, 'I'm just not sure I'm in the mood.'

We go anyway – after all I'm not in the mood for anything. It's only just gone 6.30 p.m. by the time we arrive and thankfully it's almost empty.

We sit at the bar sipping on virgin pina coladas which makes me want to laugh and cry all at the same time. Laugh because Jim is sipping on a drink with a cherry and an umbrella in it, as a show of solidarity, when really he'd kill for a beer, and cry because why did we have drinks with umbrellas and cherries in anyway? It didn't feel like we were celebrating.

My chin starts to go again.

'Sorry, I'm a mess, I don't know what's wrong with me,' I say, forcing a smile.

'Hey, come on,' says Jim, dragging his stool closer, 'Look at me.'

'I'm scared too you know.' He takes my hands in his, trying to ignore the snail trail of snot up one side where I've wiped my nose. 'I'm scared shitless to be honest.'

'But you seem . . . you're amazing . . . you're just handling this so well, so much better than me. It's like you're, I don't know, happy about it all,' I say.

He thinks about this, clears his throat. 'Well, I'm definitely not unhappy about it. I'm thirty Tess. I don't want to end up some sad old bachelor boy, no children, no life, answering the door in my underpants.'

'You do that already.'

'Oh. So I do.'

The barman places a bowl of dry-roasted peanuts on the bar which only makes me want to blub some more. Mainly because I can't even have one. No peanuts, Dr Cork said. I can't even have a goddamn peanut.

'Give it time,' Jim says, 'it's so early.'

'I know, it's just, I can't help feeling this has fucked every-thing up. You could have met someone else, got married, done it properly, we both could have. But things are going to be so much more complicated now.'

I lean back in my chair and squeeze my eyes shut. Every time I think of one consequence of all this, another rears its head, a can of worms.

'But I was never after a wife, Tess, you know that,' says Jim, making me look at him. 'All that wedding, two point four kids conventional thing was never something I dreamt of.'

I look at the floor.

'But I did, Jim,' I say, looking up at him. 'I did dream of that.'

A horrid silence. Jim stares at his drink. It's only as the words leave my mouth that I realize how true they are. I had it all planned. I don't mean planned like Vicky planned things – a subscription to *You and Your Wedding* at twenty, married and pregnant by twenty-seven. I don't mean planning your child so meticulously its birthday coincides with school holidays. The point I'm making, and the problem with me I suppose, is that I didn't realize I needed to 'plan' anything. I had it all filed under 'goes without saying'. Meeting 'The One', the white wedding, the joint mortgage and ceremonious last pill as we give up binge-drinking in preparation of our forthcoming child. The shagging – oh the shagging! – as we'd take to our bed on sun-drenched afternoons, giggling at the decadence of it all. The leaping into each other's arms with joy at the positive test and the first scan on dad-to-be's phone. And who is that dad-to-be in my mind's eye? Not Jim, my friend, the man I love platonically but hadn't even considered casting for this role. No, that man I imagined, before this whole 'life plan' went utterly tits up was Laurence. But I let him slip through my hands, just like fine golden sand, like clay on a potter's wheel, like a brand new slippery baby. Like life itself.

'This is so ridiculous,' I say suddenly.

'What is?'

'This. Us.'

My cheeks burn. I don't want to go on like this, but I've opened the floodgates now and it's all coming out.

'What do you mean?'

'People don't do this, Jim. Have a baby with their friend. We're not a couple, are we?'

Jim closes his eyes and groans.

'We were never actually an item. You're a grown man, a

64

teacher, a responsible person, *apparently*.' I hate myself now, it's not his fault. 'What sort of thirty-year-old man doesn't even have a condom?'

Jim snorts. *'What?'*

'A condom Jim, you know, a contraceptive?'

He blinks and splutters, incredulous at this last comment. 'It takes two to tango Tess and anyway, you were drunk.'

'We both were!'

'And you were wearing those knickers. Those frilly black things. I mean, they were hardly a contraceptive.'

He's gone mad.

'And there's the driving issue,' he says.

'Driving issue?!' I stare at him stunned.

'The fact you can't. And you're always putting off learning. And the fact you always miss the last tube and hate night buses and so you end up staying at mine and . . .'

'And what?! So this was bound to happen? The fact I can't drive and favour vaguely attractive underwear over enormous belly-warmers was one day destined to get me knocked up? In case you've forgotten, you were in bed with another woman when I called to tell you I was pregnant.'

'You've never said that bothered you,' Jim says. 'If you had . . .'

'It doesn't bother me. That's the problem!' I say, throwing my hands in the air. 'Don't you think it should? Don't you think it should bother me, just a bit, that the father of my baby is shagging someone else?!'

The barman clears his throat, loudly. A party of businessmen have just gathered at the bar.

Jim's got his head in his hands now.

'But don't you understand, this isn't about us anymore,' he says quietly. 'It's about this baby, a baby that needs us, more than anything now. There's thousands of women who can't even get pregnant, have you thought about that?'

I had, actually, and despised myself for being so ungrateful but I couldn't help myself.

'Forgive me,' I say. 'But I'm not feeling my most charitable right now.'

'I can see that,' says Jim, standing up and getting his coat. We leave, go home. Our separate homes.

CHAPTER SIX

'I came out of the bathroom in my knickers screaming, "Look! It's positive, we're having a baby!" Neil didn't say anything at first and I thought, oh God, he hates it. Then he dived over to the wardrobe, took out his Polaroid camera, and took a picture of me, there and then, holding the positive test. Even now, I look at that picture, stuck up on our fridge and I want to cry. I look so damn young and thin!'

Fiona, 38, Edinburgh

Gina leans back on the window of the café, folds her arms and groans.

'I suppose you're thinking, "told you so"?' she says, through half-shut eyes. 'I suppose everyone saw it coming but me.'

I put my hand on her arm. 'No,' I say, but I don't say anything else. I know the drill.

It's been almost a fortnight since Jasper dumped her – in spectacularly cruel form – by text, half an hour before she was due to meet him at a party – and she's still in self-loathing mode. This means she doesn't want my sympathy or my analysis of what went wrong, she just wants me to be her punch-bag whilst she lets it all out.

It's Sunday and this was the day I was going to tell Gina about the baby. I intended to wait until the scan like I promised Jim, but she already knows, I swear. She found my book, the *Bundle of Joy* book, you don't get much more incriminating than that. I came home from work to find her reading it in the kitchen, scoffing at all the schmaltzy pictures of women cradling their bumps.

'Check it out, how smug and tedious are this lot?' she said, pretending to stick her fingers down her throat. Gina is not what you'd call baby-friendly. In fact to be perfectly honest, she's actively Anti Baby. She and Vicky used to be the best of mates – we all did. But since Vicky had Dylan eighteen months ago and 'de-camped to the other side' as Gina sees it, their relationship has definitely suffered. Gina treats Vicks like she's holding a bomb when she's holding Dylan and when Vicky relayed the story of her horrific birth (which to be fair involved full stitching details and the way her placenta 'slid across the floor', it came out with such force) Gina was sick in her mouth.

So, I wasn't surprised in the slightest at her reaction to the book. It was only when her face fell and she said . . . 'Oh my God, is this yours?' that I went a deathly shade of pale.

'I'm doing a health piece on pregnancy, it's for research,' I lied, sticking my head inside the fridge and blaspheming at the cheese.

As if. The only 'health' features *Believe It!* magazine ever ran were ones on Chlamydia, the 'Silent Epidemic', and another, best forgotten, on 'excessive sweating'.

This was the weekend I was to spill the beans, but so far, it's not looking good. When things don't work out between Gina and men, which tends to be the norm rather than the exception, there's a set process, a series of 'modes' to be gone through, each one having to be exhausted before the next can begin.

Up until this point, for example, she's been very much in hurt mode. I got home from the cinema to find her chain-smoking in the garden, looking like she'd suffered some kind of anaphylactic shock her face was so swollen from crying.

My first thought, selfishly, was that I could do without a grief-stricken flatmate what with everything else going on. But she was so upset – distraught enough to accept a hug and that's saying something – that there was only one thing for it: A night in watching the entire box-set of *The Office*, eating oven chips and planning Jasper's downfall.

The café's emptying now, half-eaten breakfasts and bean-smeared plates left on its round mahogany tables with their retro gingham tablecloths. Used coffee cups are piled high on the original 1950s serving kiosk. The whole place seems to ooze with bacon fat.

I zone back to Gina, her fighter mode's at full throttle now, her mind churning over the last few weeks' events, scouring for evidence of when the demise began.

'I wouldn't fucking mind,' she says, downing an espresso, 'but only last week he was going on about how he was really falling for me. How I was "the most intelligent woman he'd ever met". Ha! What a load of bollocks. So intelligent I can't see what's right in front of my eyes half the time. A total, A-grade twat.'

I bite my lip and stare at the floor. It's always slightly embarrassing when Gina starts on one like this, especially in a public place. Very audibly.

'Don't torture yourself, it's best you found out now that he was a shit. Imagine if you were really into him and then found out. You'd be well pissed off.'

'Guess so,' she mumbles. 'His loss not mine and all that. Anyway, I've had it up to here with wankers, I reckon I'm better off single. I mean, what's wrong with me? Do I have "I only date losers" written across my forehead?'

'No, of course not, you moron,' I say, getting up to give her a hug but she brushes me off.

The sad fact is, Gina's always gone for men who are destined to let her down. She did have a decent boyfriend once, Mark Trelforth, all the way through university. But Mark's doting just did her head in the end, she had to put him out of his misery – the morning after the graduation ball just to add insult to injury, poor bastard.

Ever since then she's been in search of someone 'more exciting', someone 'edgy'. Mr so-called Perfect.

The problem is (as I've reminded her today) that if a thirty-five-year-old man's key qualities are that he is edgy and exciting, that he models himself on Pete Doherty, just for example, then chances are commitment and unconditional love are not likely to be his forte. But Gina hasn't quite grasped this.

The windows of the café are all steamed up from the persistent London drizzle that shrouds everything in a soft-focus haze. It's only two p.m. but it feels much later, probably because we got here two hours ago. Since then, we've drunk two lattes, an espresso and a cup of tea between us and seen two whole seatings arrive, eat and leave. First, the thirty-some-thing Islington hungover crew, with their shower-wet hair and their Racing Green body warmers. Then, the twenty-something brigade who are much cooler, therefore arrive later, and tend to be still wearing the same clothes as last night.

Through all this time, Gina has barely drawn breath whilst I've nodded and ummed and generally kept my mouth shut for so long, we've worked up an appetite worthy of an all-day breakfast.

I don't mind, this won't last for ever. After a day or so, this rant mode will subside, making way for a brief period of calm and self-reflection. This will move seamlessly into mild euphoria as Gina embraces her new-found single status, a period which usually finds her dragging me out to hideous speed-dating nights, until she finds herself another totally unsuitable man, at which point I'll be largely redundant.

I don't know why I'm going on. I'm hardly a shining example of how to do relationships in my current mess. It's just, when you've known someone for such a long time, you come to know these things. You ride the waves with them, experience their storms and their fleeting sunny days. Except, she isn't riding this, the biggest, scariest wave of my life. She isn't able to help. Because I haven't even told her.

A surly waitress plonks the all-day breakfasts in front of us and strides off, swinging her hips.

'Cheer up love,' says Gina. 'It might never happen.'

No fewer than three people have said this to me in the past week. 'Too late!' I've wanted to shout. 'It already has!'

Gina drenches everything in tomato ketchup – a breakfast massacre – and I suddenly feel a bit sick.

'Do you know what really pisses me off?' she says, cutting into her food aggressively.

'I spent a hundred quid on my dress to wear to that wanky party of his.'

'Haven't you got the receipt?' I offer. 'Can't you just take it back?'

'Possibly, but it's the principle of the matter Tess,' she snaps, stabbing her fork into a sausage. 'The fact I went and wasted my own money, money I could have spent on New York, just to please him!'

My stomach flips when she says this. New York. Shit. How could I go to New York now? Gina and I arranged to go to New York together a year ago – when we were in a pub (which is where I agree to most things). But how can I go anywhere now I'm pregnant?

Gina studies my face, my stomach rolls: does she know something? Every time we've talked in the past week, every

71

time Vicky has rung and I've made some excuse to get off the phone, I've thought this is it. This is the moment my cover is blown. But then her face falls.

'Look at us, eh?' she says, laughing. I brace myself. 'Pair of total fuck wits.'

You have to watch Gina when she does this. Tar you with the same brush as she tars herself, it's a most irritating habit.

'Speak for yourself!' I laugh. 'What's that supposed to mean?'

'I don't mean anything bad by it,' she shrugs. 'I just mean, you know, look at us.'

'Look at what?'

'Our lives, I suppose, look at our lives. We're in our late twenties, prime of our lives, witty, talented, devastatingly attractive . . .'

'Now you're talking.'

'Exactly. And can either of us get it together to find a boyfriend? Can we fuck.'

I try to think of something enlightened or positive to say, but all I can think about is the wave of nausea currently washing over me. I wish Gina would stop talking.

She doesn't.

'Do you remember when we were at uni and we used to play Would You Rather?'

Would You Rather was something we'd all play when we were too skint to go out. It mainly involved debating the lesser of two evil scenarios – the merits of shagging Noel Edmonds over, say, having to bear children to Bruce Forsyth.

When we got bored with debating the ridiculous, we'd introduce more serious dilemmas, like whether we rated marriage over kids, or whether a glittering career was more important than true love. It never occurred to us then of course, when thirty-year-olds were just people who wore court shoes – that we'd be heading towards being left on the shelf without either. (Well, almost.)

'We still don't know what we'd rather have in a way, don't you think?' says Gina. 'We still don't know what we want.'

I don't answer, I can't. I feel too rough. Plus, I don't much like the way this conversation is going.

'I mean, look at you and Jim. That was never going to work.'

She says this nonchalantly but I flinch.

'I really like Jim, you know, despite his obvious shortcomings . . .'

What were they?!

'. . . and I think he's mad for not snapping you up. But it would have happened by now if it was going to happen. You need to stop pissing about, you two, find the real thing. I always thought you and Laurence would go the distance, if he hadn't messed it up, that is. You two were so cool together. You were just too young.'

I feel the colour drain from my face. Should I have gone on the date? Should I have emailed back anyway? Maybe I am selling Laurence short assuming he'd never want to date me because I'm pregnant? He is a grown man, he can make his own decisions, after all.

'And then there's me,' Gina goes on, 'not a fucking clue what's good for me. I thought Jasper was great, so different from anyone else I've ever gone out with . . .'

So a carbon copy of every other dickhead you've dated since Mark, I want to say but I'm too busy looking at the bloodied mess of eggs and beans streaked with ketchup on her plate and trying to keep the contents of my stomach intact.

'Thank God we've got each other, eh? Thank God for you, Tess Jarvis. Who'd have thought we'd be still be living together now, eh? Right pair o' lezzers.'

73

Gina's on a roll now, but I'm not listening, I suddenly feel very, very sick. If I just keep quiet, I'll be OK. If I just concentrate, this nausea will pass, right?

Wrong.

The adrenaline rushes around my veins, my cheeks suddenly burn, my mouth fills with liquid, I'm going to throw up. I'm actually going to puke!

'Tess, what's wrong? Are you alright?' I hear Gina say, but it's too late.

I stand up, throwing my chair behind me so violently it makes an ear-splitting shriek across the wet floor. I briefly weigh up my options – the door, toilet or bag. I have the good sense – even in this state – to remember my bag has a very nice Mulberry purse in there and the downstairs toilet is way too far so I make a dash for the door.

I practically sprint to the other end of the café, pushing anyone in my path – a horsey blonde, a child – out of my way.

I grab hold of the handle of the door, fling it open, lurch onto the pavement and . . . let's just say it's not pretty. I just wasted several drinks and half an all-day breakfast, narrowly missing a yummy mummy with pristine toddler in pram.

I hear Gina swear from inside the café, then rush outside.

'Chist's sake Tess,' she says to me, arms folded, almost telling me off. 'What brought that on?'

'God knows,' I say, wiping away the tears. 'Probably just some twenty-four hour bug.'

The nausea passes as quickly as it came. After a glass of water drunk shakily and some baby wipes donated by the glamorous mother – so much more glamorous than me, at this precise moment and I haven't even had the baby yet – I feel ready to brave it home.

The plan is perfect: DVDs, toast and a full on hibernation fest for the rest of the day.

Gina puts her arm around me as we walk along the Essex Road.

'You scared me then,' she says. 'Why the hell didn't you tell me to shut up?'

'Easier said than done,' I say.

'True,' she says, 'sorry about that.'

It's a miserable grey sludge of a day, one of those that never quite gets going. In the last eight days, since the row in Frankie's, the only contact I've had with Jim has been three stilted phone conversations. We can usually yabber on for England on the phone, me and Jim. We once spent an hour debating whether Davina McCall had married out of her league when she married that fit bloke off *Pet Rescue*. Jim has been known to wander off mid-conversation then forget I am there, leaving me on the end of the phone, listening to him fart. We are so comfortable with one another it's ridiculous. But not this week. This week for the first time ever I've sat in bed having small talk with Jim Ashcroft.

But now, I don't know whether it's because I don't feel quite so sick anymore, or because I feel bonded to Gina, comforted that she's here with me, after that ordeal, but for the first time in ages I feel the tentative fingers of something like calm feather my senses.

It's still elusive. Like an under-developed Polaroid, but it's there alright and it feels good. It's as if everything that was hurled in the air, an emotional tornado, is suddenly floating gently back down to earth, to resume its rightful place.

I'd feel almost good now if it weren't for the big secret hammering away in my brain, chipping away, trying to get out. Maybe I should tell her? Tell her now whilst we're bonded in our respective misfortunes.

We turn into Blockbusters, pick up some shamelessly girly films, essential Sunday supplies, and carry on along the Essex

Road that we've pounded so many times it's imprinted on the soles of our shoes, our well charted territory.

By the time we make it home, the bottoms of our jeans are soaking wet and it feels like we'll never get warm. I go and change whilst Gina puts the kettle on, turns up the central heating and arranges our supplies in little bowls.

'Does poorly patient want a cup of tea?' she shouts from the bottom of the stairs, as I root around in my wardrobe for something to wear.

'Yes please nurse,' I shout back, smiling to myself. Is this TLC I am experiencing? Is this me, Tess Jarvis being looked after by Gina Marshall for a change? And she doesn't even know.

I pull on some old tracksuit bottoms and my netball sweatshirt. 'Officially better,' I announce, as Gina hands me a steaming mug at the bottom of the stairs.

I want to tell her. I'm burning to tell her so I won't have to handle this alone and yet, I want to savour this moment, hold it for ever. Never again, when I've told her, will we stand in this kitchen as two, single, childless friends with nothing but ourselves and the rain battering the roof for company.

We move into the lounge and collapse on the sofa. Now's your moment, 'Do it now,' I urge myself. 'Find the words, come on!'

'Gina,' I say. My heart throws a punch at my rib.

She leaps to her feet. Shit, this is it!

'I know, we'd better get on with it. Which one shall we watch?' she says, marching over to the bag of the DVDs.

She takes out *Lost in Translation*, shows it me, I nod, weakly. She crawls over to the TV, bends down, her back to me, muttering something about Bill Murray, putting it in the machine.

I think about my promise to Jim, how we said we'd wait until after the scan to tell anyone . . . but the words are too big, they don't fit in my mouth anymore, out they topple like I've got Tourette's.

'Gina,' I say, 'I'm pregnant. I'm having a baby.'

If I thought Gina was going to take this well, I was mistaken, sorely mistaken. I'm not prepared for the look on her face when she turns around. Shock is not the word. Something like disgust would be more fitting. She doesn't say anything for what seems like ages. She just sits there, DVD in hand, and glares at me.

'What?' she says, through gritted teeth. It's barely audible, a whisper.

'I'm pregnant.'

'Whose . . .?'

'It's Jim's,' I say, staring at the floor.

She looks at me through a gap in her fingers.

'How pregnant are you?'

'Eight and a half weeks.'

'And you didn't tell me?!'

'Well can you blame me?' I say. 'Look at your reaction.'

'But Tess, you're not even with Jim, you don't even love him like that. You're not in love, either of you!'

The words sting. Didn't she think I already knew that? And didn't she think I wished it was different?

'I do know that,' I say, quietly. 'But it's happened now, and we've decided we're keeping the baby.'

'What?' says Gina, half laughing, half crying. I retreat further back into the sofa.

'But you can't,' she says, 'that's ridiculous; you can't have that baby, not like this.'

'Who says?' I say, crying now. 'Why is that so wrong? We're both adults, this is not some teenage pregnancy. If I was to opt out of having this baby then I'd be opting out of life, choosing the easy way out, can't you see?'

Gina wipes her face, which is suddenly filled with steely determination.

'Look,' she says, coming to sit beside me. 'We have options (we!?); let's think about this. Because this isn't about Jim, or the baby – it's not even a baby yet, Tess, that's what Mark told me when I had my abortion and he was right, it was just a cluster of cells – the only person this is about is you. You have to be selfish.'

'But I am being selfish, I want to keep it.'

'You don't mean that.'

'I do!'

I can't believe I'm hearing this. I know this is a shock and that I'm an idiot for letting it happen but what happened to my friend just giving me a hug, asking all those questions you're meant to ask when someone tells you they're pregnant?

'I'll come with you to the doctor's tomorrow,' says Gina, decisively. 'I'll call in sick, we'll sort this out. I've been through it too remember, so I know how it feels, I'll know what to say . . .'

'No,' I say, standing up. And it feels like I've never meant anything more in my life. 'No! You don't know what to say. I'm not going to the doctor's, I've already been and that was to get my due date. December 14th if you're interested, put it in your diary. I'm not having an abortion, Gina, I'm keeping the baby, *we're* keeping the baby.'

I walk out. I slam the door shut.

CHAPTER SEVEN

'I thought the love would just be there. That I would look into my baby's eyes and we would have an instant under-standing. But when Poppy was born, I just felt terrified, like I'd been handed someone else's baby to look after. It took seven months for me to honestly say I loved her. Obviously now, I know I was ill, but I still feel guilty.'

Sam, 36, Didsbury

I am lying next to Jim, my belly against the curve of his back, the faint whirr of a dawn flight outside. After the row with Gina yesterday, the atmosphere in the house was frosty to say the least so that evening I got on a bus and came here, to Jim's place, a cosy Victorian flat in East Dulwich.

It had been over a week since the row in Frankie's and I was worried how I might be received.

I needn't have been.

When Jim opened the door, wearing his mustard dressing gown (the result of a dye disaster with a beach towel) I have never felt so welcome, or wanted to hug him so much in my life. I stood on the doorstep, a forlorn figure under the glare of the street lamp.

'Hello you,' he said, arms crossed, head leaning against the doorframe as if he was expecting me. 'Come on in.'

He led me through his narrow, bright hallway, the only thing adorning the wall a framed photo of an Americana sign:

Warning: Water on Road During Rain

Lifts my mood every time.

Jim's downstairs is open plan. The lounge is cosy in its make-do-ness. Two stripy sofas covered with dark grey throws, a huge black and white circular rug and a bobbly green swivel chair that he always does his marking on. His telly's crap – you can only get three channels if you balance the aerial on a mug – and today (like most days) there's a huge pile of marking on the sofa that he's obviously just put to one side. He moved it, putting it on the Ikea coffee table along with the remote control, the remains of a Muller Light and a note-filled copy of Shakespeare's *Henry IV*. Then he pressed down on my shoulders, sitting me on the sofa, and went into the kitchen to make tea.

It's a boy's kitchen – a dazzling array of unnecessary gadgets, juicer, pasta maker, ice-cream maker, blood-red DeLonghi coffee maker that weighs a tonne – the shine of which is diminished only by a subtle layer of grime.

On the shelves above the sink are Jamie Oliver cookbooks and a few suspect ones called things like *Nose to Tail Eating* that contain nothing but recipes for offal and pig trotter. (Jim likes to think he's a fearless cook – i.e. you have to be fearless to eat whatever he cooks.) Next to a pint glass of pennies is a herb garden that he actually keeps alive, unlike me who buys one every time I go to Tesco's only to find it desiccated on top of the fridge three months later.

'*Henry IV* eh?' I said, picking up the book, thinking a bit of idle chat might do me good. 'Sorry, but I never could get excited about Shakespeare.'

'You blaspheme!' spluttered Jim. 'It's one of the funniest, rudest books ever written.

'How can you not fall in love with such a top bloke as Hal, or a total piss-head like Falstaff? You of all people.'

'Oi,' I said. 'What are you suggesting?'

Jim handed me a cup of tea. 'So,' he said, 'what owes me this pleasure?'

That was it, I was off. I poured out all the details of the showdown with Gina and the more I said it aloud the more unbelievable it felt.

'I'm sorry for being such a cow last week,' I said, sheepishly, when I'd off loaded. 'Not to mention blabbing to Gina. You must hate me.'

'Yeah, can't stand you, hate your guts,' Jim said, totally dead pan. 'You were a bitch from hell but we'll blame it on the hormones, shall we?'

'That will be my epitaph at this rate.'

It must have been one a.m. before we went to bed. I was still pretty shook up about Gina and Jim was as confused as I was. 'Are you sure that's what she said?' he said. 'I know Gina can be unpredictable but that's just weird.'

'I know, I don't understand it either. It was like me being pregnant was a personal attack. Like something I'd done wrong. I mean, I know I can't get drunk like we used to, but I'm still me, aren't I? I'm still the person she's been friends with for more than a decade.'

Jim gave me a hug. It felt like he could squeeze the air right out of me.

'It will be alright, you know, all this,' he said, staring straight ahead, with that prophetic certainty he has about everything. 'I know it doesn't seem like it now, but it will.'

'And Gina?' I asked tentatively, as we walked up the stairs to bed.

'She'll come round.' Jim yawned. 'And if she doesn't, we'll kick her ass.'

I smiled but at the back of my mind I was still worried. How could I confide in her about anything now? And what if everyone, even Vicky, reacted as badly? What if I was utterly deluded and keeping this baby was the worst, most irresponsible idea in the world?

'All a baby needs is love,' Jim said. I play those words in my head again and again. 'All a child needs is to feel wanted.' And I want this baby. If I don't, why do I wake up, my heart in my mouth with every twinge, petrified this is the start of losing it? The fact is, I think to myself as I lay here, if I was to lose this baby now, we couldn't try for another. Not like real couples.

It is one thing to have an accident and make the best of a less than ideal situation but quite another to make something happen again that should never have happened in the first place.

This unborn child that already has fingers and toes and maybe my curviness and Jim's long legs (Eva Herzigova eat your heart out!) is a fluke, it slipped through the net. And so if fate decided it wasn't meant to be then it would be heartbreaking, but we'd have to accept it. Why did the thought of this terrify me so much?

Jim is sleeping but I can't, my mind won't let me. I know it must be almost morning because I can just about make out shapes in his familiar room in the emerging light and the photograph on his bedside table, the one in the red frame that's never meant much before, is staring right back at me now, making my mind race.

Me, Jim, Gina and Vicks sitting under the awning of our caravan, that camping trip in Norfolk last summer. Jim and I had been hopping into each other's bed when the fancy took us for three months by then. How many times have I looked at this picture? And it has never stirred much more than nostalgia before. But now suddenly the body language says it all: Gina and Vicky leaning against each other, laughing into the camera which we've got balanced on a beer crate. Me, reclining on a deckchair, feet tucked up by my bum, my head on Jim's shoulder but what's he doing? Ruffling my hair. Not a spark of sexual tension between us.

That didn't stop me getting carried away though. It didn't stop me thinking that I might even be falling in love with Jim, that he might, even, be falling for me.

I still cringe when I think of what happened a few hours after that photo was taken. We'd been to the pub that night, then walked home through windy country lanes, arm in arm. When we got back to the campsite, Jim went straight to his tent, pitched next to the caravan, and I crawled in next to him.

'Jim, we've been doing this weird on/off thing for some time now,' I said, staring at the canvas, my heart pounding. 'Maybe we should, you know, make a go of it. Go out with each other, like, properly.' After a long pause in which I wondered whether he might be about to express his undying love for me he just turned over the other way.

'Tess, you're drunk,' he said, flatly. 'We're soul-mates, something special, something really good. Let's not spoil it.'

What a twat. What an absolute wanker! So I open myself up, put myself on the line and he makes me feel so small I could have disappeared up his arse, along with his own head. *Well sod you*, I thought. But I didn't say anything, I was too mortified. I just made thoroughly mature V-signs up at the roof of the tent.

But he was right of course. Thank God somebody saw sense. Looking at us, sitting under that awning now, I cannot believe I did that. I didn't fancy Jim as much as he didn't fancy me – not really, not in the right way. It was all just wishful thinking.

And the hard fact to swallow is, if I hadn't screwed it up

83

with Laurence, I would probably never have even been in that tent, I would never have made an arse of myself, I would never have carried on having 'no-strings' sex with Jim and I certainly wouldn't be pregnant with his baby!

Under Jim's tartan duvet, I can feel that he's had got an erection. A James Ashcroft Morning Glory. Ordinarily, that's to say pre-baby, this would have meant one thing to me: a quickie, sleepy, hungover shag that would have left me with the smug feeling that I really was a thoroughly modern girl. I occasionally slept with my male best friend and we were cool with it.

Today though, it's an unwelcome pressure and I feel my body stiffen as he eases closer. He takes a sleepy breath in and as he breathes out, he kneads the inside of my thigh with his knee, trying to gently prize me open. I resist. I can't do this. My head's too muddled and weighed down. Where sex before was like an added extra, now it is loaded with meaning. It is as if the lightness had been shot out of it, leaving it withering to the floor like a deflated balloon.

Jim puts his arm around me.

'Morning,' he murmurs, then kisses my head, then slips his hand between my legs.

I gently remove it.

'Jim,' I say, pushing him gently off me, trying not to sound too annoyed, 'Jim, look . . . I can't, I'm sorry.'

He rolls onto his back and for what seems like for ever, he doesn't say anything.

When he speaks again, he sounds almost sad.

'It's different now, isn't it?' he says.

'Yes,' I say. 'I guess it is.'

He reaches for my hand, strokes it for a second or two and then turns onto his side. 'Come on,' he says, pressing his warm, long body against mine. 'Let's just have a cuddle.'

*　　*　　*

84

We must have eventually drifted off, because when I wake up again, it's 7.10 a.m. and Jim isn't in the bed. I sit up and hear the shower going, so I plump up the pillows and pick up the *Bundle of Joy* book.

I like waking up in Jim's flat. Like everything in his life – his car, his beloved books, his friends, he got it a long time ago, nurtured it, tended it lovingly and it's served him well in return.

Jim has always had to look after things, because he's never known when anything new or better will come along. He was fifteen when his alky waster of a dad walked out, leaving only his mum's income from her part-time job as a school nurse to support the family, and so he and his sister Dawn never got much. As a result, the bookshelf in his bedroom, made from red bricks and planks of wood, is full of childhood books that he's looked after for twenty odd years. There are records that he's had since the eighties, too, and all manner of retro chic – a leather chair, an orange seventies phone – none of it bought in trendy design bric-a-brac shops, but just things he's kept all this time.

Jim walks back into the bedroom, still dripping wet, wearing nothing but a teeny towel. He pulls open the curtains to reveal yet another grey May day, and stands in front of his mirror, examining his stubble.

'You love that book, don't you?' he says, peering at me via the mirror.

'Might do,' I say coyly, 'what's it to you?'

Jim shrugs. He flexes his 'muscles' in a mock muscle-man impression and twists his body from side to side.

'Grrrr,' he says, 'a powerhouse of masculinity, a finely tuned instrument, I think you'll find.' He lifts up one arm at a time, spraying deodorant flamboyantly. Beanpole thin with skin so pale it looks blue in some lights, this is Jim's running joke.

'Right. Yeah, all eight stone of you,' I say, peering at him from over my book. 'Look at your skinny arse!'

With that, Jim whips off his towel, beats his chest like Tarzan and dives into bed with me, still soaking wet.

I let out a yelp of shock.

'Aaah, you're fucking freezing, you're soaking wet, get off me!' I scream, as he blows raspberries all over my belly.

'I am Tarzan you are Jane. I am man, you are woman!'

'Jim!' I scream, half serious, half laughing. 'What are you doing you madman, you're going to squash the bloody baby!'

He suddenly leaps backwards on to his feet, a look of horror on his face.

'Shit, fuck, fuck, sorry I can't believe I just did that.' He groans, hands over his eyes. 'I forgot you were pregnant, what an oaf, you OK?'

'Yes, I'm fine, thank you very much,' I say, pulling up the duvet and picking up my book again. 'Just hurry up and get dressed will you, you big lunatic. You're going to be late.'

We are good at this, Jim and I. Larking about, joking about our bodies and our shortcomings. But my child will share this man's genes so it would kind of help if I fancied him. When I used to look at Laurence, all six foot two Adonis of him, I knew what I felt alright. We rarely lasted two seconds together (in the early days at least) before leaping upon each other in lust-fuelled zeal. But with Jim, it's never been like that, it's never been about lust or passion or animal-istic desire. Even though I did once think it might be enough, he's always been just lovely Jim to me, a feeling more than a need.

I look at him now, his back to me, in just his boxer shorts, putting on his shirt. He is certainly not Adonis, but there is something, I don't know, generically pleasant about him.

He is nicely proportioned: long of leg, a regal neck, nice

strong back and lean arms. Across his shoulders he has a scattering of freckles. That's the Scottish in him of course, from his dad's side – thank God that's all he inherited from him, that and the way he walks, arms folded, shoulders slightly hunched. I always think that's a Scottish way of walking, as if he's permanently cold.

Yes, Jim, the father of my baby, is a nice looking man. But still, my feelings for him come from my head and my heart, not from my loins like they should.

Jim is wearing the standard teacher outfit now: Gap trousers, blue shirt, and he's putting on some hideous tie. It's maroon and worryingly paisley.

'What's that tie you're wearing?' I say.

'What tie?'

'The one you're wearing.'

'What's wrong with it?'

'What's *right* with it?'

'It's a bog standard tie.'

'Exactly.'

'So, what's it to you?'

'Nothing, I'm just bringing your attention to it.'

'Right,' he says, flaring his nostrils.

'Right,' I say, stifling a giggle.

He walks to the door, opens it and stands there for a second.

'What are you now, my girlfriend?' he says eventually. I hear him chuckle to himself as he closes the door.

I'm on the bus, almost at work, when Vicky calls:

'Hi' she says.

'Hi.'

'It's me.'

'I know.'

She pauses. I know this is because she's giving me a chance

to tell her something, she knows I'm being weird. You can't hide anything from Vicky, she'll sniff you out in seconds. I wish I could tell her. God, I'm dying to tell her, she's my best friend! But I know Jim would never forgive me. Telling Gina was a *huge* mistake, I just had to tell someone and she happened to be there. The fact is that once Vicky – indeed anyone – knows, there will be months of nudging and winking and 'so when are you getting married?' and we certainly don't need that to start right now.

'Um, I'm just calling because it's only eight days till my birthday – as you know – and I am trying to organize what theme to have.'

'Right,' I say.

Another pause.

'Can I run through the options with you?'

'Um yes, it's just . . .'

'Tess?'

'Yes?'

'Are you alright?'

'Yes I'm fine, I'm just on the bus that's all. I can't really talk.'

'Oh right. You just sound weird that's all.'

'Do I?'

'Yeah, like you're not telling me something.'

I swallow hard.

'No, it's nothing. Honestly, nothing's happened,' I say, immediately regretting saying 'nothing's happened' since she'll now so know something has.

My flatmate's just turned against me and I'm pregnant by my best friend, that's all.

When I walk into reception, Jocelyn doesn't say anything, she doesn't even look at me. She just tears a Post-it note from the pad on her desk, her hair swinging, and hands it to me with a closed-off look of smug importance on her face.

It reads: Laurence rang. Can you meet him for lunch today? It would make his week if you could. Call him: 0771 6543 839.

And because I'm about to interview a woman who hijacked her lover's honeymoon and not only that but got pregnant on it, I think what the hell, it's just lunch with an ex. I get to my desk and I dial the number.

CHAPTER EIGHT

'I was thirty-five weeks pregnant when Hamish tripped over a cricket bat on the stairs and broke his ankle. I don't know who the nurses in A&E felt sorrier for, me or him. We had a toddler and a seven–year-old to look after and no day-time help in a hundred-mile radius. We must have looked comical in bed – him with his three pillows for his foot, me with my three for my bump. We had to laugh, or else we would definitely have cried.'
Siobhan, 48, London

We are outside the National Film Theatre.

He hands me two tickets . . . with British Airways written on them. You are joking, I think. Then I think, oh my God, he's not, he's actually gone and booked flights to Paris, without even consulting me.

'I took a risk,' says Laurence.

'That's not like you,' I say and for a fleeting moment, I am aware of thinking there's nothing in the world I'd rather do right now.

'Ooh, sarky,' he says, and gives a little laugh.

Then I look more closely and realize they're tickets to the London Eye. 'That's lovely, that's really sweet of you,' I stutter, 'but the queue's bound to be massive and I only have three quarters of an hour . . . I've got to get back . . . '

But he's already pulling me by the arm, and I'm running, despite myself, along the riverside, giggling like a teenager.

'Come on! Live a little, woman,' Laurence shouts over his shoulder. 'Jesus Christ, what is that magazine you now work on? Some sort of dictatorship?!'

Above us trains rumble over Hungerford Bridge and sea-gulls soar, screeching over the Thames. South Bank is swarming with tourists, loud groups of French school children with back-packs and neckerchiefs and attitude and fed-up teachers.

'No,' I shout. I'm laughing, gulping down huge balls of air. 'It's just, some of us do have a job, you know. We can't all swan about all afternoon having three-hour lunches, pulling pints for a living!'

He swings round, takes a long drag on his cigarette, and blows the smoke high up into the blue sky. 'Yeah, yeah,' he shouts, flailing his arms about. He looks so French when he does that. 'I forgot you had your fancy job in the media these days, haven't even got an hour to spare for your old friend?'

I wish I did, Laurence Cane. I wish I had five hours, five days, five weeks to spare with you. What is it about this man that can do this to me? Lead me into temptation. Get me right in the heart when I least expect it. Erase any good sense I have in one blink of those thick, black lashes?

But he does, and I'm here and he's showing no signs of letting up, so I have no choice but to be dragged, almost trip-ping over myself until we are dwarfed beneath the London Eye and its adjoining queues of people, as if standing by a gigantic ship about to set sail.

The queue snakes around white railings two or three times and stretches at least twenty people back. Laurence clocks the concern on my face.

'Chill out,' he almost laughs, massaging my shoulder. My

body jolts and I realize that this is the first time he's touched me – apart from the cave-man dragging me by the arm just now – in more than four years. It feels familiar and yet foreign, pleasurable and yet for some bizarre reason, even this makes me feel guilty. It's the incongruity of it all that gets me. I'm a mother-to-be. I should be thinking about babies' names and worrying about bonding, not standing in the sunshine of a lunchtime about to board a London tourist attraction with my ex.

Thankfully, Jocelyn had been too immersed in one of her 'brief chats' with her sister back home to grill me as I slipped out of the office. It must be brilliant to be Jocelyn: completely unapologetic, oblivious to the fact that calling Australia for an hour every day on the company's money might just be a smidgen out of order. God bless her.

Me, I try to get away with stuff but I've never been much good at blagging, not really. I was alright with the stuff that didn't matter – the minutiae of life, the exams, the money stuff, the charming my way out of fines and into clubs. But when it comes to relationships and to feelings, that little voice starts – my conscience. Tap-tapping away like an annoying neighbour. Like when I stepped out through the revolving doors of Giant Publishing this lunchtime and I looked behind to check nobody was watching, Like now, for instance, the guilt I feel, you'd think I was off to have smutty sex in a sleazy hotel not going for lunch! It's turning my stomach to mush. But why do I feel guilty?

I can hear Vicky now. A right Yorkshire dressing down: 'You did what? Met Laurence, who broke your heart? Who dumped you from the other side of the world, by email? Since when was that a good idea, you complete and utter numpty?'

And maybe she's right – she usually is – maybe this is the worst idea of my life. I could have deleted that email and Laurence Cane from my life for ever. But something told me I couldn't. Because otherwise I would never know, would I?

And that meeting the other morning; the fact he was staying across the road from me, the fact we were in the dry cleaners at the same time, with each other's clothes. I'd had his shirt, Laurence's shirt, hanging in my bedroom for a week!! If that's not some kind of sign – and I'm not usually one for 'signs' – then I don't know what is.

But anyway, I am telling myself, don't get your knickers in a twist, because this is just a single revolution of the London Eye. And he's got a girlfriend (major spanner in works). And you're pregnant (industrial-sized sledge hammer in the works). So no matter how many 'signs' there are, this ain't happenin'.

He lights another cigarette, the old Camel Lights. 'Fuck it,' he says, surveying the queue. 'Come with me, I've got an idea.'

He grabs me by the hand and drags me, again, towards a sign that says, 'Fast Track Ticket Holders'. There is a closed gate at the entrance. Oh God. Here we go. Pregnant Woman and Ex Arrested on Lunch-break . . .

I don't really have time to think about it though, because before I know it, Laurence has vaulted over the railings and is urging me to do the same.

I think, you're having a laugh, not a chance. I'm with child, I can't go vaulting over railings! But because I'm with Laurence and because he has the devil in him, and because I'm extremely easily led, I do. I hitch up my skirt almost to my knickers, do a little skip and a jump towards the railing, grip the bar with my right hand and catapult myself over it. Nimble as you like.

'Stop looking at my knickers!' I shout.

'I'm not looking at your knickers! Just get a move on will you woman!'

There's a few people in front if us tutting and looking round, but I couldn't give a toss. I'm too busy laughing and half collapsing and then we're on, it's our turn. A big white capsule draws up in front of us, the door slides open and we climb aboard the London Eye. The other half dozen people in the capsule with us all sit on the wooden bench at the centre but Laurence and I gravitate towards the glass, where we stand, side by side, London unfolding before our eyes.

'Wow. It's gorgeous isn't it?' I say, watching the river glint and meander. To my right, the Houses of Parliament glisten like a golden wedding cake.

'It's one cool city,' agrees Laurence, taking in the view. 'Hey look over there, bring back memories or what?'

I follow the line of his finger which is pointing beyond the Houses of Parliament, to Battersea Power Station, its four white steeples sticking up, like an upside down cow.

'How could I forget? I spent enough time there. In fact, I could count on two hands the number of times you came to Islington.'

'Well you had a shit bed,' he says.

'That's such a crap excuse!' I protest.

'You know how much I like my bed, though.'

'You're dead right there,' I say. 'Can't argue with that.'

I have never known anyone sleep as much as Laurence. Borderline narcoleptic. No exaggeration.

'They were cool times though, weren't they?' says Laurence. I am aware his weight has shifted slightly. I can feel the heaviness of him on my right shoulder.

'Sure were,' I say. 'Pub lunches in the Latchmere, messy nights round Jez's house, Frisbee in the park . . .'

We look at each other and crack up laughing.

'Park fucking wardens!' we say, simultaneously.

Someone sitting on the bench, obviously an English speaker, coughs significantly, but we don't care.

'What I can't believe, is the fact we were naked. Two days before Christmas!' laughs Laurence, throatily. He puts his hand on my back, firm and familiar. It momentarily takes my breath away. 'That was a great Christmas though, wasn't it? I still remember it.'

How could I forget it? I spent the whole of Christmas dinner at Laurence's parents' house, both hands stuck in glasses of iced water having – much to everyone's amusement – completely misjudged the spiciness of the chillies for the 'Algerian spiced meatballs' starter, and cut them bare-handed.

It wasn't the first time I'd humiliated myself in front of Laurence's mother. After the kitchen table incident (as if that wasn't bad enough) I stayed over in the blow-up-bed next to a snoring, beer-scented Gina, dreaming of Laurence in his bed next door. I thought I'd be able to sneak out the next day without having to show my shamed face. Not so. It turned out I'd left my trainers in the living room and had no choice but to go downstairs and get them the next morning and make excruciating small talk with Laurence's mum as she sat watching Rick Stein's bloody *Seafood Odyssey*.

'Oh, you're watching Rick Stein,' I said, stating the obvious like a total loser, picking up the trainers.

'Yes, I quite like Rick Stein,' said Joelle, not unpleasantly, but she didn't say anything else.

'He likes fish doesn't he? A lot. Rick Stein?' I said after a way-too-long pause to which she didn't really answer. So then I said, 'I like fish.' I could *not* believe it.

'That's good,' she said, with a smile that was half polite and half said 'will you just fuck off'. 'Fish is very good for you.'

'Yes salmon's my favourite,' I said. 'Then probably cod.'

After that cracking display of repartee I made a sharp exit expecting never to be back. But Laurence and I had clearly started as we meant to go on: he rang me the next weekend and demanded he come and visit me in Manchester, hurtling down from Leeds in his red Deux Chevaux to spend just twelve stolen hours together before he had to be back for a lecture, and after that we had non-stop sex for the next two and a half years. This time as an official item. I was enraptured, completely under his spell of cool Englishness and

Gallic sensuality. I treated him like an exotic pet. I showed him off, forgave his moods, lapped up his erratic affections mainly because when they did come, they were pure gold.

But it was most unlike me. Not least because I'd have never normally looked twice at someone like Laurence. Because boys like him – in my experience at least – never looked twice at girls like me. Men like Laurence – half French (French-Algerian to be exact), a bit moody, bit naughty, that mix of popular and slightly aloof – usually went for demure girls. Girls who never raised their voices, who had silky hair that fell out of ponytails and come to bed eyes. Girls with more sense than to fall head over heels with someone like him.

The timing could not have been worse – trust me to go falling in love three months before my Finals. The honeymoon period was intense and draining: he'd come to Manchester (or I'd go to Leeds), we'd spend twenty-four hours in bed only surfacing to eat then, come four p.m., we'd literally have to push each other away, I would push him into his car, he would push me onto the train, in order to have a hope in hell of doing any revision. I never told him, but I cried every time the train pulled away.

Laurence was passionate and unpredictable; he found me irresistible and sexy where boys at school had found me 'cute and funny'. He said I was the funniest, coolest, most low maintenance girlfriend ever. And he was cool, damn it. I admit he was cool. He DJ'd, smoked Camel Lights and had road rage in French. And I loved him, truly, madly, deeply. I loved him in that way that sometimes it felt like we were one and the same person. And when I looked at his face and into those dark eyes, I saw a new, confidant, sexy me.

And of course there was lots of sex, crazy-in-love sex. Hungry, lust-fuelled, we didn't care where we did it and we didn't care about getting caught. We'd have quickies at his parents' house and blow jobs in lay-bys on the Pennine Way.

In the first few months following my graduation, I stayed in Manchester and got a job at a café in Castlefield. Laurence would come from Leeds to visit and we'd shag all night getting zero sleep. The next day I'd be serving cappuccinos with the biggest ache between my legs, and a dirty great smile all over my face. Everything and nothing felt like for ever back then. For the first time in my life, I was properly in love.

And it turned out I hadn't offended Joelle at all. In fact she would make quips about 'kitchen table gate' which would make me blush and make her laugh her girlish laugh and I became part of the family; I was the daughter Joelle had never had. And I thought this was it, this was The One, and I would have bi-lingual children and marry into Bohemian Academia.

But I was wrong. And just as easily as Laurence had slinked into my life, about three years later he slinked out again, by email, when I was half way across the world.

'How is your mum?' I ask, eager to change the subject before Laurence remembers either the chilli fingers incident or the cod/salmon shame.

'Great. Well, barking mad, still constantly disappointed in me, you know how it is . . .'

'Ahh,' I sigh, nostalgically. 'I love your mum.'

'She loves you,' says Laurence, turning to look at me and holding me with that disarming gaze of his. 'She's never forgiven me for what happened.'

I look at the floor embarrassed. Below us, people scurry across Westminster Bridge getting smaller, like ants. I feel small too up here, suspended in mid-air, away from the world and reality.

'Can I ask you something?' says Laurence.

'Sure,' I say, 'fire away.'

'Why didn't you reply to my email?'

I am momentarily stumped. I'd totally forgotten about the

email. 'What email?' I say, impressed with my quick comeback.

'The email I sent last week. Asking if you wanted to go out on Friday – I was gutted when you just blanked me like that.' He says it with a smile, half wounded, half flirtatious. I go bright red.

'I didn't get it,' I say eventually.

'Right, I see,' says Laurence, obviously unconvinced. Then he takes my hands and holds them and I'm not sure where to look, this has taken me by surprise.

'Tell me the truth. I acted like a cock didn't I?' he says. 'Breaking up with you like that.'

I look straight into his eyes now, until he closes them and hangs his head. I fight a tingle of pleasure.

'I'm not going to lie,' I say. 'You broke my heart.'

I am transported to the day he finished it, everything starts to flood back. I was in Victoria Falls, I'd been canoeing down the Zambezi, but even surrounded by one of the Wonders of the World, I was sidetracked by thoughts of him. He hadn't emailed for days, and when I called, he was always mysteriously out. For the second time that night I padded across the campsite in my bare feet, into the Internet café to check just once more for messages. And there it was.

Dearest Tess
I'm sorry, I can't do this anymore. I know you're gonna think I'm a shit – please don't think that Tess! – Think of all the good times we've had!! But three months is such a long time and I miss you!! I can't do it. I've also met someone – I didn't want you to hear that from anyone else! Nothing's happened yet, but I think it might. I wanted to tell you face to face but I felt too bad. I had to get it off my chest.
I will always love you. xxx

God, I cried. I cried like my heart had been torn from my chest and then I cried some more. I couldn't do anything, holed up in sodding Africa, no phone card, no nothing. I emailed him back:

Please call the camp number at 10 p.m. tomorrow, I'll be here.

But nothing. Not a word. My feelings went from hurt to rage in a matter of hours. Who was this other girl that was so good he couldn't bear to wait for me? How had I been such a dumb ass to assume he could keep his hands to himself? How could he end a two year relationship by goddamn email? And did he think all those exclamation marks would soften the blow?!!!!

I was knocked for six after that. Half way through my six month trip around Africa, my trip of a lifetime, my last few months of freedom before making a proper commitment, I suppose. Laurence was going to concentrate on getting work experience in film (that never came off) and I was going to spread my wings before finally knuckling down to finding a job writing for a proper magazine (rather than writing about copper piping on *Kitchens and Bathrooms* magazine). I'd only ever been to Spain (and Lanzarote in 1992, but all I remember is my ungrateful brother moaning that the sand was black). I had almost killed myself getting up at four a.m. to clean aeroplanes to save up for the trip. And although I knew I would miss Laurence, I felt I needed to do this, I needed to get it out of my system, if only so I didn't feel such an ignoramus in front of Laurence's worldly-wise family.

The goodbye at Heathrow airport was agony. I cried, Laurence cried. We clung to each other, me with my hands in his jeans back pockets, in the middle of the departure lounge until the last call for the flight came and I had to run, or else I never would have gone. I didn't wave, I didn't say goodbye, I couldn't utter the words, it physically hurt.

'I love you baby,' whispered Laurence, placing a lingering kiss on my forehead.

'I love you too,' I said, taking his face and kissing it for the final time. Then I ran, boarded the plane with the taste of his salty tears still on my lips.

The plan was this: Laurence would come out and meet me five months into my trip, in Tanzania; we'd go from there to Zanzibar, spend three blissful weeks looking like the Bacardi advert in paradise before coming home and moving in together. But of course it never happened.

After he dumped me, I extended my ticket to a full year. After all, what was there to come back for now? I had a few liaisons in those last few months, but as fun as they were I was only trying – and failing – to fill the gaping hole left by Laurence. It was a veritable desert after that. Three years in a sex wilderness. Until Jim, in that May of 2006, I hadn't let a man near me – not close enough to penetrate me anyway – I was too broken, too wounded.

Laurence opens his eyes again now, his gaze intense.

'I know. I know. God, Tess, I fucking hated myself,' he says. 'Then I saw you in the dry cleaners the other day and I just thought, wow.'

'Stop, honestly,' I say, 'it really doesn't matter now. Anyway, you're happy now, you've got a girlfriend.'

I don't know for sure whether he's got a girlfriend, this is a trick statement. Last time I asked Gina whether he was still with Chloe – and I do try to leave it at least a couple of months between enquiries – he was, but he didn't mention it when we met at the dry cleaners. Chloe's another of Gina's expansive circle. She was in the year below her and Laurence at boarding school, but didn't surface (or steal my boyfriend) until she went to a barbeque that Laurence happened to be at too, while I was travelling, and ensnared him when he was at his most drunk, weak and stupid.

I hold my breath.

'Girlfriend?'

My heart pounds. Hasn't he?

'Oh, Chloe you mean?' He sounds surprised.

'Yes. The girl you finished with me for all those years ago. The girl you met, whilst I was in Africa, remember? You are still with her, aren't you?'

I say it like this more to jog his memory, because he looks like he seriously needs it, than through any sort of maliciousness. I'm so over maliciousness. Looking at it from his point of view, I was the one who left him to go off around the world after all. I was the one who chose to be without him for six months. What message did that give out about my feelings for him? What would I have thought if it was the other way round and he'd been the one to go travelling? I would have supported him but I probably wouldn't have been thrilled.

I zone back to Laurence. 'Yes,' he says finally, 'I am still with her. But Tess, listen, it's not like she was better than you. It's not like, I chose her over you.'

(Oh yeah? It certainly looked like that!)

'It's just, you know, she was here, and you weren't and . . .'

He knows from the look on my face that this isn't really washing.

'Anyway,' he says, 'what about you? You seeing anyone?'

Although I say no I have to stop and think about this one. My head is a mess of conflicting emotions, like the mishmash of lawns and rivers and parks and buildings below us. On the one hand, here I am, with the man I had thought was The One, a man I am certain is now flirting with me quite outrageously, and yet part of my brain zooms, like a telescope, to a classroom somewhere in a school, just over there where the river hugs Hyde Park, where the father of this baby growing inside me, a man with wayward hair and the sparkliest green eyes you've ever seen, is trying to excite fourteen-year-old boys on the subject of the *Canterbury Tales*. I feel . . . I don't know, unfaithful. But why? Jim isn't my boyfriend, I'm not his girlfriend. I owe him nothing and more than that, we're not in love anyway, so what's the point?

'I can't believe that for a minute,' says Laurence, bringing me back to myself. And then the carriage stops and the doors open and a voice says, 'Thank you for flying British Airways' and we step off the ride, onto the platform, go down the steps and we are back down to earth.

He grabs hold of my forearms and pulls me close. A pain shoots through my chest, making me gasp.

'Ow!'

'What's the matter?' Laurence jumps back, alarmed.

My boobs! I think. My boobs are like two giant, rock-hard bruises! And I realize I've not thought about being pregnant for almost an hour.

'Nothing,' I say, aware I must seem quite unhinged. 'Nothing, don't worry.'

'Right,' says Laurence. 'OK, well . . . that was cool, hey? Can we do this again?'

'Yeah!' I say, thinking that is so a good and bad idea all rolled into one. 'I'd love to.'

He rubs my arms for a second, then pats my bum and pulls away with a smile that tells me that if he hadn't, he may have crossed the line and never come back. I peck him on the cheek, aware of wanting to be the one who leaves first, who leaves him wanting more.

Then I say thanks for a great lunch hour, turn in the direction of the office and disappear into the faceless crowd. And as I walk back to work and back to the real world, I don't know if it's the ride or what has just happened, but my legs are like jelly beneath me.

102

CHAPTER NINE

'It was a one-night stand, that's all, someone I pulled at a salsa dancing night after too many tequilas. I was twenty-two, about to start an MA the next week. I would be lying if I said there weren't times during my pregnancy when I wished I'd not decided to keep the baby, but now my son's here I can't imagine loving anyone or anything more.'

Kate, 24, London

I really don't know what's eating Gina. It's been four weeks since I told her I was pregnant and still we are like ships in the night. Gina goes out in the morning, doesn't come home till after I've gone to bed. I spend most of my time at Jim's, not wanting the confrontation. But I miss her. And the thing that hurts the most is that I don't really know why I've lost her.

The other thing that happened almost four weeks ago and the thing that's eating me, I suppose, is that that was the last time I saw Laurence. Since then there's been the sum total of two and a half texts (the half was a round robin to all his friends notifying them that he's at a different address for a while). I really should forget it. He's got a girlfriend anyway, so I don't know where I think it is going. And I've got another man's baby on the way so really, if we're going to get technical here, the possibility of us getting together is probably more remote than the prospect of Posh letting herself go.

Jim is late. Rudely and unforgivably late. I scan the street, jiggling my legs nervously. Please don't make me hate you today, Jim. Of all the days to want to kill you, slowly, agonizingly and preferably with a blunt instrument, I really don't want it to be today.

Another couple, hand in hand, flash me a sympathetic smile as they push by where I'm sitting on the steps of the antenatal department of University College Hospital. There was a point when I was smiling back, but since my sense of humour failure approximately ten minutes ago, I can only manage a sulky look.

Where the fuck is he?

I call his mobile and contemplate hurling mine onto the road when I get his voicemail.

'Hi, this is Jim. Can't get to the phone right now but leave a message and I'll . . .'

Completely ignore you?

I wouldn't mind but this is not like him at all. Jim hates being late, he thinks lateness in other people is rude and inconsiderate. He has many annoying characteristics: uncalled for chirpiness in the mornings, talking over films and giving you a running commentary even though you never asked for one, and an unhealthy obsession with Manchester United. However, rude and inconsiderate he is not, which is why I'm getting worried.

And very annoyed.

If he misses this, our twelve-week scan, the day we see our baby for the very first time, I will never speak to him again. Maybe even deny him access to his child. OK, no, perhaps that is a bit strong, but I will never ever let him forget it, that's for sure. Of that you can be certain, James Ashcroft.

I look at my watch, it's 1.30 p.m. He is now officially fifteen minutes late. I think about just going in on my own. I have told the friendly receptionist in the canary yellow jacket I am here after all so I stand up, utter a few more expletives, (it must be the hormones. Lately I've been known to tell our toaster to eff off) and give the street one last scan, just in case.

That's when I see him.

I know it's him, because only Jim has hair that big and only Jim's head wobbles like that when he moves. But hang on, why is he moving like that? Like he's doing an impression of a train for a child, using his elbows to propel him along, a sort of demented power walk?

It's only as he comes nearer, waving like a madman at me now, that I realize he's actually limping. This doesn't concern me quite so much as what he appears to be wearing. It's a black and acid yellow ensemble, stripy at the top and shiny at the bottom, making him look like a giant bumble bee that's been on a stretching machine (then splatted by a heavy-footed predator if his current physical condition is anything to go by).

I walk towards him, squinting, trying to compute this information. Then, as if in fast forward motion, he is there before me and it all becomes horribly clear. He's wearing his school tracksuit which is caked – as he is – in mud, his face is bright purple, he's sweating profusely and he's done something sinister to his foot.

'Tess . . . listen . . . I'm so sorry, I'm so . . .'

He collapses onto the railings at the side of the hospital, one hand on my shoulder, gasping for breath.

I stand there staring at the sky for a few moments, trying to find the right words.

'You stink,' I say, eventually. 'You absolutely stink.' With that, I flounce back to the entrance of the hospital, through the revolving doors (getting my bag caught in it and having to go round several times which somewhat takes away from the intended impact) shouting back to a limping Jim as I go: 'You remove that mud, have a wash and find some deodorant. Otherwise I will erase all knowledge of you fathering this baby, do you understand?'

The antenatal waiting room is lit with harsh strip lighting that makes everyone's face look green. Jim's is still fuscia pink.

'I'm sorry, OK?'

'I know you are.'

'I had to cover for Awful, he's ill.'

'Ill?' I throw him my best exasperated wife look (I've been practising this of late).

'OK, hungover. But he's my mate, he would have done the same for me. It's not like he teaches English or Geography or anything where he could have just sat there quietly whilst the kids got on with their work, is it?' Jim says, trying to placate me. 'It was double PE, rugby union in fact and he was a scary shade of green, Tess, I kid you not. There was no way he would have made it.'

He says this with an infuriatingly genuine tone of concern.

'It was our baby's scan, Jim,' I hiss, trying to keep my voice down so the entire waiting room doesn't hear. 'And now you've probably broken your leg.'

Jim looks at me and laughs through his nose. I momentarily feel like punching it.

'Don't exaggerate,' he says in the patronizing tone he reserves only for me and Gina. (Jim is one of few people who knows how to handle Gina.) 'You always have to exaggerate.'

I hate Awful right now. I can now perfectly understand why girlfriends sometimes hate their boyfriends' mates and Jim isn't even my boyfriend. Awful (Warren Woolfall but we just call him Awful) is Jim's best boy mate, but sometimes I wonder whether Awful would like to be more. They grew up together in 'Stokey' (Stoke-on-Trent to non 'Stokies') went to primary school, secondary school, even the same university town together (although Awful only made it to Manchester Met, something his enormous ego has never quite recovered from). They had a brief spell apart between 1998 and 2000 when Awful finally found himself a Polish girlfriend called Marta whom he proceeded to treat like shit. But it clearly proved too painful to be apart, because when Jim landed a job as English teacher at Westminster City School in the autumn of 2001, who should rock up as the most unlikely pot-bellied PE teacher you've ever seen? Warren bloody Woolfall.

'I got the time wrong, didn't I?' Jim says, getting defensive now. I realize I can only string out this guilt trip so far. 'It was only when I got back to the changing rooms and checked your text that I realized it was quarter past, not half past. I did skip on the shower and get here as fast as humanly possible for a man who may be at risk of losing his foot, you know.'

'Ha! Who's exaggerating now?' I say.

'Whatever,' he says, petulantly.

'I couldn't get hold of you Jim.'

'I ran out of battery.'

'I thought you'd forgotten.'

'I'm sorry, OK?! I totally fucked up.'

Silence. I sigh and pat his knee, resignedly. Jim announces he's 'gagging for a slash' – I do hope this child has more decorum – and wanders off to the Gents. Why is nothing ever easy? Why is this, the first milestone in my pregnancy, not going like it does in the films, and why is the father of my child hobbling to the toilet with a swollen foot, leaving wafts of Impulse body spray behind him?

Thankfully, the nice lady on reception who lent it to him took pity on us and we're still going to be seen, but it's not ideal. Plus, the thing that's really concerning me now is that having drunk two pints of water as instructed (something to do with being able to see the baby properly on the scan) I am in real danger of wetting myself.

This is a strange place. But then I've come to accept strangeness as my current state of being. When I look around at all the pregnant ladies, the doctors and nurses striding back and forth in white coats, and the ancient posters about breastfeeding in which all the women seem to have hair like Lady Diana, I feel like I'm an observer, not a participant. I still feel like a fraud. A woman with a snotty-nosed toddler sitting next to her strokes her bump; I wonder if she can tell. There's something strange about those two over there, I imagine she's thinking. Those two aren't together, those two are impostors.

I look around. It's true, everyone but me looks professionally pregnant. I thought I was showing. At almost thirteen weeks, I already feel enormous, but looking at some of these women, I realize how far I have to go.

Take the girl in the far corner for example, she looks as if her waters might break at any second. She and her boyfriend can only be eighteen at the most, they look like kids themselves. The boyfriend's got his hair gelled so that it sticks together in clumps and you can see bits of scalp in between. The girl has ironed blue-black hair and a comedy sized bump protruding from the zipped front of her bubble-gum-pink tracksuit top. The entire ensemble reminds me of Mr Greedy in the Mr Men books. I smile at her, she looks me up and down. I look away, a bit scared.

Jim hobbles back from the toilets, obviously struggling with the pain but trying his best not to show it. He's just about eased himself into his chair, leaning on me for support, when scary girl in a pink tracksuit's other half pipes up:

'Alright sir?'

I flash Jim a look of horror but he looks more horrified than me, his cheeks turning suddenly anaemic.

'Oh, hi Connor,' he says, unable to disguise the dismay in his voice. 'I er, I would ask what you're doing here but I think that's probably obvious.' He gestures at the girlfriend's beach-ball of a bump. The hard stare she gives him back means I have to look away in order to keep a straight face.

Superb. As if this whole antenatal experience could get any worse, we now have to engage in chit chat with one of Jim's pupils and his mardy teen girlfriend.

'Yeah,' says Connor, his tracksuit rustling as he leans forward. 'Two weeks to go till the birth, sir, it's proper weird.'

(You can say that again.)

'Congratulations,' says Jim. 'I didn't know you were going to be a father.'

'Nor did I to tell you the troof, sir,' he says. When he smiles, he flashes a gold tooth. 'It was totally unplanned, wa'n it, Sade?' Sade raises an eyebrow – the first time her face has moved since we got here. 'First time we'd done it in all, which was proppa unlucky but that's life, innit, I s'pose.'

Jim smiles shyly at Connor, then looks at me and raises his eyes to the ceiling. Turns out he's got more in common with his pupils than he thought.

Connor fidgets, leans forward, leans back. He probably had a line of coke an hour ago I think, then cuss myself for sounding like a *Daily Mail* reader.

'So er . . . you expecting too then, sir?'

Sade punches her boyfriend on the arm. 'Connor shut up will ya!'

'What me?' Jim is thrown. 'No, but Tess is pregnant,' he says, as if I'm someone random he just met on the street.

'Is she your wife, sir?'

'No, no she's not my wife.'

'I am *not* his wife,' I throw in, just to clear up any misunderstanding about that one.

'So she's your girlfriend then?'

Jim looks at me helplessly, 'Yes,' he says. 'She's my girlfriend.'

'She's well buff sir.'

'Connor!' Sade bolts at this one. 'Just give it a rest, will ya? You're doing everyone's heads in.' Me and Jim are trying not to laugh now, me unable to hide my delight that a teenage boy just called me buff.

'Congratulations,' says Connor, before being dragged off by his girlfriend. 'I hope everything goes well with the little 'un, sir.'

'Thank you,' says Jim. 'And you too Connor.'

Jim and I are shaking our heads in disbelief when a nurse pops her head around the door.

'Mrs Jarvis?' she trills, cheerfully. 'Please come through now and when you do, bring your notes with you, will you dear?'

The room for the scan is dark and quiet, just the gentle beep, beep of some equipment or other.

I lie on my back, my skirt pulled down to my hips, a few stray wiry pubes on show. (Why didn't I think of that?).

This is the moment I've been waiting for, for seven whole weeks – the longest seven weeks of my life filled with endless fibbing and avoiding people. This is the moment of truth.

'So this is your . . . husband?' says the nurse as she rubs freezing jelly into my stomach. I tense my muscles. 'Er, no.'

'Your boyfriend?'

'Um, well.'

'Partner,' says Jim. I look at him, he winks at me. 'I'm her partner.'

It's a word I've sniggered at in the past, the kind of word Anne-Marie at work would use, due to some misplaced sense

110

of political correctness. But right now, at this moment, in this room, it was suddenly a word I liked, a word – at last – that fitted us. We were not many things, after all, but partners in this, we are.

We've been partners in crime for ten years. We've spent interminable nights together writing essays; he's been the first person I'd called when my brother had an accident, the first person I'd wanted to tell when I got my first job. He's seen me hiccupping with tears wearing slipper-socks and a bobble hat, so pissed I am trying to light the wrong end of a fag. And now we are partners in this, our biggest adventure to date, suddenly it felt good. Truly good.

We all look at the fuzzy screen in front of us and I am suddenly gripped by nerves: what if there is nothing there? My God, what if I have imagined all this! What if this is a figment of my delusional mind! I look at Jim for reassurance, he is shifting in his chair, more nervous than I've ever seen him.

And then I hear the words that make me suddenly, unexpectedly well up inside. The words that make this real.

'There we are. There's your baby,' says the nurse, pointing to the screen. And low and behold, there it is. A tiny being spinning in an air-tight orbit in the middle of me. Totally unaware of any of this.

Beside me, I hear Jim's smile. 'My God,' he says, as he draws his chair closer, looks at the screen and then at the nurse. 'Is that its heart, beating there? Is that our baby's heart?' And for the first time since I found out, I suddenly feel like this just might be the start of something good. Something unexpected, but something really good.

When we step, well, when Jim limps (it turns out he's broken his toe) out of hospital, late that afternoon, the trees along Tottenham Court Road are thick with pink blossom and there's the first hint of summer in the air.

111

CHAPTER TEN

'By the time mine and Toby's marriage fell apart I was thirty-nine, a total workaholic, childless and had convinced myself that's how I liked it. Then I went to Cuba and all hell broke loose. Three years later and I'm head over heels in love with a Cuban drummer of all things! having the baby I now realize I've longed for all my life.'

Cecile, 42, Warwick

'So what are your favourite memories? What really makes you smile when you think of Jamie?'

I glance at the Dictaphone on the spotless glass coffee table, checking the Record button is still shining red.

Danielle sits down on the sunken sofa next to me and hands me a mug of coffee that says 'World's Best Dad'.

'There's too many.' She's wearing eyeshadow the colour of sea shells. 'He was the kind of person who made every day special.'

'Wow,' I say, genuinely wowed. 'Lucky girl. So what – if you had to pinpoint one – was the best day you ever spent with him?'

I love my job. I love the spectrum of people I get to meet –

from psychos who put poo in their husband's pies to people who choose to share their home with grown pigs. But sometimes, I hear stories that do not have a funny side, which are not 'triumph over tragedy', they're just tragedy. And then I hate this bit: having to tease out the heartbreaking specifics. Danielle has told me every raw detail of her nightmare: the last time she saw her boyfriend leave the house, as he did every Saturday, to buy a Lottery ticket; the flat whine of his dead phone; the scraping at the door, the horror of what she found behind it: Jamie, legs sprawled, hands clawing the wood as blood spewed from his chest, stabbed for nothing but his i-Pod. If this were up to me, I'd stop now and give her a big hug. But I know that Judith will go ballistic if I don't get those details and send me back here to Danielle, which is just unthinkable.

There's echoey footsteps in the corridor outside, Danielle looks over at her son, Kyle, who's glued to *The Lion King*. 'We didn't get to go many places, I suppose, Jamie always having to work weekends. But there was one day last November, well it was nothing special . . .'

'Go on, I bet it was . . .'

'We went to Greenwich Park. It was really sunny, you know, one of those crisp autumn days? I was pushing the buggy, Jamie had Kyle on his shoulders, running thorough these huge piles of leaves – they almost came up to his thighs there were so many of them.'

'Sounds great fun.'

'I went off to queue for some drinks and when I came back about fifteen minutes later . . .'

Her eyes fill with tears and she has to pause to gather herself.

'I remember his face. The happiest I've ever seen him. He didn't know I was watching him, but Kyle had fallen asleep in his buggy by that point and Jamie was laying down on the grass, all sweaty from the running. He had one hand on Kyle's leg, his eyes closed and this huge smile from ear to ear. He looked so content, you know? The happiest man alive. He was just so content with his lot.'

She pauses. The tape whirrs.

'You alright to go on?'

'Yep.' A tear escapes and she wipes it away. 'And he adored his football, too, was all I was going to say.'

'You're telling me,' I say, looking at the photographs crammed onto the mantelpiece: Jamie and Kyle in matching football kits next to the Christmas tree, Jamie in what looks like the football clubhouse, shower fresh, one hand on hip, the other around Danielle. Proud and vital as anything.

'He loved to take me and Kyle to matches. Or we'd invite a few people over when there was a big match on and I'd make sausage sandwiches for all the boys.'

'Sounds like you had a brilliant time together.'

'We did. He was a gorgeous person, my best friend, the best dad in the world.'

I am aware of the warmth of the mug in my hand and an orange-sized lump in my throat.

'But it's not really the days out, it's the tiny things I miss the most,' she says, tears are streaming down her face now but she doesn't bother wiping them away. 'He used to call me every afternoon to tell me what he'd had for his lunch, now, sometimes, the phone doesn't ring all day. And he was so excitable, like a Labrador puppy my mum used to say. When the football was on, and Palace scored, he would throw himself in front of the telly on his knees, then run round the house till he found me, and snog me till I could hardly breathe!' she laughs. 'Absolutely barmy, he was.'

She walks over to the mantelpiece, picks up a photo in a silver frame and brings it to me. It's of Jamie on the sofa, Kyle fast asleep, his head lolling onto his dad's.

'He adored Kyle,' she says. ' I know what people say about teenage dads but he was nothing like that. Every morning, before he went to work he would get Kyle up, put *The Jungle Book* tape on and get him dressed singing 'Bare Necessities' at the top of his voice. It used to do my head in. Now I'd do anything to get woken up by that sound.'

Kyle turns round to see that his mummy is crying and toddles up to her side, leaning his fuzzy blonde head in her lap. I put my hand on Danielle's hand and the orange-sized lump in my throat now grates like new shoes on a blister.

'I suppose the hardest thing,' Danielle goes on, 'is that I didn't choose this, this was not my decision. Most people who are single choose to be single, don't they? To be or not be with someone, to get divorced or whatever. But I didn't choose to be without Jamie. He was taken from me when we had our whole future ahead of us.'

'You have those wonderful memories,' I offer, thinking, 'yeah, good one Tess. As if that's any compensation for losing the love of your life and father of your child at nineteen.' But what she says next surprises me.

'I know. In fact d'you know what keeps me going when it gets really hard?' she says. 'It's the fact that despite what I've been through, if I could turn back time, I wouldn't change anything. Because some people never find The One, do they? But I did, even if it couldn't be for ever. So I'm lucky.' She smiles. 'I'm one of the lucky ones.'

I stand in the corridor outside Danielle's flat. It smells of rubbish bins and fried chicken.

'You will remember to put the website at the bottom of the article, won't you?' says Danielle. Kyle pokes his head around his mum's legs. 'It's www.droptheknives.co.uk.'

'I've got it,' I say, thinking please God don't let the subs say we haven't got space on the page.

Ten seconds later, I'm running down the fire escape from her immaculate rabbit hutch of a flat, bawling my eyes out like a baby.

CHAPTER ELEVEN

'I'd always wanted to be a mum, but like everything in my life it was a case of "How?" How will I change a nappy? How will I keep them safe? But when I fell pregnant with my son, I was overjoyed. It's been tough though. I imagine what my children look like by tracing their features, but it makes me sad I'll never see their faces.'

Monica, 39, Henley-on-Thames

'Life stripped bare' is my bread and butter I suppose. People open up to me, they tell me the intimate details of their lives: the day their babies were swapped at birth, the day the family pet saved their life, the fact their husband never goes down on them, the way they feel about their breasts. Sometimes it's heartbreaking, sometimes it's cruel; often it's really hilarious. But my job is never to help, it is just to listen and to record the facts. And so most of the time I am able to distance myself from what I am hearing.

Most of the time.

This time, God, I don't know what happened. Judith would freak if she could see me.

'First rule of tear-jerker journalism,' she always says, when she's doing one of her prowls around the office, 'for fuck's sake, don't get emotionally involved.' (Judith's partial to a bit of gratuitous swearing.) 'We're not counsellors. Or a pissing charity.'

I stand on the platform of New Cross station and close my eyes to a gentle sun. 'If I could turn back time, I wouldn't change a thing.'

Wow. That's got to be true love, hasn't it? To choose all that pain and hell for just three years with the love of your life, over long-lived blissful ignorance and probably a very adequate second best? Have I ever felt like that about anyone? About Laurence? Does Vicky feel that about Rich? Mum about dad? I've no idea. What I do know, is that love like that is surely gold dust. What Danielle has lost does not bear thinking about. But what she does have, the certainty of her feelings, it blew my mind.

A train pulls up and I get in, sit opposite a rhino-sized man dressed in swathes of grey jersey, bobbing his head to something tinny on his Nano. We creak off towards London Bridge. The high rises of South London flick by like a thumbed deck of cards.

I close my eyes, the tune of 'Bare Necessities' rings in my head and all I can see is Jamie gently easing a T-shirt over his son's blond head, unaware that by the end of the day he'll be dead. Three futures wiped out.

How many sad interviews have I done before and I've never lost it like this? But the water works are turned on full pelt now. I've surrendered myself, I'm almost enjoying my tragedy-fest when the siren-like wail of my crap phone startles me from my misery.

'Hello.'

Whoever it is is laughing. 'Jesus, you sound like someone died.'

Laurence.

I'm disturbed by how quickly the sickened pit of my stomach is filled with tiny airborne feathers. I hastily wipe the tears from my face.

'Do I? No. Nobody died,' I say, forcing the corners of my mouth to curl upwards.

'Are you ill then? You sound like you're dying from a cold.'

Typical Laurence. He only had to sniffle and he'd think he was at death's door, his mum force feeding him some North African concoction or other.

'No, no I'm not ill. I'm just on a train that's all. I've been interviewing someone in New Cross.'

I'm suddenly embarrassed at my blatant lack of professionalism. I bet Jeremy Paxman doesn't go wailing back to the office after a particularly harrowing interview.

'Right, that's good. That's very good actually, because I was hoping we could meet up.'

'When?' It comes out as 'Wed?'

'This lunchtime, at Borough Market. I've got something I really want to show you.'

That feeling, a heaviness in the pit of my stomach, it's there again telling me I shouldn't go. One lunch, that's OK, that could just be for old time's sake. I would have my baby, life would be OK, life would be *great*, even, and I'd move on. But two meetings? Two's getting into something.

But Danielle's words are there again. Was she really lucky? Or did she make her own luck?

And what if Laurence is The One. What if he's my Jamie and we just screwed it up the first time around. What if this is my second chance?

'OK, why not,' I say, eventually. 'I can pretend my interview ran over. I deserve a lunch break anyway.'

'Good girl,' says Laurence. 'Do you know the bit where the cash-points are at the opening to Borough Market? I'll meet you there, say one p.m.?'

Despite my best efforts in the Body Shop at London Bridge station, applying some powder compact thingy and trowels of blusher, I don't get away with it.

'Shit. What happened to your face?' Laurence never was one to stand on ceremony.

'You look a tad . . .'

'Blotchy? It's a long story,' I say, slightly deflated.

Laurence makes a face that says, 'You said it not me.'

We both laugh shyly, then look away. We stand there like a pair of idiots for a few seconds, me taking in Laurence's face. The straight, jet-black eyebrows like blackbirds in flight, the caramel-coloured lips with their permanent mischievous curve, the sleepy lids that make him look stoned, even when he's wide awake. With a day or two of stubble, he looks better than ever. I see his eyes drift down towards my midriff and I physically flinch, then cover my belly with my bag. I suddenly panic that I'm showing through my top and wondering whether I should be here at all when he says, 'So, shall we?' And he gestures into the crowds. 'You can tell me all about the blotchy face when we sit down. I'm all ears, I promise you.'

June shines blue through the Victorian arches over Borough Market. A gastronomic greenhouse. Food paradise. I am walking in front, Laurence steers me gently from behind. I have no clue where he's taking me, in amongst this sprawling maze of cobbled pathways and yellow and red canopied stalls but I don't care, I'm just savouring the moment.

We pass stalls of olives, fruit and jam, skinned rabbits, gigantic hams hanging from the ceiling, a mountain of huge cheeses, like ancient hat boxes. Drifts of roasted coffee and just-baked bread envelop me. I can feel the warmth of the sun on my hair and every pad of Laurence's fingers on my back.

'Where are you taking me?' I shout over my shoulder.

'That's for me to know and you to find out. Now, turn

119

round.' I do as I'm told and he stuffs a chocolate truffle in my mouth. 'Good?' He leans over my shoulder and I catch a whiff of his aftershave – complex, musky, confidently sweet. It's potent with memories. 'God, amazing,' I mumble, through chocolatey teeth.

We turn a sharp corner and come to a fish stall, oysters piled on frills of crushed ice, enormous sea breams with eyes like marbles. Then Laurence slips in front of me, he gestures for my hand.

'Here we are,' he says, nodding towards a tiny door nestled in the side of a railway arch. 'This is the infamous Bedales. You're gonna love this.'

This place is seriously cool. The ceiling is low and curved, the walls are white-washed exposed brick, endless bottles of serious looking wine stacked high against them. In the middle of the room sit food connoisseur types – probably wine writers and suchlike – at benches, grazing over tasting plates and goblets of wine.

'This is brilliant,' I say. 'Beats the usual Pret sarnie anyway.' But I'm also aware that something's not quite right. It's the smell: pungent, sweaty, kind of *piggy*. And then I notice that the food on everyone's plates seems to be of the same, very limited kind: various types of pate and various oozing cheeses.

'Run a bloody marathon if you like, have wild and passionate sex because it won't harm the baby!' laughed Dr Cork. 'But avoid un-pasturized cheese, pate and large amounts of alcohol like the plague.' I'm starting to panic.

'Isn't it wicked?' says Laurence. He's standing, eyeing up the shelves of wine, his hands in his pockets, his tanned, toned forearms on show. 'Which one would you buy if you could?'

'God knows,' I say. 'As long as it's alcoholic.'

'Oh come on you philistine, you must know what sort of grape you like?'

120

'Who are you all of a sudden?' I laugh, 'Oz bloody Clarke?'

'No,' he says, flatly. I worry I might have offended him. 'But I am French, and I do manage a bar, so actually Miss Jarvis –' he unconsciously pulls up his T-shirt and strokes his belly. I catch the ripple of muscle like water-worn sand '– I do know the odd thing about wine.'

I scour the shelves for the one wine I know. 'OK,' I say, 'I know what I'd choose, it's called Tan something, followed by a long word that sounds like hermit.'

'Tain L'Hermitage?' He says it with a proper French accent like it's the most natural thing in the world. 'Yeah,' I say impressed. 'How did you know?'

'I just know,' he says. 'Bon choix mademoiselle.'

Laurence looks around the room, briefly glancing at his reflection in the mirror opposite, then sits down and clears his throat.

'So. Are you going to tell me about the blotchy face?'

'You really wanna know?'

'I really wanna know.'

And so I go through the whole story. How Danielle and Jamie met at school when they were fifteen, how much they loved each other, how much they doted on their kid, how Jamie was stabbed, lay dying in his girlfriend's arms, the last thing he said to her, the music they played at his funeral.

'And do you know the thing that kills me most of all?' Laurence shakes his head. 'She said she'd rather go through all that pain and grief and still have known him, than never to have known him at all, isn't that amazing?'

It's only when I stop talking, that I realize I'm almost crying and that Laurence is staring at me, like I'm stark raving mad.

'Wow, it really does get to you,' he says, frowning and half laughing at the same time. 'Or is it the time of the month?'

'No!'

(Fat chance of that.)

Laurence leans forward and holds my gaze. I smile nervously and look away.

'Well, if you must know,' he says, resting his chin on his hands. 'I think it's really sweet. I think you look gorgeous when you cry.'

'Sir, would you like to try the wine?' We spring apart like parents caught out having sex. A rubenesque waitress is suddenly at our table with . . . Oh *God*. A bottle of Tain L'Hermitage.

'Laurence!' I gasp. 'That cost a bomb!'

'I'm allowed to spoil you aren't I? Anyway, I want to say sorry.'

Laurence tastes the wine and nods his approval. 'And two of the tasting plates,' he says without asking me. The waitress shuffles off.

Shit. How do I blag myself out of this one?

We make nervous small talk about the clientele, the menu on the board, the couple across from us. Then, Laurence takes a deep breath. 'Listen,' he says, filling my glass. I watch forlornly, wracking my head for good excuses.

'When I saw you on the London Eye last week, I didn't really tell you the truth about Chloe. The thing is . . . we're not together.'

'Oh! Really?' I can't stop the ridiculous level of enthusiasm in my voice.

'Well, we are, but by the skin of our teeth. Man,' he takes a sip of wine, 'she's a nightmare, so fucking high maintenance.' I have to bite my lip to stop myself from smiling.

'The reason I'm living at my mate's house in Islington is not because I'm flat-sitting like I told you but because I moved out, I'd had about as much as I could take. We haven't been getting on at all.'

'Oh, I'm sorry,' I lie.

122

'Don't be,' he shrugs. 'I think the relationship's just run its course.'

I swill the wine around my glass.

'Eh, voilà!' The waitress is back with the tasting plates. I look down at the beautifully arranged morsels of pate and cheese, none of which I can eat, and think I feel Laurence watching me. We eat, in silence for a minute or two, me nibbling on a gherkin, going through my options.

Laurence chews slowly. Then, he puts the bread he's holding down on the side of the plate and smiles at me. 'It was a laugh the other day, on the London Eye, wasn't it?'

'Yeah. Best lunchtime I've ever had.'

'I meant what I said, Tess. I was a total shit for finishing with you like I did.'

'Forget it, honestly, it's in the past now.'

'No hear me out,' he says. 'I was lonely back home when you went travelling. When Chloe came along I just succumbed. It was a moment of weakness that just,' he clasps his head, 'somehow turned into five fucking years!'

'Well,' I say, trying to lighten things. 'Stuff happens, I guess. Life just throws things up, doesn't it? We can't be in control of our destinies all of the time.'

Laurence stares at me intensely. 'No, you're right.'

You bet I am.

'But I want to sort my life out, Tess, I want to – what is it they say in *Trainspotting*? I want to choose life!' He's laughing now and I laugh too, with a mixture of surprise and pleasure. 'I want to get married, get the house, the kids. The whole shebang.'

'Bloody hell,' I say, trying to sound casual and detached when really, inside, my heart's on a rollercoaster. 'Am I hearing this right? Is Laurence Cane finally growing up?'

'Yeah, I guess so,' he says, drawing his chair nearer, full of boyish enthusiasm. 'I'm sick of flailing about with the wrong woman, in a shit job – I mean, I'm a glorified barman, really, that's what it boils down to. I want to start a new career – I might even resurrect the film thing!'

I'm not sure how to react. I'm not sure what he's getting at, I mean does this, could this, whole new future include me?

'Oh no,' says Laurence suddenly. 'Look, you haven't touched your food. *Or* your wine. Sorry, I've been on a total monologue. Listen, I'm going to go to the toilet.' He stands up, he wipes his mouth with his napkin and winks at me. 'And whilst I'm gone, take that stunned look off your face. You're scaring me.'

I look down at my untouched plate and very full glass of wine and realize I have to act fast, this is Operation Foetus First.

First up, cheese and pate: I could probably get away with nibbling a bit but in my pregnant mind, I have convinced myself it is riddled with listeria. I don't hesitate, I grab some napkins, wrap it up and stuff it at the bottom of my bag, covering it with a book and my make-up bag to disguise the smell. Now, wine. I look around for a pot-plant, reasoning clichés are clichés for a reason. There's nothing near by but I spot an urn filled with a fake lemon tree just outside the door. I saunter over, glass in hand, to discover it's choked with fag butts so I figure a bit of 1992 Tain L'Hermitage isn't going to do any harm. I stand at the door, pretending to drink in the market atmosphere, dripping bits of the wine, into the urn.

I only just make it back to my seat and arrange myself to look natural when Laurence is back from the toilet.

'Wow, very impressive. I see you haven't lost your ability to speed drink, then,' he says, his face slightly damp from having splashed it.

'You can take the girl out of Morecambe but you can't

take Morecambe out of the girl!' I say. Then I say, 'Anyway, it's good to see you.'

Laurence sits down. 'It's good to see you too.' He smiles. 'Ridiculously good.'

Laurence finishes what's left of his food and I make some lame excuse up that I'm on a diet, which being a bloke, Laurence unthinkingly buys. And then we leave, me feeling confused and excited and wondering how the hell I'm going to get through a whole afternoon's work feeling this distracted.

We meander through the market, traders relaxing after the lunchtime rush, and make our way towards the Park Street entrance.

We stand in a shaft of sunshine, hugging our goodbyes next to a railway arch. A train rumbles overhead, a throng of starlings gathers above then scarpers into the blue, as if out of politeness for what's about to happen, which is that Laurence Cane takes his face in my hands, looks at me, with the sort of tenderness that almost looks like pain, and kisses me, with as much clawing relish as smokers smoked on the eve of the smoking ban.

CHAPTER TWELVE

'I thought I was just fat, that I'd just not managed to lose the baby weight (and also piled on some more for good measure). I was breastfeeding a seven-month-old baby: I couldn't get pregnant could I? Ellie-Rose's arrival five months later was all the proof we needed. I always wanted my kids close together but this is ridiculous.'

Bethan, 31, Llandudno

*'Go Grease Lightning la-la-la-la la . . . quarter mile
Grease Lightning! Oh Grease Lightning*

*'Go Grease Lightning bla-bla-bla-bla-something trial (?!)
Grease Lightning woah, Grease Lightning!*

*'You are supreme. Oh yeah it's cream???? Oh Grease Lightning
Go. Go. Go-go-go-go-go-go-go!'*

Could my life get anymore bizarre? Approximately eleven hours ago I was kissing my ex lover under sun-streamed arches feeling like we were in one of those black and white photographs by Henri Cartier Bresson. Now I am in Beckenham, singing a *Grease* anthem, very badly, into a karaoke microphone, wearing vast amounts of padding and a man's size thirty-four suit.

Trust Vicky to go for a *Pop Idol/X-Factor* fancy dress theme for her twenty-ninth birthday party on the year I am forced to remain stone cold sober. Of course she doesn't know I can't drink, she thinks I'm as pissed as she is. I will tell her soon about the baby – before Gina does – there's surely a limit as to how long Gina can keep her mouth shut. However, something in me tells me that tonight – what with me dressed as Rik Waller and Vicky as Sharon Osborne – is not the time.

I wanted to come as Sharon Osborne too but I didn't think a corset was a great idea in my condition and I decided that at least a fat suit would hide any sign of a bump. I'm kind of wishing I hadn't gone to such extremes now.

This is an insight to say the least, being sober at my best friend's birthday party. On my right, Vicky is putting me to shame with her huge, jazzy voice that wouldn't sound out of place in the final of *X-Factor*. To my left, Jim, complete with Simon Cowell high-waisted jeans and a Lego-like wig, has his eyes closed in a near-orgasmic expression, and is thrusting his pelvis backwards and forwards. Lost in music.

God, it's carnage in here. Mascara-streaked girls cavort with sweaty blokes, trays of tequila do the rounds. Hannah Burns – one of Vicks's Beckenham mates – is dead to the world (or is she just dead?) head slumped against the speaker, unaware that her jeans are hanging down by her hips and her G-string's on show.

Over in the corner, on top of a heap of coats and bags, there's a couple, limbs entwined who've been eating each other for the last four hours, eyes closed, in their very own bubble of ecstasy just like that advert for Match.com. I think she may have come as Michelle McManus (but I haven't dared comment in case she's just a big girl, it's hard to tell). Either way, I wonder, do I look this deranged when I'm drunk? It's a sobering thought. I'd claim it's enough to put me off beer for good but that would be an outright lie. Every other pregnant woman in the whole world seems to go green at one sniff of alcohol. I'm more likely to go green with envy then stick my nose in your glass and inhale, violently. I cannot believe I have six more months of this mind-numbing sobriety. Jim Ashcroft has a lot to answer for.

We finish to rapturous applause. I reckon I got away with it. Nobody would ever suspect that I would come out to any social event (let alone one where I am dressed in a fat suit) and voluntarily not drink, for starters, plus I've discovered the technique of drinking 'vodka lemonade'. Only, you leave out the vodka bit. A genius bit of deception.

'We were the business, this lot are shit,' says Jim, one arm on my shoulder, the other around Vicky. We're sitting on the kitchen worktop now, watching three girls from Vicks's osteopathy course do 'Gold' by Spandau Ballet.

'You were fucking Robbie Williams up there,' slurs Vicky. She's definitely drunk, she never swears when she's sober.

'You wanna see me do my "My Way". Dead ringer for ol'blue eyes. But I won't bother tonight. I don't want to outshine the birthday girl,' Jim teases. 'Get up there Vicks, go on.' He nudges her off the worktop. 'Go and show these muppets how it's done.'

Vicky staggers purposefully towards the karaoke machine, clearly intent on hogging it, as she has the entire evening.

'Another belting power ballad on its way,' I say. Jim laughs and turns to me. 'You coping?' he mouths to me. 'Tell me the truth.'

'I'm cool,' I shrug. Then I look down at the vast acres of shiny, navy suit covering my gigantic spongey form. 'Well actually, tell a lie. I'm absolutely boiling.'

Jim gives it up, starts laughing like me in a fat suit is the funniest thing he's seen in his life.

'Fair play, Jarvis. I don't know many girls who would have the balls to come to a fancy dress party dressed as Rik Waller. Especially sober and pregnant ones!'

'At least mine's fancy dress, you wear your jeans that high all the time.'

'Cheeky . . .!' Jim pulls them higher. 'Anyway,' he says, 'I like them like this. They show off my manly bulge.'

Jim jumps down from the worktop, shouts out in pain (the fact it hasn't got a whacking great plaster on it means Jim constantly forgets his little toe is broken) and goes to the fridge, pausing to do the chord change of 'Gold' with imaginary drum sticks.

'I'm getting a beer, want anything fatso?'

'A pint of white wine? Followed by four barrels of lager and forty Marlboro Lights. No, tell you what, I'll just have a lemonade.'

Jim sticks his head around the fridge door.

'Wise decision,' he says, looking me up and down. 'I'd say you're already piling on the baby weight.'

I'm suddenly aware of being stone cold sober. I'd like to talk to Gina, but she's doing sambucas with Vicky, Claudia from uni and a couple of other people I don't really know. She's come as the ginger one from Girls Aloud and is wearing MY BLOODY SEQUINNED DRESS!

OK, so I can't wear it – I have to wear a bra with everything now my boobs have ballooned to twice their former size – but considering we've barely even had a conversation in the past month, I think it's a bit much. Things were getting mildly better, until last week, when I had to tell her I couldn't go to New York.

Gina had just come off the phone from an hour's conversation with some bloke she pulled on the tube when I broached the subject.

'Right, so you're not coming?' she snapped, standing against the radiator in our hall, arms folded.

I forgot how scary she is when's she's pissed off. Her nostrils flare and she stares at you like you're the most useless, pile of crap in the world.

'I'm sorry, I just really don't think it's a good idea,' I mewed, hating myself for being so meek.

'I thought it was only when you were fit to drop that you couldn't fly. When you couldn't like, fit into the seat you were so fat?'

(Gina Marshall at her sensitive best . . .)

'The doctor says past thirty weeks . . .'

'So what's the problem, you're only about ten.'

'Actually I'm thirteen weeks,' I said, 'but it's not really that. It wouldn't be much fun for me for a start, would it, let's be honest, not being able to drink? And anyway, I couldn't relax, there's too much stuff going on in my head.'

Gina gave me a look as if to say told you so then stropped off to her bedroom to have another fag. I know what she was thinking – that I'm regretting keeping it – but nothing could be further than the truth. After seeing the scan, the reality if it all, I am happy to be pregnant. I just wish things weren't so messy.

Jim puts a glass of lemonade, complete with ice and lemon down next to me, plus a vodka and tonic for Vicky.

'Here you go. Go steady on that,' he says. 'I don't want that baby being a lush like its mum.'

He limps off, tries to dance with a girl in a T-shirt that says 'Louis Walsh is always right' and I know, I just know that his perpetual good mood is due to one thing: the little fuzzy picture, folded up and slipped inside his wallet. Concrete evidence that this is really happening.

Oh maybe we should just get together, do what you do when you get pregnant, do the happy ending thing – even if we have to compromise, it would make life so much easier.

The music throbs, disco lights swirl and hug the walls, as blinding and distracting as my thoughts: I'm having Jim's baby, but I'm falling in love with someone else. It's craziness when I say it like that. Should I even be letting myself? Can I even *stop* myself? I don't know anything anymore.

'God, I'm shit-faced.' Something matted and streaked with red lands on my lap. Vicky's head. 'I've just double-dropped two sambucas.'

'Where's Rich?' I say, patting her head. 'I haven't seen him all evening.'

'God knows, you know what he's like.' Vicky adjusts her Sharon wig in the reflection of the kitchen window. 'He's probably in his element, doing his Rolf Harris impression somewhere. Telling his story about the time the parrot said "fuck you" during a children's presentation – God, if I've heard that once.'

'Yeah but it is a funny story.'

'Not after the millionth time, it's not.'

From someone else, this comment could sound like a dig, but I never worry about Vicky and Rich. Ever since the day they met at the Musical Theatre Society auditions for *Oliver Twist* during the first year it's been Vicky and Rich, Rich and Vicky, and nobody can imagine it ever being any other way. The story comes round at many a drunken night in the pub: Rich had never sung or acted in his life, he only went to the audition for *Oliver Twist* because he knew Vicky was auditioning and he fancied her something chronic (it was the heaving bosoms in a wench dress). But then she got the part of Nancy and he got the part of Fagin and that's it, the rest is history. The fact they did a specially choreographed rendition of 'I Had the Time Of My Life' at their wedding complete

131

with the lift at the end (only made possible by both of them eating nothing but turkey steaks for six months) says it all. Vicky had found her Patrick. Her Pa Larkin. He was her bon-vivant, she was his salt-of-the-earth.

'Er . . . how's Gina?' I enquire, trying to sound nonchalant. She's said a sullen 'hi' to me this evening and that's about it.

'On form,' says Vicks, 'Haven't you seen her all night? Hey,' she gets a sudden glint in her eye, 'and she's got sambuca. Come with me, let's do another shot.'

'No!' I protest, rather over-zealously. 'I'm drunk enough already, I'll puke if I do.'

Vicky stops and squints at me, her glittery eyeshadow all over her face.

'Are you, Tess?' she says eventually, scrutinizing my face. 'Because you don't seem that pissed to me.'

'Riiiight!'

Suddenly the music goes off. Jim is standing on the coffee table, swaying slightly, beer in hand.

'As we can't find Victoria's betrothed . . . '

'Yeah, actually where is my husband?' Vicky says, as if she's only just remembered she's got one.

'And he is probably face down in a pint of Guinness, or talking to the dog, or whatever it is Dr Dolittle types do, I have taken it upon myself to take over Peddlar's annual birthday speech.'

'Good one Jimmy!' Gina shouts from the sidelines. (I don't know what she's on about, she's not spoken to him for a month.)

'Go Ashy!' I join in, hoping I might get some camaraderie going with Gina. She doesn't even look at me.

'Now, as we all know this has been a big year in the Moon household. Vicks has finally started drinking properly again, thank God, after what can only be described as a very selfish

132

decision, on her part, to abandon partying properly with her shambolic mates for over a year to bring up her son . . .'

I throw Jim an amused 'that's rich!' look. He realizes what he's said and instinctively covers his mouth.

'Plus.' He takes a swig of beer, tries to smooth it over. 'As everyone knows, she's been Super Mum, working really hard on her osteopathy course, only to pass with flying colours . . .'

A huge crash as someone literally falls in through the kitchen back door.

'I'm here! Everyone calm down, I can take over now . . .!'

A sea of people parts as Richard swerves towards the coffee table.

'Rich! My God!' Vicky gasps. 'How pissed *are* you?'

Rich is very pissed. Wasted actually. In fact in all the years I've known him, I've never seen him in such a state. His cheeks look like Noddy's, his Gareth Gates, spiky hair is flattened to his head. And his little belly . . . 'Baby, put your gut away!' says Vicky, tugging at his top . . . is sticking out of his 'I love my mam' T-shirt.

But Richard couldn't care less because this is his moment, this is his world, his and Vicky's world. This is his family home, the wife he loves, his annual speech.

'F f f f f f first of all . . .'

Everyone gets the Gareth Gates joke. He's got his audience captivated already.

'I just wanna say thank you to my beaudiful Sharon . . .'

Someone guffaws from the sidelines.

'For putting up with me for the past year.'

And on he goes. Shit-faced but seamless. He tells everyone, what a star his wife is, how she put him back together after his dad died, how she is a wonderful mother, has the 'best chest in Beckenham', could join a circus she's so good at juggling. How she makes him a happy man.

A speech like this – just for a birthday – could come across as twee, but somehow, Vicky and Richard get away with it. Rich jokes it's to make-up 'for all the grief he gives her the rest of the year'. Vicky jokes it's the only reason she stays married to him.

'Richard Moon, you drunkard!' Vicky gives her husband a smacker on the lips as he staggers down, eventually, from his podium. 'Where the hell have you been, I haven't seen you all night.'

There's three cheers for Vicky's birthday and then she picks up her vodka and lemonade.

Oh. No. That'll be my lemonade.

'Uurgh what's this?' she turns to Jim. I see Jim panic and turn to me. 'This hasn't got vodka in . . .' she looks at me. 'It's just lemonade.'

Oh. My. God.

Something like realization eclipses her face. I am sure something like horror eclipses mine.

She looks at Jim, he scratches his head and mutters some expletive. She looks back at me. That's it, we're caught out.

At that moment, the room stands still. There's no movement, no voices, no music, no nothing. Don't ask me how she knows, she just does. She's my best friend, she knows everything.

'Oh my God,' she says it so quietly. 'You're pregnant aren't you? You and Jim are having a baby.'

We all stand there dumbly for a second, Vicky with her hand over her mouth, shaking her head in disbelief. Then she looks at Jim, who nods his head, she looks back at me, I close my eyes. Then she erupts into the widest beam I've ever seen, throws her hands in the air and runs towards me.

'Aaaaaahh!' Vicky's ear-splitting shriek engulfs the room. 'This is the best news EVER!!' she says, hugging me so tight she almost winds me. Then she does the same to Jim, who laughs, a sweet, shy laugh. 'Rich, have we got any champagne?' She's running around the room now, flapping her arms. 'If not, go and buy some, we've got to have champagne!! Tess, this is the best news of my life! Everyone, everyone.' She stands on the coffee table herself now. 'Jim and Tess are having a baby!!'

Nice one Vicks, the room's going mad. People throw themselves at us, and then at each other. 'This has made our fucking night! We love you guys!' they gush, drunk and amorous.

And despite the fact I didn't plan this at all, it's kind of made mine too. After Gina's reaction, I presumed nobody would be happy for us, perhaps she was right, perhaps this was a disaster. But now, here, this is the reaction I yearned for (well, just their support would have done, but this is even better).

'So you're not just fat, you're preggers!' Richard chucks his chubby arms around my even chubbier middle, drops to his knees and kisses my belly.

I laugh, the first genuine laugh of the night. Rich stands up and gives Jim a high five.

It's brilliant and positive and it's what, I now realize, I really needed. But despite all of this, there's two things gnawing at my thoughts: 1) Gina is the only one not joining in. She's over there, arms crossed in a display of the most telling body language I've ever seen. 2) Vicky's already miles ahead of reality, she thinks this is it. She thinks we're getting married. For Vicky this isn't just an announcement about a baby, it's about Jim and me 'coming out' as a couple.

She's in her element now, filling peoples' glasses, her wig half way off her head, spilling half the champagne on the floor.

'Is this all we've got Rich?' Vicky holds up two bottles of Cava. 'Oh well, Moet it is not but it'll have to do!'

'Er . . .' I try to speak but Vicky cuts in.

'You're alright with a little glass, aren't you?' she says, then she shouts over to Rich in the kitchen. 'Did I drink much when I was preggers?'

'Shit-faced every night!!' he shouts back.

She tuts and rolls her eyes, then pours an inch or two in a glass, hands it to me and kisses me on the cheek.

'Vicky . . .' I just have to get it out now.

She's sloshing wine into the glasses of Claudia and her boyfriend Martin, saying, 'I always knew these two would see sense at some point. And at my birthday party too, oh God! I'm so touched!'

'Vicky . . .' I say, my voice weird – not to mention my Rik Waller fat suit – 'the pregnancy, it was an accident, you know, it doesn't change anything between Jim and I, we're still just friends.'

'Yeah, and I'm a lesbian,' says Vicky, totally disregarding me. Then she stands once more, in her stockinged feet, on the coffee table, bog-eyed she's so drunk, and raises her glass: 'Three cheers for Jim and Tess, and their unborn child!'

Unborn Child? She makes it sound like an anti-abortion rally!

'Not only are they my best friends,' she continues, 'but they have got to be the most perfect for each other couple you will ever meet.'

'Ooooh God,' I hear Jim groan from behind his glass. I feel my face redden with embarrassment and gesture for Vicky to get down.

'And now they're having a baby, I'm sure they'll bang their thick little heads together, come to ther senses and live happily ever after just as I always knew they would. Three cheers for Jim and Tess, hip hip hooray! Hip hip . . .!'

But I don't stay for the rest, I disappear into the kitchen to hide behind the buffet. For the rest of the evening, all Jim and I get is the same old stuff. 'Isn't it just the most romantic story you've ever heard? Like Ross and Rachel from *Friends* but the real life version?'

'Er, no,' I strain, wanting to either slap them or cry by the end of the night. 'It's not like that, actually, it's a bit more complicated.'

At gone two a.m. I finally persuade Jim to share a taxi. I am so tired I could almost die. Jim sinks down into the seat and flops his head on my shoulder.

'Jesus Christ,' he says, exhaling slowly. 'Was that a party and a half or what?'

I mumble an answer but I'm too tired to talk, so I just stare out of the window, at the catseyes that come at us like meteors out of the dark, wondering if he's thinking the same thing.

'Jim?' I say, when he doesn't say anything for a while. 'Are you awake?'

'Yeah, I'm awake.'

'You know tonight?'

'Mmm, I do.'

'And what everyone was saying . . .?'

'What do you mean?'

'Well, do you think we should?'

Jim lifts up his head

'Should what?'

'Just get together.'

He studies my face. The city lights dance in his eyes.

'I know what you mean,' he says, sitting up properly. 'It would make this a lot easier, let's face it. But no, no, I don't think we should just get together.'

'Really?'

My feelings are also telling me this is the right answer.

'No, because I don't want to make a relationship of circumstance, we're worth more than that. I'd rather we were one hundred per cent what we can be – which is friends – than fifty per cent of what we *should be*.' Jim can be so annoyingly wise sometimes.

'And I couldn't stand the thought of it not working out.'

'No, me neither, that would be awful.'

'Because there's so much more at stake now. So much more to lose.'

We travel in silence for most of the way, but as my house draws close, the guilt gets too much.

'You know it's funny.' I don't know how else to broach the subject so I just blurt it out. 'I met Laurence for lunch today.'

Jim doesn't say a thing for what seems like days.

'That's a bit weird isn't it? You being pregnant and all that?' he says, eventually, and I breathe a sigh of relief that's he doesn't seem that annoyed. 'Mind you, I suppose as long as you told him you're pregnant now and it's just as mates it can't do any harm.'

I shut my eyes tightly and lay my head against the window.

'You did tell him you were pregnant didn't you?'

'Course,' I say, looking out of the window. 'Of course I told him I was pregnant. What do you take me for?'

CHAPTER THIRTEEN

'I must have been the only mum to-be in Britain praying for a ginger baby. The one-night stand with Glenn was a mistake. A gigantic, horrid mistake. It ruined my pregnancy – I tortured myself from start to finish – and the timing could not have been worse. When Dave held up Ben and I saw that shock of carrot hair just like his dad's I cried tears of joy. Dave thinks it's because he was a boy, but I will always know the truth.'
Emma, 34, Portishead

The truth is, I look fat. Not pregnant, just fat. I look like those middle-aged women who holiday in the Costa del Sol out of season: thick-waisted, apple-shaped, weird, that's what.

Right, let's try the denim skirt. I rifle through the avalanche of clothes on my bedroom chair until I find it, crushed in a ball. I put it on and face the mirror. Good God, I look appalling. My eyes are dead, I've got a halo of frizz, and I've erupted in several hormonal boils. Pregnant spots aren't like normal spots. They don't collect in the same area like period spots, or even really hurt like toxic spots. They just erupt, yellowy-red, in the most unfortunate of places – the middle of the cheek, the end of the nose, like those fake spots you get in joke shops.

It's hardly surprising since I've had about five hours' sleep all weekend. After getting back at three in the morning on Sunday after Vicky's party, I was then woken up again at five by the throb of Daft Punk on downstairs and the sound of Gina and a voice I didn't recognize cackling like a pair of demented witches. When I went downstairs, cursing them as I went, Gina and a friend were coked up to the eyeballs, doing fat lines off the lounge mirror which was, for the purpose, laid flat on the coffee table.

I couldn't help but feel that Gina was making a point. No, I know Gina was making a point: look at me, young and fun, with new young and fun friend. Look at you, pregnant, and no fun at all.

And it worked, I felt like a right square stood there in my Tote socks and brushed cotton pyjamas. People on coke talk such a load of bollocks, too.

Gina: Hey, Tess! How's it going? (She'd changed her tune.)

Me: Not great, um, it's five o' clock in the morning?

Gina: Is it? Fuck. *Really?* (Eyes like globes.) This is Michelle by the way.

Michelle dabbed at a few molecules of coke on the mirror and rubbed them on her gums. I rubbed my eyes and grunted a 'hello'.

Gina: She's stunning, isn't she? Her dad's Sudanese. God, I wish I was mixed race. (Cringe.) Mixed race people are soooo stunning don't you reckon? (Double cringe.) And her mum's from Stockholm. Is it Stockholm?

Michelle: It's Stockport actually.

At which point I gave up. I closed the door and trudged upstairs, saying 'selfish fucking cow' at a level I hope she could hear. I don't care. I've spent the last few weeks worrying about me and Gina, feeling like I'm the one who's let her down by getting pregnant. Well, no more! I can't go out and get pissed anymore (as much as I would love to), I can't have that life anymore, and if she can't accept that, then what can I do?

I face the mirror, I turn sideways, I tuck my top in, I pull it out. Whatever I do, it looks crap, just like everything else I have tried on this morning. I eventually settle on jeans (again) and a white hide-all blouse from Monsoon (again). True, the level of glamour at *Believe It!* is not exactly haute couture. (I'm always slightly embarrassed when people meet my editor. What they imagine to be a Gucci-clad, Manolo-Blanik-heeled, blow-dried vision of groomedness turns out to be more of a Barratts-heeled vision in beige, with permanent sticky tissues in her cardigan pockets.) But still, they must have noticed my standards are slipping and that I'm scoffing like there's no tomorrow. Anne-Marie, for one, has noticed the number of muffins I've been putting away.

'All that wheat and sugar'll play havoc with your digestive system you know,' she chirped up the other day, just as I bit into a second banana muffin. 'Greg (Vegan Boyfriend) said that's what used to cause his candida outbreaks.'

'What's candida?' I asked. I wish I hadn't.

'A yeast infection, but not like you get in your vagina?' (The muffin suddenly hung loose in my mouth.) 'It's in your stomach?' (Anne-Marie goes up at the end of every sentence so it sounds like a question.) 'And it wipes out all the good bacteria? And if it gets really chronic your gut can perforate? And then all the undigested bits of food seep into your bloodstream.'

I decided to keep the rest of the muffin till later.

I stand front-on to the mirror once more. Yep, I'm going to have to tell work. I've had my scan now, so there's really no excuse, but I'm dreading it.

I can see it now: 'Real Life Shocker!!!! Knocked up by best mate because I couldn't drive!!'

I hear Gina clattering about downstairs and think better of having breakfast before I go so I quickly do my ablutions, slap some concealer on my zits and I'm out of the door before I have to endure any sort of run-in with Gina, or face the lounge, which if there's been no improvement since yesterday, looks like the aftermath of Glastonbury.

I get on the bus and sit at the front, early summer blowing hair-dryer-warm through the window. I sense Laurence everywhere: a sun-kissed neck, the back of a shaven head, a molecule of aftershave, a throaty laugh. Since we met on Friday, there's been a flurry of texts and emails. Friday afternoon was a write-off, mainly spent conjuring up witty email banter (i.e. writing, deleting and rewriting emails to make it look like it all came naturally) and Googling the bar he runs, just you know, so I could imagine him at work.

Saturday's text made me laugh, a lot.

Hope u have a g8 time at V's party
Don't go lookin 2 hot. I'll be jealous as hell.

There was never any danger of that of course! (Unless morbidly obese failed reality show singers do it for him.) Thank the Lord I refrained from telling him about the Rik Waller outfit. Can you imagine!? I really should rein myself in sometimes.

All weekend I was hoping he'd ring. My stomach was in my mouth every time my phone went, then up and down again like an out of order lift. Two calls from Vicky (Had I come to my senses yet? Had Jim proposed?) One from dad (mum thinks the cat's got a brain tumour. One of its eyes looks cloudy) and one from Jim.

When his name, not Laurence's flashed up, I was disturbed

to feel a pang of disappointment – how awful is that? The father of my child calls to enquire how I'm feeling of a Sunday afternoon and what am I doing? Pining after my ex! Jim was sweet too, in his sympathy rage with Gina. 'Get her on the phone now,' he demanded. 'What the fuck does she think she's playing at, keeping you awake till five a.m.?'

'Jim, just leave it,' I said. 'I know you care but you'll only make things worse.'

'Well it's not just you, it's my baby too that I care about. I don't like the idea of Gina on class As in the same house as my baby.' For a non-conformer, Jim can be surprisingly moral sometimes.

'OK, I won't talk to her now if you don't want me to,' he said. 'But I will let her know she's bang out of order.'

I feel so wrong and yet so right at the moment so . . . skew-whiff. Something tells me I shouldn't be having all these feelings, that 'permanently on heat' doesn't quite fit with the natural order of things. Take this heavily pregnant woman waddling onto the bus now, her sticky-outy belly button visible through a thin, white top. With her glossy black hair and radiant skin, she's very desirable but she's also the epitome of 'taken'. She's wearing a badge: 'Move on! I'm off the market.'

But me? What's my badge? I'm growing a new life inside me, but my own is yet to unravel.

I'm psyching myself up to tell Laurence, I can't believe I haven't told Laurence! When I think of what I said in the taxi to Jim – an outright lie, lest we forget – my stomach turns inside out with guilt. And even if I do tell Laurence and this thing works out and it's all modern and wonderful, what will our early courtship be like, realistically? I'll be the size of a weeble and yet madly in lust, wanting acrobatic sex and barely able to see my own toes. Even more of a reason to get the shags in now.

I get off the bus on Waterloo Road and walk down The Cut, planning my speech in my head.

'Judith, I have some news. It's a bit scandalous.'

No, no I can't say that. If Judith even so much as smells the word scandal her hack antennae will start twitching and before I know it she'll have me nailed down to the sofa in her office, sucking every last morsel of my story out of me with those nicotine-stained fangs.

Try again.

'Judith, I've got some news. I'm pregnant . . .'

Perhaps I should leave the 'pregnant' bit right until the end. As annoying as Judith is sometimes, I don't want to get on the wrong side of her. That's to say, I don't want to give her the impression I am anything but married to my job. It's important to get in the other person's shoes when delivering news like this and I'm guessing Judith doesn't 'do' babies. My guess would be that babies to Judith mean a pain in the arse, a staffing nightmare. When Sonya in the art department's little boy had chicken pox and the nursery wouldn't have him, Judith's empathy amounted to: 'Well bring him in here. If he's really that ill, he won't bother you and you can still get all your work done'. Not exactly Miriam Stoppard.

OK, how about, 'Judith, I know this may not be what you want to hear, I didn't either when I first found out, but these things happen and well, I've decided to keep the baby' – side-track the P word, it might go down better – 'the dad and I are not together but are very good friends and . . . '

Too much information? What about . . .

. . . 'Judith! Hi!' Suddenly I'm face to face with my editor, she's sucking on a Berkeley Menthol outside the newsagents, her mouth like a baboon's bottom.

'Mornin'.' She chucks her fag end on the floor and demolishes it with one stamp and twist of her Trailfinders sandal. 'I haven't seen you here before. Is this your normal route, then?'

Judith's not very good at small talk. Get her on the phone bidding for a story and she's as snappy as a racing commentator, but put her next to you at the office Christmas party or now, on a five-minute walk to the office, and you'd get more conversation in an execution waiting room. Sometimes I wonder if she just likes the cut and thrust of getting the story, not actually people themselves. And I'm struggling here, too, because she lets on nothing about her own life to talk about. Does she have a partner? She's never mentioned one but we can't be sure. Does she have kids? The chances are even more remote but she's never revealed anything either way. All we know is that apparently she lives in Hounslow (although Jocelyn reckons she just camps down in a sleeping bag in the office every night) and that most of the time she looks utterly miserable.

'So, er . . . how's your dog? What's his name again?' I ask – since it's the only thing I can think of to say.

She roots in her handbag for another cigarette.

'Titch.' She stops and lights it under the shelter of her hand. 'And he's fine thanks.'

And that's it. The grand total of our conversation. Thankfully there's road-works all along Blackfriars Road to drown out the silence but Jesus Christ, painful or what? It's not exactly setting us up for the conversation we have to have. And we have to have it soon. Once the day starts, she'll never have time.

When we get into the office, there's only Jocelyn in.

'Morning Ladies! And what a fintistic morning it is!' she says, inextinguishable as ever. (God, I love Jocelyn.)

Judith hangs up her coat, goes into her office and switches on the light. I hover at the doorway like a spare part.

'Yes?' she peers at me over her glasses. I notice one side is held together with sellotape.

'Um . . .' Bollocks, this is way harder than I imagined. 'Do you have five minutes?'

I've really gone and done it now.

At first she thinks I'm leaving.

'Don't tell me you're pissing off to a competitor because if that's the case, you'd better tell Jocelyn you can't come to the conference before she books it and yet more of our budget goes down the drain.'

'It's not that, I'm pregnant.' It just slides out.

She doesn't tut, she doesn't groan, she doesn't even take her glasses off and bang her head on the desk like she usually does when someone tells her something she doesn't like. She just sits down, very slowly, and says, 'Oh. I see.'

I'm stumped. Utterly stumped! Where's the snarl of abuse? The dirty look? The dismissive look (actually that's the worst).

'It was an accident, totally unplanned, to be honest it's been a bit of a nightmare these past few weeks.'

I'm rambling now . . .

'But we are really good friends, you know, and I know we can get through this. My work won't suffer . . .'

'Hang on, hang on . . .'

Judith takes off her glasses and rubs her face. I finally stop talking.

'But you are keeping the baby . . .' She frowns at me. 'Aren't you?'

Uh?

I thought she'd offer to pay for my abortion (in return for my story) or send me packing to *You're Having a Baby!* magazine with the rest of the career casualties, as she sees it, but instead, there's something like actual concern on her face. For one minute, Judith Hogg looks like she might, even, be human.

'Um, yes,' I smile, far more relaxed now. 'Of course I'm keeping the baby.'

'Good.' I get the feeling she's reining herself in now. 'Well you'd better tell Human Resources. Today, please.'

Telling everyone else in the office doesn't turn out to be quite so low-key.

Anne-Marie smacks her hand to her mouth.

'I knew it, I ber-loody knew it! I said to Jocelyn – Joss, what did I say to you?'

Jocelyn stands up behind her desk. 'What's that doll?' Everyone turns round.

'I said, there was no way one person would be scoffing that much unless they had one in the oven and guess what?!'

'What?'

'Tess had got a bun in the oven. Tess and French Fancie are having a baby!'

And that's it. That's how it happens: the wrong version of my story around the office as fast and seamless as a Mexican wave. Thanks to Anne-Marie Wright and the very wrong end of the stick.

A gossipy mumble dominoes. A couple of people offer a tentative 'Congratula . . .' then sort of tail off and look at each other, not sure if Congratulations are actually in order. Someone's mobile rings, they turn it off. Everyone is staring at me. This is a nightmare.

Say something, say something now whilst the wrong information is only just out there! But I can't, not with all these people looking at me. Not when it's an issue as huge as the paternity of the baby!! So I just stand there, like a total lemon. An audience with Tess Jarvis – except she's just frozen on stage.

I try to swallow but it seems that a coffin is lodged in my throat. I feel like I'm in a Richard Curtis film (*Nightmare, Actually*) but there's no Hugh Grant – the only bumbling fool around here being me, so this must be very much real life.

147

Jocelyn looks at me with a motherly gaze. Right now, I could just run into those huge fleshy arms.

'Well,' she says, tipping her head to one side. 'That is fintistic news. But how do you feel about it, sweetheart?' And I realize this is the first time I've been asked this. 'Are we allowed to give you a cuddle? Or do you still need time?'

The fact she actually registers that I might not feel OK about it, makes me realize what I've always suspected about Jocelyn – she's not as stupid as she looks.

'It's a bit of a shock.' The moment's gone now, my window for explanation over. 'But yes, I'm OK about it. I think. I'm getting used to it anyway!' I smile at everyone nervously, the room spins and distorts.

As if this is the sign they were waiting for, the whole office (except Barry who looks like he's about to be sick he's so shocked and Judith, who, after displaying the first hint of emotion of her entire life, is probably having to have a lie down) piles onto my desk, hugging me and commenting that yes, of course, come to think of it, they'd guessed I was pregnant ages ago!! They thought I was getting a bit podgy around the middle but assumed it was just the wheels of camembert I must be consuming with my French lover every night.

'Tess Jarvis?'

A courier – his motorbike helmet in one arm, an enormous bunch of flowers in the other – is suddenly in our office, saying my name.

'Oh. Mon. Dieu.' Anne-Marie looks like she might start frothing at the mouth. 'Only a Frenchman . . . you lucky, fucking bitch.'

'I wouldn't get too excited, they're probably from a PR knowing my luck,' I say, thinking they're not, I just know it. They're too tasteful for that.

I take the flowers (peonies and roses in deep pinks and

148

lilacs all wrapped up in ice-cream coloured tissue paper) and sign for them, my hands trembling.

'They're no freebie,' says Anne-Marie, hands on hips. 'And anyway. It's not Valentine's Day? Read the card.'

'What? Now?' I sound suspiciously alarmed.

'Yes now.' She presses her hands together. '*Please!* Obviously we're living vicariously through you since all our own lives are a disaster in the romance stakes . . .'

'Speak for yourself,' Brian mumbles from behind his computer screen.

I open the little white envelope with my thumb and slip out the silver card.

'What's it say, what's it say?!!' Jocelyn claps her hands excitedly and tries to peer over my shoulder. I gently push her back.

If it weren't for these rather unfortunate circumstances, I would probably be screaming with joy, then straight on the phone to Vicky by now but instead I just stand there, my hands trembling as I read.

'You looked stunning on Friday and I wanted you, every curve, crevasse and fucking sexy inch of you. (P.S. is it just me or are your puppies twice their normal size?)'

'So, come on, I can't bear the suspense!' gushes Jocelyn. 'You're smiling.'

'Am I?'

'Yeah! Just a bit!!'

I look up, the entire office is looking at me wide-eyed with expectancy, I take a deep breath.

'It says best of luck telling everybody. I'll be thinking of you, Love Laurence.'

There's a blanket, lack-lustre 'aagh'. I sit down at my desk. I want to go home.

Jim calls just as I am about to get on the 76 bus home.

Despite my best efforts to stop him he's been having 'words' with Gina all day.

'You shouldn't have said anything. I can fight my own battles you know.'

I say this partly because it's true but also because I feel so guilty that whilst Jim's been sticking up for me all day, I've been telling my work mates that our baby's not his. It just beggars belief.

'Yeah well, she pisses me off.' Jim rarely sounds pissed off. 'She's so fucking self-absorbed sometimes, I just wanted to give her a piece of my mind.'

'And did it go down well?'

'Not really, you know what she's like.'

'So what did she say?'

'That it's her house too, bla-di-bla and that we can't drop a bombshell like that and expect it to be just "all OK".'

The 76 approaches but I wave it on, not knowing what to do with myself. I'm three months pregnant and I don't even like being in my own house. Surely pregnancy's a time for nesting? Surely it's not meant to be like this?

'This is ridiculous,' I say, and as soon as I have, it makes perfect sense. 'I need to move out.'

I hear Jim sigh, and he doesn't say anything for a while. Then he says,

'I don't see you have a choice. Especially if she's going to carry on like this. Come over here tonight, we can flat-hunt online.'

Jim pushes his glasses further up his nose and leans right in towards the screen.

'Right, what about this one. Needs some decorative attention but with room to expand and close to all the amenities of Camberwell Green, it's a perfect first time buy.'

'Great. How much is it?' I say.

'£210,000. But I reckon we could get knock them down.'

'Still too much. I still can't afford it. I'm going to end up in a single-mothers' hostel! My baby will be wearing knitted hand-outs from old ladies. Oh God I can't bear it!'

'Shut up woman, no you're not,' says Jim, but I can tell by the way he rubs his eyes wearily that he's getting as sick of this as I am.

The fact is, I can't afford anything. In fact, it's a mystery how anyone who earns under £50,000 can ever buy a flat.

'You know there is another option we haven't discussed yet,' says Jim.

'And that is . . .?' I look at him blankly.

'Well, you could always move in here, live rent free and save up for a deposit, move out when the baby's a few months old?'

Part of me wants to say yes, now, let's just move in now! (At least I could go home at night without risking finding him snorting class As off the kitchen table.) But the other part is really scared. It would feel like being 'happy couples'; it might throw our less-than-ideal situation into sharper relief.

'That's so kind of you Jim, it really is, but I don't know, I just don't know.'

'It's OK,' says Jim. 'I know it might be a bit weird. But the offer's there, so if you change your mind, just let me know. It would be separate rooms of course, no hanky panky.'

'You're dead right there,' I say, 'look where that got us last time.'

CHAPTER FOURTEEN

'Billy was nine days old when Rob just walked out and boarded a plane for Australia. He said he loved us, but knew immediately he wasn't up to the job (right, and I knew I was!?) so we'd be better off without him. That was two years ago, now he thinks he can just waltz back into our lives as easy as that. But we've coped this long so we can carry on coping. He's got a lot of making up to do.'

Maria, 30, Cirencester

Vicky's kitchen smells of coconut and fish sauce. I sit at the pine kitchen table and inhale the aroma, hungrily.

'Come over on Saturday,' she'd said on my mobile last Wednesday as I was walking home from having my bikini line waxed. (Yet another expensive tactic aimed at avoiding my monosyllabic housemate who is intent on pulling the biggest strop Britain has ever seen.) 'It'll probably be a madhouse but I can cook lunch and we can have a proper chat.'

I knew that 'proper chat' probably meant an interrogation about my and Jim's forthcoming 'wedding' but to be honest, I didn't care. Even if Dylan had a small army of similarly bombastic mates over and the ceiling had fallen down, it would be more relaxing than being at home.

It feels like a barbershop quartet has taken residence in my brain lately. The lead: that hideous day at work and the paternity mix up, is dominating, loud as a drum. Cutting through the notes of that main melody to my life is Gina's ongoing frostiness and Jim's offer of moving in with him, and down below, throbbing intermittently, are three things: the fact I haven't told Vicky about Laurence, the fact I haven't told Laurence about the pregnancy, and the fact I lied to Jim that I had.

If anyone needed to get away for the day, it's me.

Vicky clatters down the stairs where she's been excitedly rummaging for pregnancy paraphernalia.

'Here we go, I knew I had it somewhere.' She hands me a book called *My Best Friend's Guide to Pregnancy* and goes back to the pan bubbling on the hob.

'It's quite funny, down-to-earth, possibly a bit scare mongery.'

'What do you mean a bit scare mongery?' I start flicking through it.

'Well, it's full of all the grim reality of pregnancy, you know, turning into a psycho.'

'Turning?'

'Sprouting hair all over your face, incontinence . . .'

'What? Urrgh!'

'Yeah, exactly. If the beautiful miracle of giving life is what you're after, you won't find it in there.'

I smile to myself. Whereas Vicky might once have bought into the sentimentality of motherhood, now she actually is one she takes a far more cynical line.

I put the book down and walk over to nosy at the soup she's cooking. Vicky would kick ass on *Ready Steady Cook*. She can whip up a gourmet dinner from a pepper and an old potato – a skill that comes from having to be mum for most of her teenage years. She doesn't talk about it that much, but I know it was really tough for Vicky. After her mum ran off with the twenty-five-year-old Bolivian lifeguard (quite hard to find in Huddersfield, you'd imagine, but somehow she managed it) her dad became depressed and started helping himself to the optics behind the bar every night. Immediately Vicky went from big sister to surrogate mum to Tom, who was seven, and Steven, nine. When Vicky's mum died – in an unbelievably cruel twist of fate – two months later and only seven weeks after being diagnosed with ovarian cancer, Vicky's dad lost it completely. One evening Vicky came home from school choir practice to find the police at her house. Her dad had driven to Tesco's where he'd nicked three Tesco's finest ready meals. He'd been arrested for shop-lifting, drink driving and leaving minors unattended. Not bad for a half-hour outing. The boys were safe, thank God, happily munching through a dinner of Wagon Wheels, but Vicky told me, 'That day, I knew that was it, dad had lost it and it was up to me to look after my brothers.' That's the day Vicky lost her own childhood, too, I guess; only finding sanctuary in the half hour before she fell asleep at night, where she'd listen to the soundtrack to *Dirty Dancing* and fantasize about Patrick Swayze rescuing her.

I put my arm around my best friend and dip my finger in the soup. 'Oi!' She smacks my hand. 'Get your mucky mitts out.'

'Why do I need *My Best Friend's Guide to Pregnancy* when I've got you, eh? I'm sure you're more than qualified to tell me the truth about pregnancy madness, incontinence – sorry but . . .?'

'Do your pelvic floor exercises religiously. Someone I know at work was doubly incontinent for months afterwards.'

'Oh God!'

Vicks laughs. 'Well you did ask!'

Vicky pours Thai chicken soup into two matching blue-rimmed bowls. Steam clouds the patio doors that lead to the garden but I can still see Rich and Dylan kicking a football under the willow tree that droops, sleepy in the sun.

Again, how did Vicky's life get like this and mine like mine? I'm not saying one is more or less desirable than the other, it's just, getting pregnant by my best friend and living in what feels like a ravers' commune is not what I had imagined. This is what I imagined: nice, comfortable house in suburbs, husband playing with child in the garden at the weekend, muddy wellies by the door, Ikea pine kitchen and terracotta tiles, joint mortgage, joint bills. Much like my own parents I suppose.

'Don't you two ever open your bills?' I say, clocking a tower of unopened letters beside me.

'Don't get me started.' Vicky pushes the pile aside. 'That's Richard's job. Which he'd have time to do if he wasn't so busy messing around on Facebook like he's fifteen and pretending to write his screenplay.'

Rich has been writing a romantic comedy about a zoologist (funnily enough) since before Dylan was born but so far it doesn't seem to have quite received the international critical acclaim he had hoped.

There's the bang of the back door.

'Talk of the devil,' murmurs Vicky.

'The Gerrrr . . . and Old Duke of York he had ten thousand men . . .!! He marched them up to the top of the hill and he marched them down again!!'

Richard, bent at the waist and with a giggling Dylan on his shoulders ploughs through the kitchen door.

'Hey, it's Jarvis the Hack!' (This is Richard's joke. It sounds a *bit* like Jabba the Hut) 'You didn't tell me Tess was coming over.'

'Yeah I did.' Vicky slurps her soup. 'You just didn't take it in.'

Richard tips forward so that his chubby-legged son slides off his neck then toddles over to his mum who hauls him up on her lap.

'So.' Rich pulls down his Hawaiian shirt over his belly (Rich gets all his clothes from a shop called 'Life's a Beach' which says it all really) and gives me a peck on the cheek. 'How's junior? Cookin' nicely?'

'Yeah, look I'm massive already!'

'Ooh.' Richard sizes me up . . . 'You've got a way to go yet. Vicks was the size of a bus, weren't you love?'

'Richard!' I gasp.

'So smooth isn't he?' says Vicky. 'So complimentary.'

'So how's the screenplay coming along?' I ask, changing the subject.

'Yeah fantastic, really shaping up. I reckon I'll have a draft good enough to send to agents by the end of the month.'

'Wow.'

'Talking of which . . . er . . . Vicks?'

'Yes, my darling husband.'

I smile and make funny faces at Dylan who's busy climbing all over his mum.

'Can I ? You know . . .' He gestures upstairs.

'Rich! It's lunchtime. I've made you soup and now you're just going to piss off upstairs?'

'Please, seriously, I've only got one scene to perfect and then . . .'

'And then we're going to be multi-millionaires when your sitcom becomes a hit and wins a BAFTA. Meanwhile I've divorced you and the bailiffs have taken everything we own?' Vicky flutters her eyelashes sarcastically at her husband. I smirk into my soup.

'I knew you had vision.' Rich grabs hold of his wife's face

156

and kisses her squashed, reluctant cheek. 'Just a couple of hours, I promise, and then I'll do the washing up.'

Rich skids towards the kitchen door but Vicky stops him in his tracks.

'I think you're forgetting something.' She holds Dylan out for him to take. 'It's time for his kip, put him down will you, and change his nappy beforehand.' She takes the pile of unopened letters from the kitchen table. 'And sort these out Rich, for God's sake. I already did the other pile. How hard can it be?'

'Phew, sorry about that,' says Vicky, once Richard and Dylan have disappeared upstairs.

'Don't mind me,' I say. I'm so used to Rich and Vicky's hilarious little domestics and anyway, I've always thought there was something sinister about people who never argue in public.

'So,' says Vicky tucking into her soup. 'Are you going to take the book?'

'I've got one a bit like it thanks, well, it's more women's real-life stories than a blow-by-blow account of pregnancy, but thanks. Anyway . . .' I stir my soup. 'It's not really the physical stuff that's worrying me, it's more . . .'

'More what?' Vicky puts down her spoon.

'How I *feel* about being pregnant. I mean take Julia – you know Julia? The one I did my NCTJ with?'

'The one with legs up to her neck?'

'Yeah, her. Well I went to her leaving lunch last week – she's leaving to go on maternity leave – and she was just *so* happy, *so* excited it's awful, but I couldn't relate to it.'

'How do you mean?'

'Well, at one point, one of the girls she works with asked her how it feels to be pregnant and do you know what she said?'

'A religious experience?'

'No, worse. She said she it was like having a birthday every day, she couldn't wait to open the present.'

A round ha! explodes from Vicky's lips.

'Is that how I'm meant to feel?' I ask.

'No!'

'Because I don't. I feel terrified most of the time.'

'That's far more normal Tess, believe me.'

'How did you feel when you were pregnant with Dylan?' As I say this I am horrified to realize that I don't think I ever once asked her, not properly.

'I was happy to have actually been able to get pregnant but apart from that, I was mainly bricking it.'

Vicky only ever admits emotional weakness in retrospect. It's part of this sense of duty she has that somehow she has to keep everything, and everyone together. 'We didn't have much money – I was still studying for my osteopathy course and so we only had Rich's crap wage and there was the "my mum" factor.'

'Your mum factor?'

'Well, let's face it, she wasn't ever much cop, was she? I loved her – she was my mother – but she was never much of a mum.' I've never heard Vicky say this. 'She left her husband and three kids for a man practically half her age for God's sake! She left me, when I was about to do my GCSEs. Part of me was worried . . .'

'Vicks, as if, you're a brilliant mum.'

'Whatever.' Vicky's never been much good at taking compliments. 'But it was there in the back of my mind, you know, what if I'm just not maternal. What if I turn out like my own mother. What if I turn out like my father for that matter, he was hardly a tower of strength in the face of everything.'

In that moment, I think I finally realize what Vicky had to go through whilst I was swanning around Morecambe having a real childhood. I suddenly want to hug her with pride.

'Anyway,' she sighs, 'enough about me, what about you?

I know you're intent on fighting against what is so ridiculously obvious and yes, it must feel strange, you and Jim not having been an "item" before you got pregnant. But be patient, honestly, you two are so meant to be.'

'He asked me to move in with him.' As soon as I see the expression of pure joy on Vicky's face, I regret opening my mouth.

'I can't believe you've kept that to yourself for two whole hours!'

'I haven't said yes.'

'*Tess!*' She covers her face and groans.

'No, listen, seriously, you don't get it. It's such a kind offer and obviously things being the way they are with Gina, I may be forced to take him up on it, but I just feel with us not being together it would be like playing happy couples.'

'But he *wants* you to be a happy couple. This is his way, it's a sign – don't you realize – of saying, "let's make a go of it".'

'It's not.'

'Aw!' Vicky slaps the table. 'He adores you! you adore him. What *is* it with you two?' She curls her fingers in frustration. 'I want to bang your little heads together.'

'He told me he didn't want to be with me.'

'When!?' Vicky's voice goes up five octaves.

'Norfolk, on the camping trip.'

'Right . . . But, why didn't you tell me?'

'I was so embarrassed, oh God, Vicky, I made such a tit of myself.'

It's all coming out now.

'You know when we came home from the pub on the Saturday night? Well, me being me – decided fuck it, I'll just go for it. We'd been doing this ridiculous drunkenly-going-back-to-each-other's houses thing for months by then . . .'

'Tell me about it.' Vicky rolls her eyes.

'And I thought, maybe I have real feelings for Jim, maybe I actually love him and we have something worth fighting for . . .'

'Er . . . yep . . .'

'And. So. I told him.'

Vicky's jaw drops.

'I got in the tent with him and I just said let's try and make a go of it. Let's just go out with each other.'

'And? What did he say?' Vicky's got her hands over her mouth in anticipation now.

'No, basically. He said I was drunk and that I should be glad of what we did have – that we were soul-mates.'

Vicky shakes her head. 'Jim, you *moron*!'

'I know. What a dickhead. So basically, I asked him out and the man rejected me. Did I feel like the school minger or what?'

Vicky folds her arms and shakes her head.

'Don't get it,' she says. 'I really, really don't.'

'Well, it's true. And on the taxi home from your party, he said it again. When we'd – well you, mainly – had told everyone I was up the duff and everyone was asking, were we now going to get together, I said to him, maybe we should. But he said he didn't think it was wise to make a "relationship of circumstance" and I have to say, I agree. So that's that. It's not going to happen. Which is why I feel extra weird about being pregnant.'

I carry mine and Vicky's soup bowls to the sink. 'I mean, it's all a bit twisted, isn't it? This set up. Like something out of an American sitcom.'

Vicky doesn't say anything for a while and then she says, with almost tangible disappointment in her voice.

'So, does this mean both of you are going to carry on dating other people? Or, I mean, are you going to carry on having sex?'

160

'God no. We shouldn't have been doing it in the first place.'

'Oh.' Vicky sounds genuinely bewildered, I can't say I blame her. Why do some choices you make in life seem utterly ludicrous only in retrospect?

And anyway.' I sit back down at the table. 'I have news . . .'

'Oh God, don't tell me it's twins.'

'Behave yourself! No, I'm seeing someone.'

'Who?' She says this as if me doing anything, anything at all with someone other than Jim is surely impossible.

'You're gonna hate me.'

'Try me.'

'Laurence.'

Vicky shuts her eyes in concentration.

'So, tell me again, you've told him you're pregnant?'

'Yup,' I say, thinking you loser, Jarvis. You absolute lame arse.

'And he knows what that means?'

'I assume so, unless he missed out on the birds and the bees talk.'

'This isn't the time for sarcasm. Is he willing to take on another man's child? Even though you've seen each other like, twice?'

'Er . . . yep.'

'Teeess?'

'Yes!' I say, but I know this is already falling apart . . .'

'And you've told Jim you're seeing him?'

'Um, sort of.'

'I can tell you're lying because you're biting your thumb nail and you've got that slightly surprised expression on your face.'

It's all over.

'Oh for God's sake OK!' I snap, eventually. 'No, I haven't told him. I'm sorry, I know I'm crap and I will, next time I see him, I will tell him. I promise.'

Just as Vicky can read every lying little contour of my face, so I knew exactly how she'd react when I told her I was seeing Laurence. She doesn't tell me off or even say she doesn't approve, she just gently reminds me that I ran up a £1200 Barclaycard bill due to hour-long wailing phone calls from Africa to London, and just touches on, ever so diplomatically, what the hell I think I'm doing starting a relationship when I'm pregnant. By someone else.

Then, literally five minutes after I have disclosed this information to her my mobile goes. I swear it's like it is in the films: I look at her, she looks at me, we both know who it is.

'I have to take this, it's him.'

'I know it's him. It's written all over your face!'

I walk over to the patio door for some privacy and try – and fail – to hide the very obvious smile in my voice. 'Hey you.'

Laurence sounds like he's outside. He sounds excited and kind of free and he has news, news that despite myself, and despite straining to hear over Vicky, who has followed me, banging on in a stage whisper in my ear, plus the roar of traffic in the background, makes my throat constrict with excitement and the grey fug in my head clear into a new, blue day. He and Chloe are not just likely to finish, they *are* finishing, any day now!

'I just need to wait till she's through her marketing exams – it would be pretty rough of me to dump her whilst she's all stressed out –

(Considerate? Check. Big heart? Check.)

'And then I'm going to do it, Tess. I'm going to tell her it's over *definitely*. It's just gone bad, Tess, I'm telling you, she's doing my head in. I didn't know how fucking lucky I was to have you – you were a dream girlfriend, so low maintenance! I totally took you for granted.'

'Well if you really think it isn't working then maybe yes, perhaps it's the best thing for both of you.'

(Rough translation: just chuck the miserable bitch and go out with me, you know it makes sense.)

'I think it's best, and not just for me and Chloe but you know,' he pauses, gives a nervous laugh, 'us, too.'

A lawnmower starts up next door. I can't believe I'm hearing this.

'I made the biggest mistake of my life, Tess, the day I finished with you.'

'No. No, it was my mistake too!'

Vicky rolls her eyes and wanders off.

'And I've missed you.'

I clutch the phone, and have to clasp a hand to my mouth to stop myself from actually crying out.

'I've missed you too.'

'So what do you say to dinner, eh? To celebrate? Next week?'

'Yeah, wicked.'

It's only as I'm hanging up, a smile from ear to ear, that I even bother to look up to find Vicky is jigging up and down, waving a piece of paper in my face.

'NEXT TIME I MEET HIM, I'LL TELL LAURENCE I'M PREGNANT. I PROMISE.' YOUR WORDS NOT MINE.

'*And*,' teases Vicky, poking a finger at me, 'since when did you say "wicked"? That's so Laurence!'

'Did I say that?' I say, not really listening.

'You certainly did.'

'Good Lord!' I say teasingly, doing a little celebratory dance as I put my phone away. 'It must be love, I'm turning into him!'

Vicky pulls up at Beckenham station and I open the passenger door.

'So, promise me, you will tell Laurence?'

'I promise.'

'And you'll think about Jim's offer? Just temporarily?'

'Yep, definitely I will.'

'I hope it works out with Laurence, that he doesn't freak.'

'Yeah so do I. But I do know him remember? I've got a good feeling about this one.'

'It should have been Jim, though. You know I'll always believe that? Don't you?'

'Till the day you die, I imagine, sick happy-ending-addict that you are! But this will be my happy ending, OK?' I give her a kiss on the cheek. 'If it kills me.' I get out of the car.

Perhaps it's the thought of going back home to Gina or the confidence boost that Laurence's call has given me, or just the sudden realization that living with Jim might be really, really nice, but as soon as I'm on the train, I know what to do. So I call him. But sod's law he's not in.

'Jim Ashcroft lives here. Please leave a message.'

Beep.

'How do you feel about Tess Jarvis living there too? Because she'd love to move in, if the offer still stands.'

Ten minutes later he calls. 'Hello, flatmate,' he says.

I smile as I hang up. The fields at either side of me are a vibrant, thick green. Everything seems to be falling into place.

CHAPTER FIFTEEN

'Andy was a proper rotter, I kicked him out when Millie was four months old, cut all his suits into pieces, went to town. Three weeks later he turns up on my doorstep all apologies and flowers, and I, like an idiot, jump straight back in bed with him. Bam! I'm pregnant, two babies in a one year. It was exactly the same with number two, me screaming blue murder down his mobey at him, in between contractions. Did he show up? Did he hell as like.'

Hayley, 22, Merseyside

I know something's different as soon as I walk through the door. It smells amazing for a start – fresh and floral – and all the lights are on, which means Gina's actually in on a Saturday night. I walk into the lounge and am literally stopped in my tracks. It's spotless. Not just tidy, but spotless. The cushions are all arranged, the newspapers and ashtrays have been tidied away, the rug has been hoovered. My God, the TV's even been dusted! On the mantelpiece is a vase of hyacinths and all over the room, scented candles burn. I go into the kitchen, it's exactly the same story there. Not one dirty mug, no overflowing bin, just shiny, spotless, surfaces and the smell of lemon zest. In my bedroom I am greeted by more spotlessness and a beautiful bouquet of burnt orange tulips standing on my dressing table.

'Hey.'

I look round, to find the strange, mousy voice belongs to Gina. She's wearing pyjamas, her hair all slapped back.

'Hi,' I say back, but then her face just crumples.

'I'm sorry,' she squeaks, then she throws herself against me and bursts into tears. 'I wanted to stop behaving like a twat, but once I started I just couldn't stop. And I didn't know how to say sorry and God, I've missed you so much!'

She's wailing now. I stand there hugging her, totally dumbstruck.

'So I thought if I made a gesture – coz I'm crap with words – if I cleaned up and made the house look nice . . .'

'Gina, it looks beautiful.'

'Do you think? Do you like it? I'm glad because this is to say sorry Tess.' She's in floods now, wiping away the tears with the heels of her hands. 'For being a total cunt.' (So poetic.) 'I hope you can forgive me?'

'Course I forgive you.' *I'm* crying now.

'Good coz it's shit when we're not talking.'

'I couldn't agree more.'

We talk at the kitchen table like old times until well after midnight. It turns out Gina was threatened by the pregnancy. Being the sensitive flower she is under all that tough exterior, she assumed that now I was pregnant, she would lose me *and* Jim – two of her best friends – her partners in crime for ever. There'd be no more drunken nights in the Jacuzzi, no more nights down the pub, no more lost hours at Turnmills, no more Sundays sitting in cafés dissecting her love life. I sit and I listen and I admit yes, life will change, but that doesn't have to mean I will. I was hurt too, I say, by the way she dealt with it when I needed her most. She was childish and

166

selfish. It's not the easiest of conversations, but it's definitely one of the most satisfying and by the end of the night, I think we're both secretly flattered that the other one needed us more than we knew.

But of course, there's something I have to tell her.

'Gina,' I say, when I eventually find an appropriate lull in the conversation. 'Jim asked me to move in.'

She doesn't look shocked or angry, just more surprised. 'And?'

'I said yes.' I pause. 'I think it's what we need.'

'Oh my God!' she collapses now, head in her hands. 'But it'll be the end of an era, I can't fucking bear it!'

'I know, I'm sorry, I really had to think about it. But I'll have to move when the baby's born anyway and I just couldn't see it working, me, nine months pregnant, lying like a beached whale on the sofa, you permanently having to smoke outside, get me things, massage my feet . . .'

'Yeah.' She pulls a face. 'Maybe not.'

'So when are you leaving me?'

'I'm not sure yet, but probably soon.'

'Shit this is *big*, Tess!'

'I know! I know it is . . .'

But not quite as big as what I tell her next . . .

'I knew it!' she shouts, dancing about the kitchen. 'I knew he still loved you. Laurence Cane, you sly bastard. So why didn't you tell me you bumped into him?'

'Er, because you weren't talking to me,' I point out. 'And because I had more important things on my mind.'

'Right. But what's the situation now?' she says, glossing over that minor detail, desperate for progress.

'Well, apparently it would seem it's just a case of him finishing with Chloe. Which he says he's going to do as soon as she's finished these marketing exams she's doing.'

'Good, I never did like her. Hard face, weird eyes.'

'And the baby?' she says. 'Have you told him about the baby?'

'No,' I say, thinking oh dear, this is where her enthusiasm dwindles, but she's not even fazed. She just says 'Right, OK,' then ponders this concept for a moment. Then she says, 'It's a lot to take on. I'm not denying that. But I'm quietly confidant that he's up to the job.'

I feel a momentary burst of optimism on hearing these words. Maybe I'm not totally mad and delusional! After all, Gina knows Laurence, the real Laurence. And not in a way that is warped with lust.

CHAPTER SIXTEEN

'I was in labour for seventeen hours with Gayle and for four-
teen of those, Ron was in the pub. But the day he held that
little girl in his arms, was the day he stopped drinking for
ever. She's forty now and still has her daddy wrapped around
her little finger. If I thought a baby was all it would take, I
would have started sooner.'

Miriam, 62, Isle of Wight

It took Emete approximately five seconds to read my mind
this morning. 'You're seeing him aren't you?' she said, eyes
glinting, lifting up my chin. 'The one with the eyelashes?'
Was it really that obvious?

There are however, a couple of minor details that need,
shall we say, ironing out.

a) I still need to tell Laurence about the baby
b) I still need to tell my parents

The reason I haven't done a) is because I haven't done b)
and the reason I haven't done b) is because ... Why is it?
Because I know my mother will jump to conclusions about
Jim and me and start going on about table plans? Because
when she knows the full, scandalous situation she'll kill me?

Obviously. But also because I don't want to tell my dad. It's not that he's judgemental – that he'll want to mow down whoever 'did this to me' and kick ten shades out of them – it's just, I suspect, it will burst our little bubble. And that kind of breaks my heart.

We've been so long kindred spirits, dad and I. Our own little mutual appreciation society. Now I've gone and got myself pregnant in a situation that should never have even have been on the cards and I'm worried I will disappoint him. That he'll feel like he's lost something – Me, Us. How we were.

But that's life, I guess. Nothing can stay the same for ever. And looking on the bright side, working things out with Gina and Laurence's call has given me a much needed boost. I mean the man was practically singing with joy that he was soon to be free. Surely that's a good sign that this is not just some whim. And I definitely feel more myself of late – that feeling that whatever happens, it will all be alright in the end. And so that's why I'm standing on Morecambe station, the sea air gusting through my sinuses, waiting for my dad's blue Mondeo to roll into view ready and waiting for the Big Pregnancy Announcement to begin.

Mum's still in her Lunn Poly uniform peeling potatoes at the kitchen sink when I get home. From the kitchen window, the hills of the Lake District, across Morecambe Bay, look like grey hump-backed whales.

'Can we have a chat when we've had tea? I've got something I need to talk to you about,' I say, impressively calmly if I dare say so myself, after I've put my stuff upstairs in my old bedroom and checked for the millionth time today for any calls from Laurence. (There's none.)

But whereas I was planning on a nice quiet evening in with my parents, the perfect setting in which to break the news gently, mum had other plans . . .

'Pass us the gravy will you, Lizard?'

It's delightful how my brother still uses my childhood name, coined twenty-two years ago, due to the fact that I had an allergic reaction to some nit shampoo and my entire forehead flaked off.

Don't get me wrong, I love my brother (he's blood, I have no choice) and I adore my two nieces, Antonia and Jade. It's just, I wish his wife, Joy – or Joyless as I call her – would cheer up a bit and I wish they could have come tomorrow. Now that all four are here for the day in matching white linen – a sort of chav version of the Calvin Klein Eternity advert – there's no way I'll get the chance to talk to my parents alone.

'Well, this is nice, isn't it?' sighs mum, finally sitting down. 'A proper family meal, a homecoming dinner for Tess. Welcome home Tess!'

'Welcome home Tess!' I notice Joyless hasn't shaved her armpits properly as she raises a toast. This pleases me greatly since mum is always going on about Joyless's high standards of personal grooming (Joy's had a lovely French manicure, Joy's had a St Tropez, why can't I be more ladylike like Joy? It really pisses me off.)

'And I'm so glad you did come home because your father's had a face like a wet weekend these past few weeks and now, five minutes of you and look at him – he's a new man!'

Dad opens and closes his hand as if to say bla, bla, bla. I do the same. Mum doesn't even notice.

'So how's the Big Bad Smoke?' My brother's one of these people who thinks that people who live in London are mugs and the worst thing is, he's probably right. He only earns about the same as me working for dad but still manages to live in a four-bedroom mock-Tudor show home with a home cinema and 'corner bath'.

'Great thanks, full on as usual, but Gina's good and Vicky's passed her osteopathy course and work's going well.'

'Have you met any famous people recently!?' Six-year-old Jade jumps onto her knees with excitement. Her mother promptly squashes her back down. 'Just eat your dinner, please Jade.'

'Er . . . Linda Lusardi – we did a thing on her style last week.

Jade gawps at me blankly. 'And um, Terri Dwyer, you know, used to be in *Hollyoaks*?'

'Yeah, in about 1990,' Ed smirks. 'Before you were born. Don't listen to Aunty Tess. She doesn't know what she's talking about.'

'Oh I am sorry!' After a slightly uncomfortable silence where mum is obviously trying to find something to say to diffuse the already deteriorating situation between me and my brother, she finds something. 'Tess had some news, didn't you love?' My stomach hits my feet. 'Why don't you tell us now why we're all sitting down?'

'No it's nothing, honestly mum, I'll tell you later.' I reach for the red cabbage.

'Have you got a promotion?' probes Dad. 'Has that Judith finally clocked onto your genius?'

'No, sadly not.'

'Are you finally going to move?' chips in mum, picking a bit of chicken out of her back molars, 'I always said that road of yours is a death trap.'

'No mum, I'm not moving. Well, actually . . .' I can't tell her that bit before the main bit.

I look at my brother who's staring right at me.

'Oh my God.' He's started to laugh now. 'Have you met someone, Lizard?' Dad slaps him sharply on the forearm.

'You have haven't you? Woo-hoo!' The second he makes that noise I am once more a flaky-skinned eight-year-old harbouring dark thoughts of stabbing my brother.

'Well I don't know why you're doing that,' says Mum, to

Ed. 'No I do *not* know why you're doing that,' agrees Joyless, flashing him daggers. 'It's something to be proud of, isn't it Tessa,' adds mum. 'What's he like lovey? Is he like Laurence?'

I concentrate on a spreading circle of gravy on the white tablecloth.

'I always thought you were silly to mess that one up.' You can always trust mum to be on my side. 'You should never have gallivanted off round the world, it was typical of you . . . '

Dad puts his cutlery down. 'For God's sake you lot, will you give the girl a break?'

'She's probably pregnant,' says Ed.

OH. MY. GOD.

'Well it does seem to be the season for it,' mum chirps on. 'Lisa Price is pregnant, with twins apparently, I saw her mum in Asda.'

Oh here we go.

'I think she'd resigned herself to the fact she'd never have any grand-kiddies what with Lisa turning twenty-nine this year.' God, my mum is so see-through. 'But she's seven months pregnant now, as is Fay Maughan's daughter, and I'll tell you who else is expecting.' She stabs at me with her finger. 'Shelley Newcombe, you remember Shelley Newcombe? Year below you at school, lovely figure, she's got one on the way . . .'

'So am I.'

A chill silence descends like falling snow.

'So are you what, love?'

'Pregnant,' I say. 'I'm pregnant too.'

'What do you mean you got pregnant because you couldn't bloody drive???!!'

Dad pats mum's hand to calm her down. She shoos him off.

'I'm sorry, Tony but I just don't understand.'

173

It's been twenty minutes since I confessed my big fat secret (fat being the operative word. Mum confessed she thought I'd got a little porky around the midriff 'but you did always yo-yo' she added, which was a nice touch). For the first five, everyone was shocked but elated, 'Eee, a baby by Christmas!' dad chuckled, suddenly coming alive, his big belly shaking. 'And perhaps a wedding before?' said mum, clapping her hands together. Antonia and Jade squealed with delight when they learned they were going to have a cousin. Ed just slapped me on the back. 'Nice one sis! Thought you were eating for two.'

Then of course, I had to piss on their parade – explain the whole me and Jim situation. I may as well have been speaking in Mandarin for all mum understood. (Or wanted to understand. A point well made by my dad.) I have tried before – and failed – to explain to mum this whole concept of being friends, not boyfriend/girlfriend with Jim. But she was born in the 1950s. In her head, you're friends with girls and you go out with boys. It definitely doesn't work the other way round.

'I'm not saying I got pregnant *because* I couldn't drive,' I try to explain for the hundredth time. 'It just didn't help, that's all. I ended up drinking too much, I missed my last tube.'

'Oh, marvellous, so my daughter has a drink and she can't keep her knickers on!'

'Mum it's not like that.'

'That's well out of order mum.' My brother makes a token effort to stand up for me but I know he's just *loving* this.

'Go upstairs with Joy and the kids please.' Ed reluctantly obeys mum's orders. If I didn't know my brother better – hadn't heard him shag half of Morecambe through our flimsy walls – I would assume he's gay, he's such a gossip.

Dad wanders off to his greenhouse too, having tried and failed to defuse the situation, leaving just me and mum sitting at the mahogany table amongst the half-eaten dinner. Mum watches from the patio doors, seething with rage.

174

'Yes, you just do that Tony!' she yells after him. 'Leave me to deal with the crisis why don't you! Oh, I *wish* he'd get out of this mood.'

She collects the plates and puts them into a pile.

'I'll do that,' I offer.

'No you won't, you'll talk to me. Oh my God look at your stomach.' She clocks the growing bulge as I stand up. I doubt a stranger would be able to tell as yet, but my mother watches my midriff like a hawk even when I'm not pregnant. 'My little girl!'

'Oh mother, behave.'

Mum holds her eyes shut with her fingers. I knew she'd freak, but this is way worse.

We sit at the table for what seems hours, mum interrogating me about the whole sorry story. I tell how I'm going to move in with Jim, so I will have some support, but I certainly don't tell her that I'm kind of seeing Laurence. That would just tip her over the edge. But if I felt positive and hopeful about it all before, I certainly don't now. Worst Case Scenario is the only scenario my mother knows.

And according to her, this is what I have to look forward to:

1. Jim and I having to deal with 'funny looks and constant questions', the heathens that we are, for living together but not being 'an item' (what she means by this is that *she'll* have to deal with 'funny looks and constant questions' from the girls at Lunn Poly after she tells them that her daughter's pregnant but it's not all it's cracked up to be).

2. Never finding a boyfriend. What man will want me with a child and stretch marks?

3. We will be destitute and skint (probably not being able to turn on the central heating in the winter and having to live in a 'damp flat'. Mum thinks everyone in London lives in a 'damp flat').

4. I will have to deal with the stigma of being a 'single mum' and probably end up on drugs and working in Iceland (she didn't say that, but that's the insinuation. Because of this outrageous scandal my journalism training and perfectly good job will be annulled, naturally).

5. It's very hard caring for a baby, especially alone. (Which of course she knows everything about always having had a stable, normal marriage and loving husband on hand all her life. Argh!)

By the end, I am tearing up the label from the mint sauce just to stop myself from slashing my wrists.

Entering dad's greenhouse is like entering another world. White plastic labels with unpronounceable, Latin names. Old trowels and pliers and different composts for different jobs. All over the place are tumbling piles of terracotta pots and bulging grow-bags with unripe tomato plants like giant gooseberries.

I hoist myself up on the bench.

'Hi dad, thought I'd find you in here.'

'Come to escape have we?'

'You could say that.'

'I know the feeling,' mumbles dad, clipping his tomato plants. He's wearing the gardening gloves I bought for his birthday about ten years ago. They've got holes all over them but he never bothers to buy anymore.

What happens in this greenhouse will always baffle me – how do you learn something as complicated as how to make things grow? And yet if simple had a smell, it would smell like this: of sweet-peas and green-fly and soil and the summer. It smells of my childhood. This is where me and dad used to have our little chats. I'd come in here on balmy summer evenings when mum was zonked out in front of the TV, sit up on the side – just like I am now – and stay until it went dark. Sometimes, if dad was in one of his quiet moods or shattered after work, we'd stick the radio on and I'd flick through a magazine. But often we'd really talk: About my uncle Cliff, my dad's big brother who died of cancer in 1996 and how he and my dad conquered Scafell Pike when they were, like, six (it gets younger every year, I swear). About mum and how barmy she is. 'If this greenhouse had ears we'd be dead meat,' Dad used to joke. And occasionally the big stuff. Like this, like now.

Dad takes his cracked old watering can – as old as me at least – and waters his tomato plants, as if in another world. Mum can't half be dramatic but she's right, dad's definitely not himself. For starters, it's really not like him to not want to have a discussion about that major life event I just revealed in there. But then, June is the anniversary of Uncle Cliff's death, I wonder if it might be that. Then, I wonder, if it might be me . . .

'Dad?'

'Mmm.'

He doesn't look up.

'Are you OK?'

'Me?' He still doesn't look up. 'Yeah, I'm alright, don't worry about me.'

'Is everything OK with you and mum?'

'Course,' he says. 'Everything's always alright with me and your mum.'

'Good.' I look at dad, but his mind is still elsewhere. 'So . . . dad?'

'Yes love.'

'Are you mad with me?'

'Mad with you?' He looks at me, properly now, beneath grey bushy brows. 'Why on earth would I be mad with you?'

'For getting pregnant, I mean, it's hardly ideal, is it? It's not how Ed has done things, all proper and grown up. I've basically screwed up.'

Dad takes off his gardening gloves and leans against the

old railway sleeper opposite. He looks older, diminished somehow. Less robust.

'Oh Tess,' he smiles, he's with me now. 'You didn't screw up. Nobody ever screwed up by deciding to keep a baby.'

'Mum seems to think so.'

'She doesn't, you wait. She's just worried that's all. Give her time.'

'It's going to be hard though isn't it? Tell me the truth. I mean, I know me and you always try to look on the bright side but well, I suppose I was so used to things never happening to me . . .'

'That you took your eye off the ball?'

'Basically, yes.'

'And it feels really scary at the moment I imagine?'

'Yep.' I fight back tears.

'And there's definitely no hope of getting it together with . . . ?'

'No, dad.' I cut him short.

'Because love comes in all different packaging you know. Just because it ain't Cathy and Heathcliffe at the beginning doesn't mean it can't be. Love's as individual as a thumbprint, as personal as your iris. I mean, your mum and I, that love grew, it's *still* growing . . .'

'Dad.'

'Right, yes. Sorry.' He looks at the floor.

'It's just, I felt quite positive about it all until I came home and now . . .' I hate crying in front of my dad, but I can't keep it in.

'Oh come here you silly girl.' He steps forward and wraps his arms around me. 'You can't see it now but this is going to be the making of you. Do you want to know why?'

'Why? Tell me why?'

'Because you never regret a child. No matter how much hell and strife they give you – and believe you me, you and your brother have given us our fair share of that – you never regret a child, because it's what it's all about, your family, your kids. It's the point of it all, it's why we carry on.'

'Hello and welcome to Vodafone can I take your account number please? And for the purposes of identifying you fully today, Miss Jarvis, can I take your four digit pin number?'

I'm sure this is the same girl I spoke to ten minutes ago, the last time I checked there's nothing wrong with my phone. (Like it's not receiving texts or incoming calls. Specifically from people called Laurence Cane.) I throw my phone to the other end of the bed – *Just stop being a mentalist stalker you freak!* But it goes slightly higher than planned, almost taking Ewan's eye out on the *Moulin Rouge* poster.

I know, logically, that Laurence has more important things to do than call me. Christ, he's probably finishing it with Chloe now, his girlfriend of some years, whilst I'm lying here, convinced there's a national conspiracy to stop his calls getting through – how self-absorbed can you get? But I just wish he would call, like now. Then I could get on with other things, like smoothing things out with mum.

Talking to my parents has only made me more determined to make things work with Laurence. Apart from anything else, if it's going to be as hard as mum says then I'll need to have a boyfriend just to help out. But it's about more than that. I look around our house – our flimsy 70s semi with its dodgy mahogany furniture, and feel just how rock solid its heart is. I'd been lucky enough to have that as a child, but that was down to mum and dad. Of course Jim and I could fabricate a union of sorts, pretend to have the happy ending that everyone's hankering after, but I want the real thing, I'm not ashamed to admit it. I want the romance, the ripping one another's clothes off, the Cathy and Heathcliffe thing (sorry dad), the Danielle and Jamie thing, The One.

I want pictures of our Pearl Wedding anniversary on the sideboard too, our kids round to dinner when they're married themselves. I want to have that look my mum has in her eyes, even when she's angry with dad, that thing that makes you stick around for thirty odd years.

Even now, everywhere in this house, this room, there's reminders of Laurence and our two-year relationship: the little hole in my peach curtains where we attempted to smoke a post-coital fag out of my window and nearly set fire to the house; an old Creamfields pass hung up on my wardrobe door handle (Sunday dinner with my parents when I've got lock-jaw and my boyfriend's still gurning is not something I'd like to repeat in a hurry); the little patch of silvery Morecambe Bay, just visible from my window, where we skinny dipped on New Year's Eve . . .

And my rucksack. My filthy green and red rucksack that's been to Africa, and hell and back emotionally and knows more about me and how heartbroken I really was about Laurence than anyone in the world. I go over to it idly and open the front pocket. Inside, I find a little paper bag and inside that, there's a postcard. It's from Victoria Falls and to my surprise, it's not to Laurence, it's to Jim. I sit down on my sunken single bed to read it.

Dear Jim,
Am currently lying in a hammock (get me!) watching a fireball of a sunset sink into the Zambezi river.'

Very poetic. Must have been feeling sentimental and in my writer mode.

It's incredible here. The Falls themselves are awesome (well I guess they should be being one of the Wonders of the World) I passed on the bungee jump – you know me, not one for life-threatening activities – but I did manage white-water rafting today and I thought of you all the way through.

Ooh, bit intimate

Especially through the "devil's toilet" rapid. Get caught in that and you're a gonner, for sure. You'd love it here Jim, the people, the wildlife, the crazy bus journeys (you're the only man I know who would actually, genuinely enjoy sharing your seat with a goat and five chickens for twelve hours on a pot-holed road). How's Gine and Vicks ? How's my bedroom? Have you christened the bed yet? I bet those N1 lovelies are queuing up. Anyway, just wanted to say hi. And that I miss you. Don't be a stranger. Lots of love Tess x

I hold the postcard in my hand and read it again and again, the memories flooding back to me like atoms of a whole. I'd hovered over the 'miss you bit' for ages, I remember, but I put it in the end because I decided it was the truth. During that time, I started to think about Jim in a way I never had. Was what I felt more than friendship? If I missed him, perhaps it was. And I sent postcards. Not just this one, which didn't get sent, for some reason, but lots – maybe ten – did he even get them? And if he did, why has he never mentioned them? Perhaps I was too forward. Jim and I were mates after all, we'd never even snogged at that point, so for me to say 'I miss you' was probably a bit OTT.

There's a knock at my bedroom door, I put the postcard back, hastily.

'Lovey?' Mum creaks open the door. 'Can I come in?'

'Yeah OK.'

Mum sits on my bed in her dressing gown. Her short,

181

highlighted hair is looking more grey than blonde. She smells of Nivea moisturizer.

'I'm sorry if I was negative, if I upset you,' she says, tidying a bit of hair behind my ear. 'But I did have two babies you know, it's probably hard for you to remember that, and I know how tough it is. I really, really do.'

I look at my mum, her hazel eyes a mixture of nerves and love.

'But to be honest, mum,' I say, 'with all due respect, you don't know what it is like to have it really hard, to be a real single mum, because you always had dad.'

'Maybe,' she says. 'But I do understand.'

'Really?' I frown. 'Mmm, not sure about that. And anyway, I don't know why you're worrying at all because Jim's going to be as involved as any dad, we're going to bring up the baby together. We won't be together or live together, eventually, but we'll both be its parents.'

'I know, I know,' she says. 'And we really like Jim, I'm sure he'll make a fantastic father.'

It's 10.30 p.m. when mum eventually leaves, unconvinced I can tell, and I climb into bed shattered by the day's events and a bit stressed that things seem to have got heavy. I'm just dropping off to sleep when my phone goes. I literally leap out of bed and slam it on the side of my face.

'Hello?'

'Sorry, is it late? I was just losing the will to live marking these essays on *Middlemarch*.'

Oh. Jim.

'Honestly, to give you an idea one lad has written "he" when referring to the author all the way through and another has written "do we give a shit?" in the margin. This is what I'm up against.'

I smile as I sink back into the pillow, listening to Jim's familiar voice, with its subtle northern vowels.

'How did it go with the future in-laws?' he says. 'Did your dad vow to come and "sort me out"?'

'No,' I laugh. 'He was very decent about it actually. It was mum who nearly had a seizure, but she'll be alright about it, I think, eventually.'

'I told my mum too, yesterday.'

'Oh yeah, and how did it go?'

'She cried, bless her. She said she worried I'd never have children, but that she thought I'd make a great dad, far better than my own.'

'And she's right Jim, she's absolutely right.'

'No questions about whether we were an item or not, I don't think she even registers that, I don't think she even cares!'

'I wish my mum was so relaxed.'

'Oh come on, it doesn't sound as if it went too badly and you can't blame her being a bit shocked, her always having had the traditional marriage thing – you're lucky your parents are normal! What does she think about you moving in anyway?'

'Oh she's glad about that bit. She thinks I need professional help just to cope in day-to-day life, let alone when pregnant, so she's pleased I'll have you, in whatever capacity.'

'Good, because I thought we might as well do it on Saturday.'

'What, this Saturday?'

'Yeah,' he says, 'why, have you changed your mind?'

'No. It's just . . . oh it doesn't matter.' I can hear the TV blaring downstairs – the comforting sound of audience laughter – of home and I think how much I just wanted things to be normal.

'What?'

'Well it's just not what I expected, that's all. I mean, I'm really, really grateful, *obviously* Jim. But this whole thing just isn't what I thought my life would be. It's going to take some adjusting.'

'Yeah, I know,' he sighs, 'I know you're finding it tough.'

I kneel against my window sill and we chat for ages, me looking at the starry black sky above the sea and wondering how life got so serious. I tell Jim about my dad, how I'm a bit worried he's not himself, he tells me about his pupils, how he's worried they're all thick. He laughs at my impressions of Joyless and how my mother is worried we'll be ostracized from society. Then I hang up, I pull my old polka-dot duvet around my ears and I close my eyes, much happier, actually, for having spoken to Jim. Twenty minutes later I wake with a start. Laurence still hasn't called.

CHAPTER SEVENTEEN

'Never a day goes by that I don't think of her. Is she married? Has she got kids of her own? Does she wonder about me? Giving up my baby is the hardest thing I've ever done. For years I couldn't bear to even look at the one picture I had of her in her tiny lemon hat. Now I have accepted that I could never have coped, I did the right thing. But should she ever come looking for me, I'll be right here, with open arms.
Julie, 58, Doncaster

'Christ Jarvis, we're going to need an annexe at this rate, never mind your own room.'

Jim blows a bead of sweat off the end of his nose as he struggles down the steps with another bulging suitcase.

'This is just her make-up; wait till you see the one for her shoes,' says Gina, matter-of-factly, helping Jim to push the case into the back of the white Ford estate (kindly on loan from Warren).

Jim leans deep into the boot of the car arranging the boxes, sweat soaking his T-shirt, five inches of bare back and at least one inch of builder's bum on show.

Gina watches him struggle for a moment, biting her nails,

then takes a cigarette from inside her bikini top and lights it.

'Marshall, I hope you're not slacking,' Jim shouts from inside the car. 'There's two massive boxes behind where Tess is sitting and her arm chair to get in yet.'

Gina skips barefoot onto our black-painted front steps wearing a bottom-skimming sundress, and a red, balconette bikini top that makes her D cups look positively gravity-defying.

'Alright James.' (Gina has taken to calling Jim this of late.) 'Keep yer wig on, I was just having a fag break. Ow fuck!' She literally hot foots it up the steps. 'These steps are so hot they're burning my feet!'

Perhaps summer solstice was not the wisest day to move from one side of London to the other. There's not a cloud in the sky, not a whisper of a breeze. The only sound is the odd tinkle of an ice-cream van in the dry oppressive heat.

Sitting on the front steps, I watch as poor Jim humps a linen-basket full of books on his shoulder and lowers it into the back of the car.

'I feel so guilty sat here on my arse whilst you two do all the hard work,' I moan.

'Tough.' Gina reaches behind me to get another box. 'There's no way you're carrying anything. Jim and I will load the car. Go and check there's nothing of yours left in the house if you must help, and we'll call you when we're finished.'

Just as your hair always looks better the day before you get it cut, so I feel closer to Gina the day before I'm due to move out. Since we sorted everything out just over a week ago, it's been brilliant: we've had Jacuzzis under the stars with the velux window wide open (if you ignore the faint screams from victims of knife-wielding gangsters in the estate next door you could almost be on a spa break in Bali), then cooked fajitas and eaten outside. I even coaxed her out of

Islington the other day – to see *Notes on a Scandal* followed by coffee and cake at Maison Bertaux. (Gina said she hadn't had an alcohol-free Friday night since she was fourteen. I felt truly honoured.) Gina has decided to ask Michelle to move into Vicky's old room so I don't feel guilty about leaving her in the lurch. Whereas a couple of weeks ago I couldn't wait to get out of here, now I'm gutted to be leaving. I stand in the middle of my bedroom – it looks pitiful without much in it: smears of make-up and tea stains all over the carpet, a patch of damp behind where my bed once was. The only thing that's left is a lonely looking cork board onto which is pinned a Polaroid of me and Gina, blood-shot-eyed and drunk, and a piece of pink paper with my midwife appointments written on it. Says it all really, I've come full circle in this house. But although it's kind of helped with the denial that Gina has ignored the fact I'm pregnant up until a week ago, I can hardly see me waddling around the place at thirty-five weeks pregnant, grunting on my birthing ball while her and Michelle get stoned.

I can hear Jim and Gina laughing outside and Jim say something like, 'Are we in any danger?' It must be nearly time, time for me to leave now, but before I close the front door behind me I have one thing left to do: I need to say goodbye.

The water of the jacuzzi is still, not unsettled by the usual menagerie of delinquents that frequent our house; it feels all wrong in the daytime, like a nightclub when it's empty.

'If you're thinking of having a water birth in here, you can think again,' says Gina, coming up behind me and resting her chin on my shoulder.

'You can be my birth partner if you like, fish out my placenta with a net?'

'No fucking thanks.'

'Luckily for you, that's Jim's job. He just doesn't know it

yet. Although I'm starting to think I want to be drugged from the first contraction.'

'That's the most sensible thing you've said in three months,' says Gina. 'I mean why the hell would you want to go through pain when there's perfectly good narcotics on offer?'

'Is Jim OK out there?' I suddenly remember he's probably died of heat exhaustion by now.

'Yeah, nearly finished, he sent me to get you.'

'So, you're talking to him now then?' I say tentatively, turning around to face her.

'Course I am, stupid.'

'And me?'

Gina looks sheepish. 'Don't be ridiculous.'

'We've had some great times in this room, haven't we?'

A rare, involuntary beam spreads across Gina's face. 'You fucking bet we have,' she says.

'I've had some of the best times in my life here in fact.'

'Jarvis! I'm touched.'

'And just because I'm having a baby doesn't mean we can't have more, OK?' I squeeze her waist. 'I'll miss you Gina.'

'Oh stop it, you'll make me blub,' she says.

'And I love you mate.'

'I love you too.'

'Don't be a stranger you two.' Gina sticks her head through the driver's window and rests her cleavage on the frame. Jim tries not to look.

'And don't get some weirdo in to fill my room like you did last time I went away,' I say, winking at Jim.

'Look after her won't you?' says Gina to Jim. 'And don't let her get fat and really, really boring.'

'It's a bit late for that,' yawns Jim, stretching. I punch him in the side.

'And don't take any shit – ' Gina whispers the next bit in

Jim's ear ' – Because left to her own devices, she lives like a pig.'

'Have a great time in New York! Bag a fit, rich American for me!' I yell out of the window, as Jim pulls away, honking the horn. Then I put my feet on the dashboard, and my face to the sun, leaving what feels like an old version of me imprinted in the bricks and mortar of Linton Street, having no idea at all what the new version will be.

About an hour later, having spent half of that boiling alive in a traffic jam on the Walworth Road, we finally arrive at Jim's house in leafy Dulwich.

It feels strange as we go inside, ever so slightly awkward like I've never been here before and I'm not his best friend but a guest, a French exchange student come to lodge for a couple of weeks. We go upstairs, Jim in front carrying a huge box and grunting as he squeezes past the banister. Then, rather than go into Jim's room on the right as we usually would, we walk along the long corridor to the spare room, a room I've only been in perhaps four times since I've known Jim.

'Welcome, housemate and mother of my child.' Jim plonks the box down outside and opens the door.

Gone is the broken futon, Jim's old drum kit and the bin bags full of crap. In their place is a veritable, er, boudoir, complete with a selection of Jim's old football trophies, a disco glitterball, a poster of Eminem and a bowl of pot-pourri with bits of dried orange peel in it.

'Wow. I like what you've done with the finishing touches,' I say, trying not to laugh.

'Do you think ? Oh good.' Jim's panting like a dog. There's a worrying lack of irony in his voice. 'I found the glitterball in the attic, I got the poster from the end of term sale at school and the pot-pourri – do you like the pot-pourri? – A nice feminine touch, I thought. My mum always has pot-pourri.'

Every reason why I definitely should not.

'Right, yeah, it's cool Jim, very eclectic. Although, I didn't know you liked Eminem.'

'I don't, I just thought he'd keep you company. Be someone to talk to when I'm doing your head in,' he says, perfectly seriously.

'Right, because a rapper who sings about murdering his child is just the perfect confidant for me!' I say, stifling a giggle.

'Well it was him or Britney Spears!' he says, slightly outraged by my lack of gratitude.

'I think I'd rather have Eminem. At least he still sees his kids.'

'Exactly,' says Jim. 'So we are on the same wavelength after all. You and Slim Shady will have lots to discuss.'

Jim finally kicks the last of my boxes from the hallway inside my room then flops dramatically onto my bed.

'Thanks for helping me move, you're a star,' I say, lying beside him, looking at the disco ball catch the evening light like a giant, glinting diamond.

'Well it was Gina too, I can't take all the credit,' he says, pulling up his T-shirt and wiping his face.

'You got on well today, you two, no?'

'Yeah I think she knows she pissed me off.' Jim yawns. 'But I can handle that girl, I reckon we sorted it out.'

I'm glad, I hate it when any of us aren't getting on. Whereas Jim and Vicky always get on and have a very similar temperament, as do I, Jim and Gina have a love-hate relationship and when they fall out, they really fall out.

'Do you think she'll be OK on her own?' I ask, suddenly thinking of Gina, in that draughty old house. Not quite knowing what to do with herself until Michelle moves in.

'Course she will,' says Jim. 'It'll be character building, you watch, to cope without you.'

I smile at Jim's perceptiveness – it's one of his best qualities and takes me by surprise sometimes.

We don't say anything for a while; outside the birds have broken into their evening chorus.

'Jim,' I say eventually.

'Yeees.' He's got his eyes closed now.

'I think the pot-pourri may have to go.'

One eye opens.

'You've got a cheek. I spent ages choosing that.'

'And the glitterball too.'

'What?' He sits up on his elbows. 'I'll have it then!'

'Erm . . . and the trophies too.'

'Get lost! They're my pride and joy!'

'But I love the Eminem poster!' I sit up, eyes full of enthusiasm.

'Well thank God you do have some taste.'

'I must now be the coolest mo fo mother-to-be in the whole freakin' universe, innit.'

'Mmm,' muses Jim, narrowing his eyes, his lips twitch, a giggle escapes. 'That was the shittest, dodgiest Bronx meets Peckham hybrid I've ever heard.' He clambers off the bed. 'But I'm liking it!' I chase after him giggling, beating him with my fists. 'And I'm gagging for a shower so I'll leave you to unpack!' He skids into the bathroom. 'Shall we reconvene in half an hour?'

'Yeah, if you're still alive!'

I collapse onto the bed alarmed that even this much excitement can leave me breathless these days and listening to what sounds like five hundred gallons of water being chucked from a high rise.

I get up and go to the window, take stock of my brand new vista. Rows and rows of Quality Street chimneys, cranes like dinosaurs, Canary Wharf winking in the distance. Somewhere nearby a police siren wails. But it's beautiful too, in an urban kind of way, with the band of peachy light on the horizon, like a lid's been lifted on the world. And this is a momentous day – the day I move in with a man! So how come I'm here, with Jim's football trophies on the shelves and a poster of Eminem on the wall? Whatever happened to fighting over who has which side of the bed? To christening the bed for that matter? To buying our first sofa? It's so weird, it's almost funny.

My mind drifts to Laurence. Is he out there? Packing his life into boxes too? It's been ten days now since he called when I was at Vicky's and five days since our last contact (not that I'm counting or anything). Last Tuesday, my first day back at work after I'd got back from my parents, there was a card in my pigeon hole (thankfully, in an envelope). It was of a girl, standing on Brighton Pier, her blue skirt billowing, Marilyn Monroe-esque, revealing just a hint of frilly French knickers, smiling into the camera.

It read: *'I have a confession . . . I did look at your knickers when we were at the London Eye!! . . . Sorry didn't call all weekend, Chloe's grandma's 80th in Brighton. Boring as all hell but couldn't get out of it. Did nothing but think about you (looking hot in just those knickers) . . . Wish you were here L xxx*

The devil! I read it again and again. So he hadn't gone cold, he was just fulfilling his last engagements. His last, obligatory engagements of being someone else's boyfriend.

I look over at my bag and think about phoning him but decide against it because last time I tried, I just got his voice-mail.

'Hi this is Laurence (he says 'Laurence' with a faint French accent, it drives me crazy) leave a message and I'll call you straight back.'

I opened my mouth to speak, but I couldn't, it felt all wrong. He was the one who called me to say he and Chloe were about to finish, he should be the one to call me when he's done the deed. It's not my place.

Maybe it's more complicated than he thought with Chloe though, he's obviously emotionally indebted to her in some way. Maybe he's even changed his mind. Sometimes I wonder, if I'm just totally deluding myself anyway. What man – especially a man like Laurence who could probably get anyone he wanted – would willingly take on someone else's baby and not just that but a pregnant woman! Because let's face it, I'm only going to get fatter, heavier, more tired, less interested in sex. And then the baby arrives. After that, so everyone loves to tell me, it'll be Goodnight Vienna to your sex life. We won't even have had time to say hello to *ours*.

I make a start on the unpacking but get distracted on the first box which contains all my old photo albums. Within minutes I'm drowning in a pictorial version of *This is Your Life*: all four of us in Paris back in February, cagoules pulled tight in the pouring rain; Gina on Jim's knee at Vicky's twenty-sixth birthday party (that year the theme was London Tube stations and they came as Charing Cross, 'sharing' a cross between them all evening. A lazy effort by anyone's standards); Vicky having a whitey in our second year house; Gina straddling a bollard in the middle of the street. There's one of loads of us – including Jim and Laurence – picnicking on Hampstead Heath on a boiling hot day. And this. Oh I forgot about this! My favourite one of all time. Me and Jim in the Jacuzzi in Linton Street, him wearing a Bart Simpson wig and me in a Marge one, both of us laughing so much we look like we're crying.

'Aahh, you getting all sentimental?'

Jim walks into my room, all shower fresh and leaps onto my bed.

'Do you remember what happened about half an hour after that picture was taken?' he says, taking it from me to get a better look.

'I drowned Bart in the Jacuzzi?'

'Close. I got my finger stuck in the food mixer making mojitos and we all had to go to A&E, pissed as lords.'

I shake my head laughing.

'You idiot, Ashcroft.'

'This baby's not got a chance with us two as parents, has it, poor bugger? Not a cat in hell's chance of having any common sense.'

We sit, me on the floor, Jim on the bed, looking at photos until a fiery orange sunset envelops the room.

'Hey, check this one out.' I hand Jim another picture: me, Jim and Vicky stood in front of Jim's old Polo on a day trip to Macclesfield. Vicky's hair slapped to her face in the rain, mine's a big frizz ball, blowing about in the wind. We often used to go on random day trips back then when we had two lectures a week and nothing better to do. How simple things were then, compared to now, sitting in this room! What will mine and Jim's photo albums of the future look like? Sometimes it feels like my world is doing a seismic shift beneath my feet.

'Jim?'

'Yeah?' He chuckles rather sweetly at the photo he's holding.

'You know we're friends.'

'Yes I know we're friends.'

'And you know we're having a baby together.'

'I had gathered that, yes, why, what's bothering you?'

'Well. Do you think we'll always be friends?'

Jim looks at me and frowns.

'What are you on about, why wouldn't we be?'

'Well, it's just, you know what people say about your

relationship being really tested when you have a baby?'

'What? Like, you can't ever finish a conversation and want to kill each other due to sleep deprivation?'

'Oh, you've heard that one too. Well, I suppose . . .' I pick at the carpet. 'I'm worried that since we're not even married, or going out with each other . . .'

'Our friendship'll be next?'

'Yes, if I'm honest.'

'Don't be like that,' says Jim, going back to looking at the photos. 'We've just got to make sure we make the effort that's all.'

'What, like as if we are actually married?'

'Yeah, I guess so,' says Jim. 'This is a relationship after all. A bit of a funny one, true. But it's the only one we've got so we're just going to have to try our best to make it work.'

Ten minutes later, we are sitting on the lounge floor, Morrissey on the stereo and a huge piece of paper in front of us.

'Nothing like a bit of Morrissey to make you want to jump off the nearest building on a Saturday evening I always find,' says Jim, rolling up his sleeves. 'Now, are you sure you want to do this?'

'Yep, it's definitely the way forward.'

'Well as long as we put it somewhere nobody can see it. Awful would rip the piss no end at school if he saw this. I can't have anyone think I'm running some sort of Christian Fundamentalist regime in my house.'

Jim lays down on his stomach on the black and white rug. I perch on the sofa, supervising.

He writes 'THE HOUSE RULES' in bright red marker pen, then he draws a line down the middle of the page and on one side he writes WE WILL and the other side he writes WE WILL NOT.

'You go first then,' I say, 'it was your idea.'

'OK, what sort of thing do you think should be on there?' he says, stumped already.

I start: 'Stuff that's going to help us, I suppose. Help us not wind up wanting to kill one another before the baby's even born. Oh, and boundaries.'

'Boundaries?' Jim wrinkles his nose.

'Yeah you know, they're the basis of all good behaviour and successful relationships. Our kid's going to have to have plenty of them so we might as well start with ourselves. And this is a new set up, remember from the one we had before? We're not two idiots falling into bed together drunk all the time. We're responsible parents-to-be first and friends second. We have to navigate a whole new landscape, Jim.'

'Woo! Look who's gone all grown up and philosophical,' Jim teases.

'Well it's true!' I say, rather surprised myself at that little outburst, it's usually Jim who's all Victor Mature. 'Oh for God's sake just give me the pen,' I bark, standing up and yanking it out of his hand. Then I sit down on the floor next to him and take the plunge, write the first RULE.

It's quite easy once we get started save for a few moments where the concentration goes a bit funny and we start putting stupid things like: THOU SHALT Recite Keats and Bring me Muffins on a silver platter at 5 p.m. every day (me) and THOU SHALT Bring Me Cold Beer, a Whore and a Newspaper at 5 p.m. every day (Jim).

The final, serious list, though, looks like this.

1) WE WILL NOT fall into the trap of becoming 'just housemates'. We will actually venture out with friends or together on occasions too.

2) WE WILL take turns to cook for each other and have the decency to tell the other in advance if we're going out.

3) WE WILL have one night a week when we actually

talk, about meaningful things, like the fact we're about to have a baby and who will be the next American President rather than just watch telly all the time.

4) WE WILL give me a ten point head start when we play Scrabble as Jim's an English teacher so that's not fair.

5) WE WILL refer to each other as 'partner' in front of other people, for ease. 'Father of child' is too much of a mouthful.

6) WE WILL NOT allow Jim ever to go to Blockbuster alone after two disasters in the past month (*The Black Dahlia* – a lot of men in trilbies talking in very low voices for five hours. Followed by *Pirates of the Caribbean* – surely a cure for insomnia).

7) WE WILL both read books on babies and parenting. We don't want to be the only parents who think it's OK to feed cheese on toast to a three-week-old.

8) WE WILL NOT tell anyone at antenatal classes that we are not a couple. (Jim protests this point as he couldn't give a shit what people think of him or us, but I've already been met with far too many raised eyebrows and awkward silences to have to go through that in a room of twenty strangers.)

9) WE WILL start flat-hunting for me as soon as possible after baby is born so that I don't get too used to this cosy set up.

10) WE WILL NOT shag, snog or date other people whilst I am pregnant. It's just a bit bad taste.

I physically twitch at the mention of this last one. 'Where do you expect I'd find a date anyway?' I say, alarmed how easy this stuff slips out. 'The antenatal speed-dating night?!'

CHAPTER EIGHTEEN

'Throughout my twenties, I was obsessed with not getting pregnant. I never dreamt I'd spend my thirties obsessed with the opposite. It had become like a military operation. Every time that fertile window arrived, we'd be dragging ourselves upstairs. There's nothing quite so likely to kill the romance as your husband seeing you standing on your head with your legs in the air for ten minutes afterwards, but fifteen months later and we've got our baby.'

Lucy, 37, Oxford

I come downstairs in the morning, the first of our co-habiting life, to find Jim perched on a stool at the breakfast bar, his dressing-gown belt trailing on the floor, his hair all separated like brunette bales of hay.

He's flicking through my copy of *OK!* magazine.

'I can't believe you actually buy this stuff,' he says. 'Do you reckon when we have our baby, they'd do a shoot with us?' He crunches into a spoonful of cornflakes, then looks whimsically into the middle distance. '"*Believe It!* journalist Tess Jarvis and dashing teacher James Ashcroft introduce their son, Caspian Ignatius Napoleon, whilst reclining on their chaise-longue in their beautiful country home."!'

I burst into a snigger.

'Er, *no*. But I'm quite worried how easily those names just tripped off your tongue.'

I walk over to Jim and drag the magazine over so I can read it.

There's a shoot with a pregnant Gwen Stefani and an accompanying feature about how she longed to start planning the second baby the minute she dropped the first.

My head runs away with me, something else to fixate on. 'Mmm, I guess we won't be able to plan a family like most people, will we? I guess we know already, that this baby will only ever have half-siblings, if it gets a sibling at all.'

Jim looks at me, incredulous. 'And all this thinking at what? nine in the morning? God, girls are hilarious. Anyway, nobody knows what awaits them. Gwen Stefani's a pop singer for God's sake. She'll probably be divorced in a week. Or in The Priory.'

I go over to Jim's Smeg fridge – second-hand from e-bay but still a Smeg fridge. There's no magnets or pictures on it, just a Fantasy Football league table and a note that says 'Dawn, social worker, Tuesday, 2 p.m.'. Nobody seems to bother with Dawn, Jim's sister, as far as I can tell, except Jim. His mum can't be doing with her, which is fair enough since she steals from her to fund her drug habit. But Dawn still lives with their mum in Stoke-on-Trent, which drives Jim's mum crazy. Jim took me to see his mum once, a huge mound of a lady with eye bags like dead mice and the weight of the world hanging off the end of her ever-burning fag. She suffers from agoraphobia, something which started when Jim's dad left. Not that Jim ever goes into a lot of detail, he's fiercely private and protective about his family. But anyone can see that Rita Ashcroft has been paralysed by the shit life has dealt her, so that she is now an immovable boulder onto which crashes a relentless array of bad news. The worst of which is Dawn.

'What are you up to today?' I ask, venturing inside the fridge. Inside is a huge salami; some black bean paste, four cans of Heineken and some parmesan cheese.

'Awful's asked a few lads round from school to watch football, maybe a cheeky pint or three – if her indoors approves that is.'

'Jim.' I slap down the salami on the worktop and hack off a four-inch hunk. 'In my book, joking that we're married is only two steps away from behaving like we actually are.' I take a big bite of salami.

Anyone would think I'd bitten off a piece of my own arm, the look of horror on Jim's face. 'What are you doing?' he says.

'Eating salami.'

'For breakfast?'

'Yes, for breakfast, if that's OK with you.'

'And what are you up to today, Fraulein Schmitt? May I ask? Besides eating continental sausage?'

'Shopping!' I announce triumphantly. 'I officially surrender! I feel like a heffer. I need some maternity wear.'

'What, some of those weird jeans with a girdle that make you look like you might have a baby kangaroo in there?'

'Maybe I'll get some of those, yes, or maybe some vast dungarees.'

Jim grimaces, a spoonful of cornflakes just inches from his mouth. 'Or maybe not.'

'What's it to you? It may be the only time I get to wear vast dungarees in my whole entire life.'

'Let's hope so. Although the rate you're going with that salami may mean you're in them for the rest of your life.'

'Piss off!'

'I'm only teasing.' He slips off the stool. 'I'm making eggs, do you fancy some?'

'Yeah, why not.'

'How do you like them?' he says, and we both immediately start laughing at what I'm so obviously going to say next.

'As long as they're not fertilized, James Ashcroft, I'm really not bothered.'

I used to wonder how come there were so many people in the world. Now, I realize, it's just that pregnant ladies do not tend to frequent Turnmills of a Friday night and then to bed to lie in the dark for the rest of the weekend. Now, I realize, they were here all the time. Here in Nappy Valley.

Everywhere I look, there they are: queuing up outside the Blue Mountain Café, bump-to-bump, spilling out of the over-priced boutiques of North Cross Road, buying baby grows with slogans like 'If you think I'm a mess you should see my daddy' – a bargain at twenty-two quid. If they're not pregnant, they're pushing a galactic looking pram that looks like it might take off any second it's so high tech. And there's a uniform too: for the girls, a sort of trendy granny look – all printed knee-length skirts and layers and orthopedic shoes. And for the boys, it's heavy-framed glasses, Birkenstocks and a look that says, 'I didn't bargain for this when I snogged her pissed out of my head down the Red Star.'

If I was in denial before, there's no chance of it now. I feel like a drug addict on day one of rehab, thrown into the deep end with the real hardcore set.

I cross Lordship Lane to the bus stop where a Dulwich Alpha-couple + Alpha baby in bugaboo stand in the sun, the man with his arm around the woman. She's wearing a gorgeous yellow sundress that shows off her elegant collarbones and bejewelled sandals. Her face is hidden with enormous vintage

201

shades but I can tell she's stunning, it's all in the cheekbones. With his piercing blue eyes and sculpted physique, he is no less impressive. But I can't help but think he's strangely behind in the fashion stakes with his desert boots and eighties pale denim jacket.

He gives me one of those smiles that tells me he's never had any difficulty with the ladies. I'm flattered, any attention is good attention these days.

We say 'Hi' and I gesture that their baby is gorgeous, which she is. She's got her dad's blue eyes and mum's dark hair: a pedigree baby. I notice that the label on her blanket says Petit Bateau – that figures, since we are deep in the heartland of the chi-chi baby boutique.

The man says, 'She may look pretty now but at four o'clock this morning I could have bloody strangled her!' The woman laughs and I do too. Sweet, I think. Babies are like new lovers to their parents. Any excuse to mention them – a polite gesture from a stranger for example – and they're away.

'How old is she?' I ask.

'Three months,' says the girl.

'What's her name?'

'Matilda. Tilly.'

The man has his hand on the woman's bottom as she talks. They look properly in love. Maybe it's not true what people say after all.

'She likes you,' says the girl, as I smile at Tilly and she grins back.

'Oh that's good,' I say, 'I'll have one of these come December, all going well. I'm pregnant you see.'

'Really?!' The girl gives me a beaming smile. 'Congratulations, you don't look it, not for four months, you'll probably be one of these lucky people who's really neat.'

'Rachel was big as a house, weren't you hon?' says the

man. 'I loved those gorgeous curves, myself, that belly and bum. She's gone all skinny now.' Rachel doesn't say anything.

I say, 'Well, I'm off to get some maternity clothes now, actually.'

'And we're off to get some post-maternity wear, aren't we babe?' says the guy. 'I'm treating her.'

'Oh, that's lovely,' I say, thinking Jim didn't offer to treat me to maternity wear, did he? And it was him who got me in this state.

'I'm Rachel by the way,' says Rachel, 'and this is Alan.'

'Her husband,' says Alan. Alan? I wouldn't have put her with an Alan.

'I'm Tess, nice to meet you. Do you live around here?'

Rachel looks to Alan to answer, he's clearly the talker of the couple. 'Bassano Street, warehouse flat, one of the ones with a roof terrace,' he says.

Wow, architect, I think. I bet he's an architect and she's an interior designer.

'And you?' says Rachel.

'Lacon Road just up there, just off North Cross Road.'

'Have you and your husband just moved in then?' she asks. 'I don't think I've ever seen you before.'

And that's it. I'm off. Maybe I needed to talk to someone about it all more than I thought. And this friendly couple seems as good as anyone: neutral, un-judging and actually, I decide, by the end of the bus journey, really, really nice.

It turns out I was wrong on the job front, Rachel's a make-up artist – well when she's not on maternity leave – and Alan's a fireman, which explains the pecs.

'It was great to chat to you,' says Rachel as I get off the bus on Regent Street.

'Yeah, you too,' I say. 'Perhaps if we bump into each other again, while you're still on maternity leave, we could go for coffee?'

'That would be lovely,' she says. When I get off the bus and look behind me, Alan's watching me. I wave, but he doesn't wave back.

'It looks a bit . . . baggy,' I say, staring forlornly in the mirror at the vast, white hammock I appear to be wearing on my chest.

The Mothercare sales assistant pushes her bulk up against me and hoists the thick straps upwards, grunting with the effort.

'Pregnancy is not a fashion parade, I'm afraid,' she says, pursing her coral-stained lips. 'You're already a C and are likely to go up at least two cup sizes during your pregnancy so probably best to get used to it now.'

A C cup?! When the hell did that happen? I've never been more than a B in my life and now I'm likely to become an E?! Hello!? And nobody's ever going to see them?! The one time in my life I have enormous tits and I am, to all intents and purposes, single. And have to wear a surgical bra.

'Do you have anything slightly more attractive? Something with an underwire perhaps?' I venture, tentatively.

'An underwire?!' she gasps, like I just asked for heroine. 'Pregnant ladies do not wear underwired bras, my dear. I'm afraid it's fashion selflessness from now on.'

'Oh,' I say, 'what's wrong with underwires?'

'They wreak havoc with the milk-ducts, which can reduce your chances of breastfeeding successfully and I'm sure you wouldn't want that?'

Oh yes, I'd love that. In fact do you sell gaffer tape because I'd quite like to bind my boobs down for the rest of my pregnancy just to make sure, you know, I eradicate every glimmer of hope of ever breastfeeding. No you stupid cow, of course I wouldn't want that! This is the first time I've had a baby, and in case you haven't noticed, I haven't got the faintest idea what I'm doing!

This is what I think, but of course I just pay for the hammock-bra I'm wearing, buy another two and shuffle out of the shop feeling like a total failure of a pregnant person.

'Selflessness'. The word really sticks. Perhaps I need to learn some. It's not very selfless of me to have been fantasizing about Laurence Cane all week, is it? To have been imagining cavorting naked with him, being his girlfriend, him proposing to me on Battersea Park Bandstand (not that I've considered the details at all) when I should have been reading books on why underwired bras are the devil's work. Since re-meeting Laurence, my libido has perked up no end. I get this recurring dream – it's mainly an office-based theme with us going at it like the clappers over my desk whilst Blanche Jewell gives a seminar around the corner. It gets to the good bit, where Laurence is moaning he's about to come, then the foetus starts talking, like that film, *Look Who's Talking* and says, 'Hey! That's my head! Watch out you're nudging my head!' Probably my conscience talking . . .

Perhaps it would be a good thing if Laurence never called. At least then I wouldn't have the humiliation of ever revealing the hammock-bra. Or telling him I'm pregnant.

Something about this whole prospect scares me. It leaves me wanting to phone my dad. I stand outside River Island and call his mobile.

'Hi love, how are you? Are you on the motorway, it's ever so noisy?'

'No dad, I'm on Oxford Street.'

'Right. And are you OK? Do you want to borrow some money?'

'No dad. I do earn a salary these days you know, a pittance though it is. I just wanted to speak to you that's all.'

And so we do, we chat and he doesn't ask any annoying

questions about the Jim situation (except that mum wants to know if he has a smoke alarm. With batteries in it) or about what I'm going to do, or the FUTURE which has become a dirty word since I feel like I cannot plan beyond next week. He just tells me how exhausted he is, how my brother's not pulling his weight at work. He tells me about his plants and how mum is rationing him to half an hour per evening in the greenhouse because she's worried he talks to his tomatoes more than her, and he soothes and he calms and he's just my dad, who I love. And then he tells me to go off shopping and treat myself to some 'really posh togs' which makes me laugh because only my dad would say 'posh togs' and then I say, 'Dad, thanks for the pep talk it's just nice to hear your voice.' I hang up and it's only when I do that it occurs to me that that voice was not quite right. It was not my dad's voice at all.

I decide to follow his advice anyway and head to Mamas and Papas on Regent Street. Then, I don't know what comes over me, maybe it's in a bid to feel this, that by doing things a pregnant woman does I might, eventually, feel like one – like method acting. But as if in a retail-induced hypoglycaemic fit, I shop. For England. I buy bootees and baby-grows and a quilted sleeping bag with little animals all over it. I buy a bump-enhancing wrap dress even though I don't have a bump to put in it yet, spend ages in the changing room fancying myself as a model in Jojo Madam whatserface magazine. I buy a pair of 'baby kangaroo jeans', and text Jim 'if these don't turn you on, nothing will'. I wander around the nursery department actually feeling something when I look at the blown up pictures of tiny sleeping babies. And I buy a sheep-skin throw, a sterilizer and a big, fluffy snail called Sebastian Snail that when you press a button, speaks in a voice like Prince Charles and says, 'Good morning! I'm Sebastian Snail.

And how do you do?' And then, eventually, when I think I have sufficiently immersed myself in babyness I go to the cash desk where the woman behind it asks me when the baby's due, and I cave in and buy another baby-grow on her suggestion, one that says 'Born to be Wild'. Oh dear. Then she says, 'That will be £176.50 please,' and I flinch, momentarily, but really I don't care. Because for half an hour I am like everyone else. I am like those women in Dulwich. I am like the women in Mothercare. I am what the sales assistant said I should be. I am Tess Jarvis, I am selfless earth mother. I am going to be a mother. Someone's mum! How amazing is that!

I walk out of the cool, air-conditioned shop into the thick, polluted heat of Regent Street, a sudden fizz of happiness bubbling up my throat. It is 4.30 on a Saturday afternoon, the end of a sultry weekend in London, and yet for once I don't get a twinge of jealousy when I see people walk past me, new purchases in hand, on their way for an al fresco beer down Kingly Street or a boozy barbeque. And then I see him. Across the road in front of French Connection. I wonder if he might be a mirage, my mind playing tricks. Two double-decker buses speed past and I blink hard but he's still there. He's wearing a pale grey T-shirt and a dark grey blazer and blue jeans and Converse and sunglasses on his head. I smile and wave and feel something like excitement and desire creep across my belly like sunshine on your sheets in the morning. Then I feel the sting of the four giant Mamas and Papas bag handles heavy in my hands, and the heaviness of my swollen boobs under the hammock-bra, and the excitement turn to a sudden rising panic.

I don't have time to think though, because before I know it, he's there, right in front of my face and just the smell of him – Oh! – fresh laundry, with that smoky, musky aftershave, gives me that feeling: like light-headedness but between the thighs. 'What are you doing here? Hello,' he says. Then he rests his forehead on mine and we kiss, a slow, savoured kiss in the middle of Oxford Street. I can feel Laurence's boner against my belly and hear people's tuts as they try to get round us. And it thrills me, I can't help but surrender. And somehow the guilt and panic I felt dissolves instantly, to be replaced by something like caramel drifting around my veins.

We end up going for something to eat, sitting outside Carluccio's in St Christopher's Place.

'So what's with the ten day silence, mister?' I say, settling in to get a closer look at his face. The sun's shining on it, turning it a burnished brown, I want to kiss it desperately.

'It's not like I didn't *want* to call you!' I thought about you constantly. But as soon as I started talking about it she went ape shit, bawling her eyes out and saying she'd do something stupid.'

'Shit, that's heavy, that's emotional blackmail,' I say, brows knitted, all serious, desperate to get to the next bit. 'But you did it though? You told her it was finished?'

'Well, no not exactly.'

'Oh.' I can't hide the disappointment in my voice.

'I tried to, I really tried. Please believe me when I say I will! I basically did. I just didn't say the words.'

'So what did you say?'

'That it wasn't working, that she was too high maintenance.'

'But she's got her results for the marketing exam, right?'

'Yeah, but they weren't what she was hoping for. Then there was the grandma's eightieth birthday party I promised her I'd go to. I mean, spare a thought for me, having to spend the day in a fucking retirement home, speaking to old biddies who banged on about the war and forgot what I said two seconds after I said it.'

208

He starts laughing and even though I think about my own lovely grandma and think he's a little bit mean, I follow.

Laurence is like a drug, an hypnotic, addictive drug. It's in his lazy smile, the straight line of his eyebrows, the way his dimples make him look younger than he is. It's in the close cut of his hair around his ears, his tanned neck when he leans forward to eat, it's in his toned forearms and the way he shouts 'branleur!' and does that French gesture with his hand whenever he's got road rage. And it's in the way he's looking at me now, his hands clasped beneath his chin, making me feel like I'm the sexiest woman in London. But mostly, it's how he can eradicate any maternal, nesting instincts I may have and replace them with an animal desire so instant and overwhelming, I almost have to sit on my hands to stop me from acting on it. No matter how much I pretend it's not true. I want him. I want to be with him. And sometimes, although I am almost so loath to admit it, I can't bring myself to say it, I want him to be the father of this baby. Because then it would be so much simpler, so less stressful, so much more normal. But that's not my life. That's not how things turned out.

'So anyway,' he says, changing the subject. 'Tell me again, who are the presents are for?'

'Julia. My friend Julia from work. She's about to pop anytime.' (The last bit's not a lie which makes it half alright, surely?)

'You've gone a bit over the top, haven't you?'

'She's having twins.' (What? Why did I just say that?! Now what was only half a lie is a whole lie again, at the very least.)

'Lucky her,' says Laurence. '*Not*. I mean one baby's surely enough for anyone – I could take them or leave them myself – but two . . .'

CHANGE OF SUBJECT. NEEDED. URGENTLY.

'Anyway, so,' I say, eager to pin Laurence down on the

209

Chloe front. 'Do you think you might tell Chloe soon? I mean to be honest I don't feel that comfortable meeting like this when you're attached.'

'Look I'm sorry Tess,' Laurence continues. 'But give me a fortnight and honestly!' he slaps the table, decisively, 'I swear, it's over. In my head it was over weeks ago! I never loved her,' he says, 'not like I loved you. God I loved you. I still . . .'

'Laurence.' I put a finger to my mouth. 'Don't. Don't say it. Not until you mean it.'

I want to hear those words more than anything but I also remember how much he hurt me.

'Anyway, I've got something to tell you,' I say.

Laurence leans on his elbow, taking in every millimetre of my face.

'What?'

'I moved in with Jim.'

I don't know what I'm expecting. Mad, crazed jealousy ideally. Or at least a valiant effort to appear nonchalant when oh so obviously not. But instead all I get is a sort of amused surprise.

'Jim?' Laurence crinkles his long, Gallic nose. 'What? Lanky Jim from uni?'

I suddenly feel protective. That's the father of my child you're talking about, I think. And what's wrong with lanky?

'Yes, Jim Ashcroft from uni.'

'Right, interesting.' He's smiling now. 'What brought that on?'

'He had a spare room.' I realize I'm stuttering. I suddenly feel a bit stupid. 'Gina and mine's time together had run its course.'

'Course, nice one. Well, I'll have to come over some time. Although I can't say me and Jim were ever particularly pally.'

And that's it. That's his big reaction and I'm kind of baffled it didn't have more of an impact. But then, Laurence has grown up. Why should he get all gnarled up and jealous about me living with a bloke? That, I decide, would be highly unattractive.

We pay the bill and walk out onto Oxford Street. We are just about to say goodbye and go our separate ways and then he turns to me and grabs my hand and I just know what he's going to say next and I'm wishing for it and dreading it all at the same time. 'Come back to mine.' he says.

I must be mad (definitely bad) and drunk on the sun like a big, fat bee but the next thing I know I'm in the back of a black cab, haring down New Oxford Street, embroiled in the second snog of the day and laughing at the driver who's shouting 'Get a room!' from the front of the taxi, as I constantly try to move the hair that's sticking to my lip gloss. And I'm thinking, this is the best day, the best fun, the best idea, ever. And yes I feel naughty. But I trust myself that it's all for the end result. A girl's got to have a bit of fun before it's too late, after all and I will tell him, just maybe not now.

Laurence's friend's flat is on the top floor of a terrace just down by where the canal runs through Islington.

'Well your mate's either gay or he's got a super stylish girl-friend,' I say, eyeing up the lime green cushions and silver accessories, the 'accent' wall with its flocked wallpaper and the chandelier.

'The latter,' says Laurence, 'but she dumped him and moved out, so he's left with this girly flat. Anyway . . .' The air's knocked out of me as he suddenly starts kissing me again. 'That's enough talking for one day, you sexy, *sexy girl*.' He puts his hands in my hair and pulls at the roots. ''Coz I want you.' He leads me by the head and I surrender, flopping all my bags down and collapsing with him onto the sofa, giggling. 'I want to devour you. Right now, Right here.'

211

'Oh really?'

'Yes, really.'

'We'll have to see about that.'

He's on top of me now and we're tonguing and our breathing is fast and shallow. He puts his hand up my skirt and my thighs shudder involuntarily as he runs one finger from my knickers all the way down my thigh. I slip my hand down his jeans and feel his balls, warm and deliciously familiar in my hand and we're groaning now and sort of laughing all at the same time and I think, God this is good. *Fuck,* I've missed this. Then his hands start to roam under my smock top (thank God for the current fashion) and up to my belly button Shit! Is there a bump? There's definitely a curve to that area now but you can't see it when I'm lying down, surely, or can you? I hope he won't notice, I pray he won't notice . . . Then his hands are roaming up my top and he's dangerously near the hammock-bra. Fuck, fuck, the hammock-bra! This is like a bloody obstacle course! I have to act fast and so I undo it at the back and whip it off, throwing it as far away as I possibly can. But it lands in a heap right in front of Laurence's eye level. 'Fuck me,' he says, eyes popping out of his head, 'I could fit my head in that.'

I redden, embarrassed but he doesn't seem fussed. He just kisses my neck, up my neck, biting kisses all over my jaw, and on my eyelids and then he lifts his entire body and lays down on me. He smells of sun-on-skin and fresh air and I feel him press his pelvis down into me, his dick twitch in his jeans. His hands are on my breasts now, his breathing urgent, our kisses more frenzied. 'Jesus.' Laurence stops kissing me and looks down my top. 'They're massive!' he laughs. 'They're fucking magnificent!' I laugh too but he stops me with another kiss and then he's undoing his flies and I think I might explode with desire and I can already feel the tell-take flush across my chest and the nagging, pulling throb between my legs. I lift up my skirt. I've totally surrendered and we're pushing our pelvises together slow and hard and I'm a gonner now, the pregnancy thing pushed firmly to the back of my mind. The sofa's squeaking beneath us, my breathing's rapid and I'm loving this, I'm absolutely loving this!! I've longed for this moment for so long and . . .

At that moment we roll, limbs entwined, straight off the sofa landing right on top of the pile of plastic bags. And Sebastian Snail's head.

'Good morning! I'm Sebastian Snail. And how do you do?'

'What,' pants Laurence, his face inches from mine, 'the fuck is *that*?'

I come to my senses abruptly and horribly. Sebastian Snail is suddenly a beacon of clarity in an otherwise heady, sun-drenched day of madness. 'It's Sebastian Snail,' I say, meekly, 'and I think we should . . .'

But Laurence is un-perturbed. 'Sebastian Snail, eh?' he says lifting himself up and pushing the offending bag to the side. 'Well Sebastian Snail can fuck right off because I'm in the middle of something.' I'm on top of him now and he gently pushes me off and then crawls on top of me, starts to kiss me. But it's no good.

'Sorry! Get off me please.' I hastily push Laurence off and stand up. 'I can't do this! I'm sorry, I can't do it!'

'What's wrong?' Laurence has got his pants down his ankles, he looks slightly absurd. 'Have you got your period? Because honestly, really, a bit of blood . . .'

'No!' I snap. 'Why are you so obsessed with me having my goddam period? Actually, if you must know, I won't be having a period for a long time.'

Laurence goes white as a sheet.

'Because I'm pregnant.'

'*What*? Pregnant?! *How* pregnant . . . ?' Laurence leaps up, a look of disgust on his face like I just told him I had crabs.

'Fifteen weeks, almost four months.'

'Who's is it? It's Jim's isn't it?'

'Yes, oh! But we're not an item!' I say, seeing this thought process cloud his face. 'He's not my boyfriend, I'd never lie to you about something like that! I still want to make this work with you Laurence, I still want . . .' His face goes blank, my voice trails off. 'But I know it's a lot to take in.'

'A lot to take in? Just a bit Tess!'

'So, what, you don't want me now? You've finished with Chloe for nothing?'

I've stooped low now, but who cares? I feel exposed enough already.

'No, it's not that,' says Laurence, he looks clammy with shock. 'It's just well . . .' he clears his throat. 'I just need time to take this in, that's all. I just need time to think about it. It'll be fine, don't worry.' He puts his shirt on and I follow suit, putting on my skirt. 'I can handle this, Tess, honestly I can. I'll call you really soon, I promise.'

CHAPTER NINETEEN

'I will never forget those words: "I think there's three heart-beats". I put on six stone during my pregnancy and was bed-ridden from week thirty. We slept no more than three hours a night for six months once they arrived and couldn't go out because by the time we got them dressed it was time to come home. Nothing could have prepared me for how hard it was having three at the same time. But now I look at them and I feel truly blessed.'

Michelle, 33, Amersham

Good morning! I'm Sebastian Snail. And how do you do?

Good morning! I'm Sebastian Snail. And how do you do?

Good morning! . . .

Aaah! FUCK OFF! Fuck-off-you-fucking-mollusc!

I curl the pillow so that it covers both ears and try and go back to sleep.

No good.

Good morning! I'm Sebastian . . .

Right, that's it. I throw back the duvet and leap out of bed. I surrender! I can't take anymore of this.

Ever since the heinous Laurence debacle of yesterday, the

little cinema in my head has constantly played one of two sequences. Both of them, torturous.

1) The March of the Molluscs: a horror film, starring a giant Sebastian-Snail-turned-nasty and a whole army of his similarly tormenting friends

2) The whole, sorry pregnancy announcement scenario from start to finish, in excruciating slow motion with a scene selection that seems to go something like this:

a) The hammock-bra landing on the floor right in front of Laurence's eyes, in all its head-sized glory

b) The bit where we pressed our pelvises together and bumped and ground and I thought I might, actually, have an NPO (non-penetration orgasm). Glorious. Although I can't fully enjoy that bit because then this next bit kicks in . . .

c) The point where we toppled off the sofa and onto Sebastian Snail's voice box (and the look on Laurence's face, like I'd just fallen in a cow pat)

d) Me leaping up and announcing I'm pregnant and the look on Laurence's face (like I'd just eaten the cow pat)

Yeah, he tried to smooth it over, but the fact remains, the poor bloke was horrified.

I grab a towel and go to the bathroom, on the way checking, just one last time, my mobile for missed calls. (There's none.)

I turn on the shower full pelt. The water feels good on my skin but does nothing to drown out my thoughts. I cannot believe I almost shagged Laurence. With £176.50 worth of stuff, stuff for *my* baby growing in *my* body, right at our feet! And suddenly I feel guilty, stomach-churningly guilty that I have broken House Rule #10 – not to shag, snog or date other people whilst I am pregnant – in nearly all its parts. Obviously it should have been higher up the list, but then let's face it, I'd already allowed my hormones to take over once, it was only a matter of time. But now I even feel guilty about not feeling guilty earlier.

I pump some shower gel out of Jim's Radox Active and cover myself in soap. My hands feel the curve of my belly. There's definitely a shape to it now, a shape I didn't have even a fortnight ago. But unless you saw me naked all the time – which Laurence does not – you wouldn't know. No, the man had no inkling whatsoever. It was a total bolt from the blue. But he said he could handle it. In Bedales he said all that stuff about wanting the house, the kids ... Maybe he likes the thought of having a child but not having ultimate responsibility? Yep, that would probably suit Laurence Cane down to the ground. He said he'd call. He WILL call.

There's a banging on the bathroom door.

'Yeah?'

I stick my head out of the shower cubicle.

'Are you going to be much longer?' says Jim, 'because I've got something you might like. Come downstairs.'

'Right, put this on,' says Jim.

He takes a tea-towel from his jeans back pocket and gives it to me.

'On?'

'Like a blindfold. Come on.' He beckons me to him, bossily, turns me around then puts the blindfold over my eyes and ties it, tightly.

'What are we doing?' I ask.

'Going outside.'

'Then what?'

'All in good time, Miss Jarvis, all in good time.'

He pushes me up the rest of the hall and then I hear the front door open and feel the balmy outdoors envelop me. Footsteps pass, two women chatting. Jim walks in front of me and takes my hand. 'Watch the step, there's a step there.'

'What are you doing, you weirdo?' I say, giggling, more out of nerves than anything else.

'OK stop.' He presses down on my shoulders.'Now, I can't do anything about the fact I am a useless twat and didn't have a condom, but I can do something to prevent you ever getting up the duff or having any other major accident befall you due to the lame, *lame* excuse that you couldn't drive.'

'Jim, I'm not planning on anymore unplanned pregnancies, this is quite enough of a head fuck for one lifetime.'

'Yeah, you say that now but I'm not taking any chances. So.'

He slowly takes off my blindfold. 'Ta-da!'

It takes me a few seconds to spot it and then I do: A car! A car with L plates on!

'Jim! You star! You absolute star, it *rocks*,' I gasp, truly shocked.

'It's alright, you don't have to be that excited. It's not new, it's my old car, remember my old Polo? It'd been sitting in Awful's garage for ages but I finally got round to wheeling the old knacker out and getting some L plates.'

'I don't care, it's acc, I *really* love it. Thank you!' I give Jim a hug.

'I'm glad because we're going in it today. Your driving lessons start this very minute.'

Jim drives up to Barry Road, a wide boulevard, largely empty on a Sunday with cavernous houses on either side and trees with leaves the size of spades. He parks the car with smooth, intimidating ease and gets out.

His crotch is right at my eye level and I look away politely as he hastily rearranges his balls in his jeans and then, when I don't move, he sticks his head in the car. 'So, get out then. We need to swap places.'

I look at him alarmed.

'What, now? I've got to get in the driving seat now?'

'Well you'll never learn anything with me driving, will you, you div head. Yes now, just bite the bullet. I want you, Tess Jarvis, in the driving seat.'

I have wanted this all my adult life. Someone to trust me enough to let me sit behind the wheel of a car. Mum has never, ever allowed me to even sit in the driving seat of her Nissan Micra. Dad gave me a lesson or two about a decade ago, once took me for a spin down on the shore, that was brilliant. But when mum found out she had a massive epi about me not even having a provisional licence and how we could have both got stuck then swallowed up in the quick sand and how *that* would have been a lesson to us both (no mention of whether she'd be sad that we died or anything). And so we never did that again.

Today, at long last, someone is giving me the opportunity to learn to drive and yet, now, I'm terrified. Absolutely bricking it.

Still, I get out of the car, go around the other side, Jim smirking at my face on the way. Jim gets in next to me, slams the door, then stretches his arms in front of him, cracking his knuckles.

'Nervous?' he asks.

'Just a bit.'

'Don't be. It's like riding a bike.'

First of all we go over the vital ABC – Accelerator, Brake, Clutch – even though I tell him I do, at least, know that much. We haven't turned the engine on yet.

'The main thing to remember when driving,' says Jim, putting on his serious teacher voice, 'is eeeasy does it. No sudden movements, no jerking, no showing off.'

'What about jerking off?'

'Jarvis, behave.'

'Sorry. I've gone all silly.'

'The point is,' he continues, 'you have to go carefully.'

219

'Jim, I barely know where the accelerator is so I don't think I'll be doing any Dukes of Hazard style wheel spins just yet,' I say, getting slightly fidgety that it's been forty minutes and still no engine.

'Good. I'm glad to hear it.' He's hamming up the teacher thing just to irritate me now. 'Right, I want you to turn on the ignition, start the engine and eeeease –' he does this pushing gesture with his hand so I have to bite my lip to stop myself laughing '– gently away from the curb, pressing gently on the accelerator and controlling the clutch. Off you go.'

I start the ignition and put the car in first then I press on the accelerator and . . .

'Fuck! Tess!!! *Jeeeesus* Christ.' Jim curls up in a hedgehog-like ball, hands in hair, his knuckles white. I've missed crashing into a VW van by millimetres.

'Ooops.'

'Ooops?! Tess you nearly killed us then!'

'Sorry,' I say, sheepishly. My heart's going nineteen to the dozen.

'OK. It's OK.' Jim takes a few deep, dramatic breaths. A nosy old man who was hobbling down the road and saw this farcical scene unfold stops. Leaning on his walking stick he peers into the car, his face all gnarled and interfering.

'Yeah, what you lookin' at you old git?' Jim mutters through the gritted teeth of a very forced smile.

We try again and this time I manage to do it – slightly shuddery but with some degree of control at least.

'Good, that's good! Spot on. *Now* we're cruising.'

I wouldn't go so far as to say cruising, more shuffling. On wheels. But suddenly I'm driving, I'm actually driving a car!

'So where were you last night? It's OK you can get a bit more speed up. Woah! I said a *bit* Tess!' Jim shouts as I misjudge the accelerator.

'Well stop talking then, I was trying to concentrate.'

It's a handy excuse not to answer the question. A question I hoped would never come up. When I got back from Laurence's house Jim was sitting at the breakfast bar, much as I'd left him, but wearing his glasses now and marking books. He didn't ask and I didn't explain why I was back so late, I just said I was tired and went to bed.

We carry on in silence, me looking at Jim now and again. His face is completely neutral, he's staring right ahead.

'Jim?'

'I thought we weren't allowed to talk,' he says.

'It's OK for me to talk, I'm driving. Well, trying to!'

'Right. Charming.'

'How do you think it will pan out, you know, when we meet other partners?'

Jim sighs and look at me in the mirror.

'Is this one of your this is all really fucked up and I'm quite scared questions?'

'If you like, yes.'

'Well . . .' Jim looks out of the window. 'The answer is . . . I don't know.'

'Oh.' I wasn't expecting that.

'I s'pose we'll just have to try and meet nice people, people who can accept that we're friends and who like children, preferably.'

Does Laurence fit that, I wonder? OK, he and Jim were never best buddies but they don't hate each other . . .

'We're going to take the second right,' says Jim

'OK,' I say, not really paying attention. Thank god there's not another soul on the road. Nobody moving anyway. 'So how is it going to work us living in different houses. It'll just be a logistical nightmare, won't it?'

'Now! Right! Indicate!'

'Ahhh!'

I swerve into Goodrich Street, completely over-steering.

221

Jim has to grab hold of the steering wheel to avoid a head-on collision with a skip.

'Oooh,' he winces. 'That was close.'

'You're telling me. I'm not very good at this am I?'

But we are moving forward again now, unopposed.

'You're doing fine,' says Jim. 'Just –' he clips me round the head '– pay attention! Now what were you on about? Oh yeah, well, you'll have to get a flat as near to me as possible. It might be a logistical nightmare at times, true, it certainly won't be perfect. But we'll manage, we'll cope. People always cope.'

I look across at Jim, he's leaning his head back on the seat of the car now, eyes half-shut, trusting me behind the wheel of this car. How is Jim so confident about me and this car? About how we'll cope? How come I'm not? I realize I've probably never had to 'cope' in my whole entire life, that's why. He has, in ways I don't even know.

We're going at a snail pace down Landell Street now, just the sound of birdsong keeping us company. And I can't make out if it's the fact that I might be finally learning to drive, or ten hours of sun still to enjoy, or just being here with Jim. But I suddenly feel happy, I suddenly believe this might all be OK.

'I like living at yours,' I say. It comes out of nowhere. 'I like it already, thanks for having me.'

'Don't get too cosy,' says Jim, putting on a Johnny Vegas accent, 'because as soon as that babby's born, you're out on yer ear, mark my words!'

'Jim.' I frown.

'Sorry, I always make a joke out of everything, don't I,' he says. 'Well I like living with you, too Tess,' he says, looking at me sincerely now. 'And you can stay as long as you like.'

We swap places, we've both had more than our fair share of near death experiences for one day, and decide to go to

Ikea, to get some stuff for the baby, some stuff that doesn't cost a John Lewis arm and a leg. Jim looks at me as we cruise down Lordship Lane.

'So where were you last night? You still haven't told me,' he says and I think well what's the harm in telling him (at least most of) the truth, he knows I met him for lunch the other day.

'I bumped into Laurence,' I say. 'He was shopping in town, too, and we were both hungry so we went to Carluccio's, just as mates, obviously.'

'Oh right,' says Jim, surprised maybe, but not un-cheerful. And then we don't say anything else for a while. We just sit, in comfortable, contented silence, two friends and a baby. A thoroughly modern relationship and dealing with it, admirably.

There's something about haring down the A23, seeing the blue and yellow towers of Ikea rise up out of nowhere, that makes me feel comforted and warm inside. They say, 'home, family, Saturday, normality'. They're like the visual equivalent of the theme tune to *Grandstand*. But the reality is, of course, always rather different: jostling crowds, the constant high-pitched wail of toddlers, the moaning of heavily pregnant women and the silence of their nodding-dog husbands. People, everywhere, paralysed with indecision, destined to return home with yet more box files and a peg bag.

At least Jim and I know what we've come for. We head straight for Children's Ikea to look at the cots.

'This is nice, I like this one a lot.'

Jim runs a hand down a plain, white, wooden crib and leans over it as if to test that it's sturdy.

'It's classic, well made, what do you think?'

'Yeah I like it,' I'm speaking but my brain's not engaged. I'm holding my ringing phone in my hand, deciding what to do.

'Why don't you take that call?' Jim says eventually, a bite of annoyance in his voice. I look at him, I look at the phone and the silver 'Laurence' flashing up on a blue background. 'I am,' I say, it comes out all defensive. 'I was just about to. Find out how much the cot costs.'

I walk as casually as I can away from where Jim's standing, my heart racing. I think I can feel his eyes follow me but when I look again, he's engrossed in a conversation with a sales assistant.

'Hello?'

'Tess, it's me.' I hear Laurence drag deeply on a cigarette. 'So, I've done the thinking bit.'

'Ooh, dangerous.' I'm pretending to be all light-hearted but inside I'm in knots with the suspense. 'And?'

'And, I reckon we should give this a go.'

'What, really?!' It comes out louder than planned. I look around at Jim, he smiles, a small, tight smile, I smile back. 'Are you sure? I mean, it's a lot to get your head around . . .'

'Yeah I know.' He sounds strangely calm. He takes another drag of the cigarette. 'But I've changed, Tess. I've grown up. And I'm ready for this. I mean, I'm under no illusions it'll be easy. I know fuck all about babies and kids, let me just tell you that now.'

'That's not particularly encouraging, Laurence, but at least you're honest.'

I turn to my right, Jim's standing there now, holding up what looks like cot bedding, gesturing he's going to the till.

'I am, that's the point. I'm feeling more honest than I've ever been with myself. At the end of the day, Tess, it's you I want. And if you come with child, then well, that's the way it's got to be.'

'But what about Chloe?' I'm aware of a child with a nose-bleed opposite me but I'm too stunned and glued to the spot to go and help.

'What?'

'Chloe, you know, your girlfriend?'

'Done.'

'Done?'

'I finished it.'

'No way! How did she take it?'

'Badly. She was gutted, went a bit bonkers, you know how girls do, but to be honest, she knew it was coming. It's been on the cards for months.'

'Right, so.'

'So I want to take you out for dinner.'

I can see Jim out of the corner of my eye, I smile at him but he looks away.

'Okay. Well I'm not going to argue with that. When?'

'I'll call you. I need to sort something out – I have plans young lady – but soon, OK? Leave it with me.'

I hang up, my head reeling, and walk over to Jim to join him in the queue.

'Who was that?' he says.

'Just Laurence, saying hi. Just finishing a conversation we started yesterday,' I say, as lightly as I can.

'God, he's keen. Lunch yesterday, phone calls today . . . Are you sure he's not after getting back with you? I mean he did ask you on a date before he knew you were pregnant.'

Tell him now, I think. Just tell him what's the big deal, anyway? We're just friends after all, but somehow him stood there, a patchwork baby blanket in his arms, it just seems so wrong, so I say . . .

'Don't be ridiculous. He knows I'm pregnant with your baby. And besides, dating anyone whilst pregnant, that's just *weird*.'

CHAPTER TWENTY

'I've always wanted a baby more than I wanted the big white wedding. Never in a million years did I imagine I'd be impregnated, my legs in stirrups on a doctor's couch, with the sperm of a total stranger.'

Trish, 42, Birmingham

A few days later the weather broke and so did my good mood. The clouds sagged like big fat udders, then it rained so hard that the lake in Dulwich Park looked like an out of order television. Laurence still hadn't called but I wasn't unduly concerned since he'd said to leave it in his own capable hands and we'd not made any firm plans. No, what had suddenly hit me now was that even if it did work out with Laurence it wouldn't be the end of this messy period. The fact I'm going ahead with this pregnancy means my whole life will be messy, period.

It was Julia's baby shower that did it. Anne-Marie told me to expect games like 'Guess What's In The Nappy' where the host would smear different baby foods in Pampers and we'd have to be blindfolded and guess what it was. Not this one. Oh no. I doubt even the babies themselves had dirty nappies:

there were vintage tea cups filled with big pink blooms (Julia knows she's having a girl) and ornate cake stands with immaculately-iced cup cakes. Everybody brought presents such as Elemis pregnancy massages and Jo Malone candles. I bought a cow that mooed when you pressed its middle.

If Julia wasn't such a lovely person you could really hate her. She's five feet ten with never ending legs that she always shows off in 60s mini dresses (even at nine months pregnant) bee stung lips and auburn hair that she wears effortlessly tousled on top of her head. Her photographer husband Fraser's beautiful too in a period drama kind of a way, brooding brown eyes and expensively cut hair that's stylishly unkempt – as distinct from Jim's whose fuzzy look is definitely not deliberate. I bet they'll have gorgeous kids who will model for Boden and be called things like Felix and Manon. And they're so in love, it's sickening. Even after eighteen years together they still speak to each other as if they are in the honeymoon period. Fraser was at the baby shower of course, he spent the afternoon charming the pregnant ladies and capturing the occasion on camera, leaping about in his nerd-chic cardigan.

Since I told her about the baby, Julia's been so cool, so understated about my situation. Like most married people she said, 'I think that sounds like the perfect set up! I'd love to have somewhere to go when Fraser's annoying me!' I had coffee with Rachel and Tilly the other morning and Rachel said the same thing, but I know neither of them means it, they're just trying to make me feel better. And I still cried all the way home from the baby shower. All those women had their future mapped out, they know what they're doing. They're not flailing around like Jim and I, going against the grain and pretending that it doesn't matter.

But it does matter. I really wish it didn't, but it does. It matters that I'm not having my first baby with someone who's in love with me. It matters that my life will be for ever compli-cated and never will I be able to have a three day love-in with Laurence or any other future boyfriend because I will have a baby permanently suckling at my nipple. And perhaps most importantly, it matters that this baby, who didn't ask to be born, will have a mother who, at almost thirty, cannot drive herself home, does not carry condoms and has a very warped idea of 'friends'.

It is in this unhelpful mood that on the Thursday after the baby shower I turn up to see Dr Cork for my sixteen-week scan. She's deep into some classical music when I walk in, sitting at her huge mahogany desk, in the middle of writing a prescription. 'Isn't this just wonderful?' she muses, eyes closed, pretend-conducting with one, sinewy arm. 'It's Vaughan Williams "The Lark Ascending": makes me feel happy to be alive!' I look at her glumly.

'Now.' She eyes me up and then my midriff, myopically. 'Are we sixteen weeks yet?'

'Yep,' I say, as cheerfully as I can muster. Dr Cork does not seem the type to suffer mopers readily.

'This pregnancy is going along like a train, is it not?' she enthuses, marching over to the stereo – also housed in more imposing heavy furniture – and switching off the music (Dr Cork is a big fan of the inverted question) 'Onward Christian Soldiers!' (Not to mention the odd religious declaration.)

'Now, pop yourself on that bed and pull your top up for me. Let's see how strong this little one's ticker is.'

I climb up onto the bed. Outside it's drizzling. I can see it land in smears on the window pane then dribble downwards miserably like custard pies. I pull my top up and roll my knickers down to my hips. Dr Cork presses the ultrasound on my belly and smiles at me. I have always taken a kind of twisted delight in the fact she has a thirty-a-day-Benson-and-Hedges smile and she's a doctor, nobody's perfect after all. She

228

slides the ultrasound around me this way and that and smiles at me again. And then we wait. Five seconds. Seven seconds. It's got to be more than ten seconds now. She re-positions it and clears her throat and smiles at me again. She looks worried, should I be worried? Should we have heard something by now? What if we never hear anything, would that be the end of the world? Perhaps I'm not meant to be a mum, not this time. Perhaps I will walk out of here and never have this baby, start over with Laurence and have a new baby, with none of these complications. It occurs to me that I am maybe not as horrified by this possibility as I should be. Or perhaps this is just my mind playing tricks on me, throwing dark thoughts in there just to freak me out. This particular dark thought thuds away somewhere in the recesses of my mind. Thud, thud, thud. Then I realize that this thud is not the thud of my dark thought at all, but of my baby's heart, clear and regular as a metronome. It fills me with relief, a sudden, delicious relief that almost makes me laugh out loud, 'There it is! I heard it!' But there it is again, along with the wild joy, that faint but definite tinge of anxiety. This baby's coming, like it or not.

I'm sitting in front of Dr Cork now, she's scribbling notes, intermittently looking at me from beneath her frizzy, black fringe.

'So,' she says, 'baby's strong as an ox but what about mum? Mm? How's mum?'

'Yeah great,' I shrug, after a pause. It always takes me a moment or two to realize that 'mum' means me.

'And dad? How's dad feeling about impending fatherhood? Excited?'

'Oh yeah, he's *really* excited.'

'Started painting the nursery yet?'

'Well, no. Well, basically.' I take a deep breath. 'I'm sort of in what would be the nursery so, erm, I'm not sure how we'll work that one out.' I laugh, nervously.

229

Dr Cork crosses her legs and ponders this for a second. The creak of the floorboards in the room above seems suddenly deafening. 'So you are in what would be the nursery . . .' her voice trails off. 'You mean, you're *both* in what would be the nursery? So it's a one bedroom flat, right?'

'No, it's got two.'

'Oh.' She looks stumped. Dr Cork's the sort to want to get everything right. 'So, you're not in the same bedroom at the moment but . . .'

'We're not together,' I cut in. I can't bear to drag this out any longer. 'We're not a couple. Basically what happened was, we were friends – friends who occasionally had sex, admittedly, but we were still just good friends.' Dr Cork straightens up in her chair, suddenly intrigued. 'Then one night we both got really drunk at Jim's place – Jim's the dad by the way – and I never learnt to drive, because my mother refused to get me driving lessons in case I blew up the engine or killed myself by crashing into a lamppost on the first lesson.' She smiles, amused. 'And I didn't want to get a night bus home because there's always loads of strange characters on the night buses and also I was drunk, I was four-pints drunk *at least*. And one thing led to another and we ended up having unprotected sex, on my most fertile day of the month as luck would have it.' I raise an eyebrow, sarcastically. 'I didn't have a condom which is bad, I know. But neither did Jim, although I'm very careful not to fire the blame. (This is bollocks, I'm always firing the blame.) And I was wearing these stupid frilly tie-at-the-side knickers for the simple reason that they were the first thing I pulled out of my drawer that morning although Jim doesn't believe that, he thinks I'm a prick tease.' Dr Cork gives a phlegmy chuckle.

I cannot believe I am telling my doctor this stuff! If she didn't have a packet of fags and a bottle of Jamesons in her top drawer (oh yes, nothing gets past me) I definitely wouldn't be. 'And so that's how I got pregnant and come to be having a baby with my friend – who's not my boyfriend, never has been my boyfriend, and never will be my boyfriend. And the most infuriating thing is it was all so, so *avoidable*.' To my horror, I start welling up. Dr Cork passes me a tissue with a look on her face that tells me I am definitely not the only hormonal nutter to breakdown in her surgery.

'So there's no way getting pregnant could change your feelings about . . .'

'No. Everyone says that and before you ask, it was a mutual decision. Not to suddenly become an "item" that is.'

'OK but you're living with him, right?'

'Yes.' I wipe my face with the tissue, a big clump of mascara comes off. 'He was kind enough to offer me to live rent free in separate rooms until the baby is born and I've saved up for a deposit on a flat.'

'And then what are you going to do?' she asks, in that no-nonsense way that she does.

'Move out, I guess, into my own flat as near as possible to Jim so we can share the childcare, "co-parent" – I think that's the modern term,' I say, all too aware that 'co-parenting' does not seem quite so cool in reality.

'Oh, so he wants to be involved then?'

The very fact she asks this, the possibility that he might *not* want to be fully involved seems bizarre to me. I realize I have not even considered that. Perhaps because Jim has never given me reason to.

'Oh yeah, Jim wants to be involved alright. He'd start antenatal classes now if he could, buy a pram just to practise with if I let him. He's more excited about having this baby than me.'

'So you trust and like this man then, he's a good friend, not some sort of . . .' She leans in and whispers the next bit, 'fuck buddy?'

I shake my head, embarrassed but it's only when she says this that I get an inkling as to how the majority of people might see our situation: girl has casual sex with boy, girl gets knocked up, boy runs a mile at the first sign of a bump. But that's not Jim. We're not that cliché.

'No. *No*.' I lean forward, emphatically. 'We're really close. Jim's a gorgeous person, I think you'd like him. He's funny and genuine and totally individual. He cries at stuff on the news and he's great with his family – and that's saying something because they're like the Addams Family – and he's dead sweet with his mum. But he's tough, too, do you know what I mean?'

'Mm-mm,' she nods, smiling.

'He doesn't put up with any of my hormonal rubbish anyway and he's loyal, he's solid as a rock, is Jim. He'd never let you down.'

Dr Cork sits, hand over mouth, digesting this information for a minute or two. Then she leans forward, splaying her hands on the desk and she says, 'So, forgive me. Do tell me if I am speaking out of line here but as I understand it, this fella, this Jim –' she counts each point on a pale, bony finger '– he's loyal, he really wants to be a dad, he's agreed to let you live in a house rent free whilst you save up for a deposit. He makes you laugh, he's genuine and to top it all off, it wasn't just the once you two got it on, was it? I mean you'd been having on/off sex for a while, yes?'

'Yes,' I say, meekly.

'So, do tell me if I'm just being a nosy old Irish pain in the arse,' she says. She smiles. I smile back and fill up with tears all at the same time. 'But why aren't you together again? Because I can tell you, those sorts of men don't come around very often. Most men in this situation would run a bloody mile and I should know.' She cups her mouth with her hand as if she's telling me a secret, saying, 'You don't get to look this haggard if you haven't had your heart broken a fair few times. Plus,' she adds, her eyes narrow and glint, 'I think you love this fella, don't you?'

I give a short embarrassed laugh. Put like this, she has a great case, it is hard to see why we're not together. But it's the last bit that puts a spanner in the works. That's the broken fuse in this particular circuit.

'I do love him, we love each other. But we're not, I'm not "in love with him",' I finally manage.

'Ah,' she says, with a slow smile. 'That old chestnut.'

I walk through Camden Passage towards the tube gawping at things I can't afford. That was a bit heavy for a check up. I certainly didn't bargain for that when I went in today. But I like Dr Cork, I like her hard-living ways and her tough love approach. She makes me think.

However, I also know I'm right. I do love Jim, but it's not the sort of love to build for ever on. Love is what happened when I saw Laurence standing across the road from me last week on Regent Street and I felt that thrill take hold like a temporary insanity. Love is what happened when he called, asked me out to dinner and I couldn't even hear his voice, the rush in my ears was deafening. Love has to be intoxicating, maddening, about I'd-die-for-you passion – *especially* at the beginning – or else we'd all be up the duff by our mates, walking down the aisle with Mr Platonic, surely?

When I finally get to the office at 11 a.m., Jocelyn's got 'that look' on her face.

'Why have you got that look on your face?' I ask, hanging up my jacket.

'What look?'

'The look that says, "I've got something to tell you but you'll have to pin me down and extract it with pliers before I do".'

'Oh well, now that is rude,' she says, podgy hands on generous hips. 'I was just happy to see you that's all.'

Today Jocelyn's wearing a Pucci-esque print blouse knotted at the front to reveal a doughy, pale midriff and cropped, white trousers with a broderie anglaise trim.

'Now, how is the little mite?' she adds, unperturbed.

'What? Oh, the scan. Yeah, good thanks Jocelyn,' I say. 'Its heartbeat's going strong, my blood pressure's all good.'

'Great. Daddy come then?' She says it like this is the second of a hundred planned questions and she needs to say them really fast in order to get them all out.

'No he's teaching.'

'Teaching? I thought he worked in a bar?'

'Yeah he does.' My conscience squeezes my insides. 'He's teaching in a bar. New barman, you see. He's teaching him the ropes.'

I pick up the *Mirror* from Jocelyn's desk and walk over to mine before she asks me anything else, cursing myself for that astronomical cock up. It never ceases to amaze me how huge, fat lies just fly out of my mouth. It's as if I committed the ultimate scandal when I got pregnant in the first place and now I think 'what the hell!' A few more mini scandals won't hurt. Except they do, I just don't know how to stop.

Anne-Marie is standing on a stool writing out the new Features List on the whiteboard when I get to my desk. Next to my name she's put:

Murdered swinger

Dating Guru Dog

I still love my elephant man

I am too busy concentrating on this to notice the message written on a Post-it stuck to my screen. It is written in Anne-Marie's hand-writing and starts: HE WANTS YOU BAAAD, GIRLFRIEND . . . Which really makes me laugh because she never uses phrases like that. Our new black intern from

234

Atlanta, does. The note continues ... Laurence called, 10.10a.m., he says meet him tonight, 8p.m., Angel station. Wear something foxy, he's going to spoil you!

I read the note, forget, for a joyful, fleeting moment, all my worries and all the complications, before my stomach swarms with realization and dread.

'Did you um . . .' Anne-Marie is still writing on the white-board, I talk to her back, unable to swallow. 'Did you actually speak to Laurence? Anne-Marie? Chat to him about the baby, about him being about to be a father . . . or anything . . . by any chance?'

Because if you did, I will kill you. And then myself. What sort of fantasist would that make me look!

Anne-Marie continues writing on the board and I'm not sure she's heard me then she mumbles, so vaguely and quietly I have to crane my head to hear it.

'The scan . . . yeah, um . . . ' I can't tell if she's deliberately trying to make this agonizing for me – she can be warped like that – or if she's just trying to zone in. There's an awful few moments where I anticipate the worst and then she says, 'No, no, come to think of it. I didn't actually speak to him.'

I mouth 'thank you' and internally punch the air.

'He obviously tried to call you.' She steps down from the stool and turns to face me. 'But he must have got diverted to Joss's phone because he left a message. I just took it down for you.'

'Oh.' I beam at her now. 'Thanks, Anne-Marie. That's really great.'

Jocelyn comes waddling around the corner, thighs brushing, her bright hair swinging. 'So, has she seen it?'

'Abso-bloody-lutely!' Anne-Marie clicks the top back on her marker pen and smiles inanely at me like a proud aunt. 'She's a fucking lucky bitch, that's for sure. The most romantic

235

thing Greg's ever done is to invite me to a Vegan March and even then he was dressed up as a pig so it wasn't exactly . . .' she makes a thoroughly un-erotic face, 'erotic.'

I can't concentrate for the rest of the day, excitement fizzing up inside me, making me feel that should it spill over, I'd start laughing manically and never be able to stop.

An email from Vicky slightly takes the sheen off things . . .

From victoria.peddlar@hotmail.com
Dead bored, client cancelled, nothing to do but sit here and ponder your love life (you know you love it.)
So how's it going? Have you practically got his n' hers dressing gowns now? Is it making you feel different living together? Bet it is . . .!! You are SO Ross and Rachel! Rich is doing my head in, haven't seen him for about a fortnight. He spends all his time locked away working on his screenplay (so deluded) When he does finally come downstairs I can't get a word out of him.

I email her back, giving nothing away:

To victoria.peddlar@hotmail.com
From: tess_jarvis@giant.co.uk
Nope, sorry. No declarations of love just yet and the chances of me getting a dressing gown that matches Jim's (Have you seen Jim's dressing gown?) are nil.
p.s. Rich is clearly a frustrated 'artiste', try to give him a break?!

After what feels like the longest afternoon in history I'm finally on the bus home, crawling up the grimy Walworth Road with its pound shops and African restaurants, consumed by the vital question: what the hell am I going to wear? Do I go with the smock look and chance looking a bit frumpy but not drawing attention to the growing bump which could, I'm sure, be very off putting, mainly because it's just at that stage where I look like I ate all the pies then ordered some more. Or do I go for something tighter, feel potentially sexier, but also look fat with colossal boobs? It's six of one and half a dozen of another.

I hang my bag on the banister and shout through to the kitchen, 'Busy day at the office, dear?'

'Barely drawn breath,' shouts Jim with mock seriousness. 'Absolutely chocka block.'

I tie my hair back and saunter into the kitchen, looking forward to our usual post-work debrief but am stopped in my tracks. 'Wow,' I say, drinking in the scene before me. 'You *have* been busy.'

The place looks like Heston Blumenthal's laboratory. Pots boiling on every ring of the hob, every inch of the worktop covered with vegetable peelings, spice refills, scatterings of flour and smears of sauce. The washing-up bowl is piled high with pans and roasting trays and all sorts of cooking paraphernalia I can't even identify and right in the middle of all this is Jim, apron splattered with something tomato-based. He's pulled out the extendable table and dressed it in flickering tea lights. The Divine Comedy plays softly in the background.

'Bloody hell, whoever's coming round is in for a treat.'

'Nobody's coming round,' Jim says cheerfully, taking a heavy earthenware dish out of the oven. My smile dissolves. 'I just thought since you'd been living here a fortnight now, I'd do us a Jim spesh, cook us something proper, make an evening of it, you know.'

'Jim.' I figure it's best just to get it out now. 'I can't stay, I'm really sorry, I'm going out.'

'Oh, are you?' Jim looks at me, he looks a bit disappointed but not, I hope, actually pissed off. 'Oh well, no worries. It was no big deal although –' he says it with humour but I

237

can't help think he is a little miffed '– I would draw your attention, Miss Jarvis, to the house rule?'

'Oh no, I *know*, I'm so sorry, I feel really bad! I should have rung.'

'Offal and line-caught cod with broad bean puré ratatouille, too . . . Oh well, more for me.'

'What a shame,' I say, thinking, bloody hell, that was close. Lucky escape on the offal front. 'It sounds amazing Jim. It really does.'

Jim dithers about, I need to get ready but feel bad just dashing off upstairs when he's gone to such an effort, then he says, 'So where are you going? Have you got a work thing on? I thought you were going to tell them you needed to cut those down?' He shoves a tray of courgette in the oven. I look at the clock and realize I have approximately twenty-five minutes to get out of the door.

'It's not a work thing,' I say, his concern making me feel even more wretched. 'I'm meeting Laurence and some other people (lies! All lies!) Just for a pizza. Sorry, I should have told you earlier . . .'

'No, it's OK,' he shrugs, before sticking his head in a cupboard, scouring for some herb or other. 'Well, maybe I'll ask Gina round then, she's back from New York.'

'Good idea,' I say, a smidgen jealous that she called Jim to say she was back and not me. 'Well she'll definitely want to show off her pictures and be up for some free food. Give her a ring now, before she eats.'

I slip out of the kitchen, have a two-minute shower – cutting my leg shaving in two places in the process – and throw open my wardrobe to weigh up the options. I try on some maternity-could-pass-as-non-maternity wear but none of it gets me excited. Then I have a brainwave – the lightweight jumper dress – not too try hard, conceals any sort of slightly inappropriate bump (I don't want to wave it right in front of his face. There's plenty of time for that, when I'm enormous, and we can no longer pretend it's not happening . . .) but it also shows just the right amount of leg to be sexy. I team this with suede, knee high, three-inch-heel fuck me boots and the best smoky eyes I can muster. As I grab my bag and run downstairs, I can hear Jim on the phone to Gina talking about wine, so, I assume, she must be coming. That's good I say to myself, good he's not wasted all that gorgeous food. But there's another feeling there, nestling beneath the surface. A feeling that's ever so slightly taken the edge off tonight like arriving on holiday to find that it's raining.

'Right I'm off,' I say, getting my keys off the breakfast bar. 'Have a great night.'

'You too,' says Jim, as he takes something out of the oven. Then he turns around, looks at me, then does a double take.

'Wow,' he says, vegetables sliding to one side. 'You're a bit dolled up, aren't you? For a pizza on a Thursday night?'

CHAPTER TWENTY-ONE

Frank was conceived on a pool table in a Greek taverna. I hardly expected to see the guy again let alone have his baby. But Stef came to visit when Frank was five months old. That was ten years ago now and we've been married for five.'

Claire, 30, Worcester

Angel station echoes with wet footseps and every time a dark head emerges at the top of the escalator, the gathering thump-thump of my heart. I am standing beneath the clock, next to a busker playing 'Have I Told You Lately That I Love You' on the pan pipes, self-consciously folding my arms across my dress and trying – in vain – to breathe in.

I spot another dark head coming up the escalator. Oh God, is that him? It's the right, dusty-dark skin tone, the long, elegant nose. I walk towards the barrier giving a little wave, the nerves making my fingers flutter like leaves. I'm arranging my facial muscles to look calm and collected when the man lifts his head up and I realize oh, it's not him at all.

I look at the clock, it's now 8.10 p.m. Ten minutes late and no phone call, no text, no 'I might be a bit late', which is a bit weird since he's the one who organized this whole evening but I'm not unduly worried. By 8.15 I *am* worried. By 8.23 I'm pissed off. But then, just as I'm about to consider the option that the little scally has stood me up and whether I should leave a semi-abusive message on his phone, there he is, the eyebrows first, then the dark, mischievous eyes, darting from one side of the concourse to the next. The way he looks self-conscious as if he doesn't want me to see him looking for me, is really, incredibly cute. He's wearing perfectly worn-in cords and a loosely knitted, expensive-looking polo shirt. All is naturally forgiven. But then he could have been wearing a nylon shellsuit and all would have been forgiven.

'Oh, so you finally decided to rock up then, what time do you call this?' I say, coyly, reaching on my tip toes to give him a kiss. But he doesn't kiss me back, he looks down so I miss his mouth and get the middle of his nose.

'Sorry.' He takes my hand at least, swings it back and forth. 'I . . .' He looks around, wipes imaginary sweat from his brow. 'I had something to do in town and it took longer than I thought.'

'Oh right.' The queasy emptiness of disappointment. 'Well if something's happened or you've just had a really shit day then.'

Then no, NO! don't say we can do this another time!

'No it's cool.' He eventually pecks me on the mouth. 'Come on, let's go, let's walk and talk.'

'So, how are you, good day?' asks Laurence. We step outside into a sudden beam of sunshine, the air smells of wet tarmac and roses from a nearby flower stall.

I went to the doctor's to hear my baby's heartbeat, the one that's beating right now, with mine . . . I decide that might just be too much information.

'You know, usual nonsense at work. I have to do an interview next week with this woman who reckons her cocker spaniel guides her on her choice of men.'

'No I meant, how are you? You know . . .' he looks at my stomach. He has a look of Gina when he does this, like I might smell if she got too close. 'Do you feel sick? I mean, is there anything you can't eat? Is there anything you'll only eat, like I dunno, pickled onions, isn't that what pregnant women eat?'

Laurence lights a cigarette and takes a hard, sucking drag before blowing the smoke out sideways. I look at him and laugh.

'No, sick bit over thanks. There were a few nasty accidents at the beginning, but I promise I won't barf on you in the restaurant. Just perfectly normal cuisine will do. Only thing I really can't eat is shellfish, pate, and un-pasturized cheese.'

There's no mention of Bedales.

We walk along Upper Street, navigating the heaving crowds of young, free (and babyless) types whose weekends begin on Thursday nights simply because they can't wait till Friday. The weather's been undecided of late – buckets of rain followed by brief explosions of sunshine and consequently rainbows, one of which arches the sky now, making the puddles we're dodging glisten, multi-coloured.

We swerve to avoid a man with a dog and Laurence's left hand brushes mine. My instinct is to grab hold of it but there seems to be a great chasm between us. Laurence seems distant, it's in his body language, the way he's smoking with one hand and has the other in his pocket.

I ask him about his day too but I don't get much out of him except the fact that he's pissed off with his boss, who's an 'arrogant cock' (Laurence does have a touch of the wronged teenager about him sometimes, it comes from being permanently lectured by his lecturer dad) and pissed off with the chef who's 'a useless cock'. That's it then, I decide. He's just pissed off full stop. It's nothing to do with me, or the baby, or anything I've done and once he sits down and gets a drink inside of him, he'll be fine, I'll be fine, everything will be fine.

We continue on past The York where students sit on the cobbles outside, cradling pints of cider. I think back to all the times we made this walk from the tube to my house on balmy summer evenings when we were going out. Laurence always held my hand back then, firm and warm like he was proud of me. Despite not always being the most reliable boyfriend in many ways, he was always the one to instigate public displays of affection: he'd have me sit on his knee whilst he stroked my thigh in the pub, sneak up behind me and slip his hand down my top when I was standing at the bar. But that was OK because he was not some leering bloke, he was my boyfriend. My cute-as-hell, amazing boyfriend. Of course I'd protest, girlishly, roll my eyes in agreement when Gina looked at us and laughed, 'Jesus man, she's going to turn into bread if you knead her anymore,' but secretly I loved it. Of course I bloody did!

'So where are we going then?' I say, cheerfully, looking up at Laurence and trotting to keep up. I'm secretly hoping it's Frederick's near Camden Passage or maybe he's gone for cosy and intimate at The Elk in the Woods or gone French and candlelit at Le Mercury. I really don't mind as long as we get to eat soon, otherwise I am at risk of eating my own arm. Laurence doesn't answer and I worry that perhaps it's not the etiquette to ask. Then, he suddenly stops in the street, stubs his fag out and says, 'Just wait there.'

He disappears into a smart looking restaurant with dark wood tables and stark,white tablecloths.

This has got to be it, no doubt he knows the management. Laurence is such a networker, he probably knows everyone in the catering business. He's probably reserved some little nook just for us.

He chats briefly to the barman, me standing on the pavement

feeling like a bit of an idiot. Then, rather than usher me in like I expect him to, he strides towards the door, swings it open, mumbles some expletive then marches on ahead, leaving me behind. 'Come on, let's just go,' he says, lighting another cigarette. I try to keep up like some stupid confused lapdog. 'What happened?' I shout over the traffic.

'Nothing,' he says moodily.

'Did they pretend they knew nothing about your booking?'

'Yeah, something like that. He was just a tosser anyway, let's go somewhere else.'

We walk on and on, the day has faded to a cool, lilac glow and I can feel the life force slipping out of me, and my 10 p.m. curfew – at which point I lose the ability to communicate, fast-approaching. We cross the road to Le Mercury. Something about the noisy clatter of my stiletto boots is suddenly making me feel ridiculous, overdressed. Clearly this is not panning out to be the occasion I had envisaged.

My hopes are lifted however when Laurence storms inside and starts talking to someone who looks like the manager. He's probably family, I think, Laurence has got something up his sleeve I just know it. But then I can see the man looking around as if for spare tables, then shake his head and gesture, apologetically. Laurence looks flustered and walks towards the door. My mood plummets.

He hasn't booked anywhere has he? Like so many of Laurence's big ideas, grand gestures, it just didn't materialize. I'm getting a horrid, all-consuming sinking feeling that this whole evening is a bit of a chore for Laurence, that I am an inconvenient distraction from whatever he was doing beforehand. That he's changed his mind.

He's strutting towards me now that same petulant expression in his face. 'Come on,' he says again, 'let's go.' But I've had enough. I stop in the street and fold my arms. 'You didn't book anywhere did you?'

Laurence turns around – his eyes are dark and pretty as a fawn's (God, I wish he wasn't so beautiful) – and gives me a self-incriminating huff.

'I don't mind (that's a lie) but just tell me because you know, I'm pregnant, I just need to eat. Otherwise I'm going to start digesting my own stomach.'

Laurence rubs his forehead and sighs as if puzzled by how this could possibly have happened. 'OK, look I'm sorry,' he says. 'I was going to take you to this wicked French restaurant, spoil you rotten and make it really special. But then I got waylaid and you know how it is, I just ran out of time.'

'Is it the baby Laurence? Because if it is, just tell me. If you've changed your mind?'

'No it's not the baby.'

We end up in Pizza Express – which is fine if I had been led to believe it was going to be that sort of night, but sitting there, totally overdressed in my mini dress, smoky eyes and heels, I feel utterly humiliated. We even have to go for a drink nearby because there aren't any tables free until 10 p.m. By the time we actually eat I am so hungry I practically inhale the pizza. Then that's about it, that's the sum total of our 'romantic' night. We make small talk and a weak attempt at gazing into each other eyes, as if by running through the actions, the feelings will come but I know his heart's not in it and I wonder if mine is still. He's made me feel stupid, and already, sitting here munching on dough balls, the bright overhead lights blaring, I'm not sure we can go anywhere from here.

He doesn't talk about Chloe and I don't ask him. He doesn't say anything else about the baby, and I don't tell him. I immediately slip into a carb-induced near-coma after eating anyway and can barely manage to keep my eyes open let alone have major discussions about the future.

We're standing outside the restaurant now, it's suddenly freezing cold.

245

'Let's go for a drink,' says Laurence suddenly.

The thought of alcohol is for the first time, abhorrent.

'Nah, thanks I don't really fancy it. I can't really drink, Laurence, I'm pregnant, remember.'

'Come back to my place then,' he says, lighting a cigarette.

'No, honestly, I'm knackered.' I fold my arms in an attempt to keep warm.

'I'll call you a cab in an hour.'

'Laurence, *no*.'

'Right.' He looks away smiling but defeated, then pulls the collar up on his top. It suits him, draws attention to his naturally sucked in cheeks.

'OK, well . . . I'll call you this weekend then,' he says, stepping forward, hands in pockets.

'OK.' I suddenly feel desperate to get home. 'Thanks for the pizza.'

Laurence gives an embarrassed laugh through his nose. 'Whatever,' he says. 'I promise to do better next time.'

A cab approaches, I hail it, kiss Laurence on the cheek and get in. We go over Blackfriars Bridge, London opening out into a fairground of colour, boats gliding beneath us, life moving on. And I know there won't be a next time.

As soon as I put my keys in the lock I can hear laughter. Gina's laughter.

The house smells of struck matches, stewed fruit and Gina's perfume. Van Morrison is playing. My CD.

'Hi guys,' I shout, as I walk through the door.

'Hi,' they both shout back, in laughter-punctuated unison.

Gina's reclined on the sofa, her newly tanned feet on Jim's knees. There's two empty bottles of wine and one still on the go.

'Hey, stranger.' Gina wipes an actual tear of laughter from her face. I don't recall ever seeing her laugh like that.

'How was Le Cane?' she gives an exaggerated wink.

'Yeah, great thanks.' I sound completely unconvincing. 'How was New York more to the point? Hilarious, obviously.'

The snipeyness comes from somewhere I don't recognize. Thankfully they're both far too pissed to notice.

'Amaazing,' she gushes.

'You've got to see the pictures,' says Jim.

'Me and Michelle want to live there, I'm telling you, best city in the world.'

'So did you pull?' I ask, feeling suddenly sickened by New York, by this, by everything. 'You know me,' slurs Gina.

'I'll take that as a yes, then. And the food? Did you have pancakes, eggs sunny-side-up and all that? You still look skinny.'

'Amazing, stuffed my face.' She pokes Jim playfully. 'But it was nowhere near as good as what I ate tonight.'

'Oh yeah, how was the dinner, Jim?'

'OhmiGod, *lush*,' gushes Gina, totally cutting in.

'Great, perfect actually,' confirms Jim, through drunken, half-closed eyes. 'But we're a bit pissed, sorry.' For some reason his apologetic grimace makes me want to punch him, square in the face.

'You don't have to apologize,' I say. 'Anyway, I'm knackered. Have a good rest of the night, I'm off to bed.'

I brush my teeth vigorously and spit into the sink. Where the hell did that come from? That feeling, just then? It was like milk turning sour, a curdling of feelings. And I didn't recognize it, I definitely didn't like it. Downstairs, I can still hear the gentle lull of 'Coney Island'. I bet Gina went to Coney Island when she was in New York. I bet she's telling Jim all about it. I walk onto the landing, I hear the lounge door open, hushed laughter in the hallway, the creak of the front door. Gina's leaving. I go into my room and watch from the window. Outside the night is black and starless and I can see the smoke from Gina's cigarette trail behind her as she walks away. My rooms feels cold, I shut the curtains, get straight into bed and turn out the light.

I'm just drifting off when it suddenly occurs to me, the feeling, that feeling, it's jealousy. I'm *jealous*?! Must be the hormones I think. Just the hormones, messing with your head. Two hours later, I'm still wide awake.

CHAPTER TWENTY-TWO

'My waters broke at 6.10 p.m., ten minutes after the last boat to the mainland. Angus was delivered by the landlady of The Jura, on our living room floor at ten to two in the morning. He was the eighth baby she'd delivered and the seventh Angus in our family. The next day, it was wonderful, half the island came to wet the baby's head.'

Gillian, 61, Isle of Jura

I realize now, as I lie in bed meeting the steely glare of Eminem, that I must have been suffering from a severe case of pregnancy battiness to even *think* it could have worked out with Laurence. After forty-eight hours of mulling it over I can see that my expectations were a joke. I mean, what on earth did I think he'd say when I told him I was up the duff?

'Brilliant! I have a fetish for lactating nipples, and women who cry at not being able to work tin openers, especially when the baby in question is not my own, and sleep deprivation? Love it to bits! Who needs eight hours sleep when you can have three!'

Vicky called me at work yesterday, 'just checking up' on whether I had met up with Laurence and if so, if I had fulfilled my promise and told him I had a bun in the oven. (I didn't tell her about Sebastian Snail. There are some things in life that other people just do not need to know. Even your best friends.) I could have relayed the Pizza Express date in every gruesome detail but frankly, I couldn't be arsed. The fact is, it was a non event, so non, I told it her it hadn't happened at all, that he'd never even called.

'So does this mean you're not going to be seeing him anymore?' she said, breathily. 'And that you and Jim are . . .'

'No,' I snapped. 'It doesn't mean anything. *Nothing* means anything. Ever again.'

'Right, I'll shut up then,' said Vicky, sharply. And that was it, she hasn't asked about it since.

The pneumatic drill starts up outside. They've been digging up Lordship Lane for weeks now. I close my eyes, an image of Laurence slides onto my eyelids and I allow myself, just for a moment or two, to indulge in reverie, to imagine what it might have been like if things had been different: if I'd have held on longer, for example, told him about the baby when we were further down the line with our relationship. If we'd got married, moved to France. Maybe I'd have a job on *Paris Match*, we'd live on a tree-lined boulevard in an apartment with shutters, I'd spend weekends riding a basket-fronted bicycle dropping baguettes into said basket whilst wearing a flimsy skirt and permanent expression of gay abandon on my face . . . But then I figure it's all irrelevant anyway because in the end, in the words of Queen, nothing *does* really matter because life will just do what it wants anyway and the more it strays from what you expect, the harder it is to envisage what exactly that might be.

I throw back the duvet and stand up, pulling back the curtain so hard it almost comes off its runners.

I peer down onto the street, there's one there already And it's only eight o'clock. A yummy mummy-yummy daddy twosome with yummy baby in yummy pushchair. If I squint, the bloke looks a bit like Laurence: tall, olive-skinned, same perfectly shaped head. I watch them saunter in the sun to the end of the street, the guy stopping to give the baby a drink, to stroke his hair, to tenderly get something out of the girl's eye to . . . .*Oh pack it in you ridiculous woman, he's probably gambled their life savings away.*

I go back to bed. When I wake up, forty minutes or so later, Saturday is hotting up outside and a full on row hotting up in the kitchen. I recognize Jim's voice immediately, agitated but in control. But there's another voice, one I don't recognize at all. It's a girl's and it's teetering on the brink of hysterics.

'Jim *please*, why not? You're supposed to be my brother.'

Ten years I've known Jim, and I've never met his coke addict sister once. I'm a mixture of grotesquely fascinated and a little bit scared.

I sit down at the top of the stairs and wrap my nightie around my knees so I can hear better, like I used to when I was little and mum and dad had friends round for a cheese fondue. (There was something in that emmenthal. They always ended up screeching at the top of their lungs to 'Born in the USA'.)

Jim's voice is weary but firm.

'Look, if it was anything else you needed I'd help you, you know I would. I did, in fact, only last week and you totally took the piss.'

Dawn had been an hour late to her meeting with her Addiction Project Manager and high as a kite. Jim had taken a whole day off work to attend it with her. He was not amused.

'But I can't have you come and stay, I'm sorry, it's just not fair. Tess is pregnant and to put it bluntly, I don't feel comfortable having you in the house when you're like this. How do

I know if I can trust you? It's not as if you have the best track record with mum.'

'Thanks a fucking lot!' As Dawn lifts up her face I notice that although she was probably once really pretty, she looks haggard; closer to forty than thirty-three. 'Do you really think I'd sink so low as to steal from my own little brother?'

'Yes. You've done it to your own mother, why am I any different?'

'Because you are! Because you're my brother, because we've always been in this together, you've always looked out for me.'

'Not anymore, sorry Dawn. I'll have my own baby in a few months, I can't be babysitting you anymore.'

Curiosity is getting the better of me now, I creep downstairs, as quietly as I can and peer through the banister where I can get a closer look at her.

She's tall and skinny like Jim, with high-lighted hair pulled back in a messy bun and the same prominent nose. But she's glamorous, too, in a bling kind of way. She's wearing tight cut-off jeans, a cropped leather bomber jacket and sky-high, wooden-heeled shoes with gold studs on. Every time she shakes her arms about, which is all the time, the twenty or so bangles that take up her left fore-arm, jangle noisily.

She leans against the worktop and bites her nails. The skin on her midriff is mottled, like salami.

'You think I'm such a loser, such a waster don't you Jim?'

'No, *you* think you're a loser. I just think you need help.'

'Yes Jim!' Her voice reverberates around the kitchen. 'That's what I'm asking for, that's why I'm here. God, you're so fucking righteous. You're not so perfect yourself, you know. At least I stayed with mum when dad left. At least I didn't fuck off to my mate's house when she needed me most and had the pigs ringing her up in the middle of the night for the next six months.'

Pigs? Police? Has the father of my child got some dodgy criminal past he's just omitted to tell me about?!

'Oh fuck off Dawn, that only happened about three times. It wasn't just you who was dealing with dad leaving, and anyway you've more than made up for it since. At least I didn't start stuffing cocaine up my nose when things got a bit heavy. At least I sorted my life out.'

'I am sorting my life out, that's why I want to come here, to get away from the dealers and mum and fucking Stokey which is doing my head in.'

'Oh, and you think you won't be able to get hold of drugs here? In London? Jesus, Dawn, you're so naïve. You're already high anyway, I can see it in your eyes.'

There's a long silence. From the corner of my eye I see Jim hang his head then go over to his sister and try to hug her.

'Look I'm sorry, OK?' he says. 'Perhaps if it was another time and Tess wasn't pregnant.' But she brushes him off . . .

'Dawn,' Jim shouts after her, following her to the front door. 'Oh for fuck's sake, don't be like that, look . . .'

But it's too late, she's gone, her wooden high-heeled clogs clip-clopping down the front path.

Jim slams the door shut. 'Oh sod yer then, you stupid coke head bitch,' I hear him mutter as he trundles off in his dressing gown. I can't help but smirk. I've never known Jim speak like that before. But he hears me.

'Tess.' His expression is one of surprise and embarrassment. 'Have you been sitting there all the time?'

I cower, guiltily. He gives an amused tut. 'Oh marvellous,' he says as he shuffles off back into the kitchen. 'So now you really know the truth about my mental family.'

'So, is she alright? Why can't she come and stay?' I ask, getting up from the stairs and following him in the kitchen.

'No,' says Jim, pointing at me. He takes two crumpets out of the bread bin. 'Just no, alright? You've got no idea

253

what she's like. And anyway, you shouldn't have been listening.'

'Sorry,' I mumble. 'Although I have to confess, I did hear everything. So, what's this about you and being in trouble with the police, eh?'

'Oh nothing, it was just a bit of joyriding.'

'*Joyriding*!!? Just a bit of joyriding?!'

'*Yes,* so?' The crumpets pop up and Jim takes them out of the toaster and drops them on the side. 'My dad had just left, I went a bit off the rails, give me a break.'

'Did you get a criminal record?' I'm shocked, Jim's always seemed so in possession of himself, I can't imagine him caving in to teenage angst. I follow him into the lounge.

'No, just a caution.'

'Did you cause any damage?'

'What, in our two week reign of terror around Stoke-on-Trent?' he scoffs and for a moment I see that beanpole of an attitude-ridden teenager. 'A tree and my mate's collarbone. And the bloke's car, obviously. Unluckily for us, he was a local policeman.'

I start laughing. 'You idiot, Jim, that is so you. Is there anything else you want to tell me? A secret past as a rent boy? Dawn said there were a *few* calls to your mum from the police?'

'Drunk and disorderly.' Jim bites into his crumpet. I get the feeling he's actually showing off now. 'I got arrested for being drunk and disorderly the week after that.'

'No way! Really? Did you have to spend a night in a cell?'

'In hospital. Me and my mates were legging it away from the police and I got impaled on a fence.'

'That's hilarious!' I double up laughing.

'It's not funny, Tess', he says. 'I nearly lost my right bollock. Two millimetres to the right and there wouldn't have been any baby Ashcroft.'

Jim slurps on his tea, I get the feeling that's the end of the conversation. He's got two days' growth of stubble and hasn't bothered to put his contact lenses in today, or yesterday come to think of it. Not that I saw him much yesterday, he was out at Awful's all evening then went straight to bed when he got in. Although that could have been the fact I was hogging the sofa with an Alice band in my hair and toothpaste on my spots.

'You're so good with them, Jim,' I say, looking at him as he rubs the side of his face, all stressed out. 'With your sister, your mum.'

'Yeah well.' He smiles, matter-of-factly. 'I don't have much choice, do I? They're my family.'

'Do you want to talk about it?'

'No, don't worry. I don't want my dysfunctional family to put a dampener on your Saturday morning. Or mine for that matter. Oh, but I know what I forgot to tell you. A bloke called this morning, Fraser is it?'

'Oh! She had it?'

'Yeah, little girl, seven pounds something. Everything's fine, all fingers and toes, mum and baby well . . .' He stops, he thinks. 'What else are you meant to ask when someone's had a baby?'

'Her name, Jim. What's her name?'

'Oh.' Jim wipes away a bit of butter that's running down his chin. 'Something fancy and foreign, to be honest I only asked out of politeness.'

'Jim! The name's the most important bit. Was it Esme?'

'No, it definitely wasn't that.'

'Giselle?'

'*Gisom?* What? No. I'd have remembered something so ridiculous.'

'Manon?'

'*Manon.* Now, you might be onto something there. Yes,' he says, suddenly, decisively. 'It was definitely that.'

'I knew it,' I say, smugly, sipping on my tea. 'I knew they'd call her that.'

'Only a girl,' mumbles Jim, shaking his head, 'would get excited about guessing a baby's name.'

An hour later and I'm laid out on the sofa, Jim is curled up on the bobbly armchair, one foot tucked under the other, the Travel section of the *Guardian* folded back so he can hold it with one hand. With his other hand, he's twirling strands of hair round till they become stiff like meringue, at which point he moves onto another one which means his head is now covered in dark little spikes.

I look at him out of the corner of my eye, the sun streaming through the window makes the skin on his legs look even more translucent and his hair more glossy. Deep chocolate brown.

He has a nice profile Jim – something about the full, expressive lips, part gormless, part looking as if they are always just about to say something.

'What?' Jim clocks me looking at him.

'What?'

'What are you looking at?'

'Nothing,' I say, 'I'm not looking at anything.'

'Good,' says Jim, going back to his newspaper. 'I thought I had something hanging out of my nose.'

'What's that your reading?' I ask.

'The 50 best Family Breaks.'

'Any good ones?'

'Yeah, fifty.'

'Can I read it after you?'

He nods and yawns.

We decide to go for a driving lesson.

Jim drives down Lordship Lane, one hand on the steering wheel, leaning into the window with the other.

'Are you OK, Jim?' I ask.

'Yeah, why?'

'You seem distant that's all.'

'No I'm fine, just a bit knackered.'

Silence, we drive on, around the bustle of Goose Green roundabout and up Dog Kennel Hill.

'Are you up upset about your sister?'

'No, I'm alright,' he says, tersely. 'Stop going on.'

He indicates, then turns left into Sainsbury's, I look at him, confused.

'Where are you going?'

'Where does it look like?'

'You didn't say you needed some shopping.'

'I don't,' he says, 'we're having a driving lesson, aren't we?'

Jim's moodiness is very off putting, totally foreign to me and I don't know how to react. But I imagine he is, secretly, upset about Dawn, so I don't push it, I just keep quiet.

We drive around the car park, packed on a Saturday morning with families pushing trolleys back to their four-wheel drives. We drive right around to the far right hand side, then Jim pulls up into an empty corner and turns off the engine.

'Right,' he says, a little more cheerful now. 'We're going to master the three point turn.'

We swap places, me trying not to show my nerves at doing something that sounds scarily advanced.

'OK,' says Jim. 'The three point turn is all about getting you out of awkward places, about turning the car in the opposite direction in as few moves as possible.'

'I.e. three?' I say.

'Yes,' he says, 'although there's no need to be pedantic.'

I resist the urge to rise to this, if anyone's being pedantic it's him! Jim explains the process and we attempt the first one but my mind's all a tizz and I screw it up, stall on the first move.

Jim sighs, wearily.

'It's OK, you're rushing, take your time,' he says.

I take a deep breath, start again. I put the car into first gear turn to the right. 'Now what?' I say.

'Reverse,' he says, 'put it into reverse.'

I try to put it into reverse but the gear slips and the car shrieks in protest.

'What the hell are you doing?' says Jim.

'Trying my best!' I say. 'Give me a chance. Jim?'

I look at him but he's already looking right at me.

'Yeees?'

'Do you think we'll go on family holidays together? I mean, what do you think our kid will do for holidays, us not being together?'

Jim raises an eyebrow as if to say, 'you never cease to amaze me.' Then leans back on the head rest, his arms behind his head.

'Is this to do with that article I was reading?' he says. 'God, you're so sensitive aren't you? You're always obsessing about something.'

He has a point. Now that my fantasy – as deluded as it was – of Laurence and I working out, perhaps even being a family some day is well and truly off the agenda, my thoughts are focused on Jim, the baby and I, and how we're going to navigate our increasingly complex landscape.

'It does at the moment, yes,' I say, annoyed now. 'This being quite a big deal, having a child, especially like this. Don't you think about things like that?'

'Not when we're trying to do a driving lesson, no. Now, left arm down, try and do the neatest little curve you can.'

I'm offended by his dismissive attitude but I try to do as I'm told. I rev too much though and my curve is way too wide.

'Tess! Can you try and concentrate? *Please.*' He looks out of the window and mutters an expletive.

I take my hands off the steering wheel and glare at him, seething.

'Well you wouldn't be a very good driving instructor, would you?' I say. 'Totally losing your rag when I'm trying my best.'

Jim gives a frustrated laugh. I crane my neck to look at him but he's looking out of the window. 'You are upset about your mum, aren't you?' I say. 'We can do this another time, you know, when you're in a better mood.'

'I'm not in a mood!' He makes me jump, I start back. 'Just, get on with it, OK. Just do the move?'

'Yes sir,' I mutter. 'Whatever you say.'

I drive forward a bit and put it in reverse again. Jim looks at me, then clears his throat.

'If you want an answer to that question no, I don't suppose we would go on holidays, not if you had a boyfriend. I'm not Bruce Willis, you know. Now, left arm down, try again.'

This time I do it right and make a neat little curve, just as he said, so we're facing the sea of parked cars.

'What do you mean by that?' I say, knowing perfectly well what he means. We poured over those pictures in *Vanity Fair* for ages in the office. Bruce Willis, bare-chested, masterfully steering that speed boat whilst his ex-wife, Demi Moore, suns herself, hair blowing in the wind, her arm around Ashton Kutcher, the archetypal blended family on holiday. I remember thinking, how brilliant, how utterly modern. But also how utterly unlikely that that could ever work in real life.

'You know what I mean,' says Jim.

'Yeah, OK, I know what you mean. But it's not all down to what I do, is it?' I point out. '*You* could get a girlfriend.'

'I could, you're right. And I'm sure I will bag a hot, twenty-year-old. But then I wouldn't expect you to holiday with us.'

'I'm not suggesting you would!'

'Good! I'm not suggesting I'd ask you!'

'Right so, we can safely say our child would never go on holiday with his biological parents then?'

'I think yes, we can safely say that.'

'Get on with it then,' says Jim

'With what?'

'The three point turn, Tess! Of which you've done two points so far. Very poorly.'

I look at Jim, his green eyes bright with exasperation, his hair still in stupid peaks, his face baggy with sleep. He's wearing an enormous hooded top with the name of a hip-hop rapper on it that he's never even heard of but he got it from a sixth-form sale and therefore assumes it must be cool, a pair of baggy, chav, Adidas tracksuit bottoms and his Reebok Classics. But it's oddly attractive, worryingly so and for some stupid reason I put my foot on the clutch, put the car into first, and give it far more gas than is strictly necessary.

'Brake! Tess! Put your foot on the brake!'

I do, just in time. Inches from a smart black Saab. Jim looks at me, stumped, and opens the car door. Then he gets out, closes it behind him and very calmly walks away.

I sit in the car, wiggling my knees, my heart palpitating, my mind racing. What's wrong with me? My emotions are all over the place. Vicky's *Best Friend's Guide to Pregnancy* warned me I'd lose the plot but I didn't expect it to happen quite so quickly. And completely.

A knock on the window. Jim's back, carrying drinks from Sainsbury's Starbucks.

He opens the car and gets in, hands me one hot paper cup

260

and starts slurping on his own. 'Finished?' he says, 'coz I reckon I am.'

'Yep.' I stare straight ahead. 'I think I've got it out of my system now.'

CHAPTER TWENTY-THREE

'I'd travelled from Zimbabwe alone to have my spinal tumour removed. I knew there was a fifty per cent chance I could be paralysed from the waist down. When I woke up, a nurse gently told me I was one of the unlucky ones. In the next breath she told me I was pregnant. I called the baby Kayode – it means "he brings joy". He is my one and only reason for living.'

Betty, 39, East Finchley

It wouldn't be so bad if it was just my own feelings and expectations (dashed as they are) with regard to Laurence, that I was having to manage. But no, thanks to Anne-Marie and my own cowardice and stupidity, there is also most of my colleagues'.

'So go on, tell all, do you still have sex when you're pregnant? Or do you get that –' Anne-Marie pokes one curled fist with her finger '– nudging the head feeling.'

'Shh! Christ, Anne-Marie.' Jocelyn looks around to check nobody heard. 'This is a family restaurant and that is *difinitely* below the belt.'

I give a non-commital laugh and pray they'll shut up about Laurence. In fact, if I'd known that we'd get onto the subject of Laurence at all, I might have chosen to go with another group for this morning's task.

Judith had one of her rants this morning. We were called into her office to be told that none of us had a clue who our readers were and that we were living in La-La land where everyone worked in the media and went to Yo Sushi for lunch. (What planet is she on? I'm lucky if I can afford a Boots own sushi on my measly wage.)

She demanded we get into groups then dispatched us all off to different eateries where we had to have lunch and 'chat to *Believe It!* readers' and do a vox pop about whether or not Fern Britton really had deceived her fans by having a gastric band op (most of our readers just wanted to know where they could get a gastric band op themselves). I chose McDonald's on the South Bank because it was nearer and I could have murdered a filet-o-fish. But now I wish I'd gone with Barry's group to Nando's at the Elephant and Castle, at least I wouldn't have been subjected to this interrogation from Anne-Marie (journalists are always the worst).

Putting aside the minor detail that I am no longer seeing Laurence, let alone that he was ever the father of my child, the longer this farce about the paternity goes on, the guiltier I feel. At first, before I was showing, before I moved in with Jim, before I felt this close to Jim, it was an idiotic blip, something I really believed I could reverse in a second – it would just take a lot of guts and explanation about being put on the spot and the emotional rollercoaster of those first disorientating weeks. Now, however, it's become like a dark, spectre-like shadow that wakes me in the early hours, tugging at my conscience. Sometimes I can't get to sleep again till dawn, the shadow taking over my entire bedroom and enveloping me in panic. Despite the fact that neither Anne-Marie nor Jocelyn has met Laurence, in their heads he's the stuff of dreams. He's French, he sends me flowers on a whim, he romances me with spontaneous dinners. And better than all of this, it's a whirlwind romance, a full-blown love-affair-and-baby, all in a matter of months, what could be more romantic than that? It's pathetic, I know, but part of me doesn't want to shatter their dreams. The fact my own are not exactly intact any longer is by the by.

I watch Anne-Marie pick moodily at her fries. She's wearing the sullen expression of someone who knows they've crossed the line but I know she's still dying for an answer to her question.

'I take it that question is off limits then?' she says, after nobody's said anything for five minutes.

'Okay,' I sigh. 'Yes, course one can still have sex when one is impregnated and no, I have not yet experienced the nudging the head feeling.'

Jocelyn tuts, but she wanted to know the answer just as much as Anne-Marie, I know she did.

'Well *I* want to know about the romance,' she says. A wave of nausea engulfs me. 'I bet he thinks you're so beaudiful, doesn't he? So natural, as God intended?' She closes her eyes, dreamily. 'A naked pregnant woman is magnificent, I've always thought.'

Anne-Marie laughs, a bit of burger bap spraying from her mouth. (She made us promise we'd never tell Vegan Boyfriend. Faced with a Big Mac, her will power was pushed just that bit too far.)

'I don't know about that, Joss,' I say, cringing at the memory of the one and only time Laurence saw me without my clothes on. 'I don't look that hot with my clothes off, believe me.'

'But it all happened so fast, that's the beauty of this!' she gushes. 'Normally, by the time a woman gets pregnant, she's been in the relationship for years and, you know,' she screws her nose up, 'he's already a bit over her.'

'Jocelyn!' Jocelyn stuns me with her lack of sisterhood sometimes.

'But you, you and Laurence, this all happened in the first flushes of love, a baby born of real passion!'

Oh God, PLEASE shut the fuck up.

'I bet he'll be, like, Fit Dad at school,' says Anne-Marie, picking the gherkin out of her Big Mac.

Why does something tell me Anne-Marie felt like this about all her mates' dads?

'So when are we going to meet him, this Laurence?' says Jocelyn. 'Yeah, when can we see the fittie in the flesh?' adds Anne-Marie.

'Soon,' I say. 'Maybe at my leaving do.'

Maybe like, never?

'Anyone for a hot apple pie?'

The afternoon at work is unbearable. Jocelyn and Anne-Marie just won't let the Laurence thing lie. What does he looks like? Olive-skinned? Ooh! The baby will tan well. Will he speak French to it? Bi-lingual kids, how exotic! Sonya, our level-headed picture editor who has a child herself, has some more realistic questions, funnily enough. Don't I worry a new-born will scupper any chance to really get our relationship off the ground (it's already underground, thanks very much). Have I thought whether this might just be lust rather than love and when the reality of a baby comes along, we'll suddenly feel in too deep? (He worked that out already.)

Sometimes, being pregnant feels like you're one of those bags of bird seed that hang from a washing line: everyone can come and have a peck at you, chew you around, spit you out. Don't they realize my head's already fit to burst with my own questions and worries and fears without having theirs crashing the party too?

The office finally descends into the 5 o'clock silence, everyone suddenly realizing they'd better do some work. There's the soft patter of keyboards, like the first fall of rain on a windowpane. A dramatically loud sneeze explodes from Brian Worsnop's nose. I blow some crumbs from in between my keypads, and idly click on my inbox.

From: victoria.peddlar@hotmail.com
Seeing a client in town later. Fancy meeting me and G in CaH for a half shandy? about 7pm? . . . x

Thank God for mates.

The Coach and Horses is empty inside, everyone's outside on the street, drinking in the sun. Gina's sitting on a stool on the elevated section, Vicky doing some pummelling thing to her back. I stand there, my two bags of shopping pulling on my arms.

'Hi,' I say eventually, after nobody notices I've arrived.

'Oh hello,' says Vicky, as if she was, actually, engrossed in massaging Gina's vertebrae one by one. Gina's got a knack for commanding this type of undivided attention.

I put my bags down on the floor with an exaggerated groan and sit down on the stool opposite.

'Can I have a go after her?'

'I'm expensive,' says Vicky. 'This would set you back forty quid if I was doing it at my practice I'll have you know.'

I bend down to get a look at Gina who's got her chin on her chest and occasionally mumbles sounds of appreciation when Vicky gets to a particularly tight knot.

'That'll be all the shagging you did in New York then will it, Gine?' I almost shout, so she can hear over The La's 'There She Goes' bouncing from the jukebox.

'Traipsing around every goddamn record shop in

266

Manhattan with Michelle more like.' I move a corkscrew of hair that's dangling in front of her face.

'I take it the honeymoon's over already then?' says Vicky, matter-of-factly.

'No, we're still very much in love, thank you. Although *obviously* she could never replace you two,' says Gina. Then she says, 'Actually that's a lie, ha! She's moving into your room in a few weeks, Tess.'

Vicky pats Gina on the back. 'That should do you,' she says, sitting back down to her glass of wine. She's got her hair up today – she looks lovely with her hair up, like a young Felicity Kendall but a lot less posh.

I order my half shandy from the bar and sit down. The pub smells of dust, of sunshine on velvet. 'So what's this business about Laurence?' says Vicky. It takes me by surprise.

'What business about Laurence?'

'About it all being on again. I thought he hadn't even called.'

Gina grimaces as if to say 'oops, sorry' and takes a swig from her bottle of Becks.

'OK so we did go out. But I didn't bother telling you because it was a bit of a disaster.'

Gina looks at me as if to say 'news to me' which of course it is.

'Basically, I told him I was pregnant . . .'

Someone outside drops a glass and smashes it. Everyone cheers. We wait for them to stop.

'And, surprise, surprise, he didn't want to know.'

'He did finish with Chloe, though? Right?' Vicky says, already indignant on my behalf.

'Yeah,' I say, 'he did at least have the decency to finish his first relationship before he finished his second. But, to be fair, he didn't know I was pregnant when he finished with Chloe, he clearly got more than he bargained for.'

'Right, so, he didn't actually do a runner the moment you

told him?' Gina is eager for her friend not to be demonized, for all this not to reflect too badly on her.

'No, not exactly. He freaked a bit when I told him – as you would, I suppose – then he said he needed time to think. Then he rang me when I was with Jim in Ikea buying cots of all things and said he'd *had* time to think and thought he could handle it. Then we went out for dinner but I got the feeling he really wasn't into it, then he said he'd call, but he hasn't. That was two weeks ago. I mean, I don't really know why I'm so surprised. The man dumped me, by email, for another woman, why the hell would he want to know me now, pregnant for God's sake!?'

'Oh, come on!' says Gina, flopping back into her seat as if I am being completely disingenuous. 'There's loads of time yet! He could still call.'

I raise a 'get real' eyebrow at her.

'He ain't gonna call, Gina, let's face it. I think after two rejections, I kind of get the message.'

'Oh mate, I'm sorry,' says Vicky, doing her best to look genuine. 'Perhaps it was never meant to be in the first place – he is a Scorpio after all and you're a Sagittarius, biggest clash ever.'

'Thanks for trying to make me feel better,' I smile. 'But I don't think astrological clashes are to blame for this one. Let's face it, he's always been an arse. . .'

Gina has to leave early. Gina always has some better invitation up her sleeve. Vicky's a bit drunk now, she puts her arm around me and gives me a consoling hug.

'Oh, Tess Jarvis.' She squeezes me tight. 'Sorry about Laurence, seriously, I am. I know you know what I think about Laurence, but I also know how much you liked him, so I'm sorry for you.'

'Honestly, don't be, I'm just mainly cringing now,' I say.

'I cannot believe I almost shagged my ex when I was pregnant with another man's child!'

'What? Did you?!'

'Oh God . . .' I wilt inside. 'I didn't tell you about that bit did I?'

When Vicky really laughs, she doesn't just shed a tear or two, her whole face contorts and she makes these gasping sounds like she's having an asthma attack.

'Alright,' I say, after five minutes of this. 'It's not *that* funny. Laurence clearly didn't find it that funny anyway.'

'God, sorry,' she says, blowing her nose on a napkin. 'It's just, that impression of Sebastian Snail on repeat play does me in. Hey, but look on the bright side.'

'Yeah, I know,' I say, because I know exactly what's coming next, 'at least I didn't shit myself.'

'So what about Jim?' says Vicky when we've finally calmed down.

'Well, I probably won't tell him that I nearly had sex with Laurence, that might be a bit off.'

Vicky nods, vigorously.

'But I think I might tell him that I was dating him. We had this house rule you see, that we wouldn't snog, shag or date other people whilst I was pregnant. But Jim'll understand. He knows how things don't always happen in the right order.'

'Er, I wouldn't,' says Vicky.

'Why not?'

'Well, put it this way, how would you feel if he suddenly announced he'd been seeing someone, what if he got a girlfriend?'

'I'd be happy for him.'

My mouth moves but it's not attached to me.

'Really?'

'Really.'

'You wouldn't be jealous?'

'No!'

'Tess, I don't believe you. I think you're in love with Jim.'

'Victoria!' I'm almost laughing now. 'Just stop it will you, just give it up!'

'Fine,' she says, raising her hands in defence. 'But I will just say.'

'Go on,' I sigh, 'what will you just say?'

'That I've been thinking of what you said happened in Norfolk, you know, Jim pushing you away like that. It just doesn't make sense.'

'Well it happened, OK? God, don't make it worse by making me feel like I imagined it!'

'There's something I didn't tell you,' she says.

'Oh? Like what?'

'It's something Jim told me.'

She sees my eyes light up, I know she does.

'A couple of months before we went camping, we all went to that restaurant called Ping-Pong, remember – you couldn't come? Anyway, we all got really pissed and ended up in LUPOs. Jim was wrecked and started on about you . . .'

I take a shaky breath in.

'Basically, he told me he'd never loved anyone like he loves you. He said you were his dream girl.' Her eyes are filling with tears. 'Isn't that a gorgeous thing to say?'

'Oh come on, he was pissed.'

'He said it, Tess.'

'I'm sure he did, but did he mean it? He's never said it since, has he?' I look directly at her now. 'Anyway, his feelings had obviously changed by the time we went to Norfolk. We're just friends, Vicky. It's a shame, I know, but that's the truth. And anyway, if it was going to happen, it would have by now, surely.'

'You said it yourself, Jim of all people knows that things don't always happen in the right order?' says Vicky, hopefully.

'I know but look, you know how it's meant to be. Look at you and Rich, fell instantly in love, couldn't live without each other from the start and you're *still* madly in love.'

Vicky makes a puffing sound with her lips.

'Well you are, aren't you?'

'It's not all passion and swinging from the chandeliers.'

'No, but you've got Dylan, you haven't got loads of time. But you're still in love with each other.'

'I don't really know anymore.'

'Oh Vicky, you are.'

'We haven't had sex for ages. We've barely communicated for weeks. He's obsessed with this stupid thing he's writing, spends hours up in the spare room thinking he's some sort of genius when he could be helping out with me and Dylan.'

Vicky surprises me with her lack of support. She was always into him doing his writing, his amateur dramatics. They were always the fun couple that did themed parties and put on plays and did choreographed dances at their wedding. I'm worried, now, that a light really has gone out in their relationship and I just haven't noticed.

'Maybe he's offended you're not supporting him.'

'Maybe,' she says. 'But the bottom line is, he's pissing me off. He's all jolly and friendly to the neighbours and Mr Life and Soul of the Party but what actual use is he to me, as my husband?'

'That's a bit harsh.'

'Oh I don't mean it,' she sighs. 'We're just going through a rough patch that's all. We just don't like each other that much, you know?'

'Shit, I'm sorry and I've been so wrapped up in myself I haven't even asked how you are.'

271

'It's alright,' she says, 'nobody asks you about your relationship once you're married. And anyway.' She smiles at me now. 'This is just the reality of being married. That mad passion you had at the beginning, that feeling that everything about them, everything they do and say is absolutely fascinating, it does die eventually, you know. Or else it sort of gets buried deep, and unless you bother to dig, now and again, you forget it ever existed.'

'God, sounds depressing.'

'It's alright,' she says, seeing the look of dismay on my face. 'We're not getting divorced just yet you numpty! It's just, this is the reality of being married, Tess. It's not like it is in the films, it's real life.'

CHAPTER TWENTY-FOUR

'Three weeks after Eliza arrived, Nick confessed he'd slept with an Israeli air hostess whilst away on business. "How could you?" I said, "Our second daughter barely out of the womb!" He looked at me – I was feeding her at the time – eyes cold as ice. "It's taken two babies to realize I didn't want any," he said. Then he turned around and walked out.'
Camilla, 34, Richmond

Yesterday was awful. Jim and I went to a barbeque at Vicky and Rich's house; the first of the summer. Gina was there too of course, plus the usual suspects from Vicky and Rich's work and a couple of next-door neighbours. I know exactly what Vicks will have been thinking, 'Let's get all our lovely mates round, the sun'll be shining; Rich'll get his barbeque shirt on, charm the crowds and I'll remember why I married him.'

Right, well, it didn't exactly go to plan.

For starters, it pissed it down so we all had to make do with grilled sausages eaten on our laps in the lounge. Not able to take on his usual role as King of the Barbie, Rich tried his hand at Domestic God but only succeeded in irritating Vicky by getting under her feet and 'annoying people by laughing too loudly'. (Like she can talk ... Poor man can't do right for doing wrong at the moment. I can definitely see his side of things.) Finally he'd had enough and trundled upstairs, no doubt to work on his epic. To cut a long story short, the atmosphere left a lot to be desired already without Jim getting drunk, *dirty* drunk. More drunk than I've ever seen him in my life.

I wouldn't have minded if it had been the final of the World Cup or he'd won the lottery or something else that warranted that level of inebriation, but it was a family barbie for God's sake (a daytime one at that) and Jim was careering round Vicky's lounge like that guy from *Shameless*.

At one point, he went to put his can on a table, misjudged and fell into mousy Amanda, neighbour to the left of Vicky and Richard, who has a blushing problem at the best of times. She let out a yelp like a hyena, toppled sideways into the mantelpiece and ended up knocking down a vase which then smashed into smithereens. (She was mortified. Jim was too, for about five seconds, until the short term memory loss kicked in.) Jim can drink, don't get me wrong, but his drunk self is usually just a more vivacious, cheeky version of himself, not this staggering, slurring alky that I didn't recognize.

The worst thing was, I felt somehow responsible for him. Whereas before I got pregnant I would have laughed and pointed with the best of them, shouted 'nice one Ashcroft!' Just like Gina did. (Before plying him with more booze so that she could laugh at him some more.) This time, I felt I had to apologize for him as if everyone was thinking, 'and you chose to procreate with *that*?' Except I didn't so much choose to as just 'ended up doing', of course. Not that I could really stand on a chair and shout that disclaimer at the top of my lungs.

Vicky took it all in her stride as usual, chatting to the

swaying, hiccupping state before her as if he was behaving completely normally. But whereas anyone asking him whether he was excited about the baby would usually have him launching into an endearingly animated monologue about how many inches it is now, how it can suck its own toes and all manner of other useless trivia that he hoovers up from the back of my *Bundle of Joy* book; this time he responded with a dismissive shrug. He said, 'I don't even know what I'm supposed to be excited about yet.'

'You know what it is, don't you?' said Vicky, taking me to one side on the landing. 'He's pissed off with you, about Laurence, for Laurence calling you in Ikea. I mean, come on! It's obvious, he's *jealous*. Men always get drunk when they're jealous.'

'I don't think so,' I said, thinking he's not getting away with it that lightly. 'He's been getting pissed and acting like an idiot all week. He's probably having one of those helpful pre-baby crises that men like to have. It's a pity the women carrying their babies can't get loaded as well, or else we might have the luxury of having one of those too.'

That shut her up.

Still, once at home and in front of the telly – having single-handedly propped Jim up all the way back then thrown him on his bed where he immediately fell asleep with his shoes on – I pondered what Vicky had said today, and in the Coach and Horses last week. True, the drunken antics – the night with Gina, with Awful and now the barbeque – had all come after the night he cooked for me – the night I couldn't stay in because I was going out with Laurence. It suddenly occurred to me: could Gina have told him the vital detail? That I was actually going on a date with Laurence, not just meeting him and some friends for an innocent pizza? A quick text confirmed that no, she had not. (Gina is lots of things but she is not, to be fair, a grasser. What comes around goes around, after all.) But even if she had, OK, I would have broken a house rule, but that's it, it's just a technicality. It would piss him off but it wouldn't break his heart. It certainly would not mean that this bizarre behaviour was some sort of Shakespearian display of unrequited love.

It only takes the events of the very next morning, to confirm things on this front.

At 10 a.m. Jim's shuffling out of the bathroom as I'm about to go in. Skin all flushed from the heat of the shower, water dripping from his eyelashes.

'Morning.'

'Oh, mornin',' he croaks, as if he's forgotten I live here. Then, when I don't move out of his way. 'Everything alright?' He doesn't say it unkindly, but I can tell, what with the tight-lipped smile, that I'm annoying him. 'Did you want to say something?'

'Me? No.'

Doesn't he remember yesterday? 'I just wondered how your head was that's all.'

'Fine,' he says, nodding, beer fumes exuding from every pore. Then he sighs, and solemnly announces, 'I think I need to lie down.'

And that's the end of that. Jim doesn't mention anything at all about the night before and taking his cue, nor do I. When we meet, two hours later as arranged for coffee at the Uplands cafe; he just sits down, Adidas top zipped up, hair even more freestyle given that he passed out whilst it was still damp, and casually chucks a newspaper in front of me.

'You look a lot fresher after that hour's kip,' I say, cheerily, ordering a cappuccino. 'You look almost human.' Then I realize that the newspaper he threw in front of me is not a newspaper at all, it's a property paper. South London Property.

'There's a few gooduns in there, have a look,' says Jim,

casually, not even looking up from the menu he's now reading. 'We could arrange some viewings for next week if you like, I've circled a few I think have potential.'

My face falls.

'Oh, thanks.'

We haven't even mentioned me moving out since I moved in. We've talked about it theoretically, mainly me getting stressed about the logistics, but we haven't actually talked about me flat-hunting, not yet.

I open the paper, the blow still raw, making my blood pump and the words blur.

I suppose I thought we'd put it on the back burner, that we knew it was something I had to do, but that we didn't want to think about – I know I didn't. Clearly, as far as Jim is concerned that's not the case at all. Clearly he can't wait to get rid of me.

I watch him, legs crossed, twirling his hair, oblivious – seemingly uncaring – to the mayhem going on in my head. It's not like him to be so crass.

'So . . .' when I speak, my voice sounds strangled. 'When do you think I should be buying somewhere?'

'You what?' mumbles Jim, not really listening. Then, having ordered a black coffee from the waitress, 'Well, we're in July already, and you don't want to be traipsing around places when you're heavily pregnant, so –' he folds the menu and then his arms '– in the next month or so?'

Whatever happened to 'you can stay as long as you like'?

Whatever happened to the house rule that said I should start flat-hunting 'once the baby is born' to avoid getting cosy?

Too late, I realize, I already got cosy.

'OK,' I say.

Get a grip, Tess, you just presumed. Typical you, you always presume.

277

'Good idea.'

'I thought the one in Camberwell sounded good,' continues Jim. My God, he's keen, he's even done his homework. 'Kitchen/diner, big bedroom – so there's the option of making it into two, or at least things won't feel too cramped if you have to share with the baby . . .'

I try to picture me in a flat on my own with a baby – feeding it; dealing with its crying in the middle of the night. The reality's so different from the idea. And I've got used to living at Jim's, more than that, I *love* living at Jim's. I love having someone to eat breakfast with, to cook with, someone to remind me to defrost the chicken. I got used to Jim laughing at the radio in the morning, his first hour-long wee of the day and his crap taste in films. I can't imagine having nobody to chat to about my day at work or to jump on my bed on a Saturday morning like we're kids at boarding school, or even to bicker with, like we're married.

'Camberwell's miles away,' I say, fighting the tears that now threaten to fall.

'Well you'll be hard pushed to afford anything around here,' says Jim. I can't believe how matter of fact he's being. 'For £190,000 you'll be looking at ex-council in east Dulwich, whereas in Camberwell, you might, if you're lucky, get something in a nice small block.'

'Right,' I say, 'I don't know if I realized that.'

'My God,' I sigh, as we're gathering our stuff, ready to leave the café, I'm eager to talk, as if by talking I'll reduce this sudden anxiety I'm feeling, let the air out of it. 'Six months ago I'd never in a million years have imagined me being a single mum. If you'd have told me I'd be buying a flat on my own for me and my baby, I'd have laughed in your face!' I try to sound jovial, but inside I feel anything but.

'Oh,' says Jim, 'really.'

I carry on.

'Yeah, honestly, I thought becoming a single mum happened to other people, to, you know – and I can say this to you – to chavs who lived on council estates and got knocked up by blokes who'd been inside and . . .'

Jim snorts 'And who are you?' he says, 'the Queen of Sheba?'

'You know what I mean,' I say, but he's wandering off towards the door, 'I'm only being honest.'

We walk towards North Cross Road, everything feels heavy and I find it hard to keep up.

We stop by the Saturday market, me buying two brownies that cost a silly £2 each, in the hope of cheering Jim up, maybe we can have them later, for afternoon tea? I suggest. 'Maybe,' he grunts, 'if I've finished my work.'

We've just paid for them and are wandering towards home, dodging the couples and the prams that seem to be there on purpose, singling us out, the local frauds, when I see a couple walking towards us that I know I recognize but it's not until they're right in front of me that I realize, it's Rachel and Alan walking towards us with Tilly in her pram.

It's no wonder I didn't recognize Rachel at least. Gone is the glamorous dress and glossy-haired groomedness. In its place, drawstring trousers and a faded T-shirt. But she still looks beautiful and she's still smiling, blissfully happy. She's obviously not one of these girls who always has to look perfect.

'Hello you!' I say, kissing her on the cheek. 'Hi Alan.' Alan gives me a nod.

'Jim, this is Rachel and Alan. The ones I met at the bus stop, the Rachel I met for coffee the other day? And this is Tilly, their daughter, she's so good, I don't think I've seen her cry yet.'

'So er . . .' Rachel nods towards Jim

'Oh, sorry! Yes.' I smile bashfully because I know what she's getting at. 'This is Jim as in *Jim*, as in father of my child.'

'Hi,' smiles Jim, used to this kind of bizarre introduction by now. 'Wow, she really is a beauty, isn't she?' he says, sneaking a peek at Tilly, who's sitting, wide-eyed in her pram. And it's clear from the way he momentarily come out of his mood that he really means it.

We chat for a while, the conversation moves onto the labour (inevitable with anyone who's got a baby): twenty-seven hours, room like a war zone, Rachel thought she was going to die. (It only fuels my argument for a general anaesthetic at the very first twinge.)

'She was incredible, weren't you babe?' says Alan, eyes glowing with pride. Rachel shakes her head with embarrassment. 'I tell you,' he says to Jim, 'when you see her give birth, you'll just be like, wow, women are awesome.'

'He doesn't even know if he's going to watch yet, do you?' I say, nudging him, Jim doesn't say anything. I'm a bit put out.

'You'd be mad to miss it. You've got to see the birth! I mean, it's not pretty, probably put you off sex for a while!'

Rachel laughs nervously, Jim and I do too out of politeness and something else far more complicated. 'But I wouldn't have missed it for the world. Best moment of my life.'

They tell us about the craziness of the first few days, the sleep deprivation, the all-consuming love that Rachel says took her completely by surprise. They are honest and positive, but what strikes me most of all is how much of a unit they already are. One minute a couple, the next, a family.

We say our goodbyes, cross the road to go home, but my

280

head's in the clouds, whirring, thinking. I hadn't really thought about whether or not Jim would come to the birth – I suppose I presumed he would, but what if he doesn't? Do I even want my friend to see me in that state? Blood everywhere, probably losing control of my bowels? But then the alternative – because there is no way on this earth I'd want my mum to come with me – seems so desolate, so lonely. Suddenly everything seems a bit lonely. There's a spreading unease in my guts, a feelings that I don't really belong anywhere.

I just want to keep talking.

'Rachel and Alan are nice, aren't they?' I say.

'Yeah,' sighs Jim. 'Wasn't sure about him but she's lovely.'

'The baby was cute.'

'Dead cute,' says Jim.

'But they looked knackered didn't they?'

'Yeah,' laughs Jim, but I can tell he's not really interested, 'absolutely shattered.'

We get home, open the front gate. A cloud eclipses the front garden, turning it dark. I can't stop thinking how they seemed, the three of them there, I can't help thinking that won't be us, we won't be a family. I try to imagine Jim at the hospital, cheering me on, I try to imagine those first few nights with a new-born, us in separate bedrooms, but I can't. I think about what I imagined having a baby would be like and it definitely wasn't this.

Jim searches about in his pockets for the front door keys, I stand there thinking for the first time, that I don't really want to go in.

Keep talking.

'They seemed really in love, you know, *together,* considering they've got a small baby.'

Jim lets us into the flat and turns off the burglar alarm.

'Yes,' he says, 'they did seem pretty solid.'

'It's a lucky baby, that baby,' I sigh. So does Jim, but not in the same way.

'For a start, she'll be streets ahead in the looks department.'

Jim throws the keys onto the table, opens the cupboard and takes out a glass.

'Imagine having parents who look like that!'

He turns on the tap, fills the glass and downs it in one.

'It's a rare thing to have parents who are so in love. I know I felt secure to have my parents, it will be hard for our baby . . .'

'For fuck's sake, Tess!'

Jim slams the glass down on the side. I nearly jump out of my skin.

'Shut the fuck up!'

I look at him, stunned.

'Why do you keep doing this?'

He turns round, tears fill my eyes.

'Yeah that's right, you cry, go on.' He puts his head in his hands. 'It's all about you, isn't it? Never anybody else. You don't get it, do you?' He glares at me now.

'Get what? I'm sorry. Why are you so upset with me?'

'You're always putting this down, our baby, this pregnancy, you're always comparing us to other people.'

I stand there, bewildered.

He storms through to the lounge, picks up my book, the *Bundle of Joy* book, and hurls it on the floor.

'Have you read this?' he shouts.

'Yes, you know I have,' I say.

'Have you read all these stories?'

'Yes!' I protest, 'of course I have.'

'Are any of them fucking perfect?'

I can't answer, I'm crying too much.

'Because they're not, are they? None of them are. None of them prove this theory you seem to have that everyone except you has got it so good. Well you don't know anything Tess, you know shit about real life which surprises me considering the people you meet and talk to every day in your job. At least this baby will have a father.'

'A brilliant one,' I say, walking towards him, he turns away from me.

'At least I want this baby Do you know about my dad?'

'What, that he was an alcoholic?'

'That he beat my mum to a pulp?'

'I'm sorry. I didn't . . .'

'In front of me and my sister?'

I close my eyes.

'I'm sorry,' I say, 'I didn't . . . you never told me . . .'

'It's alright for you, Tess, with your dad who really loves you, who thinks you're the best thing since sliced bread. Mine was a total arsehole, he chose booze over his own family. Then he fucked off out of my life and he never came back. This is my chance, don't you get it?'

He's still shouting but his voice is cracking.

'My chance not to screw up, not to be like my dad. When you told me you were pregnant, it was the best fucking day of my life and yet you put everything down, put a downer on it all. Just because it's not totally perfect.'

I try to say something, but I'm appalled with myself, I can't find the words. Then to my horror, Jim bursts into tears. He stands there, quivering like a little boy. I walk towards him. I want to hold him, now, more than anything in the world. I want to take everything back, I want to start again.

I take another step, I hold out my arms.

'Not now,' he says, then he walks out of the room. Ten seconds later, I hear his bedroom door slam shut.

I stand in the kitchen, the blood rushes in my ears. I am glued to the spot, I am appalled with myself. I am a bitch.

283

An absolute bitch. How could I have been so insensitive? So blind, so self absorbed?!

I pick my book up off the floor, put it on the kitchen table and go into the lounge. I lie down on the sofa and close my eyes. I hear an aeroplane overhead, but not a murmur from upstairs. Then I close my eyes, jaw jammed shut, and the tears flow. Tears of self-loathing. I think of Jim upstairs and I wrap my arms around myself and imagine, really hard, that I am holding Jim.

I must have drifted off because the next thing I know, Jim's sitting on the sofa.

'Hello,' he says. 'Did you fall asleep?'

I blink at him. 'I must have nodded off.'

'I'm sorry Tess.'

'No, Jim, *please*. I'm sorry, *so* sorry. I had no idea how I was coming across.'

'Yeah but I shouldn't have sounded off like that, it was dramatic and unfair of me, you weren't to know all that stuff. Even *I'd* forgotten that stuff.'

We don't say anything for a minute or two, next door some music starts up, then Jim takes a breath, he starts to talk.

'I miss him,' he says. 'I think that's the thing. I've never admitted that to myself before, but I realize, it's true.'

'Your dad you mean?'

'Yeah, him. He was a total shit, but he was still my dad. And he wasn't always like that,' he continues. I just let him talk. 'It was the booze that did it, he was an alright dad before that.'

'What was he like?' I ask.

'Just normal. He'd take me fishing and to the park, kick a football around with me, boy stuff I suppose. But when it all kicked off with the drinking, I don't know, he just changed almost overnight. Suddenly he was so apathetic about life, about us, everything.'

'That must have been really hard to take.'

'I was only a teenager, I don't think I could make sense of it, I just felt ... I don't know ... confused and pissed off with him.'

'Totally unsurprisingly.'

We talk for an hour, Jim opens up like never before. He tells me how his dad used to come home in the early hours, how he came to dread the sound of his drunken singing outside his bedroom window. He tells me how he often scraped his dad off the kitchen floor then listened to his parents' screaming matches in the bedroom next door. There was the time he saw his dad throw a steel lamp at his mum, slicing into her temple. I listen, appalled; he talks and talks. Then, when he's finished, we eat the brownies and Jim laughs, embarrassed at how I must really be worried about having this baby, now I know where he really comes from (I'm not). Then he says, Let's go somewhere.'

'Where? What do you mean?'

'Let's go to the seaside, to Whitstable, let's just book a B&B.'

His face lights up because he's guessed what I'm thinking.

'Separate beds of course, don't look at me like that!'

CHAPTER TWENTY-FIVE

I'd just landed the job of my dreams – secretary for the MD of Yorkshire Fittings. I'd been to Leeds and spent the best part of my first salary on a Biba dress and chisel-toe shoes. Then I found out I was thirteen weeks pregnant. I was devastated. In those days you didn't work late into pregnancy, so it hardly seemed worth even starting. Worst thing was, I never did get into that dress after that, even after our Steven was born.

Janet, 56, Pontefract

The morning's clouds eventually crack under the pressure of a fiercely hot sun. Every man and his dog has got the same idea – escape the City, head for the coast and the A2 is packed, the traffic crawls and my bum cheeks are fused to the seat with sweat. Jim's got a cheesy piano house mix-tape circa 1998 thumping out of the sunroof. I can't resist doing a piss-take 'rave on' gesture out of the window.

'Can you stop doing that?' says Jim.

'Doing what?'

'That thing with your hand. It's really embarrassing.'

It amuses me greatly that he's embarrassed since it happens so rarely. I carry on, he shakes his head with despair.

Driving to Whitstable feels like driving to the end of the world. Steep chalky cliffs rise up on our left, on our right, the gently undulating downs of Kent. The only sign of civilization for miles is a fragmented town built into a craggy hillside. Even the names of the places: Gravesend, Ebbsfleet, have a world's-end feel about them. It's hard to believe that such a sparkling, white-washed gem, lies in wait, some thirty miles south.

Eventually though, we turn off the motorway. Charmless dormer bungalows lead into the town with its tea rooms, tiny doorways and shops that sell doorstops that say 'Gone to the Beach'. Red-faced men and sun-kissed girls with bikini straps dangling, pour out of pubs, drinking in the sun.

The cry of gulls is everywhere, it reminds me of home.

'So where is this place then?' Jim leans forward in his seat like an elderly driver. 'You booked it, this ninety quid a night place.'

'It's my treat, Jim,' I protest. 'One night's not going to break the bank and anyway, you deserve it, it's the least I can do. Especially when you consider I don't pay you any rent.'

The B&B's called Cove House. It's tucked behind the sea-front amongst the rickety old fishermens' cottages in one of the sleepy lanes.

The heat hits us like a wall when we get out of the car. The white of the buildings dazzles against a deep blue sky.

'Check it out.' Jim stands, hands on hips in front of the smart, double-fronted house with its white clapboard façade. Baskets ablaze with magenta flowers hang at both sides of the front door. Somewhere in the eaves, a wood pigeon coos.

The owner – a large woman with a sun-worn face – shows us to our room then she leaves and we look at each other and burst out laughing. 'Nice work Jarvis!' 'Oh my God it's gorge!' I squeal, 'I'm so clever!' Stripped wood floors, roll-top bath, a huge white, Victorian wardrobe with pebbles trapped in the glass. Oh, and one, (all be it a beautiful white cast iron one) bed.

'Just the one bed then?' smirks Jim

'Oh!' I clasp a hand to my mouth. 'Sorry I must have thought double meant twin.'

What if he thinks I did it on purpose? What if he thinks I've set him up?!

'It's alright,' says Jim, clocking the worry on my face. 'We did, once or twice, sleep in a bed together remember, so I'm sure we'll cope.'

We could have spent all day marvelling at the Molton Brown goodies and the widescreen TV but a perfect square of glistening sea is calling us from our sash window so we dump our stuff and go.

Jim buys a tub of cockles from a van and we wander along the sea wall, following the curve of the beach full with pale bodies laid out like fish drying in the sun.

'So, Jim?'

I have an uncontrollable urge to ask him questions.

'What do you want to do with your life? You know, what are your dreams for the future?'

'Bloody hell,' laughs Jim. 'What kind of a question is that? I can barely get my head around today, let alone the future.'

'OK, but do you want to carry on teaching?'

'Yeah,' he shrugs, 'definitely, I love it.'

'And what about ambitions?'

'Just to be happy.'

We step onto the beach, the shells crunch beneath our feet. 'You alright?' Jim asks.

'Yeah, why wouldn't I be?'

'Just checking, that's all, that you're not withering in the heat.'

We walk for almost an hour Jim making me laugh with stories of the kids at school. How they take the piss out of his car, his clothes, his *everything*.

'Doesn't it bother you?' I say. I hate to think of him being taunted, poor bloke!

'Don't be silly,' he laughs. 'They're just kids, it goes the territory, you've got to rise above it and just get on with the job.'

The beach widens and gets quieter, upon the verge of grass to the left is a cluster of brightly painted beach huts.

'Now you're talking,' says Jim. 'I could really fancy one of those.'

'What would you do in it?' I ask.

'Nothing, that's the whole point. A bit of musing, a game of scrabble, a few sundowners with someone special.'

We've gravitated to the beach now, we're lying face up on our towels.

'Do you reckon you'll ever settle down?' I say, it just comes out.

'I don't know,' says Jim. 'I hope so, one day.'

I close my eyes, light dances on my eyelids. I can hear the chatter of children and the womb-like rush of the sea.

'I suppose,' he starts. Then he pauses, he takes a breath. 'I suppose I've never had much evidence, you know, that it works.'

'What works?' I say, turning on my side to face him.

'Well, *life*,' he says, picking at his towel. 'But mainly commitment, you know, relationships, *love*.'

I open my mouth to speak but Jim carries on.

'I suppose what I'm trying to say is that I stopped believing, when I got to be a teenager probably, in that happy ever after thing. It never crossed my mind after that – that I'd ever be married with kids, it's just not something I envisaged.'

'Maybe having an alcoholic father who beat up your mum, and a crack addict sister didn't help,' I blurt out. 'Oh God, sorry.'

'It's alright,' shrugs Jim. 'It's taken me all this time to realize it myself.'

'Do you think you ever will?' I ask. 'Get married that is. Obviously the kid thing's somewhat taken care of . . .!' 'Maybe,' he shrugs. 'Yeah, I think so. I'll probably end up like this friend of mine, he was just like me. Dodgy childhood, various short-term girlfriends, could never get it together and then, one day, he just met the right girl.'

'And then what?' I ask. He looks at me and the sunlight pierces his eyes turning them a kaleidoscope of green and gold.

'And then that was it, he did it, didn't he? He fell in love.'

I sigh, contentedly, and feel the warmth of the pebbles on my hand.

'Who's that friend, then?' I say, after a pause. 'You've not mentioned him before.'

'Oh just a lad who teaches at school,' says Jim.

'Well, good for him,' I say.

I lie back down.

'Anyway,' says Jim, when we've drifted off into our own headspace for a few moments. 'Enough about me, what about you, eh Jarvis? What are your big plans?'

'Oh I dunno,' I say. 'Become a better writer.'

'How do you propose to do that?'

'Get a job on a better magazine. Maybe do a creative writing course.'

'Really?' says Jim, sitting half up. 'You never told me you wanted to do that.'

'Well there's only so long one can stomach triumph over tragedy, and besides, I want to write proper stuff.'

'Proper stuff?'

'Yeah you know, proper creative writing, fiction, poetry. I'm so impressed with Rich doing his script.'

'Come on then,' says Jim, sitting up, suddenly excited. 'Let's do it, let's practise now.'

'What do you mean?' I say, screwing up my face.

'Describe the sea,' he orders.

'Describe the sea?'

'Yeah describe the sea, you know, as if you were writing a description.'

I sit up, cross-legged on my towel and frown at him, but secretly, I'm already loving this.

'What?' I say, 'like I'm reading a book aloud?'

'Exactly that. Look at the sea, really look at it, think about how you can describe it in as original and powerful a way as possible and then do it. I want to see you really use your powers of imagination, all your senses. No clichés please.'

'Bloody hell,' I laugh, 'I'm glad you're not my teacher. You're scary.'

Jim doesn't flinch.

I look out at the sea – beautiful but fairly uneventful today, close my eyes and pray for inspiration.

'Right,' I start. 'No, sorry I feel like a tit.'

'JARVIS.'

I try again.

'The sea,' I start, resisting the temptation to just take the piss, 'was gun-metal grey and gentle waves dawdled to the shore, as if from a long and satisfying walk.'

'Nice,' says Jim, sounding annoyingly surprised, 'original, nice personification. Bit overdone perhaps, what with the walk analogy.'

'Yeah, yeah, I already thought that as soon as it came out of my mouth,' I say, surprised at how seriously I'm already taking this. 'And "gun-metal grey",' I say, critiquing myself. 'Bit of a cliché?'

'Possibly, yes.'

And so over the course of the next ten minutes, the sea becomes elephant grey (if it's a rough, stampeding sea), stone-grey, moon-grey (that was Jim's. Very nice). We particularly like my suggestion of dove-grey for a peaceful sea, perhaps very early in the morning.

'Now your turn,' I say. 'What about the clouds, the sky?'

291

'Right,' says Jim with comical seriousness, reaching for his sunglasses so he can look at the sky.

The scoop of skin revealed by his round-neck T-shirt is already turning rhubarb red in the sun . . .

'Wisps of clouds like cotton wool . . . punctuated an azure-blue sky,' he begins. 'And as the day came to a close . . .'

'Hang on, hang on,' I cut in. 'If "cotton wool clouds" isn't a cliché, I don't know what is and "azure-blue sky"?! That's worse than "gun-metal grey sea" surely!'

'Yeah, alright,' says Jim, with a mixture of hurt and amusement. 'You win. You're right, it's harder than it seems.'

We really get into it though, this becomes our game for the whole weekend. Seagulls no longer merely squawk or screech, they bleat and whine, the sun becomes a cracked egg, a girl has skin the colour of Dime bars. And I lose count of how many times Jim tries to better his crap cotton wool moment ('clouds like starved sheep' causes the orange juice I am drinking to come down my nose I am laughing so much). It became an ongoing competition to out-describe one another and kept us entertained all day long.

'You're good, Tess,' Jim said, as we collected out stuff from the beach. 'You're a better wordsmith than me and I teach creative writing. Why don't you start writing yourself? Go to an evening class or workshop?'

'Think I will, although I'd die of embarrassment if had to read it out and besides, I'll have a baby.'

'I'd look after the baby,' says Jim.

'Really?'

'Yeah,' he backtracks. 'If I could have Friday night out, and maybe Tuesday night out. Then there's the football on a Saturday . . .'

I give him the withering wife look.

'I'm only jesting,' he says, 'kind of.'

*   *   *

By the time we've left the beach, it's gone six p.m. As we stroll back to the B&B, along the parched grass behind the beach huts, our shadows are long in front of us and the only sounds are the distant whirr of a lawnmower and the surge of the sea.

'Do you want to go in the bathroom first? Since it will take you about five times longer than me to get ready?' Jim asks when we get back to the coolness of our room. He switches on Sky Sports and takes off his T-shirt, flopping onto the bed. Then immediately bolting upright.

'Ow shit!' he shouts, 'Jesus that hurt!'

'Oh my God!' I look at him, horrified. 'Look at your sunburn!'

Jim's arms, Jim's neck, Jim's chest and shins . . . Jim's everywhere that wasn't covered with clothes, is a violent shade of pink.

'Oh Jim,' I say, covering my mouth, 'that looks so sore.'

He gets up from the bed, wincing, and shuffles over to the long mirror.

'Oh for fuck's sake,' he says, examining himself. 'Why do I always do this?'

'Because you think you've got Mediterranean skin?' I say, shaking my head. 'I mean what factor did you have on? Four? You're Scottish, Jim. Deal with it.'

Thank God I thought to bring the Aloe-Vera.

'Look at the colour of you,' Jim tuts, sitting opposite me on the bed as I reach for the cream. 'You've gone nut-brown in a day for God's sake.'

'I've got my dad's Cornish heritage to thank for that,' I say, gently smoothing the cream in on his ankles, trying desperately not to press too hard. 'Does that hurt?'

He shakes his head.

'That's why I'm this weird mixture of dark hair and blue eyes but with mucky coloured skin.'

'Are your eyes blue?' Jim says.

I look up at him and flutter my eyelashes, self-consciously.

'They're not, they're kind of sea-greeny-blue.' He peers at me. 'Gorgeous colour, actually.'

I pump some more cream out onto one hand, then take Jim's foot in both. I concentrate on the ankle and the instep, going in tiny circular motions, then take each burnt little crisp of a toe, rubbing it in gently.

'You've got nice feet.' I say. 'Not like my podgy horrible ones.'

'Oh well, let's hope he or she gets my feet then. And preferably your everything else.'

The evening sun floods the room. Through our open sash window, we can still hear the hiss and crackle of the sea as it laps the beach then retreats. I finish one foot and move onto the other, Jim closes his eyes, completely relaxed.

'There you go,' I say, putting the bottle to one side. 'That should be nice and cool for you now.'

'Thanks,' says Jim. 'That feels really nice. Although I'm sure I'm supposed to be the one giving you a massage.'

I run a bath, add a few drops of my mother-to-be bath oil and sink into the steamy, fragrant water, my bump sticking out like an island. Next door I can hear football commentary and the odd empassioned cry from Jim. 'Back o' the net!' 'That was shit!' 'What a fucking beauty!' It's oddly soothing.

I turn on the hot tap with my foot, lie back and close my eyes. 'Cotton wool clouds'? How crap is cotton wool clouds!? And clouds like skinny sheep? Where the hell did he get that from?! I picture us on the beach, wandering down the sea-front, the sight of Jim padding down the beach with two ice lollies running down his hands. I picture him next door, caked in goo, enough heat coming off him to cook an egg, and I can't help but smile.

'Have you gone to sleep in there Jarvis?'

Shit, my eyes flick open.

'No,' I shout back. 'I'm getting out now.'

I haul myself out of the bath, wrap a towel around me and open the bathroom door, stepping out in a billow of steam.

'Right,' says Jim, easing himself off the bed. 'Cold shower I think, for me.'

The shower goes on, I hear him yelp and chuckle to myself as I open my case.

It's a beautiful summer's evening, I want to dress up, but everything I try on just doesn't look right. In my head, I am thin with a massive bump. In reality, I am curvy with a small one. I try everything in my case, until all that's left is a black, strappy knee length dress cut on the bias. I slip it over the thick straps of my maternity bra and stand in front of the full-length mirror. God, how depressing. How come you always looks so much better in your imagination? Saddlebags are spreading, I'm sure my thighs touch down to my knees but it's all I've got, it will have to do.

'Wow, nice dress.'

Jim emerges from the bathroom in a miasma of Lynx, his sunburnt nose glowing like a beacon.

'I look like a whale, don't lie. A fat, dumpy blobby whale.'

'You do not,' says Jim

'I bloody do. Look at this.'

I hold up every item of clothing I have tried on and rejected.

'This looked shit, this looked shit, this doesn't even zip up . . . !'

Jim sits down on the bed and sighs.

'You're pregnant you idiot, of course you're going to get bigger.'

'I look rubbish.'

'You look *lovely,*' says Jim. 'You look beautiful, actually.'

295

He looks at me through my reflection in the mirror. 'You *are* beautiful, actually.' He says it so quietly I hardly catch it.

I pretend like nothing's happened, I smooth the dress down and step back a little. 'Well it'll have to do,' I say, smiling at him. But my heart's beating like a bird.

Did he just say I was beautiful?

The town is heaving, the air thick and sticky. We look in restaurant windows but everywhere looks so cramped, so hot. Then Jim has an ingenius idea.

'How about The Neptune? The pub on the beach. We could sit outside? Have fish and chips?'

The Old Neptune stands, a run down old house, alone at the end of the main stretch of beach. It's a local's favourite and it's packed tonight, but there are ten or so tables outside on the sand and we manage to bag one, sheltered by the sea wall.

We sit down, me facing outwards. There's nothing in front of us but an inky calm sea.

'I had a great day,' I say. 'I love it here.'

'Me too,' says Jim. 'I haven't had such a good day in ages.'

Nostalgia catapults me back in time. Back to that day at the harbour in Whitby when he sat like that, face to the setting sun, and said that too.

'I just got déjà vu then,' I say. 'Of that day in Whitby, remember? After we cleaned my parents' caravan.'

'Oh God,' says Jim, 'I remember. We sat outside a pub near the sea then, too, only you weren't preggers so we were drinking.'

'Yeah,' I say, 'and we were snogging.'

'*And* we were shagging,' Jim says.

We both laugh shyly and look away.

Jim goes to the bar to order the food. I take off my flip-flops, sink my feet in the still-warm sand. It's almost dark now and the only source of light is a warm glow from the pub windows and a cloudy moon, leaking across the sky.

Jim comes back and our food arrives in minutes.

'It's funny how things have turned out, isn't it?' I say, the vinegar from my chips, making my eyes smart.

'Who'd have thought it, eh? That day in Whitby? That we'd be here now, me up the duff, about to have a baby in four months time! It's all good,' I say, feeling suddenly warm inside.

'Do you mean that?' says Jim.

'Yes, I do. It may not have seemed like that at times, I know I've driven you mad lately, but I don't regret this Jim, you do know that don't you?'

'Yeah,' smiles Jim. 'Course I do.'

'And you know, whatever happens,' I continue, 'our baby will never have to deal with its parents getting divorced, since we were never together in the first place. That's a very good thing.'

'A very good thing.'

There's the sound of raucous laughter from the pub, and the constant rush of the sea. On the table opposite, a gang of teenagers, in a uniform of leggings and denim minis are gathering together for a photo.

Jim puts his fork down and smiles at me, a serious smile.

'You know today,' he says. 'When we were on the beach?'

'Yes.'

'You know that lad I was telling you about? The one who teaches at my school?'

He's got a look about him now that I don't really recognize. He looks kind of vulnerable. He looks down at his plate.

'Well the thing is, well, you know when I was saying I'd turn out just like him, that maybe I'd . . . well the thing is . . .'

The high whine of my mobile suddenly erupts into the night.

'Oh God.' I see mum flashing up. 'I better take this, she starts worrying if I don't.'

'Hello.'

I mouth 'sorry' to Jim and wander down the beach. Mum sounds agitated and kind of serious. It's dad. She's worried about him, he's very withdrawn and behaving strangely.

'He's alright mum,' I say, 'just give him some space. You know he gets a bit down sometimes, he'll be up again in no time.'

The sea laps the shore sleepily.

'I'm not sure love,' she says. 'He's been like this for weeks. He's worse this time, I can't seem to get him to snap out of it.'

I try to reassure her and ask to speak to dad but he's watching telly and doesn't want to come to the phone, which I have to admit, isn't really like him.

'Is everything OK?' says Jim when I go back to our seat.

'Yeah, it's fine. Dad's just a bit moody that's all. Mum gets all stressed about it – he does this sometimes – but I know he'll snap out of it, she just needs to give him some space. So, um, what were you saying before?' I say, after we've talked about my dad some more. 'Oh nothing,' says Jim, taking a sip of his Stella. 'It doesn't matter now.'

We walk back to the B&B in almost total darkness, the sound of revelling from the pub getting gradually fainter. We watch some telly, then get into bed, both of us almost perched on the side, hyper aware of the space between us. We talk for a bit and then silence, darkness.

'Jim,' I say, but from his even breathing I can tell he's asleep. 'I think I just felt the baby move.'

CHAPTER TWENTY-SIX

'I was getting too big to hide the bump at work. My GP gave me an address for a Georgian building near Lancaster Castle. The placard on the front read, Ferry Road Moral Welfare. As soon as Lilian was born, I knew I couldn't give her up. As miracles would have it, three weeks later, I received a telegram from my aunt, offering to take us in.'

Geraldine, 82, Barrow

The night we get back from Whitstable, I have a fitful sleep. The baby flutters, as do thoughts around my head. I felt closer than ever to Jim after this weekend, as if every moment spent in Whitstable was a treasured memory just waiting to happen, a perfect red balloon floating in a clear blue sky. It was like old times when we were carefree and just friends. But these were new times, too, wonderful new times! Times, I realized as I lay, willing sleep, that I don't want to end in six months or so when I have to move out.

Morning seems to take an age to arrive. When it finally does, I look out of the window onto the greyest, most unlike-July day you've ever seen, and I get that feeling – I used to get it when I was little – did this weekend happen? Or was it just a figment of my imagination?

I am standing on my bed, arms folded now, nose inches from Eminem.

'So Slim,' I sigh (I reckon Slim Shady and I are enough acquainted with each other now for me to abbreviate), 'what do you reckon, dude? Eh? What will become of me at the end of all this?'

Eminem glares right back at me from beneath his baseball cap, his hands down his baggy pants, his feet wide apart.

I sigh, I step down from my bed as gracefully as a baby elephant. 'Right, OK. I take it there won't be much in the way of enlightening insights from you, then?'

The house is silent, Jim having gone to work at the crack of dawn to get on top of the end of term reports and I miss his presence and his shuffling about.

I get dressed (Slim and I like to have our little tête-à-têtes in just my pants) and sit cross-legged on the bed, plucking my eyebrows. My eighteen week bump protrudes like a modest little Buddha's and I notice that the beginnings of a line running from underneath my bra to my belly button is appearing, chestnut-brown and defined, like a henna tattoo.

I dawdle, leaving for work ten minutes late, but weirdly, I couldn't care less. Rachel's at the bus stop when I get there, Tilly good as gold in her pram. It crosses my mind that nine fifteen on a Monday morning is pretty early for a woman and her baby to be out and about, but then Rachel strikes me as one of these Super Mums. She's probably off to some sort of baby yoga group in town.

'Look at you! How many weeks are we now? It's definitely grown,' she says as I approach the bus stop. She's wearing huge vintage shades today, a bo-ho top and long trousers, and a cream pashmina arranged around her shoulders. She's back to her usual glamorous self.

300

'Eighteen,' I say. 'Almost half way!'

'Wow, how exciting. Try to enjoy it, I wish I'd enjoyed mine more. Pregnancy for me was pretty stressful.'

This surprises me, she looks like the sort who would have revelled in her pregnancy – spent the entirety of it in the Lotus position wearing Isabella Oliver maternity wear.

'So where are you off to today?' I say, 'and where's Alan? Work I presume. I suppose I've only bumped into you at the weekend before.'

'Well, no, he got made redundant, actually,' she says. 'He's not working at the moment, so, he's just at home.'

'Oh, sorry to hear that,' I say, thinking that's odd, I'm sure he told me he was a fireman.

'Yeah, it was terrible timing, just before Tilly was born. It hit him really hard.'

I don't want to say the wrong thing or something useless like 'I'm sure something will come along' so I just change the subject.

'I felt it move for the first time yesterday.' I feel sure she'll be touched I told her something quite momentous, that perhaps by sharing, she'll share more with me but she doesn't answer, she's suddenly not listening. She's looking nervously up the road, like she's just seen a ghost.

'I have to go,' she says, wrapping her pashmina tighter around her shoulders. 'I have to go, I'm sorry, I'll see you, OK?'

'Sure,' I say, concerned. 'Is everything OK? Do you need any help?'

But it's too late, she's gone. She's running up the hill, with Matilda in her pram, towards a black car that's pulling over.

'So how exactly does Bruno guide you on your choice of boyfriend?'

Anne-Marie snorts, I put my finger to my mouth to tell her to shut up and move the phone to the other side of my desk so she can't listen in.

'Well he wags his tail if he likes 'em, you know.' The woman on the other end of the phone has got the strongest West Country accent you've ever heard. 'And he bites 'em on the leg when he don't!'

'Right.' I rub my forehead. I was hoping it would be more sophisticated than that. 'And is there anything else, you know, more specific?'

I come off the phone forty-five minutes later. The only more specific thing I learned was that Bruno sniffs around their crotch if he thinks they look iffy, then barks at the door, till she finally sends them home.

'That sounded abso-bloody-lutely priceless,' laughs Anne-Marie, as I flop dramatically back on my swivel chair, groaning with the pain of it all.

'Painful more like,' I say. 'The dog's totally normal, it's got as many special powers as you or me!'

'Oh worry ye not,' says Anne-Marie, typing manically. 'Just make it up, the real nutters never notice. And anyway,' she says, 'you've got far more important things to think about. How is French Fancie anyway?' I feel the blood rush to my insides. 'You haven't mentioned him for ages.'

'He's great,' I say, pretending to fiddle with the batteries on my Dictaphone. 'Nothing to report, everything going smoothly.'

'Aahh,' says Anne-Marie, 'look at you, all in phase two. Make the most of it because phase three is when the little annoyances creep in and then you start to fucking hate them.'

The red light on my phone flashes.

I pick it up.

'Hello, Features.'

'Hello, it's Becky in reception here, there's a man downstairs saying he's here to see you.'

'Oh, Really? I'm not expecting any man, what's his name?'

'He won't say. He just keeps saying "Do I look like a terrorist to you?" I think you'd better come down.'

To be fair, my dad couldn't look less like a terrorist if he tried. His shirt is unbuttoned, he's wearing long Bermuda shorts, sandals with socks and he's eating a portion of McDonald's fries. He looks like an overgrown teenager.

'Dad!? What are you doing here?'

'I've come to see you of course, aren't you pleased to see me?' he says, going to hug me. I hug him back but his embrace is loose, not an embrace at all.

'Course, yeah but . . .'

'Not that I could bloody get in the place for love nor money. These idiots obviously think I've got bombs in my shoes.'

'*Dad!*' I say, through gritted teeth. 'They're just doing their job. It's standard security, everyone's got to give their name and get a pass.'

He shrugs moodily and carries on eating his fries.

'Tony Jarvis,' I say to Becky the receptionist. I mouth 'sorry'. She gives me a confused smile back and hands me the pass.

'Um, do you want to come and sit over here dad?' Dad trundles behind me as I make towards a big red leather sofa in reception.

Dad smooths the big rubber plants on either side with the palm of his hand.

'These are flagging,' he says. 'Need a bit of a dust and some attention, these do.'

'Right.' I frown. 'I'll let Becky on reception know. So dad, is everything alright? To what do I owe this lovely surprise?'

'I just wanted to see you that's all. I've been to that Tate Modern, eh, loads of rubbish in there, isn't there? I couldn't find anything decent to look at. They had loads of boxes in the main entrance, looks like they're packing up the place.'

'Dad, that's an art exhibition, a Turner Prize-winning one.'

'A what?' He makes an unimpressed grunt. I look at him worried. Dad knows exactly what the Turner Prize is, he's normally quite interested in culture.

'So, where's your office then?' he says, offering me a chip (I decline).

'Fifth floor, just above *Gardener's World* magazine, hey, I could get you a subscription if you like, for your birthday?'

He looks right through me and carries on munching. I wonder if he actually heard.

'So . . . is mum OK? Are you and mum OK?'

'Oh yes, me and your mum are OK, we're always OK,' he says, as he always does. I breathe a sigh of relief. My parents divorcing is one of my all-time greatest fears. But all the same, I'm panicking slightly, there's something seriously not right with my dad.

'And Ed? Is everything OK with Ed and Joy and the girls?'

'Mmm,' says dad with his mouth full, 'stop asking so many questions, everything's fine.'

I sigh, we sit in silence for a moment or two then I say.

'Dad, look, I'm not being funny, but it's just quite random that you came, on your own, you know, without calling first? I'm just worried that's all . . .'

'I just wanted a change,' he says, 'isn't a man allowed a bit of variety in his life when he wants it?'

'Course dad. Course you are.'

'Well, there you are then,' he says.

Five minutes later, he says he's off, off to that wheel thing he saw on the river.

'Now, just don't tell your mother I came, will you? She'll only worry. Promise me?'

'OK,' I say meekly, 'I promise.'

I watch my dad's short stocky legs as they make towards the exit, wandering if I can keep the promise I just made.

CHAPTER TWENTY-SEVEN

'The Ex Sex was incredible, far better than it had ever been when we were actually going out. A month after we'd done it for the fourth time – drunk of course, after a wedding – I found out I was pregnant. "You're not going to keep it, are you?" he said, the fear of God in his eyes. "Yes," I said, "Of course I'm going to keep it. It's the only good thing I'm ever likely to get from you."'

Sufia, 35, Manchester

'Needs a lick of paint, a bit of updating but space wise, you ain't gonna get better than this for the money,' says Craig from Kinleigh Folkard and Heyworth (or Kinleigh Fuck Hard and Pay Less as Jim and I have taken to calling it), throwing the keys up and down in his hand.

We're at the second viewing of a flat in Camberwell. A second floor, one bed flat in a faded Victorian mansion block. It's got potential – light, high ceilings and for the price (£189,000 – right at the top of my budget) it's big. But nobody's lived in it for years and apart from a pink mattress pushed up against the wall, there's no sign of life. I look around it, struggling to imagine myself living there.

'Is there an option to knock this wall through and then create two bedrooms and make the bedroom into a lounge?' says Jim, knocking on the wall as if he knows what he's talking about.

Craig from KFH strokes his goatee – trimmed within an inch of his job – and repositions his feet, wider still. 'I can't see why not,' he shrugs. 'But wouldn't you just rather have one big bedroom?

'She's expecting a baby in December,' says Jim, his voice echoes in the empty space. 'So an opportunity to make it into a two bedroom flat, would be ideal.'

'Oh, congratulations . . .' Craig's eyes plunge to my cleavage. 'I did wonder if you might be expecting.' He suddenly frowns. 'But, so . . .' the cognitive process is obviously just spluttering into action, 'why are you not looking for a place together?'

'We're not together,' says Jim. I'm hurt how readily.

'Oh, right,' the concentration is etched on Craig's face. 'But the baby . . .?'

'Is mine,' says Jim.

Craig pulls a face.

'It's complicated,' I say with a half-hearted smile.

Craig nods, clearly embarrassed that he now seems to be witnessing the messy aftermath of a nasty split. Why would he know we'd never even been together?

'Well, being a parent is the hardest thing I've ever done, that's for sure,' he says, carrying on breezily. 'Our little bruiser's five months now. My missus said the worst thing was the breastfeeding coz, er . . . I couldn't exactly help her with that bit!' When he laughs, he reveals a set of perfect veneers. 'But, I mean . . .' he puffs out air through his lips then assumes a solemn face, like putting on mask. 'I can't imagine what it must be like on your own.'

Jim's stretches his lips as if to say sorry. I shrug. I'm used to this now, then give Craig my best empty smile.

Is this what I have to look forward to? Being a pitiful figure in society's eyes? Craig from KFH will probably go back to his wife and say 'quit your whinging, woman, I saw a girl in a hell of a worse state than you today.' He probably thinks Jim's a total bastard and just dumped me, which of course could not be further from the truth.

I stroke the walls of the flat – flakes of peeling paint fall to the ground. I try to think of something to say that sounds like I really want it. Like I'm a serious buyer.

'So I could definitely convert this room into two then?' Craig nods. Jim smiles encouragingly. 'But what about the décor? I mean . . .' I'm looking for any excuse to not take the flat. The thought of leaving my cocoon at Jim's fills me with a nauseating dread.

'It's purely cosmetic,' says Jim. His face is animated, full of enthusiasm. 'You've got to imagine what it'll look like when you've got all your own stuff in. And I'll help you decorate. Me and Awful could do it in a weekend.'

Yeah, alright I want to say. You don't need to be so bloody positive about it all. You could be more devastated to see me go.

'I think you should put an offer in,' says Jim. Craig looks at the floor and taps one, shiny shoe, eager not to look too pushy but I can practically hear the £ signs rotating in his eye sockets.

'It's a great location, it's got loads of potential and it's big, Tess. Better a big flat that needs work than a swanky one you couldn't swing a cat in.'

'So, er . . . is that a yes then?' ventures Craig, when Jim and I have stood looking at each other for a few moments, both trying and failing to read each other's thoughts.

'Yes,' I say, 'it's definitely a yes.' I'm smiling, there's no way I want Jim to see how I'm really feeling but my throat aches with the effort of it all.

We decide on an offer of £185,500, Craig calls the vendors and it's accepted on the spot.

'Awesome!' beams Craig. He attempts to give me a high five but my hand misses and almost smacks the side of his head. 'You just got yourself a belter of a flat.'

Jim steps forward and gives me a big hug. As I hold him tight, possibly longer and tighter than I should, I am sure I feel him pull away.

One thing that's been happening since we went to Whitstable is that Jim's been going out a lot more. It's like those first few weeks we lived together when we used to stay in and just chat were a novelty, and now he's eager to keep his distance. I feel more alone in the house somehow, like we're not a unit, albeit a somewhat unconventional one, anymore.

Jim pops his head around my bedroom door where I'm lying on my bed reading the *Bundle of Joy* book. 'So er . . . see you later then.'

'OK. Go easy on Awful, you know what a light-weight he is. I don't want him getting another crippling hangover and you breaking another toe covering his lesson.'

'Yes dear,' jokes Jim, then he cranes his neck to get a look at what I'm reading. 'You still reading that book then?'

'Looks like it,' I say, suddenly self-conscious. 'I'm on number ninety-six so just another five to go.'

Jim's face disappears from my door then reappears and hesitates as if he's not sure whether to speak or not.

'You're not obsessing about what I said to you, are you?' he says. 'You know, about how you were always comparing us and should read some more of those stories if, you really want to know about real life.'

'No, don't worry, I'm not that paranoid!' I lie.

'Good. I wouldn't want you to beat yourself up. Now I'll probably be late so I'll see you tomorrow, OK?'

'OK,' I say. 'Have a good one.'

I hear the click of the front door and then the silence descends, deafening as a storm. I lie there, the book laid on my bump and I look around at this room that won't be mine soon, that will be our baby's room, not even a room in my house. Will it be a girl's? All flower fairies and gingham? Or will it be a boy's, with pirates and trains? I imagine Jim coming in here in the middle of the night to soothe our baby to sleep when I'm not here. Will *he* be OK on his own, let alone me? It's, like, we're both fast-tracking to single parents status, without having practised as a couple first.

I get up off the bed and on some sort of auto-pilot, go into Jim's room. It smells of him – of Lynx (Jim's never been one for aftershave), the papery smell of bookshops, the slightly metallic and woody smell of school.

I browse his shelves full of books. Books that tell a million stories, not just the one between the covers. There's a Faber and Faber collection of war poetry, lots of Iain Banks, every single William Boyd. There's a 1970s handbook entitled: *How to Get Defined Abs in Thirty Days* sporting a picture of a man in knee socks and very short shorts. On the bottom shelf there's the Asterix collection (trendy cool) the Famous Five (classically cool) and a series about a pony called Gill (*Gill's Gymkhana, Gill's New Stable . . .*) – not so cool at all, he kept quiet about that one).

I sit on his bed then lie back onto the tartan pillows. They smell of boy, of Jim. I take the photo – that same photo in the red frame of us in Norfolk – and I hold it close to my face, then up above me so I can see it in the weak evening light. Gina and Vicks leaning into each other, me, already a shitty shade of brown after one day in the sun, sitting on the deckchair, leaning into Jim. I look closely at my face, and I see it now, like seeing a vital clue in a forensic photo.

All that stuff about it being a ridiculous idea to ask him

out, that Jim's rejection saved me from myself, was a lie, a total lie! Inside I was crushed, in some small way I suppose I always have been. But I put it to the back of my mind and I tried to believe what Jim told me: we were friends, soulmates. Best not to ruin it, eh? And besides, how can you be in love with someone who's not in love with you back?

But I seem to have managed it nonetheless. Because I *am* in love, I am ridiculously in love with Jim Ashcroft: His skinniness, in all its Scottish, transluscent glory, his stupid bouncy walk and his worrying taste in ties. I love the way he stirs his tea for *hours,* how he uses a letter knife to open his post. I love to watch as he reads a newspaper, mouthing the words, and want to lay him down and ravish him when he comes in from football all sweaty and alive. But most of all I love the way he takes things as he finds them – me included – like it would never occur to him to be so arrogant as to want to change *anyone.*

I put the photo back and am overwhelmed with a sense of missing Jim, of wanting to be near him, of sadness that I, we, seem to have totally screwed this up. Fucking hell Tess, Why didn't you push it? push it when we were in Whitstable, tell him how you feel? Take a risk!

I have a sudden urge to look at the baby pictures he showed me the other night. I want to imagine what our baby will look like. I want to feel close to Jim.

I remember he kept the photos in albums in a long white Ikea box. I lay on the floor and look under his bed, rammed full with old trainers and three inches of dust. I see the white box and start to pull it out but then another box, a dark red one next to it, catches my eye. It has a little label on the side: 'letters and stuff' written in Jim's writing, in bright green pen.

Curiosity gets the better of me. I slide it out, put it on the bed, then get up on the bed too and open it, sitting crosslegged. Inside, there are a few letters from his mum which I

don't look at, that feels too private and some sweet postcards from Annalisa. They're all about people Jim's probably
never heard of, a Reiki convention she went to, the fact her
ex is about to have his house repossessed and all signed off:
I kiss you, lost boy! She's barmy, Annalisa, nutty as they
come, but she 'got' Jim, and she was probably secretly gutted
when he emailed to tell her our news, even though she'd
never have said.

There's two letters from Ken Livingstone's office (*Dear Mr
Ashcroft, I am sorry to hear you feel you must dispute your
parking fine . . .*) – and a collection of postcards tied together
with an elastic band. I know I recognize the writing on them,
but I can't quite place it. Then as I see where they're from –
two from Lake Malawi, one from Harare, one from a safari
camp in Chobe, Botswana – I realize that the writing is mine.

I take one, the one from Malawi and angle Jim's poise
lamp so I can see it clearly:

Dear Jim, it says.
Am ill, (could s**t through the eye of a needle as my dad
would say) which is why am lying in my tent writing this
now. Not the best week: had camera nicked at Lilongwe
station, got so caned on Malawi Gold hash cakes (was
upset about camera) that I hallucinated, fell down ditch
and sprained my ankle and now this, clearly the onset of
malaria. Missing you guys like mad, especially you, miss
our deep chats and your impressions of Broke-Snell. (Does
she still drop a foie-gras-flavoured one every time she
leaves? Hee hee!) Call me you b***rd! (V's got the number
of this camp.) See you soon (if I don't die before then, that
is), Love ya loads Tess xxx

So he got them, he got the postcards! But he never mentioned
them. So I was right. I put the elastic band back around them,

just the way Jim had done before me, so that they are contained, compartmentalized, filed for no future use.

I put them back in the box, slide it back under his bed, then go downstairs and eat two bowls of Frosties without the milk because we haven't got any and I can't be bothered to go and get some.

I watch *When a Man Loves a Woman* on DVD, more because I just want to have a good cry than because I actually want to see it (I know the lines off by heart). And it does the job, I cry my eyes out. And then at eleven o'clock, I hear the key turn in the lock which makes me jump because I wasn't expecting Jim back so early and I look a total state: swollen eyes, swollen lips, the works.

'You're back early,' I say, having turned the DVD onto TV and slapped my face a bit in a last ditch attempt to look normal.

'*Jesus,*' gasps Jim. 'Look at your face. You've been crying?'

'Doesn't take much,' I say, forcing a smile, gesturing to the empty DVD box. 'It's a right weepy, gets me every time.'

Jim just stands there looking at me. He knows I'm bull-shitting and that surely just watching a film, even a tear-jerker, can't render anyone in this state. He takes off his coat and sits down on the chair opposite, not on the sofa next to me, I notice.

'It's the moving thing isn't it?' he says, so softly it makes me well up again.

'Yeah, I s'pose. It freaked me out a bit.'

'Look, I'm not going to chuck you out before the baby comes,' he says, as if that's going to make me feel less like a stranger in my own (albeit) temporary home than I already do.

'I know,' I say, chin trembling. 'But I don't want to outstay my welcome, you know. And I have to get used to this idea of being a single mum, Jim. This is going to be my life, my future.'

Jim sighs, looks at the floor, then at me again, his face serious.

'Look, if it makes a difference, I really feel for you, OK? I probably haven't been very sympathetic, getting at you for being ungrateful and you probably feel like you have to hide your feelings now. But I know it must be tough for you getting your head around being a single mum, the flat, moving out, everything happening so fast.'

'And you too,' I say.

'Yeah well,' shrugs Jim. 'I'm not the one who's pregnant, am I. And I'm sorry, I'm really sorry Tess, because I know that you wanted it so desperately, the whole in love thing and it just didn't happen for you.'

I look at him, I try to speak but I can't, something inside me breaks.

That's all I need to know now.

CHAPTER TWENTY-EIGHT

It was Harry who wanted the babies. I was quite happy with the cockatoos and safari twice a year. Then I got food poisoning from a scallop and low and behold I was pregnant. Sperm of Adonis! We've got four children now but still, every time I eat scallops Harry always jokes "oh here we go, in one end, out the other. Should I be painting the nursery?"!'
Lillian, 50, Aldeburgh

In Whitstable I had been high on life and possibility but now it feels like those twenty-four hours really were spent at the end of the world in a lawless bubble with no connection to my real life, because since then, all of Jim's behaviour suggests I read it wrong. And now there's the flat – a sure sign that life has to move on and I feel like I've come full circle, I feel as dislocated and scared as I did during those mad few days after having found out I was pregnant.

It's a breezy, cloudy Saturday, the weather as indecisive as I am and so I go into town, mooch around for a while before meeting Gina for the 4.30 p.m. showing of *Ocean's Thirteen*. I'm just in Cath Kidston convincing myself that I simply

314

cannot live another day without an ironing board cover with little sailing boats printed all over it when Gina calls.

'Hey you.' She sounds really 'up'. 'Are you out and about?'

'Yeah, just in Cath Kidston in Covent Garden, about to make what I fear may be a hormone-induced purchasing disaster.'

'What is it?'

'An ironing board cover with sailing boats all over it.'

'Oh Jesus, thank God I rang. Listen, I know we're meeting to go to the cinema later but since you're in town already, I wondered if you'd come and meet somebody with me first.'

'Who?'

'Simon. This new guy I'm seeing. Honestly Tess −' she sounds fizzy, like she might be about to explode '− ohmiGod, he is such a sweetheart, sooo different to my usual type −' (yeah, yeah) '− you'll love him, I promise.'

'Alright.' It's not like I'm doing anything else. 'When and where?'

'I thought we could go for lunch, maybe in China Town? Shall we meet at the arch on Gerrard Street, at say, twelve thirty?'

'Promise I'll be able to get crispy duck?'

'Bloody hell you really are obsessed with food, aren't you?'

'Yup.'

'OK, I promise we'll get you a crispy duck.'

'That's swung it for me. See you there.'

Gina's hair is down and very big, she's wearing full make-up, a fur gilet over a purple, pussy bow-tie blouse, denim hot pants with turquoise tights and knee-high boots.

'I see you've gone for the demure, dress down look, then?'

'Do you like it?' she beams.

'I *love* it. Very glamourpuss.'

'Oh good. Simon says he loves it when I really go for it on the clothes front. He can't bear women who wear boring clothes.'

315

(Good sign: not boring. Bad sign: could potentially mean we've got another pretentious and flaky wannabe actor/Mexican juggler/tattoo artist on our hands.)

Gina looks me up and down.

'So, how's the er . . . bulge?'

'Bulging,' I say, pulling back my cardigan.

'Fuck me,' she applies a thick coat of lipgloss. 'It's fucking humongous!'

Which makes me feel just fabulous.

It's only when we start walking . . . in the opposite direction to China Town, that Gina confesses there's been a change of plan.

'Simon's really sorry but he can't get out of work, he's suggested we meet him at his office instead.'

'What, on a Saturday?'

'Yeah he works *really* hard.'

I stop and stand in the street.

'Right, so it's now gone from Chinese banquet to no food at all in my friend's boyfriend's office?'

'Er . . . yeah. Sorry.' She winces.

'You owe me you do.'

Gina has surprised me many times with her choice of boyfriend but this time I'm stunned. Not only does Simon work as a business manager in HSBC (a BANK, lest we forget: Despite the fact that Gina works in a bank herself, she doesn't touch bankers of any description with a bargepole . . .) but he also works in a boring office with not so much as a notebook on his desk as a show of creativity. He wears a suit, every day, has a short back and sides haircut, freckles all over his cute, boyish nose, and cannot be more than five feet seven. He reminds me of Michael J. Fox.

The other thing that surprises me is that I know, within seconds, that this guy is the real thing. That this is the one for Gina.

'Tess, this is Simon. Simon, this is my best mate, Tess. She's the one who's up the duff by her friend, you know the one I was telling you about?'

'Hi Tess, how's it going?' Simon flashes me a sweet, what-are-we-going-to-do-with-her? smile and gives me a firm hand-shake, eye contact and everything.

'Hi Simon, I'm good thanks, nice . . .'

Office, I meant to say, but at that point, Simon is unable to hear what I'm saying because Gina has suctioned herself onto his mouth and is snogging him like he's about to go to war. Not that he's complaining of course. In fact, there's a good ten seconds of snogging during which I have no choice but to pretend I am engrossed in a leaflet about pensions.

'So,' says Simon, eventually, stroking Gina's back. 'I don't know about anyone else but I'm starving. If nobody's fussy then I've got some ham sarnies and a bag of Wotsits in my bag, we could just share those?'

And so that's how I come to spend my Saturday lunchtime in the office of the Shaftesbury Avenue branch of HSBC going three ways on a ham sandwich with my loved-up friend and her equally loved-up boyfriend, feeling like I'm in a docu-mentary about surrogate parenting. But you know, I didn't mind. In fact I would go so far as to say it was fun. I liked Simon, he didn't make me feel like a gooseberry. He was funny and genuine and laughed *with* me not *at* me when Gina wheeled out the one about Luisa Vincenzi (she cannot help herself that girl).

But most of all, I liked how he was with my friend and the way she didn't stop laughing for a whole hour in his company.

I finally say goodbye to Gina at around two p.m. We were meant to be going to the cinema but I figured, what with the pleading look she gave me when Simon said he was getting off at three p.m. and did she want to go with *him*, that she'd gone off the idea. It's fair enough. If I had the choice between heavy petting at the back of the Soho Curzon with my new boyfriend and sitting next to me as I whinge about heartburn all the way through, I know what I'd rather do.

I cross the road, filled with a pleasant motherly satisfaction that Gina may, at last, have finally found a good one. There's no time to hide or run away, they're just there, as if in fast forward. Laurence, hand in hand with a girl. And I know, because of what Gina has told me of the cat-shaped eyes and the tiny piercing above her painted mouth that it's Chloe.

Laurence looks petrified, like he just bumped into his mother whilst off his head on drugs.

'Hi,' he says.

'Hi,' I say.

'How are you?'

'Good, you know, getting bigger, you?'

'Yeah good, we're good, everything's um, good.'

Chloe gives me the once over, then she looks up at Laurence, genuine confusion on her face.

'Hun, don't be rude.' She nudges him in the side. 'Aren't you going to introduce me?'

She's well spoken, exotically pretty in a trendy London way with her spotted neckerchief and her kohl-rimmed eyes. Her eyes are quick, intelligent, not the sort to suffer fools. But they're warm, too, there's certainly no sign of the mad hysteric Laurence made her out to be.

'Er, this is Tess,' says Laurence, gesturing towards me but managing to look the other way. 'Tess, this is Chloe.'

She gives me a friendly but knowing nod.

'So when's the baby due?' She smiles. She's just being curious, but Laurence is squirming, desperate to leave.

'December. December the fourteenth.'

'Ahh, you're so lucky. I can't wait to have a baby. Part of

318

me wants to chivvy along the wedding bit just so I can get up the duff!'

'*Wedding?*' I shoot Laurence a look. I think I see his eyes flicker then drop to the floor. 'Yeah, we're engaged. Getting married in September, although I'll believe that when it happens!'

That figures. Back together with her the minute I drop my bombshell. Proposal to follow, all grand gestures but no feeling behind it, no conviction.

'Congratulations.' I force a smile. 'So that must be quite a recent thing, then? A whirlwind wedding?'

'Are you joking?!' laughs Chloe. 'Longest engagement in history this one! He proposed to me three years ago.' I feel my skin go cold. 'It took him another nine months to actually get me the ring but then he still wouldn't actually commit to a date. I had to give him an ultimatum in the end. I chucked him out, sent him packing to stay in my old flat and told him if he didn't have a firm date for the wedding, if he didn't sort his head out in three months, we were over.'

She keeps talking but I can't hear properly, there's too much clatter in my brain as the pieces fit together like a Rubik's cube, which then sits, heavy and solid, at the pit of my stomach. I keep glaring at Laurence, but he doesn't look up, not once, what a total, spineless twat.

'Wow, that's hardcore, but it obviously did the trick.' I smile, eventually. Then, I can't resist it: 'Laurence was obviously ready for the whole wedding and kids thing. The whole *choosing life* thing, though, weren't you Laurence? He just had to have a bit of time to get his head together.'

Just keep walking, just keep walking and don't look back. I feel like I've been winded, I feel kind of breathless. So not only did he not finish with Chloe but he was engaged to her? All that time?! What a fucking mug I've been! How naïve can you get? The thought of us in that flat, *her* flat, me pregnant, exposed with that hideous bra on the floor and the Sebastian Snail thing, oh God! I can never look at that snail again.

I take a sharp left into Romilly Street, I've no plan, my legs are just walking. It's bright, the afternoon's clearing and Soho's bright young things are lounging outside cafés, aviators on, shirts open, one hand smoking a cigarette, the other around the bony, brown shoulders of some other bright young thing, chattering, laughing. An urban aviary of exotic birds. I've seen this so many times. This place is scattered with the remnants of me, but right now, my heart pounding, it feels like it's a scene in a different universe, like I am witnessing it from within a sound-proof glass box.

I can hear my own breathing, everything looks strange. Once, I was one of those bright young things, I felt right here, I fitted in. Now, I'm not so sure anymore. Does a single pregnant woman fit in anywhere?

A gaggle of hens wearing pink feathers in their hair and printed T-shirts topple out of Kettners champagne bar, venue of many a 'sophisticated' night for the former me, followed by hours of sweaty dancing in some basement club. There's the oxblood banquettes of Pollo's Italian restaurant, the one nearest the door surely indented with the shape of me; Bar Italia where I once fell down the stairs and gashed my leg. I walk down Frith Street, the shock's subsiding now, leaving a sense of numbness, of resignation. I jump onto the curb as a motorbike carrying two rowdy guys zooms past me, startling I close my eyes and can almost taste the cheap French wine and chicken escalope for a fiver that I existed on as a trainee journalist, as I pass the dim windows of Café Emm on Frith Street.

And then there's here, our all time favourite, the Coach and Horses, and somehow, even that looks different today.

Like going back to your childhood home to find another family living there.

What a summer this is turning out to be. It was only three months ago that I staggered out of this pub resolving that I would sort out my life, make decisions, move forward. Well, I certainly did that! Although I wasn't expecting to have so little say in the proceedings. I didn't expect life to have such plans for me.

Part of me wishes I could just rewind. Be in that place where my story was yet to be carved out, where there were still so many options, so many roads to choose from. So much hope. I just wasted two months of my life. Laurence took me for a total ride! I'm single – *still* single. Even Gina has managed to sort it out on that front. And the one thing I want, always wanted, really, the very thing that would make this all OK, is never going to happen. But well, that's life I guess, you can't have everything you want. And I've got a baby, a Jim baby, nobody can take that away from me And if this hadn't happened, something else would have. Of that you can be sure.

When I get home Jim is sprawled on the sofa, remote control in hand. When he hears me drop the keys on the kitchen table he turns around.

'Oh hello, what are you doing home?' he says. 'I thought you were staying out with Gina.'

'Change of plan,' I say, taking off my shoes in the hall and going back into the kitchen. I spot a little note next to the phone: 'Tess, V rang, call her back.'

'What time did Vicky ring?' I say, picking it up.

'Oh about fourish.'

'Did she sound OK?'

'Yeah, fine.'

I put it down, thinking I'll call her in a bit.

My Place in the Sun is on the TV. Jim turns the volume down with the remote control.

'So er . . . what's the deal with Gina? Is she ill?' concern crosses his face. 'Are *you* ill?'

'No, I'm fine.' I see Jim's gorgeous face looking up at me and I desperately want to leap on top of him for a hug, like the old times, but I know that wouldn't be appropriate anymore; that we don't fall into bed with each other anymore, that we are friends, slightly frayed friends at that, and that we observe each other's personal space. But I want to tell him everything all the same. About what Laurence did, about today. He's going to be the father of my child, shouldn't we be one hundred per cent honest with each other?

I sit down beside him and I just come out with it.

'Jim, listen, you know when I went out for lunch with Laurence and then I went out for a pizza and you cooked that amazing offal (not even a flinch at the blatant oxymoron) well, I wasn't totally honest with you.'

'Oh right.' Jim sits up on the sofa and turns the TV off.

'The thing is, Laurence and I weren't just meeting as friends. We were dating, we were a sort of item. I know there was the house rule so I wanted to be honest with you. It's been niggling at me ever since.'

Jim's face is a blank.

'What, even though you told him you were pregnant?'

'I didn't tell him – well, I did eventually, but not at first like I told you I did. I told him when we'd already been seeing each other for a while.'

'Why? Oh . . .' Jim gives a shy laugh, like 'silly me'. 'Of course, that would be suicide.'

'I wanted him to fancy me, I didn't want to scare him off. I thought we may even have had a chance.'

'Seriously?' Jim looks a bit shocked.

'Yes. I mean, I know it sounds stupid, but the things he

322

told me about really wanting kids and wanting to get married, I really thought he'd changed and that maybe after the baby was born that we could take it slowly, give it a go.'

'I see. So, what do you call seeing each other?' says Jim 'I mean, did you have?'

'No! God no, although we nearly did. I went back to his house at one point, things got a bit fresh but something got in the way.'

Jim frowns at me. 'Like, a baby I would presume.'

'Yes, the baby. Of *course* the baby,' I say, thinking I cannot believe that Sebastian Snail is etched more in my psyche of that moment than the bloody baby.

'Anyway, that's when I told him.'

'And he couldn't handle it, right?'

'No, course he couldn't and anyway, it turns out there was another complication.'

I tell Jim everything: about how Laurence told me he'd finished it with Chloe and how she was a total bunny boiler and how none of the above was true because all the time he was bloody engaged to her! I tell him how I was just a distraction, a last chance saloon at some no-strings fun, how he clearly spun me a load of crap just to get in my knickers.

'He's such a wanker Tess, you do know that don't you?' Jim says.

'I do now!' I say, smiling, ironically.

We don't say anything for a while, I look out at the front garden, the leaves of the cherry tree blow prettily in the breeze.

'So er . . .' Jim starts to speak, I look at him, but he's not looking at me, he's staring intently at his finger. 'Did you love him?'

And even though I sit there and think, no, I love you, you bloody fool. I say, 'Yes, at one point, I really think I did.'

323

CHAPTER TWENTY-NINE

'There was no way Mike was in denial. It was like we were both pregnant. If I wanted treacle pudding and custard in bed whilst watching Sex and the City, *Mike would join me. If I scoffed cheese on toast in the middle of the night, so did he. We both put on three stone by the end. Problem was, I lost half of that when our daughter was born. A year later, Mike still looks four months gone.'*

Steph, 28, St Albans

How did that happen? I've just woken up and looked at my I 'heart' the Algarve alarm clock and it's 11.10 a.m. I sit up and push myself up against my pillows. Everything feels strange; silent and still like we're snowed in outside, or like I've slept through my alarm and missed a flight somewhere fantastic that all my friends are on right now, singing and drinking beer.

I lie still for a while, the kick kick of our baby like the ticks of a clock, time ebbing away. Then I get up, knock on Jim's door but there's no answer, and when I go in the bed's made so I figure he must have gone out.

I go downstairs in my nightie, stand in the kitchen not quite sure what to do with myself, the only noise, the low purr of the fridge. Out of the corner of my eye I spot last night's note about Vicky's call. Bollocks, I didn't call her back. Yet again I was so wrapped up in my own dramas I totally forgot. I ring my mobile from the landline and it immediately springs into action, rotating like an electrocuted rodent on the coffee table. I scroll through to V.

'Hi, it's me, are you alright? Sorry I totally forgot to call you back last night.'

'Not to worry.' Her voice is sing-songy, more relaxed than she's sounded in ages. 'It's probably better you waited until this morning anyway.'

'Why? What's up? What's happened?'

'Hang on.' Vicky mumbles something, obviously to Rich, I can hear Dylan chuntering in the background. 'I'm just going next door.'

I hear a door close, then a big sigh, then: 'It's alright, we've sort of sorted it now, but Rich and I had a bit of a hoo-ha last night,' she says. (This probably means they almost killed each other, Vicky always plays her own life down.) 'You know my birthday party? You know how Rich went awol for ages and Jim had to start the speech and then when he did turn up he was pissed out of his head?'

'Yeeah.'

'Well, it turned out he was snogging some girl outside. He confessed to me yesterday.'

'*What?! Who?!*' ('Whatabastard' is on the tip of my tongue, but somehow I sense that would be inappropriate.)

'Oh, God, I don't know some bird, a friend of a friend of someone from my course.'

'Yeah but, hang on.' I put my feet up on the coffee table. 'How come you're so calm about it? I'm worried, are you drunk?'

'No! Give over. Honestly, Tess, the sucking up and beating himself up about it all is doing my head in more than what

325

he was like before he confessed!' she laughs. I don't. Has she gone mad?

'Listen, what are you up to today?' she says.

'Er, me? Nothing. Jim's gone off somewhere, I'm just skulking around like a bush pig.' The pneumatic drill starts up on Lordship Lane again.

Vicks laughs. 'Do you want to meet? Rich has got Dylan all day and evening – for obvious reasons. Gina's going to come too, I could tell you all the gory details then?'

'Oh, OK.' I don't sound convinced.

'Don't worry !' she laughs. 'Honestly, it's not as bad as it sounds, I'm kind of glad it happened, actually. Anyway, are *you* OK?'

'Yeah, yeah I'm fine, well there's things to tell you too.'

'Sounds ominous, let's meet. We've clearly got ground to cover.'

We meet at JACK'S bar underneath the railway arches near Southwark station. Everybody's sitting outside amongst the hanging baskets and enormous spider plants. Laidback Ibiza chill-out tunes float from the speaker. For a second, when I spot Gina and Vicky, already tucking into a bottle of white wine I ache for old times, for last summer, before life got so bloody *grown up*.

I can hear Vicky's flat Yorkshire tones from a mile away.

'Thing is,' she's saying, 'he was so wasted he can't even remember who she was. She's irrelevant, anyway, as far as I'm concerned. It's why he did it that's important.'

Gina listens, aghast.

'But he got off with someone, and you're married don't you feel a *bit* fucked off?!'

'Hiya.' I put my bag down and swing my legs over the bench, rather ungainly what with the bump, so I'm sitting opposite them. 'I caught that last bit but you might have to rewind, go right back to the beginning.'

326

So she does. She tells me how Richard had been acting really strange for ages and how everything came to a head last night. They had a huge row about the fact that the dishwasher had been broken for weeks (she was making a stand against doing anything about it because she always sorts everything to do with the house out, apparently. Rich didn't even notice she was making a stand . . .) Then it transpired that Rich was also making a stand, in his way, against being constantly nagged. *Then,* in the heat of the argument, he dropped the bombshell that he'd snogged someone at Vicky's party and that he had been racked with guilt and self-hatred ever since, which actually was the real reason he couldn't face her. Then, he burst into tears.

'He actually got down on his knees at one point,' Vicky says, half laughing, half crying. 'He was so obsessed with this notion that it meant nothing and that I believed that and you know, I know it might sound strange but I really do.'

Gina and I nod in unison because actually, come to think of it, the thought of Richard snogging someone else other than Vicky and it meaning anything is totally preposterous. And we just know him, we can feel what he felt when he sobered up the next morning and remembered. He probably cried then too, sobbed like a baby then signed himself up for some public stoning. It's just not Richard. Rich is many things, but he'll never be a philanderer.

'Anyway,' continues Vicky. 'I blame myself, partly.'

'Really?' I say. 'How's that?'

'Well poor Rich,' she says. 'He must have felt pretty shut out since Dylan was born. I'm so obsessed with being the perfect mum and not ballsing it up like mine did, he probably just wanted some attention. I seem to have turned into a nag, which I vowed I would *never* do. And I just think, I don't cut him much slack. Just because I've had to work out how to do everything, had to develop such heightened life skills – out of necessity and survival more than anything – I

327

expect him to too. But really, I never married a man who would earn a lot, or be good at DIY or paying the bills, or mending the goddamn dishwasher did I?'

'And, I've been so ungenerous about the script writing thing. I mean I know it'll probably come to nothing but he's proud of it, and it's a creative outlet for him and to be honest, I'm just bitter and twisted and jealous because I no longer sing, I mean, why do I no longer sing?' she says, exasperated with her own lack of initiative.

I watch Vicky as she talks, that wide open face, the broad smile that comes often and easily, the clear blue, make-up-less eyes behind which lie no secrets, no mind games and I think how much I admire her. She looks in the mirror and she sees who she really is, and I wonder, do I do that?

We chat, the sun shines high and the barman brings me a virgin Mary and I imagine I am, actually, sitting with my mates at Café del Mar and I forget about me. Then Vicky slaps a hand to her forehead.

'Oh my God! Tess! There's me banging on about me and I haven't even asked about you, so what's happened?'

'Shit, yeah.' Gina's spine straightens. 'What's happening re Laurence?'

'Oh God.' I drape myself dramatically across the table then go through the whole story. Vicky, bless her, has the decency never to say 'I told you so' or even look like she's thinking it, but I know she is. Gina just hides behind her sunglasses, but I can tell by the way she's twirling her hair and kind of pouting, like an embarrassed teenager, that she feels partly responsible, just for being an acquaintance of his – even though I don't blame her at all.

'Ah,' she grimaces when I've finished, 'so it turns out, he's still a total shit, then, that he hasn't changed one bit.' Which I appreciate, because I know the effort it's taken her to say that.

'Oh Jarvis,' sighs Vicky. 'You've really been through it

this past month haven't you, eh? Life's had it in for you.'

'All my own fault no doubt, the muppet that I am. But you know the worst thing about all this?'

'No what's the worst thing?' they say.

'I think I'm in love with Jim.'

The squealing and hitting me over the head till I have to almost cower to protect myself goes on for at least a minute. Gina has to have a fag to celebrate.

'Oh my God, I knew it!' Vicky wags a finger at me. Her eyes light up with knowing delight. 'I knew that face of yours, that smile, every time anybody ever spoke about him!'

'Yeah,' adds Gina, taking a drag, 'and that look of love when he got wasted at the barbie and everyone else thought he was acting like a knob end.'

'Er, actually,' I correct, 'I did not love that. *You* didn't have to mop up his wee when he missed the toilet bowl later that night.'

'Oh will you listen to her!' laughs Gina, '*how* married?!'

Despite myself I blush, with happy embarrassment, but then the reality of the situation wipes the smile of my face.

'Anyway,' I say, 'it doesn't really matter what I feel because it still ain't happening.'

Their faces fall, 'Eh?'

'Jim doesn't feel the same way, I know he doesn't. There was a time, we had this day in Whitstable, right, and it was glorious and wonderful and I thought, maybe, he did feel something but since then, honestly, he may as well be camping outside that solicitor's he's so desperate for the flat to go through . . .'

'What do you mean?' says Vicky, her whole body deflating.

'Well, I only put an offer in because Jim was so enthusiastic about the idea. And then you should have heard him, he would have been down there decorating if I'd have let him this weekend. He wants me out, asap.'

'I don't believe it,' says Vicky, shaking her head.

Gina takes off her sunglasses.

'That's because it's bollocks,' she says.

'How are you so sure?' I say. She's looking sheepish now and I'm a bit unnerved.

'I just am.'

'Er, like how? Gina? You can't say something like that then not say anything else.'

'Look, promise you won't be mad with me?' she pleads, getting hold of my hand. 'Because if I had known then what I know now there's no way it would have happened.'

My heart is pounding. 'No, I won't be mad at you.'

'That night, when you went out with Laurence, basically, well . . .' She looks away, embarrassed, I've never seen Gina like this. 'I made a move on Jim. Oh God! I was so drunk!'

I gasp, not out of horror, but just shock. Jim's the last person I thought Gina would have gone for!

'I'm sorry Tess, I had no idea you felt like you did I thought . . . oh fuck.'

'Yeah, oh fuck Gina,' mumbles Vicky, shaking her head in disbelief.

'But listen,' she says, I sit there, open-mouthed. 'nothing happened, I swear nothing happened, do you know why?'

'No, why?'

'Because he wants you. Only you, Tess! He said if he was going to kiss anyone, it would only be you. The thing is, I've always fancied Jim.'

'OhmiGod,' squeaks Vicky. This is getting farcical now.

'When you two were attached to each other at the hip all the way through uni I was so fucking jealous.' I've never seen Gina so transparent before, it's like she's turned on a light and we can see right inside her head. 'I used to fantasize about going out with someone like Jim – so caring and funny and *creative,* properly creative. Not a pretend creative which is all I ever seemed to get. But I knew even then he was in love with you, it was so bloody obvious. Then, when you got pregnant, I was kind of mad with you, you know? Because it seemed such a waste. You didn't even want him and now nobody could have him – least of all me!'

Vicky looks at Gina, gobsmacked. I just sit there wondering if I'm dreaming.

'OK,' says Gina, when we don't say anything. 'You can both stop looking demented now. Tess, it's OK, I'm in no way a threat. Jim and I would never work, I'm too intolerant, he's too laidback and anyway, I'm totally in love with Simon, but I'm telling you, Tess . . .'

I look at her now and I find myself smiling.

'I'm telling you because I love you. I love you guys to bits, you and him. And I want you to know the truth and to sort it out, and –' she lifts her hands – in exasperation – to fucking get it together. Like, come on!!'

I sit there and I feel, I don't know what I feel, an explosion of joy, I suppose, and of gratitude. I get up, go round to the other side of the table, and as I do I sense just a twitch of a flinch from Gina – my God, she thinks I might hit her! But of course, I don't. I take her glass from her hand, sit down beside her and wrap my arms around her bare, tanned shoulders. 'Thanks Gina. Thank you,' I say, 'I love you too.'

I am practically sprinting – well running as fast as my condition will allow me – along Blackfriars Road, planning what I'm going to say in my head. The sky is clear, my head's clearer than it's ever been. I've got my hand over my mouth, I feel like I might overflow with happiness. I get my mobile out to call Jim, to ask when he's coming back. I want to see him – but as I do, my mobile rings. It's Ed, my brother. 'Tess? he says. 'Can you come home? Like, right away? It's dad.'

CHAPTER THIRTY

"We adopted Kira just before Christmas. By New Year I was at my wits end, we just weren't getting along. Then one snowy day in February, something clicked. I suddenly fell in love. I have since learned that it sometimes isn't immediate even when the baby's biologically yours. I can't believe I worried so much.'

Annabel, 36, Exeter

It turns out that whilst I was losing sleep over my loser of an ex, my dad was in his greenhouse knocking back three quarters of a bottle of vodka, and twenty-three paracetamol.

Lancaster Royal Infirmary is not a white, bright, modern type of hospital; it is very much an infirmary, for the infirm: dark stone, Victorian, ivy gripping its walls, like sadness has gripped my poor dad's mind. My brother is waiting for me outside when I get there, unshaven and blotchy-faced.

'Tess.' He hugs me tight when he sees me. It's only the second sober hug we've given each other in our lives. 'Thank God you got here. He keeps asking when you're going to arrive. I'm telling you, he just wants to see you.'

We go inside, the smell – of dust on red-hot radiators,

disinfectant and congealed gravy – makes my legs buckle. I have never seen my dad with anything more serious than a dodgy stomach and here I am, in this depressing place, where even your footsteps seem to echo like a ghost and it just seems so wrong, so shocking.

I follow Ed down the corridor, past a woman with swollen feet in a wheelchair, a jaundiced man with a packet of cigarettes in his pyjama pocket. We get in the lift with a male nurse and a man, also in a wheelchair, with snow white hair and pupils like frog spawn. He looks at least a hundred and fifty.

The lift stops at the next floor. 'Alright Albert, this is us,' says the nurse, as he rolls the man out into the empty corridor.

'So how is he?' I say, turning to Ed. 'Does he look really bad? Should I prepare myself?'

Ed puts a brotherly arm around me.

'No, no, he doesn't look that bad. He's just really tired and you know, emotional.'

It turns out that for once in his life my brother has been the master of understatement.

My dad, my bold, funny dad who once actually made me wee myself in a Lake District gift shop he was making me laugh so much, is sad, properly sad.

The round shiny cheeks have had the air sucked out of them, his eyes are sunken and dead. His skin, pale as the moon, seems to hang off his face like wet clay. This is not my dad.

I try to smile, not to look shocked but my mum takes the words right out of my mouth.

'I know, he looks bloody awful, doesn't he?'

Even in this state, dad manages to crack a smile.

'Hi dad.' I walk around the bed and kiss him softly on the cheek. 'How are you feeling?'

'Stupid, hungover, *blinding* headache,' he mumbles. I sit down beside him and he takes my hand. 'Now I can sympathize why you two used to take to your beds all day after a night on the hard stuff.'

I look at mum, she smiles but her lips are quivering. I notice that dad has a drip in his hand.

I pick up a bunch of grapes from the bedside table next to him. 'Is this all they brought you? Tight or what?' Mum makes a half-hearted effort at a noise that means 'charming'.

'Thank God for your daughter, eh?' I take the Terry's chocolate orange I bought in Euston station out of my rucksack. 'I brought you this.'

Dad pats my hand, 'Good lass,' he says. 'My favourite, that.'

'And this.' I get out the Vaughan Williams CD, the one featuring 'The Lark Ascending' on it. 'My doctor introduced me to this. She says it cheers her up, makes her feel happy to be alive.'

Mum fusses with his blankets.

'Well let's not get ideas above your station,' she says. 'Out of hospital will do for a start, full of the joys of spring is something to aim for.'

We sit – me, Ed and mum – around dad's bed, the curtain pulled around the cubicle. It hasn't been the four of us like this since about 1999. Mum wants to tell me the whole story. Ed says he's heard the story at least three times now what with Joy having come to visit and the two nannas calling mum. Mum says she doesn't think it's healthy not to talk, not anymore she doesn't, which makes me wonder what else she's got to hide. The story goes: Mum woke up at two in the morning on Saturday to find dad not in the bed. When she came downstairs he wasn't in the house either. She says, 'I thought, oh marvellous, he's only gone and slept walked and is probably wandering down bloody Glebe Close right now, stark naked, how on earth am I going to live that one down?' Then she spotted the little torchlight on in the greenhouse.

He confessed to the pills immediately, apparently. 'Although I would have known sooner or later because I count those pills religiously, every single night.' (proving that she's even battier than I thought.) Dad never wanted to actually die, he'd never do that to her, to us, she tells me, talking about him like he's not even there. No, my dad just wanted to make it all go away for a bit, to go to sleep and then wake up when things felt better.

Mum says the paramedics were amazing. One of them looked like that 'really dishy one' from *Relocation Relocation*, apparently. And the hospital staff – apart from one 'girl with a face like a slapped behind' who's probably just finished with her boyfriend – have been fantastic. Absolutely faultless.

Dad joins in occasionally, but mainly he lies there with something like an apologetic expression on his face, or maybe it's embarrassment. And it's ironic, this is the most tragic day our family has ever experienced – the day my dad ends up in hospital because he feels so utterly desolate that he wants it all to stop? And yet strangely, in some way, I know that this time, right now, will be a good one in the Jarvis memory bank. Bitter sweet, but sweet all the same.

At 7.30 p.m., an hour and a half after I arrive, Ed goes home to put the kids to bed and mum suggests we go to the canteen to give dad a rest.

'Danny Ford Café', no doubt named after a person who is no longer with us, which kind of puts you off your food for a start, is empty apart from two heavily pregnant women in dressing gowns and a man with some kind of brace around his head.

A mural – a depiction of all the seasons from snowmen and Santa Claus to a huge bonfire made from tissue paper, probably done by local school kids covers one wall, the other is painted a sickly green. The tables and chairs – in white and red plastic respectively are stuck to the floor. I wouldn't be surprised if a fair few people hadn't sustained an injury worthy of a week's stay in hospital after forgetting this fact and head butting the table when they stand up.

We queue up, mum buys an egg mayo sandwich and I get a bacon roll. Then we sit down. Mum folds her arms.

'You must be wondering what all this is about,' she says. The only sound apart from her voice, is the random clink of cutlery, like an avant-garde percussion piece.

'Well, yeah, I suppose so. It's a bit out of the blue,' I say, conscious of not being too dramatic. She's probably had enough drama to last her a lifetime in these last twenty-four hours. 'I mean, dad's depressed obviously, but I had no idea how bad he was, I mean how long?'

'All your life.'

I blink, I don't compute.

'He's suffered from depression all your life.'

'But how, I mean how can he have? He's always so . . .'

'Happy?'

'*Yes.*'

'Oh Tess, he has been happy in his life. My God, when you two came along, it made him the happiest man in the world. But just before you were born, your dad had a nervous breakdown.'

'What?' It comes out as a whisper.

'He took an overdose; far, far more serious than this and I very nearly lost him Tessa. My first and only love, very nearly gone.' She smiles, she's wearing the same pink lipstick she always wears, but her eyes well up with tears.

'Oh mum, I had no idea.'

'But, listen.' Mum comes to sit beside me and gives me a hug because I'm crying too now. 'I had you and your brother, thank God, or else I don't know how I'd have got up in the morning. And I had to carry on, I *did* carry on. It was very hard because your dad was in hospital for weeks and even when he came out he wasn't fit to do much for six months . . .'

'So you knew.'

I lift my head from her shoulder.

'Knew what?'

'You knew about being a single mum and there was I telling you to shut up! Oh God, mum, I'm so sorry.'

'Don't be daft.' She gets hold of my head and makes me look at her. 'I just wanted you to know I could empathize that's all, I didn't feel I could tell you why at that point. I wish I had now.'

'So, why didn't you tell us?' I say, leaning back on my chair.

Even now, mum can't help herself. 'Don't do that Tessa, please,' she says. 'You can break your spinal column like that.' Then she continues, 'We wanted to protect you, we wanted to give you the best start in life, the most normal family life possible. You wait.' She pats my bump. 'When you have that baby you'll feel like that too. The thought of anything shattering their world just breaks your heart, and so we agreed never to tell you, I mean, it wasn't like your dad was suicidal all the time.' She laughs through the tears. 'But our little plan didn't quite work out, did it?'

'So, you weren't really happy, when we were younger? You just pretended to be, for mine and Ed's sakes?'

'Oh Tess, don't be silly.' Mum takes a packet of tissues out of her handbag. 'We've had more happiness, more joy from you two than any parent could wish for.' She looks straight at me now. 'But it hasn't always been easy, no. It certainly hasn't always been what I expected married life to be like. But I wouldn't change it because I love him, you see, that silly man in there. He drives me up the wall with worry but I couldn't do without him.' She takes a tissue from the packet and dabs at her face. 'And he *certainly* couldn't live without me.'

'No,' I say. 'I can see that.'

When we get back to his room, Dad's propped up on his pillows looking physically much brighter.

'I have to chat to the duty shrink,' he says, tentatively. 'But as soon as they've referred me for whatever it is they refer you for . . .'

'Psychiatric care, Tony.'

'Yes,' says dad, 'that stuff. Then I can go home.'

'What about the drip?' says mum, standing at the foot of his bed.

'They're going to test my liver function but they say I'm probably OK by now. All rehydrated, good to go.'

'Dad, that's brilliant news,' I say, sitting back down on the seat beside his bed again and opening up the Terry's chocolate orange. 'Shall we have a segment? To celebrate?'

Mum starts rummaging in her bag, bottom in the air. 'Well I'm going to ring your mother,' she says to dad. 'Otherwise we'll have another one in here, dropping dead from worry.'

Mum leaves and dad and I sit in silence for a few moments, the smell of chocolate orange filling the room as we eat. I could talk about the weather or the sorry state of hospital food but instead, I take a leap into the dark.

'Mum told me,' I say. 'About your depression.'

Dad breaks off another segment and sits there, holding it.

'She did? Oh.' He doesn't look up. 'She's a sly one, that mother of yours.'

We carry on eating, neither of us saying anything and I realize that perhaps, all those times in the greenhouse, we only ever talked about my problems, or about my uncle, my dad never really talked about himself, and I never really asked.

338

'You didn't actually think you could hide it from me for ever, did you dad?' I say eventually.

'I was hoping I wouldn't have to. I was hoping it would never come back.'

'But it did.'

'Yeah,' he sighs, 'the bugger came back.'

'And it's likely to again in the future?'

'I suppose that's what being a depressive means.'

'Well I know I'm a lot younger than you and I don't know much about life and all that but dad, I really hope from now on you feel you can talk to me about how you're feeling, eh? I mean, really feeling. What do you think?'

Dad smiles at me then covers his face and makes a sound I've never heard him make before like he's having trouble breathing. I worry he *is* having trouble breathing or that his headache's come back but then I realize, that for the first time in my life, I am watching my dad cry.

'Come on dad.' I rub his arm, but inside I'm shocked to the core. 'Come on, it's OK, I promise you, it'll get better.'

'I'm the one who should be saying that to you,' dad says, drying his eyes with the bed sheets. 'I feel I've let you down, you and Ed, you must think your old man's a right basket case.'

'Dad, shut up, OK? Stop talking rubbish. You could never, *ever* let me down. That thing you did – hiding your illness from me even when you were at rock bottom, that's the biggest sacrifice a parent could ever make. That's not to say I'm not annoyed with you.'

Dad sniffs and manages a smile.

He takes hold of my hand 'My Tess,' he says, 'you know, you always were that bit special.'

'Special needs?' I joke.

'Yeah, well, that as well but no, I mean properly special. My special girl.'

'Why?' I say. 'That's such a lovely thing to say but why?'

'Because I very nearly never got to meet you, that's why. I very nearly wasn't your dad.'

'Right, that's all done!' mum suddenly barges in through the curtain, a trail of Paloma Picasso behind her. Dad squeezes my hand then lets go. 'Your mother's happy you're coming home, where I can keep an eye on you. Now, shall I chuck these grapes out or has anyone brought a spare Tupperware?'

I spend the night at mum and dad's. The next day, dad's understandably quiet and not at all his old self but he begs me to go back to London, promises he won't be on the vodka again in a hurry.

'Now don't you go worrying about me,' he says, before I get in the car with mum to go to the station. 'Just look after yourself and that baby, OK? Love you, girl.' He hugs me and kisses the top of my head. I get in the car. As we drive away, I have a sudden bloom of clarity. I know what I have to do.

I get back home at two in the afternoon and the house is still eerily quiet. 'Jim?' I call out but there's no answer. 'Jim are you in?' Nothing. I run upstairs, his bed's made, just as it was the day I left for Morecambe. I go back down to the kitchen and look at the notepad near the phone – perhaps he's left a note to say where he is but there's nothing. I go to the fridge to get a drink. The note is written on a pink post it note.

Dear Tess,
I can't handle it – this just good friends thing, the Laurence thing. I thought I could but I can't. I've gone away for a couple of days. I'll be OK, please don't worry. I love you,
Jim x
    p.s. Jocelyn rang
Shit.

CHAPTER THIRTY-ONE

'I was pregnant once. I was twenty-eight and had just been promoted to news editor on the Essex Chron and Echo. My boyfriend didn't want the kid, he was twelve years older than me and said if I kept it, I could forget ever realizing my dream of working on a National. I never realized that dream anyway and I never got the kid. I've never really forgiven him for that.'
Judith, 41, Hounslow.

I have to find him. Whatever it takes, I have to find Jim.

There's only two places I think he can be. I'll try one and if he's not there I'll go to the second. I run upstairs, throw a few things into a bag: knickers, moisturizer and the *Bundle of Joy* book, I don't know why, I just get the feeling I'm going to need it.

The house is full of Jim: His Adidas top hung up on the banister, his socks on the radiators.

In the kitchen sink is a mug, *his* mug that says, 'Why am I such a Mug?' And a plate still with the remnants of marmite crumpets smeared on the side and I wonder, what was going through his head when he ate breakfast this morning? I dread to think.

I go into his room, it smells so much of him, and I ache for him. I want Jim. I walk over to where the computer is on a small desk in the corner, piled high at the sides with assessment papers, meticulously put together lesson plans, a copy of *Henry IV*. I log onto Google and thank God when I find what I am looking for. He didn't try hard to conceal it, did he want me to know?

'B&Bs in Whitstable'. It's still typed into the search box. I am not surprised, not really, it was either there or home and I know that home is hardly a sanctuary for Jim. There's a train in just over an hour. If I hurry, I might just get there. So, I get my bag, keys, phone and purse and run to the bus stop on Lordship Lane.

But just as I am about to cross the road, I see Rachel. She is not at the bus stop as usual, but this side of the road, a little bit along, carrying Matilda.

I try to look calm, but I can't hide the fact that I'm flustered. 'Hi,' I wave, 'how are you? Good?'

'Hi,' she says, but she is looking down, the brim of her sun-hat is covering her face.

'Are you OK?' I walk towards her, a bit worried now. 'I haven't seen you since . . .'

'Not really.' She looks up at me, her eyes are full of fear, her right eye is swollen, half-closed and bruised.

'Oh my God, what happened to your face?!' The train that leaves in less than an hour is calling me but I can't *not* do something, I can't ignore this. 'Look, do you want to go for a coffee?' I say, 'We could have a chat? I'm worried.'

'I can't,' she says, and at that point, a car rolls up, a black Golf, the same car I saw that day, and . . . Alan is driving. It all clicks into place. He doesn't look at me, he just stares straight ahead. She gets in the back, sitting Matilda on her lap, puts the seat-belt on and she doesn't look at me either. Then he revs the engine and it is only as he screeches off that

I meet his eyes; cold, dead eyes, glaring at me and then she's gone again, and I am left standing on the pavement, feeling sick to the stomach and resolving, that whatever happens after today, I will find her too.

The number 36 bus crawls down Kennington Road but my heart is racing and I'm thinking of Jocelyn. Why did she call me on a Saturday? She never calls at the weekend. I think about calling her and asking her what she said but I'd rather spare myself the details. I am a coward.

Instead I take the note, curled up in my palm and look at it again 'I love you,' he's written. Not, 'love Jim', or 'much love, Jim', but I LOVE YOU, and the urge to find him and to explain everything is so strong it's like a madness has taken over me.

The bus takes an age, all the time the stress building inside me, making my fingers curl inwards and the muscles of my face contort. As soon as the bus doors open I jump off and leg it, bag tearing over the tarmac behind, holding my bump into Victoria station. I have three minutes to spare: 'Platform 2 for Dover Priory!' shouts the voice over the tannoy. But I haven't got a ticket, fuck it, I haven't got time to get a ticket. I run over to the gate, it's worth a try.

'I need to get that train and I don't have time to get a ticket can I buy one on the train?' I plead, breathlessly.

The man shakes his head. I hear a whistle blow.

'Please?' I beg. I can feel the panic rattle inside me like a kettle on the brink of boiling and the tears start to well. ' I have to meet my, my . . . the father . . .' Showing the bump works a treat, the man sighs and nods. 'Thank you so much!' I shout and as I run off down the platform I blow him a kiss.

I only just make it on as the doors are closing and then we creak off into the wide, sunny blue. We pass Battersea, Clapham, kids playing in playgrounds, the multi-coloured bustle of Brixton Market. In fifteen minutes we have left London behind and all there is at either side are fields of barley, silver-green, swaying in the breeze, like plants on the ocean floor. I am aware now, with some distance between us, what a cobbled together life I have left back there, and how much this, whatever I am rolling towards, feels like my one and only chance of happiness.

The countryside stretches, sun-soaked at either side. The hot summer has already blanched the fields and it is only July. Soon, in a few days, Jim will break up for the summer, then it will be August, autumn and where will we be then?

A bunch of girls get on at Rochester. They look about eighteen, no more than twenty. The stereotypes are all there: the rebel with her kohl eyes and bleached blonde hair; the Prom Princess, I bet she gets all the boys; the ring-leader, ponytail swinging, commanding respect from her disciples as if she were Jesus. The outsider sits next to me: overweight, awkward in her own skin, hiding behind a strawberry blonde fringe. And where am I? Age twenty, in this group of girls about to hit the seaside? There I am, that one there, laughing along with the ring-leader, thinking I have life all worked out and that everything's going to fall into place just because I am me, because I am lucky.

We finally get to Whitstable, I follow the old fashioned sign labelled The Sea Front. But the way it takes me is not the tourist route, it is not the Whitstable of that day Jim and I spent together. This is normal life: streets of terraces, kids playing outside on their bikes in the evening sun. I reach the harbour, the smell of the sea hits me, catapulting me back, the memory as strong as a photograph. Beyond the boats, which sit in the deep, walled-in marina, is a huge yellow crane, dipping then rising, lifting bundles of stone from one point to another. It is noisy and dirty but somehow just being here relaxes me.

I walk along and reach the quiet of the beach, to the yacht club where the masts creak in the heat. Outside the club is a family with a little girl, probably aged about seven. She's wearing pink towelling shorts over a striped swimming costume. She's sitting on her dad's knee, swinging her legs and drinking coca-cola through a curly straw and I wonder, at what point, life stopped feeling like that.

I really have no idea where Jim might be right now, I don't know what B&B he chose, or if he even booked a B&B at all. I know, almost certainly, he won't be in the one we stayed in – it would be far too indulgent for Jim – and besides, there's too many good memories there. But I have an idea that's worth a shot.

The Old Neptune. I can see it in the distance like a ship itself, moored up on the shingle beach, all lopsided and white-washed. It's 6.15 p.m. and still warm. Jim wouldn't be in a hotel room in weather like this and yet, with his skin, I can't see him laid out frazzling on the beach either. I pass The Whitstable Oyster Company with its red and white table-cloths and London clientele – mainly wealthy couples in their 60s who take a gin and tonic in the afternoon. I am nearly there now, I check the masses of people laid out on the beach, just in case but I know I've got it right, I just know he'll be there.

But he's not.

I look outside, scan each and every table rammed with rowdy, faceless tourists who clock my anxious face then move their feet and peer under their tables as if they think I am looking for a lost bag. I go inside the pub where a few local fishermen are gathered around the ornate bar supping pints of ale, their bellies protruding from their over-alls. 'Has a tall, dark-haired guy been in here recently?' I ask. 'Northern accent? Good looking?' 'Wouldn't know if he had, love, three sheets to the wind now,' one says, the others laugh and look at me, like I am from some other planet. I check inside the toilets but then I give up. I think about calling him on his mobile, but that just seems crass, it has to be a last resort. And so I stand on the beach for a while, deciding what to do. I look out at the sea and take a moment to try to describe it, just like Jim and I did on the beach, but the words won't come, it's like my imagination disappeared with that day. Or is it that I can only do it when I'm happy?

I leave the beach, take the steps that lead me onto the main promenade and decide to carry on, what else is there to do? The beach widens, that same stretch we sat on, then the shingle thins and in ten minutes or so I am at that cluster of beach huts again, standing bright like boiled sweets in the sun. I stop by them, aimless now, peer into the ones that seem to have entire beds in there, sofas, armchairs, mini interior design projects with pretty bunting and vintage kettles.

'Ah, so *you* fancy one now, do you?'

I start and look around me, I can't tell where the voice is coming from. And then I see him. Jim. Sitting on the steps of a ramshackle hut, a pint in his hand, squinting in the sun.

'Hello,' I say, I can't help but beam. He's got his jeans rolled up and already his shins are burning. 'What are you doing here?'

'Shouldn't I be the one asking you that?' he says. 'I'm having a sundowner, well, an early one anyway.'

'Can I join you?' I ask tentatively. He gestures beside him, and I sit down, the shells crackling like fire beneath my feet.

'You didn't have to come, that wasn't the idea. How did you know where I was, anyway?'

'You left the computer on, B&Bs in Whitstable was still typed into Google.'

He tuts.

'Couldn't even find one, anyway, everywhere's booked up, start of the school holidays for some kids, I s'pose.'

We sit, unsaid words humming like bluebottles above our heads.

'Jim, are you OK?' I say, unable to bear it any longer. 'I'm so sorry you must be so angry with me.'

'No,' says Jim. 'Not anymore.' He takes a piece of paper out of his jeans and unfolds it. 'I wrote this for you. I know it's not going to change anything, I was maybe just going to keep it, never even show it to you, but it helped to write it.'

I take the piece of paper. 'Shall I read it now?'

'Na,' Jim scrunches up his nose, 'read it another time when I'm not here.'

'What's it about?' I say.

'Oh nothing, it's just to say thank you, that's all.'

'Thank you? What for?'

'For making me feel this. I did it, Tess.' He looks at me now. 'I did it, I fell in love, didn't I?'

'Like your friend from school,' I say. Jim looks down and smiles, because he knows what I am thinking and he knows I am right.

'Yeah,' he says, 'like my friend from school.'

I feel dizzy, it's like all my feelings, every good, happy feeling I've ever felt is rolled up and fizzing in my head like a ball of dynamite ready to explode.

'But Jim.'

'No, honestly, don't, it's alright,' he says. 'I know we can't have the happy ever after and all that, but as far as I'm concerned, I am happy. I'm glad I know you, I'm glad all this happened, it's made me feel things I never knew I was capable of feeling. And even if I never feel this again, I know I felt it once. And that's enough. Maybe that's enough.'

'But *Jim*,' I put my hand on his arm. 'You *can* have it, don't you realize?'

'What?'

'That thing, that happy ever after thing. Well, not that, that's all bollocks, but me, us, a real family.'

He looks at me stunned.

'I feel it too, Jim. I love you too!' I say, eyes shining.

'Love me?'

'*In* love with you, then. God . . .' I laugh. 'So love with you it's ridiculous!

'What? But what about Laurence? What about what you said . . .'

'Laurence? I never wanted Laurence, Jim, Laurence was just a distraction. I only ever wanted you but you didn't seem interested. I mean, for Christ's sake you couldn't get me into that Camberwell flat quickly enough, you did a better job than Craig from Kinleigh Fuck Hard and Pay Less at getting me to buy that flat!'

Jim looks at me incredulously and laughs.

'Only because I couldn't handle it any longer! You being in my house, the dreading you leaving, the wanting to have sex with you, like *all* the time, have you any idea what that does to a man? And to love you,' he rests his head on his knees and looks at me, 'God, I wanted to love you so fucking much.'

The heat of the day has made the sky hazy so that it melts into the sea and you can't see where one starts and the other begins.

I look at Jim. A speedboat cuts through the horizon, like a zip. Then he turns to face me, 'Come here,' he says. And when we kiss, falling back onto the sand as we do, it feels like I might combust with joy, and the feeling that nothing, ever, in my whole entire life, has ever felt this good.

'So you know Jocelyn . . .' I say. I have to be brave. We're lying next to each other on the sand now, are hands entwined, looking up at the cloudless sky. 'What did she actually say?'

'God knows,' says Jim. 'Some babble about a silver teddy bear she saw and will we be having a christening?'

I smile, I squeeze his hand tight. I *am* lucky, after all. And I feel, for the first time in months, that I am not hankering after the past, or wishing for the future I am just here, in the here and now.

CHAPTER THIRTY-TWO

New Year's Eve, Five Months Later.

'We went to Memphis when I was six months pregnant. Everybody said it was a girl: the hotel receptionist, an old blues singer called Razor who still busked on Beale Street. An Elvis impersonator outside Sun Studios. There was no competition for a name when he finally arrived, would you believe it, on January 8th. The King is reborn!'

Sarah-Jane, 41, Cardiff.

'Let's hear it for Victoria Peddlar – woo hoo!' Our lounge erupts. The MERRY CHRISTMAS banner above the hearth flutters with the man-made breeze.

Jim curls his fist, pulls his elbow tight to his chest. 'Come ON!!' he shouts, his jaw clenched, so serious is he in his support. I watch him, wedged in between Awful and Rich and involuntarily snort into a giggle. He's been 'wetting the baby's head' for six weeks now.

Vicky hoists herself up from her chair, takes her place on the makeshift stage in front of our bay window and rests the mike on her bump. It protrudes, perfectly spherical from her gold, sequinned dress like a religious relic, crying out to be touched.

The dress is short, girlishly mini and her hair – the result of four hours in Aveda this afternoon, a Christmas present from Rich, is newly highlighted and pinned up at the back of her head. The Christmas tree lights flicker behind her, making her dress twinkle like there's a magic spell in progress, like she's about to disappear in a puff of smoke.

She pulls her broad smile into a comical grimace – it's the nerves – and tidies a tendril of hair behind her ear. She looks vulnerable and beautiful, you can almost hear the pride smoke from Rich's face. The backing track starts and then, she starts to sing – 'Mack the Knife' – by Frank Sinatra. And yeah, she's definitely still got it.

Mum and dad are first to the floor. They don't have to say anything or look at each other's feet, they just take their positions, as naturally and automatically as getting on a bike. Mum stretches one dumpy arm so she can reach dad's shoulder. Dad's hand – rough, suntanned, lived in – goes to rest on the small of her back. I wonder how many times they've performed that ritual, and how many times they will in the future. Somehow, just knowing they will, makes me feel good. Whatever happens, whatever shit hits the fan, the wheel keeps turning after all. Life carries on.

Everyone's up and dancing now, our tiny lounge, hotting up with the heat of bodies. Rich – resplendent in a gold sequinned blazer is dancing with Rachel, relaxed in a tasteful, moss-green dress. She and Matilda have been a regular fixture in our house since she finally did it, she finally left Alan and moved in with her mum. The first time Matilda had a full-on meltdown (at our house on Boxing Day as it happens) I detected delight on Rachel's face. Turns out she wasn't an unusually good baby at all. If I'd have seen my mum have three shades kicked out of her every time I made a sound, I might learn to shut up too.

I am sitting on the arm of the bobbly green armchair now (Jim says some things are staying, end of story) watching the scene unfold. It's funny how it takes a party to bring people truly together. As if for those few hours, we have a pass out from life and the things that separate us. Even Joyless has cracked a smile, being flung about by my brother whose rather erratic dance moves are more like those of a ten-year-old page boy at a wedding reception than a grown man. Gina, spilling out of a midnight blue prom dress is engaged in a semi-choreographed routine with Awful, all kicks and jazzy hands. Awful's taken his shoes off and his feet stink, but Gina doesn't care because Awful's not her boyfriend. That guy with the freckles mixing cocktails in our kitchen is. Turns out I was right about her and Simon. It's been six months now – the longest Gina's ever had a boyfriend – and she's finally got herself a bed, in his house, they moved in together back in October.

Vicky belts out the last few verses. She doesn't dance or sway when she sings, she just closes her eyes and this sound, from somewhere in her guts pours out, rests on your skin like warm candle wax. The cocktails make their way around the room on a tray held high above Simon's head, Gina takes one then snogs him full on the mouth in full view of my mother who stares then looks away as if she didn't see in the first place. Outside, a gaggle of rowdy party goers bang on the window, 'Happy New Year!' They shout before running away. Awful pulls a moonie and my mum makes this sound like she just sat on a whoopee cushion. And then I see Jim, eyes shining, face flushed pink from dancing, hair slightly sweaty at the sides, making a beeline for me, parting the crowds. He takes me by the shoulders, 'Would Madam care to dance ce soir?' he says. And I laugh, because that's what he used to say to me when we used to go to Frankie's. But he's not talking to me, he's talking to the little dark haired thing curled up in a sling on my chest. He's talking to our daughter.

Freya Kate Ashcroft decided to begin her journey to the outside world whilst her father was on a school trip with his mobile turned off. So whilst Jim was having a jolly old time, laughing at a matinee performance of *The History Boys* with a bunch of sixth formers, I was puking into a bucket with every contraction, then leaving obscene messages on his answer phone. (I know, he played them back to me).

Gina was the only person I could get hold of (something my mother will never forgive herself for. She was in Matalan buying a blow-up-bed.) I admit, I did have my reservations, you never can tell if Gina will be sober on a Saturday afternoon for one thing. But she was brilliant. She mopped up when my waters broke and fixed up the Tens machine. She walked around the block with me and didn't bat an eyelid whilst I gripped lampposts and made a noise like two sumo wrestlers having sex, as people walked past. When the midwife claimed my contractions still weren't close enough together for me to come into hospital Gina got feisty, accused her of never having had a baby (she'd had five. That wasn't such a good move). But apart from that, she was fantastic. I could never have got that far without her.

So much for the 'Home from Home' room at the birthing unit. If this was home, I dread to think what hell is like. My Knickerbox nightie and aromatic candle from Mamas and Papas, never saw the light of day. My bare arse did, hanging out from a backless hospital gown as I wandered like a lost farm animal around the birthing unit, stopping to have contractions on the stairwell.

By the time Jim got there, bursting through the delivery

suite doors, the fear of God streaked across his face like fresh blood, I was off my head on gas and air begging for someone to finish me off. But eventually she arrived, our girl, as cone-headed and wise as Gandalf. She was like a soul slipping from one world to the next like an arm through a sleeve. And then well, nothing else mattered.

I'm in the kitchen now, boiling the kettle for the bottle of expressed milk I spent forty minutes attached to an electric breast pump for, so I could drink tonight. Jim says I look like I'm employed by Willy Wonka when I'm expressing, like I should be in a sterilized room in the Chocolate Factory with other mums, making The Super Sonic Mummy Milkybar.

My mum comes shimmying out of the crowd. She's tipsy and all glammed up in velvet and I think how much I love her. She stands next to me and peers into the sling at her sleeping grand-daughter and puts her hand to her heart, as if to say, 'will you just *look* at her.'

Mum's chilled out so much in the last few months. Where as before dad's 'funny turn', the hazards of having her grand-daughter at a party would have been too much to bear (epilepsy from the lights, burst ear drums from the noise.) Nowadays, she's much more relaxed. It's like she's spent the past thirty years since dad's first 'funny turn' worrying about the very worst that could happen. Then the very worst *did* happen and she saw, we all survived.

We watch as dad twirls Julia around the room. She's back to her size 8 self, looking sensational in a monochrome mini.

'He's alright now, isn't he, your dad?' says mum.

'Yeah mum,' I say, 'course he's alright'.

Alright, not *just* right, not perfect, but who is? He still has to go down the 'barmy army HQ' for therapy, but he's off the drugs and more importantly, now that his secret's out, we talk about it – The Black Cloud – it's become part of us.

Vicky finishes to rapturous applause and waddles off to sit down again. She's singing again. She got her first couple of gigs at office Christmas parties and has more lined up for next year. Rich sent his script out to twenty agents: got no reply from eight, a thanks but no thanks from eleven and a 'Shows great promise' plus a page's worth of suggestions from one. But 'one is all you need' he says, and he and Vicky are revising it, who knows, maybe they'll play the leads when it's finally on TV! It probably won't mean they hit the big time, but boy, it would be great if they did. They're going to be a family of five, come May, after all. Yep, there's two Moons under that sequinned dress.

I go upstairs with Freya and sit down on the feeding chair, next to the window. It's strange, now that this room is finally decorated – lilac walls, white floorboards, flower fairies, the lot, it's like it was never my room, that that part of my life never even happened.

She sucking sweetly now, outside, there's a fine wintery drizzle falling like gossamer beneath the glow of the street lamp. I look at the red neon clock on top of the drawers: 11.26 p.m., half an hour left until next year. I wonder what this year will bring: great days, shit days, shocks and surprises; moments of joy, The Black Cloud . . . If there's a guarantee of anything, it's that life won't leave a thing out and yet this year, it's like I'm ready for it. For the first time in my life, I don't feel scared.

I hear the familiar whistle and two-steps-at-a-time of Jim coming up the stairs. He sticks his head around the door.

'Everything alright?' he says. 'Can I come in?'

'Course.' I smile and Jim sits down on the tiny pink stool we bought from Ikea and draws it close to us, his legs up by his shoulders like a gnome.

'Wow, she's going at it like Lisa from *The Simpsons*, isn't she?' he laughs, watching her suck like she's not been fed for a week.

'She got your hair,' I say, stroking it. 'It's all growing in different directions.'

'She got my gorgeous feet too, though. And her mother's eyes.'

The floorboards reverberate with the thump, thump of the music. We hear the familiar delighted shriek of my mother and laugh with recognition.

Jim strokes Freya's head.

'I can't believe how much I love her,' he says.

'Jim Ashcroft,' I say, 'you're so bloody soft.'

11.40. Twenty minutes until 2008. We can hear the intro to The Killers, 'Mr Brightside' and Gina shout, 'Oh my God, I *love* this one!'

Jim smiles at me, then leans over and kisses me on the mouth. 'I've got something to ask you,' he says, 'something I need to clear up.'

I kiss him back. 'Oh yeah, what's that?'

He gets off the stool and onto his knees and I laugh, nervously, because I've got an idea what he's about to do and I don't know, I don't know how I feel about it. We're alright as we are, aren't we? And I don't know if I want that – not just yet! The big white wedding doesn't quite appeal anymore and I don't know if I fancy the house on a cul-de-sac and our wedding anniversary picture on the mantelpiece, and the Center Parks holidays. I don't know if I want to be like everyone else and to have the 'normal family', what the hell does that mean, anyway? Everyone's a weirdo if you look closely enough.

But he's on his knees now and he's got a glint in his eye and he's taking my hand and I'm wracking my brains for the right thing to say and then he says, 'Tess?'

'Yes?' I say, as if I'm on the precipice of a cliff, about to fall over.

'Will you go out with me?'

And then I burst out laughing and Freya startles and Jim laughs too and searches my face. And then I lean over, careful not to squash her, cup Jim's face in my left hand, snog him within an inch of his life then say, 'Yeah, why not?'

11.51p.m.

'Come on Jim.' He hastily zips up his jeans. I pull on my skirt then look at myself in the mirror and gasp at the messy hair and tell-tale flush all over my chest.

'It's nine minutes till New Year, we'd better put her down and get downstairs, *pronto*!'

'Let's take her,' says Jim, turning to me suddenly. 'It's her first New Year, let's see it in with her, it won't do her any harm.'

I look at our daughter, that hilarious, permanently alarmed look on her face, cooing up at the disco ball still, not even the promise of sleep.

'Alright,' I say, 'as long as you understand, you're putting her down tonight.'

'Fine,' says Jim, 'but you can drive your brother to the station.'

I pick her up out of her cot, an exquisite nocturnal creature, and pass her to her father who kisses her soft head.

'Come on then, you one hot mamma,' Jim says, slapping me on the arse as I switch off the light.

I turn to him, 'Shit, do you reckon my mum'll be able to tell?' I say.

'Na,' says Jim 'She's half cut.'

11.56p.m.

We're all holding hands now, sweaty from dancing, eyes shining with pleasure and booze and the knowledge that this is one of those golden moments.

11.58p.m.

Two minutes to go . . .

11.59p.m.

Till what? The next chapter of our lives I suppose. And what will become of us then?

12.00

HAPPY NEW YEAR!!! The party poppers go, the music goes off as we hug and cheer in our lounge, our family's lounge and enjoy this moment like it's the last on this earth.

As if watching from above, I see us now, kissing, cheering, jumping up and down. We are canny and stupid, blessed and doomed. But right now, in this room, we are just *here*.

Outside, fireworks zoom, then bloom in the sky with a crackle and a pop. The music starts up again, mum and dad take their position. I look at Freya, her eyes wide open over Jim's shoulder, then I catch my dad's eye, over my mum's. I think back to that day in the greenhouse, it seems like a lifetime ago now. But I think, no, I *know* now, how right he was.

THE END

Epilogue

'I didn't even fancy him: lanky, pale as anything, this *really* dodgy hair. We were 'just good friends' but you know what they say about 'just good friends?' Took us nine years to do the inevitable, *once* without a condom to get me up the duff and five months of shambling about before we actually got together. He says I loved him all along, but I'm not admitting to anything. As far as I'm concerned, he got me pregnant, then we fell in love. A bit topsy turvy, but we got there in the end.'

Tess, 29, London
From *Bundle of Joy: 102 Real Stories of Motherhood*

SUBSCRIBE NOW
6 ISSUES
JUST £6

Keep up with what Katy Regan did next by subscribing to *Marie Claire*.

Each issue will be delivered direct to your door, so you'll never miss an issue.